SEX TOYS OF THE GODS

SEX TOYS OF THE GODS

CHRISTIAN McLAUGHLIN

A DUTTON BOOK

DUTTON
Published by the Penguin Group
Penguin Putnam Inc., 375 Hudson Street, New York, New York 10014, U.S.A.
Penguin Books Ltd, 27 Wrights Lane, London W8 5TZ, England
Penguin Books Australia Ltd, Ringwood, Victoria, Australia
Penguin Books Canada Ltd, 10 Alcorn Avenue, Toronto, Ontario, Canada M4V 3B2
Penguin Books (N.Z.) Ltd, 182–190 Wairau Road, Auckland 10, New Zealand

Penguin Books Ltd, Registered Offices:
Harmondsworth, Middlesex, England

First published by Dutton, an imprint of Dutton Signet,
a member of Penguin Putnam Inc.

First Printing, October, 1997
10 9 8 7 6 5 4 3 2 1

 REGISTERED TRADEMARK—MARCA REGISTRADA

LIBRARY OF CONGRESS CATALOGING-IN-PUBLICATION DATA
McLaughlin, Christian.
   Sex toys of the gods / by Christian McLaughlin.
      p.   cm.
   ISBN 0-525-94058-8
   I. Title.
PS3563.C38364S49   1997
813'.54—dc21   97-23041
                                                                      CIP

Printed in the United States of America
Set in Janson Text

PUBLISHER'S NOTE
This is a work of fiction. Names, characters, places, and incidents either are the product of the author's imagination or are used fictitiously, and any resemblance to actual persons, living or dead, events, or locales is entirely coincidental.

This book is printed on acid-free paper. ∞

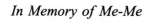

In Memory of Me-Me

ACKNOWLEDGMENTS

The author wishes to thank the following for their inspiration, support and assistance: Peter Alexander, Bananarama, The Bangles, Kyle Barnes, Blaire Baron, Tim Bauer, Glenn Berenbeim, Blondie, Kera Bolonik, Book of Love, Peter Borland, Jim Burke, Belinda Carlisle, Matthew Carnicelli, Conan Carroll, A Different Light, Arnold Dolin, Pamela Eells, Eighth Wonder, Scott Fifer, George Fletcher, Kent Fuher, The Go-Go's, Ellie Greenwich, Doris Guerrero, Richard Gurman, Julie Halston, Chris Hermening, Dan Hunt, Joanne Johnson, Josie and The Pussycats, the Kaplan-Stahler Agency, Kilgore, Mariella Krause, Maxine and Sally Lapiduss, Cyndi Lauper, Lee Liedecke, Madonna, Jim Martin, Michelle Martin, Stephanie Martini and Family, Harlan and Heather McLaughlin, Mom and Dad, Mindy Morgenstern, Michael Musto, Andrew Nicholls, Stevie Nicks, Yvonne Orteig, Angela Otey, Susan Ottaviano, John Pardee, Tresa Redburn, Jennifer and Ruth Richardson, Robert Rodi, Chris Rooney, Lisa Rosenthal, Jeffrey Smith, Terry Sweeney, Darrell Vickers and Jamie Wooten.

Very Special Thanks to Valerie Ahern, Robert Drake, Terry Maloney and Christopher Schelling.

From *The Rock-lopedia—A Comprehensive Guide to Popular Music*
Editor, Paul Suarez (Hawthorne, 1992)

*POP-TARTTS, THE. This all-female California band burst upon
the New Wave rock scene with the Top Ten single "Sick of You"
in 1982, then quickly recorded* Kittens with Whips *(1983). Consisting of lead vocalist Marina Stetson, guitarist Betty Fonseca,
guitarist/keyboardist Angela Autry, and drummer Sherry Neth-
erland (née Niehoff), the group made up for what it lacked in
training with energy, enthusiasm and style, and their debut album went platinum. Citing influences ranging from the Shangri-
La's and the Beach Boys to Blondie and the Ramones, The
Pop-Tartts put a sharp, bittersweet edge on Valley Girl culture
with a string of clever hit singles (mostly written by Fonseca and
Autry). The quartet had improved considerably when they scored
a gold record and a Grammy nomination with their follow-up
release, the much smoother* Pandora's Box *(1984). Alas, as the
band entered its most creative period, internal strife (brought on
by nonstop touring, personality conflicts and some of the most
notoriously decadent partying of the eighties) tore the group
apart. The Pop-Tartts dissolved after their less successful but
musically superior Grammy-nominated 1986* Kung Fu Grip.
*Fonseca immediately went on to form the San Francisco–based
alternative act Bubonic Pest (see entry), and in 1988, Stetson's
solo debut,* Marina Stetson, *a lightweight pop affair, yielded a
#4 and a #22 single. Just before its release, Netherland was
killed in a grisly motorcycle accident. Stetson's next album,*
Rainwater Lullaby *(1991), proved to be more of a swan song,
failing to crack* Billboard's Top 100.

Part I

Wren and Heathcliffe had been sleeping together since she first took him in that spring. Wren's housemate Jason felt a certain amount of sympathy for Heathcliffe, but it was unnerving and depressing to keep bumping into him in the kitchen, which was right off Wren's room, where he would stare with dead, vacant eyes as Jason cooked pasta or grilled the occasional turkey burger. Heathcliffe had been living with a woman who'd abused him, and now he carried his long, lean form with a numbed heaviness some took for quiet dignity but was actually closer to autism. Wren didn't care—every night and more than a few afternoons she could be found in her bedroom, cuddled up to her new best friend.

That was how Jason found them when he dashed into the house on North Orange Grove Avenue and didn't see or hear Wren getting ready for the showcase they were both due at in fifteen minutes. He went to her door and knocked. "Wren?" He pushed it open. She was crumpled on the futon in a pair of boy's long underwear and a tie-dyed T-shirt, sound asleep, a thick lock of black hair snaking into her open mouth. Not quite the perky pixie in her head shot. Heathcliffe was between her legs, spacing. He lifted his large head from her thigh and stared at Jason.

Jason ignored the Doberman and hesitantly stepped into the hovel of a room. "Wren, wake up!" He crouched halfway down, careful not to let the knee of his jeans touch the grimy, grayish blonde hardwood floor, and gently shook her arm. "Wren? Wren, it's late. Wake up!" No response. "Wren?" He tried to lift her by the shoulders. Her head lolled stuporously as she groaned something incoherent, releasing a puff of noxious breath in Jason's face.

He shook her harder. What kind of a bender had she been on last night? The first performance of the showcase, "An Evening of Original Comedy and Drama," had hardly given anyone reason to celebrate. Missed lighting cues, dropped lines, over-the-top performances—all to be expected in showcases, those collections of scenes intended to expose unknown actors like Wren to the agents, casting directors and creative types that could mold their future stardom. Normally, unlike the previous "Evening," more than three people showed up to see the things, however. Gail Ann Griffin, the personal manager mounting the showcase as a vehicle for seven of her nine clients, had assured everyone she had a well-packed house confirmed for the second and final night. Jason, conned into serving as "house manager" for the production by his friend Andre Nickerson (who wrote it), had only twelve people on the list so far but had said nothing. And now it was one hour to curtain, and Wren wouldn't wake up. "Wren! You've got to get ready!" Heathcliffe, alarmed by the commotion, shuffled into a corner and started to nibble his balls.

Wren's eyelids fluttered, and she seemed to be coming out of her coma, steadying herself. "What—Jason? What's goin' on?"

"We have to be at the showcase in a few minutes. Are you okay?"

"Sure. I'm great." She closed her eyes and splatted back onto her pillow.

Jason stood up. "Wren . . . I really have to leave."

"I gotta quit drinking," she murmured. "Last night . . . oh, man . . . and I couldn't get to sleep so I took a few barbs. What time is it, anyway?" She snatched at her nightstand in slow-motion and knocked her Fossil, cigarettes, and an ankh to the floor.

"Six-forty-five," Jason said.

"I feel like shit . . . I don't think I can go on," she rasped. Jason waited for her to add something—an apology, a message for Gail, a goodbye—but she'd apparently lapsed back into dreamland.

Jason couldn't believe he was going to have to be the one to inform Gail of this unscheduled deviation from the program. He headed for his room, then spun around on the besmirched kitchen linoleum, picked up the dog's water bowl, rinsed the hair out and refilled it. Heathcliffe stood up, but in the process got turned around and lost track of the water. "Jesus Christ," Jason mumbled.

He yanked one of his two blazers out of the inhumanly narrow closet then glanced at his answering machine. The digital readout indicated he had one message. He hit Play, any fantasies of a job interview evaporating as Andre's involuntarily affected purr issued forth.

"Hello, dear. I just tried to ring you at work, but that corpulent cunt of an assistant manager picked up. I love that little musical tone she puts on. 'Video *Xplo*sion . . . I'm a retail *whore* in polyester pants and a gold lamé belt . . .' " Recently Marilyn, the cunt in question, had come out of the back of the store while Andre was returning some tapes and utterly alienated him by proclaiming Liz Taylor "way out of her league" in *Suddenly, Last Summer* and then asking him to please not block the check-in station. "This showcase is wearing me out. I've barely had time to work on my new spec script at all. The absolute only consolation is Ryan Olstrum . . . I think I'm developing a mad crush on him. And I think he may *have* a *problem.* She seems to slip into character just a smidge too easily. And I'm so proud of Fawn. She was *dead-on* last night. Don't you think she was *dead-on*? Anyway, the reason I called is to insist you join us for the après-showcase fiesta at the Dresden Room. You simply must see the Marty and Elayne show. They're like sixty-year-old Vegas satanists with a lounge act. You will not *believe* their rendition of 'Stayin' Alive.' Okay, I've got to take my panties out of the dryer. TTFN." Ta ta for now. "Having a problem" was hip slang borrowed from Andy Warhol and meant someone was gay. Ryan Olstrum was a handsome, wholesome, towheaded Gail Ann Griffin client from Minnesota who Jason thought was about as gay as Ron Howard, but Andre had been awhirl in florid romantic hallucinations since Ryan had spoken the first line of dialogue in his scene, a domestic sketch about two white trash male lovers in a Norman, Oklahoma, trailer park.

Jason figured Andre was the queeniest queen to ever graduate from their alma mater, Fairmont West High School in the Dayton suburb of Kettering, Ohio. He regularly wore makeup, referred to any guy who he even imagined exhibited the slightest trace of homosexuality as "she," and always said *forward* instead of *straight* when giving directions. Jason thought that Andre assumed *he* had a problem, too, which he did, but it was not something they ever discussed.

Jason reset the answering machine and hurried out the back door to his 1982 Subaru hatchback, a vehicle that had lost much of its will to live after Jason put it through a two thousand-mile drive to LA upon graduation from Columbus State in May. As glad as he was that the showcase would be over tonight, there was no way he wanted to spend two hours or more in a smoke-drenched cocktail lounge nursing a vodka gimlet and eating deep-fried appetizers he couldn't afford, hoping Andre or his best friend, Fawn Farrar, a Texan oil heiress and the unofficial star and bankroller of the show-case, would pick up the tab. No matter what the venue, the self-delusion would be approaching toxic levels with Fawn doubtlessly telling Andre what a brilliant writer he was as he dutifully raved about her performances in the scenes he'd written and assured her that stardom was right around the corner. The reality was that Fawn was a reasonably attractive, utterly mediocre dime-a-dozen blonde actress whose millions had been thus far powerless to purchase her the show-biz career she desperately craved.

Andre was currently ensconced in the $10 million Beverly Hills house purchased for Fawn by her husband, Giles Burke. The estranged newlyweds had never moved into their dream home and now paid Andre three hundred under-the-table smackers per week to house-sit five thousand square feet of black-marbled, white-walled unfurnished splendor, a job that left him ample time to pursue an incredibly ill-advised writing career.

Andre saw himself as Bret Easton Ellis, Tennessee Williams and Susan Harris melded into one, but he had the discipline of a wild rabbit and talent that made VC Andrews look like John Kennedy Toole. His literary output consisted of an obviously unsold *Fresh Prince of Bel-Air* spec script in which Carlton had gay sex and a *Murphy Brown* he was now finishing which guest starred Madonna. He'd also cranked out forty pages of a torrid epic novel about twin sisters born into poverty in the Cleveland slums and their rise to control a male modeling empire, and various finished and abandoned one-act plays that had provided the fragments that formed "An Evening of . . . ," six vignettes running the gamut from uninspired to horrendous.

Agreeing to house manage the showcase had been a stupid idea, Jason lamented with chagrin as he popped a self-compiled Marina Stetson Greatest Hits cassette into his tape deck (including a healthy dose of songs by the Pop-Tartts, the seminal eighties all-girl rock band she'd fronted). He felt his car shudder and nearly stall as he turned right on Fountain. Andre had insisted Jason would make scads of "connections" that might prove invaluable in getting out of the video store and starting a real future in the entertainment industry. Jason doubted anyone from a major record label would show up and offer him his ideal job— an A&R position where he would spend every day developing a solo career for Susan Ottaviano or refining Bananarama's itinerary or powerlunching with Sophie B. Hawkins. But Gail Ann Griffin put on an impressive facade—she managed Turk Marlowe, star of the syndicated late-night crime hit *Leather & Lace*—and Jason had almost convinced himself that she might actually introduce him to *someone* who might help him get out from under Marilyn's fat thumb and her $6.95 per hour Customer Service Nowhere Express. But last night's puny turnout seemed to verify that Gail was as much a deadbeat as all of her non-Turk clients.

The showcase was at a shopworn Equity-waiver theater in one of the more frightening Hollywood neighborhoods. Jason parked in front of what looked like a crack house, locked on The Club and carried the deli trays he'd picked up earlier at Pavilions around the block to the lobby entrance, hoping his car looked shitty enough to deter the locals from assuming he had a really boss sound system.

Ryan Olstrum and his partner were rehearsing in the lobby, using mock-Texan accents to spout Andre's dialogue.

RYAN: "Don't tell me that when we lay down to sleep together in bed you're thinkin' 'bout her, 'cuz I jest don't believe it."
PARTNER: "Stop that goddamn whinin' and git me another beer. She's movin' back to this mobile home park and there ain't nothin' we can do about it!"

Jason suppressed a laugh and began to lay out the refreshments on a black paper tablecloth—cookies, sandwiches, veggies and dip —before stuffing gold-glittered folders with programs, photos and résumés. Gail arrived shortly. "Hi, darling," the newly very blonde talent broker trilled, embracing Jason for a cheek brush. She kept her hands planted on him as she surveyed the lobby with darting, ferrety eyes. She was wearing a black-and-green suit that Bob Mackie might have designed for a women's prison warden. "Everything looks perfect, Jason. Is everyone here?"

Uh-oh. "Wren can't make it tonight. She's sick."

"Sick? She's sick?!?" she barked, shaking him by the shoulders. "That goddamn irresponsible moron is calling in sick to *my* showcase?!" Gail screeched, cordial act shelved, since no powerful guests had yet arrived. Andre emerged from the forty-seat house and gave Jason a look of horrified delight at Gail's tantrum. He flitted across the cramped lobby to where Jason had been setting up cups, ice and bottles of soda and cheap champagne.

Gail went to the pay phone and called Wren. They watched her facial contortions as the phone rang and rang before Wren's machine picked up. "This is Gail Ann Griffin and I am very disappointed in you, Wren. We need to have a discussion about *professionalism* and *commitment* before I can do another thing for you. Please call me as soon as you're *better.*" She hung up abruptly and said to no one in particular, "We'll just have to cut that scene."

"What about me?" whined Wren's instantly hysterical costar, dropping a deviled egg back onto the hors d'oeuvres platter. "Gail! You can't punish *me* because that little bitch is flaking out! I need this showcase! I've paid—"

"Myra, for God's sake, calm down," Gail said. She took the forty-four-year-old substitute teacher from Hermosa Beach by the arm, consoling while conveniently leading her away from the expensive edibles at the same time. "We'll find someone else to play the part. How about Fawn?"

Andre jumped in immediately. "Gail, there is no way in hell Fawn can memorize a whole new scene *and* prepare for the rest of the showcase."

Gail's surgically rejuvenated features narrowed into a hateful scowl. How dare this pillow-biting hack defy her? "Then I'll just play the role myself," she said. "Come on, Myra. Let's rehearse."

She dragged the startled woman toward the stage, leaving Andre to comment, "*She's* playing a seventeen-year-old? Oh, good Christ, she is going to ruin my scene!" He pranced to the red-felt-draped bulletin board and tore Wren's head shot from the cast display. "Damn you!" he spat at it, handing the photo to Jason and pulling him toward the rest room.

Inside, Andre bellied up to the sink and began to apply eyedrops. "That pool man overdid the chlorine just a *tad*. I look like a fucking wino. And is it me, or is Gail destroying this showcase?" he hissed at Jason. "She doesn't give a frog's fat ass about theater, and casting herself as Trixie proves it! I wish I could take my name off the program. But I wouldn't, for Fawn's sake. She's really doing some nice work, don't you think?" Jason nodded. "She looked so pretty last night. Poor Fawn. She is simply in a tizz right now. Whirly-twirly. Edgar Black is going to be here from the Conan Carroll Agency."

"Yeah, Wren mentioned that at some point when she was conscious," Jason said. His other housemate, thirty-one-year-old ice princess/agency assistant Tricia Cook, worked for Edgar.

"Fawn's dying to impress him. She rented a suite at the Peninsula, and she and her scene partners have been rehearsing all day for her acting teacher. I'm worried, though. Fawn is the only one of Gail's clients with any talent, if you ask me. Except for Ryan." He licked his lips.

"They're rehearsing right outside," Jason remarked.

"I know," Andre sighed. He put his ear to the door. "Oh, my God! Listen."

Jason did and heard Gail's voice quietly say something tense yet supplicating. Ryan replied more vociferously. "I'm not too crazy about playing a fag, that's all."

"Darling, I told you. People are not going to see you as *gay,*" Gail crooned. "They're going to see you as *versatile.* Let's keep this just between us, but you are doing the nicest work in this showcase." Jason rolled his eyes, but Andre was totally absorbed.

"Look, Gail," Ryan said. "I'm a pro, and I'll do it, but you never see Brad Pitt playing a homo, do you?"

Jason looked to Andre for some response to this mutinous exchange. Andre shook his head and waved a hand toward the door dismissingly. "He's in denial," he diagnosed. "And so is Brad Pitt."

They came out, and Gail sank Nails by Jessica into Jason's forearm. "I have to get into costume, Jason, but tonight make sure everyone signs this." She handed him a hefty guest book that could have been purloined from a Long Island Mafia wedding. The only pen he could find was a green felt-tip marker. He arranged them next to the stack of program folders as Gail clattered away to the single four-by-five-foot dressing room.

"I need a drink," Andre sighed. He made himself a white wine spritzer. "Oh, my God! I forgot to tell you the *dish.* Fawn and Giles went to dinner at Beaurivage Sunday night—*and* frolicked in the moonlit Malibu surf until four a.m." Fawn and her husband had officially separated but were now dating. With a nine-figure fortune, his parents were the richest people in Dayton and did not approve of Fawn, who, after all, came from Odessa, Texas, and whose family was worth a paltry $11 million. Practically white trash. "Those two have buckets to work out, but they're making progress," Andre said. "I think he's threatened by her career." Jason bit back laughter. "I see them reuniting after her next boob job and taking a second honeymoon to Fiji. Now, when I finish my *Murphy Brown,* we're going to have a reading at the mansion. I want you to play Miles." He handed Jason a spritzer.

"Who are you going to be?"

"Corky. Who else?"

"Excuse me, young man." Jason felt a tap on his shoulder and discovered a woman near seventy who looked eerily familiar despite a serious hooker makeup job. "I'm Dottie Wax. You might remember me from *No Place Like Home,*" she added hopefully. Jason absolutely remembered her as the Donna Reedish mom on the *Leave It to Beaver*ish early-sixties sitcom. He could not tear his gaze from the sideshow attraction of Dottie's wrinkled, decrepit anticleavage surmounting the most flagrant abuse of a bustier since *Wild Orchid 2*, although he knew he must.

"Hi. I'm Jason Dallin."

"I'm here to see the showcase. Is Gail here yet? She's my personal manager, you know."

"Gail is, um, rehearsing at the moment. She's going to fill in for somebody in the show tonight." God, that outfit. He couldn't believe this was the woman to whom he'd eaten Frosted Flakes every day after school throughout fourth grade.

"What fun!" she cackled, eyeing the makeshift bar.

Andre rescued him. "My stars, if it isn't Dottie Wax!" He pressed his lips to her liver-spotted hand. "I'm Andre, and while I pour you a glass of bubbly, we'll talk about the huge part I'm going to create for you when I have my own TV sitcom."

"Oh? Are you a producer?" she asked hungrily. "You know, *No Place Like Home* just sold to Nick at Nite!"

People were starting to arrive. Nobody in casting or agenting, but people. When most of them left the "Company" space blank in the guest register, Jason figured they were pals of the performers, and God knew sitting through this showcase was the ultimate test of friendship. Tricia came in, followed by her boss, Edgar Black. She gravitated toward Jason, more solicitous than she'd ever been at home. "Good evening, sir," she said. "Jason, this is my boss, Edgar Black. Edgar, Jason Dallin, my housemate."

"How are you." Edgar shook his hand, then accepted a program folder. He was tan and leathery and resembled an aging Grant Goodeve. "Tricia, why don't you get us a couple of drinks." She scurried to obey while Edgar disinterestedly scanned the contents of the folder and generally peered around the lobby like Robin Leach at a welfare hotel. He withdrew Fawn's head shot and snorted at her minute resumé. Tricia handed him a cup of wine. He took one sip and tossed it in a nearby wastebasket. "Jesus! What was that? Night Train?"

"Fawn Farrar," Tricia said, ignoring it. "That's the client Gail was so adamant about."

"She's kind of cute," Edgar opined.

"Yes . . . a bit like that English actress Linda Hayden. From *Baby Love*?" Tricia agreed.

"Who?" Edgar asked.

"Linda Hayden. She did some Hammer films in the early seventies and had a kind of Lolitaish sophistication, but her career never really—"

Edgar interrupted her. "Where's your other roommate?" he asked, studying the bulletin board. "What's her name? Hen?"

"Wren . . . but I don't see her photo. Jason, Wren *is* going to be acting tonight? Isn't she?"

"Actually, Tricia, she's sick. She couldn't make it."

"Unbelievable. Edgar, I just—"

But he'd already gone in. Jason stayed in the lobby during the opening scene, about an aerobics instructor who improperly touches a student during a gym class. He nibbled the food that had been left behind by the small but ravenous audience and perused the program. Gail had of course put her lengthy bio on page one: Originally from Tennessee, she was a graduate of the Burt Reynolds Theatre Institute, had appeared on *"Charlie's Angels, The A-Team* and *Facts of Life,"* and led "support therapy groups for artists in Nashville, Los Angeles and Golden, Colorado."

Andre was listed last of all, under "Playwright." "ANDRE NICKERSON studied drama at Wright State University and UCLA. His work has been performed in Ohio, Los Angeles and London. Recent projects include a *Fresh Prince* episode and *Kiss the Fallen Angels Goodnight . . . Forever,* a novel-in-progress. Andre resides in Beverly Hills." Andre né Andrew had dropped out of Wright State during his second semester, but the UCLA part was technically true—he'd completed an extension course there in soap opera writing—and he'd also visited London, where it was conceivable that someone had read *something* he'd written aloud, even if it had just been a mash note. Andre must have done the actors' bios as well as his own—Fawn's single on-air credit, a nonunion adult chat line commercial, had been whipped into a sparkling paragraph that made her sound like the brightest young starlet since Emily Lloyd. Jason flipped the program closed and noticed at the bottom of the page in tiny print, "House Manager Jason Dallin."

He wanted it removed as soon as he sat down in the theater. Complete with costumes and props, Andre's scenes seemed even more pathetic, like a retarded child gussied up for a cotillion. And

the actors were making even more egregious fuck-ups tonight, perhaps agitated by their personal manager's presence backstage. Ryan
Olstrum's gay trailer park interlude went over like a dead baby joke
at a Gerber stockholders' convention. Afterwards, two people walked
out. Then, without warning, like a car crash turning a dull intersection into a horrific bloodbath, the Myra/Gail scene began.

The derisive chuckling started as soon as Gail made her entrance
(dressed in a hastily tossed together Esprit Juniors ensemble borrowed from Fawn) with the line, "Mom! I can't come to the phone!
I have a pimple!" It was so absurd Jason almost cracked up himself,
but by the time Edgar got up and left, the audience was maintaining
an appalled silence. Fawn's comic scene was next. Jason waited for
Edgar to return, but it didn't happen.

Finally, it was time for the last segment, an insanely out-of-
context vignette starring Fawn as a mentally unstable TV producer
who realizes she's inadvertently married her rapist. Played out in
twelve hysterical minutes of sobbing, heavy breathing, and mock
strangulation, with Fawn's hunky partner shirtless, it was Andre's
dramatic pièce de résistance. And resist it the audience did.

At the curtain call, Gail came out and bowed alongside her clients, although she'd mercifully changed back into her Bob Mackie
drag. Fawn hauled Andre from his seat and introduced him as the
writer. Amazingly, the very light applause continued. Jason ducked
into the lobby and assumed a discreet post from which to watch the
pointless but obligatory shmoozing.

Andre led the way, arms wrapped around his friend Ingrid, who
was in typical form tonight—white makeup, wearing a Carnie Phil-
lips number, telling Andre what a "gift" he had while scarfing leftover hors d'oeuvres and complaining about Tom Cruise playing the
Vampire Lestat. Fawn exchanged her torn slip costume for a cocktail
dress and cornered Gail, who was holding court by the drinking
fountain. "Where's Edgar Black?" Fawn asked confidentially.

"I don't see him," Gail said. "But he signed in. There's his
assistant." She nodded toward Tricia, a front-runner in the Most
Boring Woman Alive sweepstakes, engaged in a monologue for an
obviously sorry-he'd-asked Ryan Olstrum.

"I don't care about his *assistant*—" Fawn began, then noticed
Andre beckoning her to join him where he'd been conferring with

Jason. Gail spun on her heel and started accepting compliments from one of her friends as Fawn squeezed between Jason and Andre. "*What* is going on?" she demanded quietly.

"Edgar Black walked out in the middle of the showcase. Specifically during Gail's little performance. Did you see how she *looked*?" Andre hissed.

"Those were my clothes," Fawn stammered.

"Honey! He*llo?!?* You're a lovely young lady—she's a thirty-eight-year-old woman playing the daughter of a forty-five-year-old! It was absolutely my most embarrassing moment ever. Edgar couldn't take it."

She turned on Jason. "What other agents are here?"

"I don't know, exactly . . ."

Fawn said, Keeping the volume, if not her West Texas accent under control, "Are you telling me Edgar Black was the only fuckin' agent here and he *walked out*? Before my scenes?"

Andre and Jason were slow in verifying this, so Fawn sashayed back to Gail and broke in with, "So *one* agent shows up for this whole damn thing and leaves before he sees *me!?!?*"

Dottie Wax chose this moment to tap Fawn on the shoulder. "Dear, you were just marvelous tonight. You all were! I know every single one of you will be a star."

Fawn whipped her head around and snarled, "Can you please just shut up?" Dottie recoiled, blanching.

Gail tried to put an arm around Fawn. "Fawn darling, let's not get excited. Something must have come up for Edgar . . . Maybe he was paged . . . I know I can get you a meeting . . . he owes me a favor."

"And you owe me about two thousand dollars for . . . this!" Fawn threw her arms up and around helplessly then ran back into the house. Tricia shook her head gravely.

"Well . . . ," Gail said to everybody staring at her. "We've all been under a lot of pressure and I think everyone could use some relaxation. Let's all meet at El Coyote in twenty . . . 'kay?"

Just then Fawn reappeared laden with her belongings. She went straight for the exit. Her scene partner blocked it. "Hey, we still going out?"

"I want to be alone," Fawn tersely replied, *sans* irony. She went out the door but was back in seconds. "Andre. *Come on.*"

"She's upset . . . I'll call you, Ingrid. You too, hon," he asided to Jason before tailing after her.

Gail quickly regained control and cemented the El Coyote plan with as many of the rapidly dispersing assemblage as possible. Jason declined. Spending another five minutes with Gail and the Desperate Actor File was out of the question. In any case, he wasn't about to reenter El Coyote, a trendy dive on Beverly with food evocative of the cafeteria at a Tijuana reform school.

"Then would you mind closing up for me?" Gail had the nerve to ask him, holding out the key.

After the last person left (Dottie Wax, who slipped Jason one of her lavender cards in a grotesquely flirtatious parting gesture), Jason threw out the party trays and empty bottles, figuring the local derelicts could worry about recycling when they went through the Dumpster at their convenience. He collected discarded programs and folders from under the seats and brought them with him, not wanting to trash perfectly usable head shots even if casting people would surely be doing exactly that to them soon enough.

Tricia picked up the stack of new Rolodex cards and examined them. Unbelievable. She had explained it to Misty the receptionist twice before, and the dumb bunny just didn't get it. There was a right side and a wrong side and almost all these cards had been typed on the wrong side. It was so obvious! Cards typed on the wrong side had to be inserted into the Rolodex backward and didn't flip properly. As if there weren't already enough impediments to efficiency at this agency. Tricia considered retyping all the defective cards herself but ended up filing them as was. What she needed was an intern.

She went through the morning's breakdowns—detailed lists of roles to be cast in upcoming films, TV programs and major theater —and left messages with several casting offices requesting scripts her boss Edgar didn't already have. She then double-checked her list of actors who still needed to drop off a new supply of head shots— she hated submitting photocopies of pictures to casting directors, it was so unprofessional—and phoned them all, letting her pleasure in waking a few of the irresponsible clients up add a note of cheer to her businesslike tone. She then went into Edgar's office and filed another set of those damn Rolodex cards, running across a flyer for "An Evening of Original Comedy and Drama." She wondered how that screaming queen Andre had gotten his work produced—she guessed it had something to do with Fawn Farrar, the client Gail was trying to ram down Edgar's throat. Edgar had missed her performance last night, and Fawn's overwrought histrionics would certainly get no endorsement from Tricia. She studied the flyer. All of the actors in the showcase were listed in alphabetical order except Fawn, who was first. If this wasn't a mistake, it was quite unfair. And how many times had Gail put her own name on the flyer? "Gail Ann Griffin presents . . ." "Directed by Gail Ann Griffin" "A Gail Ann Griffin Production" "RSVP Gail Ann Griffin Management." Unbelievable. And Wren! Tricia had tried to help jump-start her housemate's career by introducing her to Edgar, and the thanks she got was Wren getting trashed and missing the showcase.

Edgar's desk was a mess. Shortly after she'd been promoted from receptionist to Edgar's assistant, she'd straightened it one afternoon while he was at a screening. When he returned and summoned her into his office, she'd expected to modestly deflect a shower of gratified praise at her initiative and skill. Instead, he closed the door and sprouted horns, fangs and warty green skin.

"You know something? I had a desk at the William Morris office while you were still sucking your thumb in kindergarten! So what business do you think you have coming in here and taking CHARGE of my fucking office!" He pounded his fist on the desktop, and his attractively arranged pencil-and-pen holder, framed photo of him and Faye Dunaway and sterling silver dish of Certs clattered loudly, making Tricia flinch.

"I'm sorry, Edgar," she began, almost in tears. "I thought—"

He stood up and leaned forward, as if preparing to swoop down and eviscerate her. "Haven't you ever heard the expression, if it ain't broke, don't fix it? Well, apply it, you dripping snatch!!"

Tricia had broken down in sobs and scurried out of the office. She'd spent a good twenty minutes in the ladies' room, and when she got back, Edgar had left for the day, the new files she'd organized scattered all over the desk and floor like victims of a massacre. The next day he apologized and bought her a gift basket from See's.

She was still sitting at Edgar's desk, remembering she'd forgotten to brew his coffee, when he breezed in. "Oh, excuse me. Would you like me to sit out there today?" He was in his charming mode this morning. Tricia relaxed as much as she ever did at work and made a chuckling noise in her pretty white throat.

"I thought you might leave the business after that showcase last night," she said, hastily rising and scooting around the other side of the desk.

"What an abortion! Gail Ann Griffin owes me dinner at Morton's and a case of cigars for *that* flea circus," Edgar squawked. Now he was in his quaintly gruff Damon Runyon persona.

He handed Tricia two photos and résumés of busty, shellacked starlets. "Set these young ladies up to meet me, please." Back to charming? "I need some new blood around here. Jesus Christ, my clients bore me to fuckin' death." No, gruff was definitely incumbent for the time being. "And do a real ass-lick submission letter for this movie-of-the-week." He handed her a breakdown. "And make sure we cc my delicate jewel Lori Openden at the network because these casting cows aren't giving me dick till she makes a call."

"Right away," Tricia said. She closed the door as much as possible without latching it then headed for the kitchen area to start two pots of Edgar's special high-octane Brazilian blend. Then it was back to her desk to catch the phone.

Hector the mailroom gofer passed by with the day's load. "Here you go, Trish," he said, depositing the pile on the desk. She nodded austerely, not about to respond to anyone referring to her by the hated "Trish." He trundled off and she divided the mail according to classification, then seized her Tiffany letter opener—a gift from her parents on her thirtieth birthday—and began to review the pix and résumés sent in by actors seeking representation.

She had a process of elimination. Anyone not in at least one of the unions—SAG, AFTRA or Equity—took the wastebasket plunge first. Then she scrutinized the remainders more carefully, discarding any hopefuls whose "bios" (as Tricia thought it hip and show-bizzy to dub résumés) boasted the deadly combination of what appeared to be day player credits plus no current acting class info. Neophyte professionals *must* study their craft in order to perfect it—if these people didn't realize the importance of this, they were wasting her time. Next in the trash went tasteless bimbo shots (Edgar had enough of these sluts parading in and out already) and anyone whose cover letter contained more than one typo. Any submissions that survived the purge were given to Edgar, who sometimes actually called them in for a "consultation," provided they were good-looking and female.

Today Tricia had tossed all but one. Her name was Violet Cyr, and Tricia saw that she had a Sherilyn Fenn insouciance tempered by the dewy-eyed wholesomeness of a young Karen Allen. And the Julia Louis-Dreyfus hair was definitely "in," Tricia noted, fingering her own straight-as-a-pin, perm-resistant ash-blonde locks with an unconscious touch of resentment. Violet's bio impressed Tricia instantly—she had "Theater" listed first and had most recently appeared in two Broadway shows as well as *Tony 'n' Tina's Wedding*. She'd also had the female role in the national tour of *Speed-the-Plow*. A sprinkling of television and film credits and training at The Actors Studio and Playwrights Horizons completed the package.

"Dear Edgar," Violet's note read. "I'm back in L.A. after three years in New York and need a great agent. I would have sent this to you FedEx in a crate of Dom Pérignon padded with crumpled hundred-dollar bills, but am terrified of appearing pushy." Tricia wasn't wild about the note—too irreverent—but decided to call her in to meet Edgar anyway. She laid the photo on top of the two he had given her this morning—both Playboy Channel types, one of whose bio was printed on pink paper and had *The Jane Whitney Show* listed under "TV," meaning God knew what.

"Tricia," Edgar buzzed on the intercom, "coffee, please?"

"Sure, I'll get it," she replied. She went into the break room and turned off the coffeemaker. The dark, aromatic brew, purchased by the pound in gold foil bags at a staggeringly expensive shoppe in The Beverly Center, continued to bubble as Tricia conveyed it to Edgar's office, but she was incapable of enjoying the rich scent. In fact, she could barely feel the heat emanating from the two Pyrex decanters onto her china-doll skin. She didn't hear Edgar mumble thanks when she set them down, one on a special hot pad.

Coffee was an autopilot function for Tricia and had been ever since she'd discovered why Edgar got two pots nearly every morning. One he drank. The other cooled, then disappeared with him into his office bathroom, where under the sink he kept his enema kit.

Violet Cyr decided there was an excellent chance she'd made a mistake with this laundromat. It was true she had miraculously been able to park five feet from the door and the dryers were, as advertised, "Free!", but the change machine had given her grief from the get-go, rejecting all three of her ones so that she had to feed it a ten and then try to stuff the ensuing jackpot into her tiny purse. And to make the hot July afternoon seem even more oppressive, a kamikaze toddler had come in off the street and was barreling around ululating like a chimp with distemper while his father, fat and sweaty and dressed as an extra from Robert Altman's *Popeye*, argued in French or Portuguese on the pay phone.

Violet attempted to read a John Irving novel, but her concentration was shot when the three-year-old ran up to her and shoved his hand up her skirt. "Gaaalrr!" he shrieked. Violet was too flabbergasted to say anything—the crazed, grimacing tot had a feral glint in his eyes as he kept his hand on her thigh, centimeters from her muffin. Thank God she'd worn tights. The kid cackled something and whipped his hand out and torpedoed off in another direction. Violet looked at the father's back and butt cleavage—he bellowed foreign condemnations into the receiver, oblivious. This was almost wretched enough to drive her to her mother's Maytags in Calabasas. Almost but not quite.

She had a horror movie audition in an hour that she'd submitted herself for via a *Drama-Logue* listing. The sides hadn't been available when she stopped by the office, but she figured a cold reading would suffice for *Teenage Brides of Christ II*.

The devil-child tipped over a trash can and crawled inside. Papa yakked and scratched his ballooning stomach, red-faced. Violet ignored them, bored with the surrealism of it all. The three-year-old emerged from the garbage with two long, serrated bread knives and began marching around, rubbing them together and barking.

"Sir? Could you please control your child?" Violet loudly requested after the tot began hacking at the seat of the chair next to hers. "You! On the phone!" she yelled.

"Eh?" he said. He dropped the receiver and grabbed the kid, knives and all, and sat him on one of the washing machines before recklessly seizing the weapons by the blades and pitching them back into the trash. Then he picked up the dangling phone and resumed the conversation. Between the noisy traffic on Fountain and the in-your-face nuts, she might as well be in New York, Violet mused. At least her Greenwich Village garret had had a washer and dryer at the end of the hall. She'd been back in L.A. two weeks. *Sunburnt*, the play she'd been in, had closed on Broadway after a five-month run. A savagely witty ensemble piece about the sexually frustrated Miami Beach cabana club set circa 1958, it had been only a modest hit. The good news was that it was soon to be a major motion picture. The bad news was Nicole Kidman wanted to play Violet's role, a brash girl from the wrong side of the tracks married to a semiretarded society bozo. And since Mrs. Cruise was "producing," Violet was history. Everyone had been ever so sympathetic and sweet when the news was handed down, especially the actors who were going to be carried over to the film. Violet flashed a "them's the breaks" smile, hugged congratulations, then went back to her apartment and cried for two days.

Her chance at stardom cruelly snatched by the capricious whims of Fate and CAA, Violet decided to go west. Fuck New York. Fuck Broadway. Fuck trying to hail a cab with four bags of groceries in the rain. Fuck the blind guy who sold pencils at 53rd and Lexington. She'd purchased one of those pencils once and the damn thing broke in her hand at a *Guiding Light* audition, driving a splinter into her palm so she bled all over the casting office carpet.

She'd done one L.A. mailing with a cute cover letter two days ago to five agents based on client lists she'd researched at Screen Actors Guild. A childhood friend was now a hotshot at ICM, her mother had waited a whole thirty seconds to remind her when she'd picked Violet up at the airport, but Violet knew that a meeting there would just be a mercy fuck and she preferred to save it as a last resort. She hoped to land a few casting interviews like today's and maybe a little recurring soap work on her own and had submissions ready to mail to *General Hospital, The Young & The Restless, Days of Our Lives, Hearts Crossing* and *The Bold & The Beautiful* on her way home. In New York, she'd done six months on and off on *One Life to Live* in 1991 and had good tape, or as good as one could get playing a nymphomaniac in prison who foils the unjustly jailed heroine's escape by revealing the secret plan in exchange for sex with a hunky guard. At least she hadn't been on the show a few years earlier, when Viki went to heaven in a space shuttle piloted by the guy who did Piglet's voice in the Winnie-the-Pooh cartoons.

Fawn Farrar listlessly picked at her salmon omelette. She hadn't touched her grapefruit half, Equal-sprinkled and garnished with an organic cherry, and had only swallowed enough fresh-squeezed orange juice to wash down a mouthful of vitamins and what Andre called "healing herb-tabs." He came into the bedroom and put a saucer of toasted crumpets on the breakfast tray. Fawn was propped up in his bed in a dark green camisole, her hair exploding around her head from a lethal combo of sleep and residual mousse. She'd come straight back to the mansion with Andre after the showcase to sob and Gail-rail and eat Godiva chocolates during *Beloved Infidel* on American Movie Classics until she fell asleep fully clothed.

"Oh, Fawn . . . your dress!" Andre took a padded hanger from the closet and rescued her new $900 shmoozing frock, which was now crumpled on the floor.

"Who cares? I don't ever want to see that dress again," Fawn pouted. Andre hung it up in his closet, already entertaining the notion of having it altered for himself.

Fawn picked up the phone and hit redial. "Are you calling Gail again?" Andre asked. She nodded. "Well, you aren't going to leave another message, are you?"

"You bet your little white ass I am," Fawn growled. Then: "Gail, this is Fawn Farrar, and I expect a call back at my Vista Laguna number right away." She clicked off. "I'm gonna take a shower. If she calls, tell her to hold."

Nobody called but Giles, wanting to know how the showcase

went and if Andre knew where Fawn was. "She's here, honey, and she's on the warpath." He explained what had happened. "We were all just sick. I haven't seen Fawn so upset since her under-five was cut from *Loving*. Uh-oh, here she comes. I'll tell her to call you later, sweetie. Bye."

"Okay," Fawn said. "That's it. I'm going over there right now." She began to violently do her hair while Andre laid out the spare outfit he'd found in the trunk of her car.

"Oooooh . . . sounds like a catfight," he clucked.

Apparently every unemployed tart in Hollywood had dragged her ass off the StairMaster to read for this epic, Violet noted as she entered a casting waiting room cram-packed with *Red Shoe Diaries* types. She wended her way through the silicone jungle to an unoccupied desk and snagged the last set of "Veronica" sides.

There was one seat left, on the floor next to a small couch. A blonde Amazon uncrossed her bare legs so Violet could squeeze in. The blonde had a chain tattooed around her ankle and was fanning herself with a set of sides while bitching about the building's non-validated parking.

Violet started to read the script pages. Her character seemed to be a nun trying to warn the other sisters that a psychotic killer was on the prowl. The second scene was attached, a flashback in which Veronica discovered her boyfriend *en travestie* having sex with her slutty little sister, a trauma so profound it presumably drove Veronica straight to the convent. Violet experienced the unsettling sensation of hearing a helium-inflected female voice reciting the same lines she was reading to herself. She looked up and saw a chipmunky ingenue with breasts as big as Buicks contentedly gurgling the over-ripe dialogue aloud to the palpable displeasure of the assembled bevy of auditionees.

One exasperated Uma Thurman knockoff stomped to the still-vacant reception desk, picked up the phone and dialed. "Is Murray there? . . . *April*." She rolled her eyes and planted a hand on her outthrust hip. "Yes, I'll hold . . ."

The chubby, flustered casting assistant emerged from the inner sanctum. "I need my phone . . . ," she miserably implored April, just before Murray got on the line.

"Goddammit, Murray, this fucking *Teenage Brides* audition is running late and I'm not going to be able to make my other one. I don't remember the name of it!" She slapped her head shot down by the phone then actually started leafing through a three-ring binder lying open on the desk.

The casting assistant indignantly reclaimed it. "There's a pay phone outside . . . you really can't—" she began, shaking her head.

"I'm *at* the thing now, Murray!" A loud, piercing beep emanated from the pocket of her miniskirt. "Fuck. I'm being paged."

A bony woman with a coal black bouffant came out and whispered something to the assistant, who then called, "Violet Sire?"

Violet gratefully stepped forward. "I've got to make a call," the casting assistant tried once more as April checked her beeper.

"Okay, fine! I've been here almost an hour. Does anyone have change for a dollar?" Actresses being actresses, everyone ignored her. The assistant led Violet into the office, where she was introduced to Fonda, the bouffanted casting director, and the film director, a blonde Asian smoking Camels in a Nine Inch Nails T-shirt and NYU cap.

"Did you get that Ami Dolenz appointment?" Fonda asked her assistant.

"No! I couldn't . . . this girl was using my phone and wouldn't get off . . ."

"Someone waiting to see us? Who?"

"I didn't check her name . . . ," the assistant whined.

"April," Violet said brightly.

"Come on. I'll take care of this," Fonda said, marching off with assistant in tow.

The director was engrossed in Violet's résumé, so she sat down. "Shit! Did you just get here from New York?"

"Two weeks ago," she said.

"I've been here a month! Wow. We haven't auditioned anyone from New York."

Sensing preferential treatment, Violet adjusted her body language and turned up the warmth. "I was just in a show at the Virginia Theater called *Sunburnt*. Did you see it?"

"No," the director replied, lighting a new cigarette from his smoldering butt. "I never went to any plays. Except *The Real Live*

Brady Bunch." He wanted to talk about living in the Village and how much easier it was to get good pizza there than in LA, so Violet happily went along, peripherally imagining annoyed bimbettes storming out of the waiting room with places to go and people to eat as she and this film school tyro shot the breeze. Finally his attention drifted to the sides and he started explaining the character of Veronica to Violet.

"She's the heroine—a beautiful young girl who doesn't really know why she's in a convent. And the betrayal issues she's dealing with, because of her boyfriend, she's feeling them again now, because the other nuns don't believe her when she tells them there's a murderer loose. This is horror, *so make it as big as you can.*"

The kind of direction an actor can only dream of being blessed with. Why not "be as bad as possible"? Violet smiled and said, "You got it." She read the first speech, agonized: "You don't understand! Sister Mary Timothy didn't just *disappear!* She's here, somewhere in the convent. I can feel her . . . and something else, *SOMETHING EVIL!*"

Fonda cracked open the door and slipped in. "Wait a sec, stop. Fonda, she's not right for Veronica. She's too strong. Too in command," the director announced, puffing madly and regarding Violet like he was popping a stiffy. "Give her the Theresa sides."

"Who's Theresa?" Violet asked.

"The villain. She's possessed by the spirit of the killer from the first movie, the ex-altar boy. Did you see it? Me neither. Anyway, in this scene Theresa knows Mary Timothy has sinned by masturbating and she wants to punish her, but she's also very attracted to her . . . well, the dead ex-altar boy's evil spirit is, anyway. 'Kay? You'll be great. The nudity's really tasteful. I'm going to call her back for the producer, Fonda. We lived a block apart in New York for three years!"

"Is there a script available for me to read . . . before?" Violet asked, slightly disturbed that the words *masturbating, punish* and *nudity* had occurred in the same speech.

"It's still being written," he said.

"Well, when does the movie shoot?" Violet continued, hoping she wasn't out of line.

"Next Wednesday."

"Okay, let's go," Fonda snapped. "Ready, doll? Love the hair. Gorgeous."

As long as she was sitting in traffic on Olympic, Violet figured she might as well put the top down for the first time. A baptism. Even though she was still pissed off at her mother.

It wasn't that she didn't like the Honda Civic del Sol—it was a year old and ran like a dream and had a false-front cassette deck that was currently enriching her world with The Cranberries' debut album. It was the fact that her mother had traded in her perfectly serviceable if no-frills Fiat for it without asking. "That was not a star's car, dear," she'd told Violet. "I didn't want you driving onto the studio lot for some producers' callback in that shabby old thing."

"I liked it. It was *my* car, Mom."

"This is your car, too, darling. And it's very hot right now. I saw one on *Melrose Place*. Now let me get Brian's number at ICM for you—"

"Mom, I think I can find a phone number for ICM if I need one. They're listed."

"Well, excuse me for trying to help your career develop, Miss New York Attitude."

"Mom? Remember the movie *Frances*?"

Her mother wanted her to move in "just for the summer," insisting Violet needed to hold on to her savings. Placing a higher value on her sanity, Violet woke up the next morning at six and quietly drove off, returning at two for a passive-aggressive luncheon climaxing with Violet's announcement that she'd rented an apartment in Beverly Glen Canyon. It was a steal at $575 with all bills paid. In denial, her mother pulled out composite cards and started recommending head shot photographers.

Violet turned north onto Beverly Glen and pulled into her space under the carport fifteen minutes later. She lugged as much laundry as she could around to the back of the house then dropped it all and screamed when she saw a guy sitting on the stone bench outside her apartment door.

"I look that bad, do I?" he said, pretending to adjust himself via his reflection in a window before bending over to help gather some stray pieces of laundry that had spewed from the basket.

Violet made no move to pick anything up. "Goddammit, Dave! What the hell are you doing here? Trying to give me heart failure? Jesus H. Christ." She turned around and stalked back to her car for the rest of her stuff. Dave shoved his hands in his jeans pockets and followed her.

"Nice to see you again, Violet. I've been jolly-jack splendid actually, thanks." She knew he was smiling, and she could really do without seeing it—or the rest of his fucking handsome face. It had been almost a year. Their last meeting had gone badly. They were eating chicken scarpariella at DaRosina on Forty-sixth Street. He was back in New York and asked her to return to L.A. To marry him. She said she couldn't. He accused her of seeing someone else. She reminded him that he had left *her* four months ago. He said she was selfish and on a star trip. She called him a manipulative, hopeless cocksucker and bolted from the table. He took off after her and knocked their bottle of wine onto the floor, where it exploded spectacularly. He was yelling after her from the rain-whipped corner when an *American Gladiators*-type hauled him back into the restaurant because there was still the matter of the bill. She thought he'd gone back to England or Ireland to work for his brother. Her mother called him "the love of your life," a terrible expression that made Violet think of bad Olivia de Havilland movies.

"How did you get this address? Like I even have to ask," she muttered, slamming the trunk shut and imagining her mother trussed up inside like the rat-fink stoolie she was.

Dave peeked into the Honda. "Nice car. Quite successful, aren't you?" She didn't think he was being sarcastic but gave him a bitchy look anyway. "Your mum told me where you were."

"She'll have to be punished," Violet deadpanned.

Dave followed her back to her door. "I tried ringing you up in New York. I wanted to catch your show."

"Well, it closed, Dave. You'll have to see the movie." She put the laundry down and started fishing for her house keys.

"I heard. Sorry. The stupid cunts." She smiled. She couldn't help being amused when he called men cunts. "Can I come in then?" She shook her head.

"Violet," he said quietly, putting his hand on her arm. "Look at me?" She finally did, hating the way he made her feel like a real woman and hating herself for wondering if she was having the same effect on him.

She looked into his very blue eyes. "You can't keep crash-landing into my life whenever you feel like it. I could be totally in love with someone else at this exact second." It might be a good idea for him to believe this until she formulated a strategy.

"Your mum said you weren't seeing anyone."

God, was she dead.

"Of all the fuckin'—" she began.

"The least you can do is let me buy you a lemonade. There's that café I passed down the road." He cocked his head south.

"The Four Oaks? It's seventy-five dollars a plate."

"I miss you."

"Yeah? I miss *Twin Peaks*."

He looked down and kicked a pebble with his cowboy boot. "Everything has to be a joke then?" he asked quietly.

The flip act was temporarily down. That was a start at least. But Violet wasn't ready to let up. "I think the joke is that you expect me to pick up where things left off."

"How do you know what I expect?"

"How am I supposed to know one damn thing about what's going on with you? It's been a year, Dave. A real kooky shitstorm of a year. And you missed it. I've changed."

"No, you haven't. You're still the bloody queen of drama."

She inserted her key into the dead bolt lock. "Get bent."

"I love you."

"You're not coming in."

"Then let's go."

"I'm busy."

"So'm I. Got a mobile pet-grooming business. Me van's out front."

"I really resent this." She stowed the laundry under the stone bench and wrenched her key from the lock. "One glass of lemonade. That's it."

"We'll go somewhere with free refills."

Fawn insisted on driving to Gail's alone. She needed to focus her anger at the betrayal and abject mishandling of her career by that pathetic excuse for a manager and then destroy her. And fire her. And get all of her pictures back. Who the hell did that deadbeat think she was dealing with? She'd be sorry when Fawn hit it big and told the world what an incompetent leech Gail Ann Griffin really was.

Fawn checked herself in the rearview mirror. There was just enough wind to lift and rustle her hair dramatically without mussing it. She blotted her lipstick and admired her Armani sunglasses. She was a beautiful young woman driving a Mercedes 300 CE down San Vicente Boulevard. People probably assumed she was already a star. She flicked on her stereo and sang along with "I'm Every Woman." And what about that new hair of Gail's? How *dare* she use Fawn's colorist and ask for the exact same shade of blonde? It was like plagiarism. Gail probably subconsciously wanted to sabotage Fawn's career because Gail's own acting had been such a failure. *Charles in Charge*? *The Last American Virgin*? She called those credits? Please!

Gail was probably sweating out some of her many toxins in the Sports Connection steam room right this minute instead of trying to procure auditions for her clients. Well, if she wasn't home, Fawn would just wait for her. She wondered if Gail did a lick of real work for *anyone* except Turk Marlowe. And what good did he do Fawn? Mr. Hot-Shit Series Star. She'd had one lousy reading for his show, *Leather & Lace*. It wasn't Fawn's fault it hadn't gone too well— she'd had no time to prepare, and everyone knew how mean Barbara Claman, the casting director, was.

Fawn pulled up to Gail's place. She worked from home, of course, the bottom half of a Spanish duplex on Sixth Street. And there was Gail's Eddie Bauer 4×4 right in the driveway. Fawn dialed Gail on the car phone and tapped a fingernail against the dashboard as it rang four times before her machine picked up. At the beep, Fawn said, "Gail. I know you're there. Pick up the damn phone *right* now. I am *not* playing games anymore!" She hung up and stormed to the front door and rang the bell. Nothing. Fawn cupped a hand around her already shaded eyes and tried to see through the front picture window, but heavy lace curtains prevented peepage. She rang the bell another time, waited for a count of "ten Mississippi," then proceeded around the side of the house to the back door. Gail had her washer and dryer in an alcove off the kitchen, and she'd better be in there doing laundry, Fawn thought furiously. She wasn't. Fawn rapped on the back door one time, then grabbed the knob in a fit of pique. It turned in her hand and the door opened.

Fawn walked into the sunny Williams-Sonoma catalog kitchen. "Gail?" she called. She entered the dining area, from which she had a full view of the living room. No one. "Gail?" she called again. Becoming a tad unsettled, Fawn headed down the hallway toward the bedrooms. Gail used the first one as an office. Her computer was on, the cursor flashing blankly on an empty screen. Fawn continued to the master bedroom. The door was open. Fawn screamed.

"Jesus! Gail, what happened?!"

Ms. Griffin had been tied to her wrought iron bed frame with what looked like Laura Ashley scarves. She was wearing black silk stockings, matching garter belt and nothing else. Her large bare breasts were crisscrossed with some type of welts or scratches. Her eyes bulged madly over a black leather *thing* stuffed in her mouth. Fawn scrambled to her side and wrenched out the wet makeshift gag. It seemed to be some kind of jockstrap! "Gail, are you all right? What in the name of—"

"You stupid bitch! What the fuck are you doing in my house?" Gail shrieked. "Get out!"

Fawn took a step back, bewildered and horrified. She heard a noise behind her and squealed, whirling around to behold Turk Marlowe, hardbodied star of syndicated TV's steamy adult thriller *Leather & Lace*, emerging from Gail's bathroom stark naked. His erect penis, trussed into a combination cockring/testicle harness, was almost as huge as the latex dildo he brandished in one greasy hand.

"Oh, my God! What kind of perverted sicko are you?" Fawn shrilly demanded of her personal manager.

"Get out of my house!" Gail barked, struggling uselessly against the knotted scarves.

"What the hell is she doing here?" Turk asked mildly. He grabbed a towel from a chair and ridiculously tried to conceal himself.

"You are fired, Gail!" Fawn exclaimed, not about to be cheated out of this moment by some kinky sex tableau. "That showcase was the biggest rip-off I've ever seen! You couldn't even get one lousy agent to sit through the damn thing! You and your nonexistent acting ability! And playing a teenager? What a fuckin' laugh!'"

"You should talk!" Gail hissed, breasts heaving with rage. "Maybe if you hadn't insisted on that fag Andre and his piece-of-shit scenes, people would have been able to make it to the end! Turk, get this talentless cooze out of my face! Now!"

"That's it! You got this comin', missy," Fawn drawled. She slapped Gail. Turk instantly seized her from behind and dragged her away from the bed.

"Get your hands off me!" Fawn roared, wrenching free and facing the two of them with abject hatred. Turk's towel had fallen free in the fracas. Damn, that's a big dick, Fawn thought for a nanosecond before addressing Gail: "I don't need you, you filthy slut! You can take your sicko boyfriend and go straight to hell!" Fawn sobbed, backing toward the door before breaking into a hysterical sprint back to the safety of her car.

Jason woke up that morning awash in relief that he didn't have to go to work all day. He burrowed his face into the foam pillow he'd had since junior high and slid a hand into his Jockeys, encountering a rigid penile salute. Rolling onto his back, he popped it through his fly, then remembered the conversation he'd overheard last night before falling asleep. He reflexively pulled a sheet over his softening penis and lay still on his air mattress, mortified.

"Did I tell you I saw Jason whacking off the other night?" Tricia's flabby boyfriend had chortled from their room, although with the open windows and tiny patch of dried backyard that separated their rooms, he might as well have been sitting on Jason's bed.

"God, Zach," Tricia said. "What were you doing spying on him? Do you have some latent tendencies I should know about?"

"Very funny. And I wasn't *spying*. I was just standing here. He had one of his blinds open and the TV on or something and I saw a shadow on the wall—him, pulling his pud."

"Unbelievable. Where was I?"

"Asleep. You always fall asleep during *Arsenio*."

"I do not."

"You do."

"That show is terribly overrated."

"Actually it's in last place."

"He was *masturbating* with the blind open? That's disgusting."

"Is he home now?"

"Who, Jason? I think he went to El Coyote with those showcase people. That girl Fawn was quite dreadful. Zach, you didn't eat all those Mint Milanos, did you? Unbelievable."

How could he have been so stupid? Damn that fucking broken blind that wouldn't come down all the way. How could he have left a light on? That was beyond stupid. He wouldn't be able to face those two again. Or Wren. Of course Tricia would tell her.

He looked around his twelve-by-seven-foot room and hated his life and everything in it. It all sucked. It had sucked from the day he arrived in L.A., May 25, 1993. Jason and Andre were carrying the first load of Jason's stuff into the bedroom Andre had sublet him and were greeted by the sight of Wren on her hands and knees in a coked-up frenzy, resolving a wet, greenish shit stain courtesy of Heathcliffe smack dab in the middle of Jason's carpet.

"I'm soooo sorry about this," she insisted. "He's really a good dog. He's just real sensitive. Did Andre tell you he's an abuse survivor?"

"And a retard," Andre added, doubtlessly thrilled he'd pawned this roommate and Tricia off on his mother's best friend's son from Ohio. Jason had bought a cheap little rug from Pier 1 to cover the indelible stain, but on hot days he thought he could still smell something foul and fecal.

There was the wooden wine crate he used as a desk. On top was a folder with copies of his résumé and job application letters he'd sent to all the major record companies in town and the inevitable "Thanks-but-no-we'll-keep-you-on-file-B'bye" rejections he'd received from practically all of them. If anyone asked why he saved them, Jason would have said he planned on hanging them in his office at Sire Records when he was promoted to VP, along with a personally inscribed Debbie Harry poster and snapshots of himself with members of The Go-Go's.

A more accurate theory would have been that when the stockpile of rejections grew fat enough, it would impel him to move back to Columbus. An option that lately seemed more and more shamefully attractive. He admitted to himself that he had only been in Los Angeles less than two months, and that he technically did have a job in show biz. The problem was it was the lowest possible position on the entertainment industry food chain. After everyone was done with a project—writers, producers, casting directors, agents, actors, publicists, cineplex ushers—it ended up trickling down to a VHS or laserdisc to be rented to Mr. and Mrs. John Q. Cheesepuff when there was "nothing good on." The absolute only consolation would have been free dick flicks, but the store only carried heterosexual porn along with the odd, unsatisfying "bisexual" title.

No matter how many Glade plug-ins or sticks of incense from Yellow Springs he employed, there seemed no way to eradicate the cigarette stink that permeated the entire house, despite the supposed confinement of Wren's smoking to her dingy boudoir. Jason dreaded going into the kitchen for toast and yogurt because of the mess he'd glimpsed in the sink on his way in last night, a compost salad of vegetable peelings tossed with coffee grounds and Marlboro Light butts. Wren was a "Vitarian" and did not cook any of her food. She believed it destroyed the nutrients. She had a rationale for coffee, but it was so out there Jason couldn't remember it a day after she told him. Kitchen cleanup appeared to be solely Jason's responsibility—Tricia usually ate out, and any cooking she did went straight from freezer to microwave and was eaten off disposable Chinette with plastic utensils. Jason was too quiet and nice to ask if Vitarianism also forbade Wren to sweep up the hairstorm Heathcliffe shed weekly.

Jason got off the mattress, which he had to pump up every other night because of a slow leak. He stretched his long, hairy legs, still muscular even though he hadn't been to a gym since he graduated. He jogged around the neighborhood far less often than recommended by *Men's Workout* magazine, no issues of which had yet made it to his new address. That was another problem. Wren retrieved the mail from the box and tended to leave it in obscure piles just about anywhere. Jason had found a two-week-old letter from his mother in Wren's bathroom when he went in to get a plunger. Not that Mom had anything real to say to him anyway.

He opened the miniblinds. It was a fabulous Southern California day. He could drive to the beach if every mile he put on his car didn't put it an inch closer to its imminent death by natural causes.

And who wanted to go to the beach alone anyway? Who would want to stay in this dirty, dangerous city and be surrounded by glamour, success and free-flowing wealth with no way to tap into it? If his twenties were going to be spent behind a video counter, why not in Ohio?

For one thing, his car wouldn't survive a return trip. What if he sold it, packed up his meager possessions and mailed them to his dad's house and took a Greyhound back? He still had a few college friends in Columbus. Maybe bartending school, then a job at The Garage, the best gay dance club in town? The guys there were a hell of a lot realer, nicer and more approachable than the self-obsessed pricks in L.A. His parents wouldn't have to know where he worked, exactly. Not that they'd even necessarily notice he was back in the state. There was always grad school to consider, too . . . a thesis on female sexual identity and its emergence in the girl groups of the early sixties.

He sat back on the mattress and started to sketch out a relocation budget on a writing tablet. The phone rang. He hesitated, afraid it was Marilyn calling him in to work. Fuck that evil cow—he'd say he had plans. "Hello?"

"Bonjour, mon petit." Andre.

"Hey, what are you up to?" Jason half-sighed.

"Packing is what I'm up to. Holy shit, honey, have I got dirt for you. The bottom line is Fawn and myself are leaving for Texas on Saturday for the rest of the summer."

What the hell . . . ? "Texas?"

"She's taking a little hiatus from acting. Her family has a lake house near San Antonio, and she's going to record a demo there. She's got a magnificent voice."

"Wow. For a record company?"

"Yes. Fawn Farrar Records. It's kind of like a spec album. To show off her talent for labels, producers." Or *showcase* it, to be more precise. "You know how the music biz works."

"But who's going to sit the mansion?"

"Well, you are, darling."

"This is for the bath lights," Andre told Jason, indicating a switch-plate set in a marble column adjacent to an expansive sunken tub garnished with a blaze of vibrant potted flowers lined up on the two marble steps descending into the empty basin. "And this dial controls the whirlpool jets. You probably shouldn't use this bathroom, though. But if you do, move these plants and wipe the marble completely dry. And definitely don't use these." He scooped up several decorative Hello Kitty soaps from a silver filigree bath caddy mounted on the wall. "They're imported." He deposited them into the pocket of his silk robe. Jason noticed a miniature champagne bottle of bubble bath and a loofah mitt on the shelf. God only knew the sudsy debaucheries that had taken place in here since Andre moved in. They were off the master bedroom, which was stunning even devoid of furniture. The all-glass south wall offered a 70mm cityscape and a partial view of the house's epic swimming pool, a perfect square that filled most of the backyard and was transversed by a glassed-in bridge that connected this bedroom with the sunken den on the other side of the house.

Jason's belongings were in the servants' quarters off the kitchen, a bedroom nearly double the size of his Orange Grove Avenue digs. Four pieces of Louis Vuitton luggage and a round box containing a cowboy hat, Andre's, waited at the front door for Fawn's arrival. She and Andre were flying first-class to San Antonio in three hours. The mansion orientation had been ridiculously simple. All Jason had to do was dump the garbage, turn a few lights on and off, and make sure the fountain and waterfall outside the main entrance didn't overflow. Easy as pie. Speaking of which, Andre had whipped up a chocolate-raspberry tart and left it for Jason in the vault-size refrigerator, fully stocked apparently moments before Fawn decreed their musical Texas retreat. Jason wouldn't have to go to a grocery store for weeks. And while he was practically levitating off the dog hair–free tiled floor with the exhilaration of being in such a roomy, immaculate kitchen—the built-ins!—with bougainvilleas outside the picture window, Andre told him rent on the Orange Grove house would be "comped" for the duration of his mansion stay. "You're being such a doll, it's the least I can do," he trilled like a fairy godmother, continuing the tour with the offhanded disclosure that Giles Burke was paying *ten grand* a month in upkeep on the one-story, half-acre hideaway.

The doorbell rang "Fur Elise." "Oh, for fuck's sake! Fawn!"

Andre wailed. "Tell her I'm just finishing dressing!" He scooted off to his room, leaving Jason to stride across the enormous foyer to answer the double doors. Fawn was in a simple summer dress, a floppy sun hat decorated with dried roses, shades and red ropers.

"Hi, darlin'!" she said, giving Jason a passionless hug. "All moved in?"

"I just have another carload to bring over. This is the most beautiful house I've ever seen, Fawn. Thanks for—"

She clomped into the foyer, pausing in the rectangle of sun pouring down in celestial shafts through a skylight. She struck a subtle pose before asking, "Excuse me, but where's Andre?"

"He's almost finished dressing," Jason dutifully assured her. "He explained everything to me, and wrote it all down in a notebook, so . . . it should be easy."

Fawn nodded absently, meandering over to the window to gaze at the pool. "We're putting the house up for sale, so the realtor may be dropping by with people." Jason was unfazed. The L.A. real estate market was so depressed it could take years to unload a mausoleum like this. "It's for the best, I guess. There's too many painful memories."

"I thought you guys never lived here," Jason said.

"The associations are still very— They hurt." Fawn sighed as if she were in a soap opera workshop. "I don't know what's going to happen with me and Giles. But thank God I have my music to help me work through it. You know about the demo, right? I even wrote two of the songs."

"Andre told me," Jason said.

"Told you what?" Andre flounced in and poked Jason's cute ass with an impertinent finger.

"That you went skinny-dipping with that teenage gardener in *my* swimming pool," Fawn sassed. Andre's mouth popped open in horror, and Jason wondered if it were true. "Now let's get a move-on. I need to buy gum."

Andre and Jason somehow wedged everything into the packed Mercedes. Jason kissed and embraced them both. Doors slammed, precision-tuned German engine ignited. Fawn turned the car around and started down the curvy, quarter-mile driveway. Then she stopped, lowered the window and waved Jason over to her face.

"Sweetie, I almost forgot. You might be seeing my mother-in-law, Maggie Burke. She said something to Giles about coming in from Dayton to 'decorate' the house. So it'll sell faster." She shook her head wearily. "She's kind of a pill. Just stay out of her way. Ignore her. I do. Bye!" And they were gone.

Jason went back into the house. He loaded the CD changer with The Pop-Tartts, Hazell Dean, Eighth Wonder, Shakespear's Sister and Kate Bush. Then he opened the glass doors onto the patio, stripped naked and with a quiet whoop jumped into the pool.

"Violet?" Tricia chimed, peeking into the waiting room. "Tricia Cook."

"Hi," Violet smiled, rising from the teal sectional sofa and shaking Tricia's cold little hand. "It's so nice to meet you."

"Follow me," Tricia replied. "Edgar had to step out for a few hours, but I'm sure he won't mind if we use his office." She ushered Violet in. Tricia was actually quite frightened at the possibility of Edgar returning early from his lunch with Drew Barrymore to discover her behind his desk, which she'd taboo-shatteringly straightened.

"So I won't be meeting Edgar?" Violet asked lightly, as if it didn't matter that she'd be frittering away the afternoon with his powerless secretary.

"Well, today you're meeting with just me. I'm a subagent and I work very closely with Edgar." A secretary. The phone rang. "Yes?" Tricia answered. "I'm sorry, Lucy, he's not in. Is there anything I can help you with? . . . Tricia . . . Fine, I'll have him return." She hung up and rolled her eyes. "Now where were we?"

"You were just about to pick up my photo and tell me what a bright future I had in L.A.," Violet said playfully. She crossed then uncrossed her legs, realizing she'd tarted it up outfit-and-makeup-wise just a tad in anticipation of meeting a man, not a girl who looked like an Episcopal missionary.

Tricia smiled. Violet had a spunky, relaxed quality she liked but would never admit aspiring to. She picked up Violet's "bio" and they discussed *One Life to Live* and *Sunburnt*, Tricia paraphrasing a recent *Variety* piece about its imminent cinematic adaptation and saying she just didn't "get" Nicole Kidman. Violet took her demo tape from her purse and handed it to Tricia. "My best soap stuff is on here, plus two scenes from *Law & Order*. I didn't put any of my L.A. work from the eighties on it 'cause I look really young and it was for shows like *Knightrider* and *Archie Bunker's Place*. And I was cut out of *Bad Lieutenant* entirely, except for fifteen seconds of screaming."

"I'm sure this will be fine," Tricia said, placing the tape in the in-box. "So you left L.A. in 1990 to tour with *Speed-the-Plow*."

Violet nodded. "It was a fabulous experience. I loved working with Perry King."

"I remember when it played the Henry Fonda Theater," Tricia said wistfully. "I terribly wanted to go but I couldn't afford a ticket."

"Darn, I could have comped you," Violet laughed, but Tricia was staring into the air somewhere to Violet's right.

"What is it he said?" Tricia asked rhetorically. "The pursuit of Fashion is the attempt of the middle-class to co-opt tragedy."

What the fuck was she talking about? "Who?"

"David Mamet."

"I'm really not sure," Violet said.

"It was in *Writing in Restaurants*. Have you read that?"

"No, I haven't."

"Oh, you simply must. I love his theater, and his screenplays, especially *House of Games*, but he also writes the most hortatory essays." *Hortatory???* "The fashion piece basically said we appropriate styles of dress so that we can absorb, vicariously, you understand, the experiences of groups alien to us who seem to represent tragic or romantic elements missing from our own lives. For instance, the straight community is influenced by the gay fashion world, which is really just borrowing from the fifties, because it finds that era so tragic."

Violet nodded thoughtfully. What the hell was this, Honors English 12?

Tricia leaned forward confidentially. "So, did you ever get to meet . . . Mamet?"

"One time. We had dinner with him opening night in Chicago. We talked about the Berlin Wall coming down and he tried to guess my cup size."

Tricia flushed visibly. The phone rang. "Yes, hello? . . . Yes, it is . . . I'm sorry, he's out of the office until this afternoon . . . No, he *isn't* here . . . I see . . . Yes . . . , Sir, I have nothing to do with his personal affairs—just leave me your number—hello? Hello?" She hung up. "Unbelievable. Yes, uh, Violet, why don't I schedule a scene for you?"

"A scene?"

"You'll do a monologue or a duet for myself and the other agents." Tricia began to re-create the disarray she'd tidied on the desktop. "Actually, they do tend to prefer duets. Do you know someone who could be your scene partner?"

"I really don't."

"Oh, fine. Monologues are fine. Something modern. Mamet, perhaps?"

"I'm sure I can come up with something," Violet said quickly. "So this is like an audition for the agency? I don't mean to sound stupid, I've just never done anything like this."

"It's quite standard for new actors," Tricia informed her. This person could really become annoying, Violet thought. "I've been in the agency business for over five years—"

Edgar's intercom beeped. "Tricia, can you please cover the front desk? Misty thinks she has food poisoning."

"I'm in a meeting right now—" Tricia responded.

"She's in a *meeting*," the intercom voice sarcastically relayed to someone. "Who are you, Sue Mengers? Finish it and take over the phones. Now."

Tricia stood up. "Will you excuse me? I'm terribly sorry about this."

"Don't worry about it," Violet said, poised for a quick getaway.

Tricia nodded, forcing what she thought was her warmest smile, which squizzled into a miserable grimace as Violet walked out and Tricia scrambled for tissues to blot her tears of humiliation.

Jason never would have heard the doorbell if not for the quiet part of "Live to Tell"—he was startled to recognize the tinkling notes of Beethoven preceding Madonna's confession that if she ran away, she wouldn't have the strength to go very far.

He darted toward the door in stockinged feet, sliding up to the peephole, the music thumping and soaring gorgeously behind him.

Standing on the doorstep-cum-footbridge spanning the decorative waterfall pond was a hunk. Jason opened the door.

"Hi," the hunk said. He had dark eyes and black hair and black jeans and a solid white T-shirt stretched snugly over a solid chest. If Jason could have picked a custom-built man out of a catalog for home delivery, this would have been it. The hunk was holding an amazingly cute pug who appeared to be grinning at Jason like a dragon outside a Chinese restaurant. "I'm sorry to bother you," he, the hunk, said, "but I live next door, and the way the acoustics are in these hills, your music's really loud up at my place . . ."

"Oh, God," Jason said. "I'm sorry." He zipped to the wet bar and lowered the stereo volume. "I feel so isolated up here, I didn't think about . . ." The hunk had stepped in during the interim. Could he possibly, please Jesus, *have a problem?* "Normally it wouldn't be any problem, but my wife's meditating." Damn. "My name's Hank Rietta, by the way. And this is Nabisco. Say hi, baby." He raised the dog's tawny forepaw to Jason.

"Jason Dallin," Jason said, giving first the paw then Hank's large hand a firm shake.

"You didn't buy this place, did you?" Hank asked, shifting Nabisco in his arms. Despite the wife, his deep voice and flexing muscles made Jason dizzy.

"No, I'm just watching it for Fawn and Giles. The owners." "Live to Tell" ended and the CD changer replaced it with an obscure track from Marina Stetson's almost-as-obscure second solo album.

"Wow," Hank said. "Maybe you better turn this song up."

"Why?" Jason wondered, always excited to discover a fellow Mariniac.

"I guess I should tell you who I'm married to," he smiled. Hank began to dance in place, mouthing the lyrics to Nabisco. A rather bizarre spectacle.

Oh, my God. "Marina Stetson?!?!?" Jason blurted, the very possibility spinning him out of control.

"Bingo. She claims that not one person owns a copy of this album. I'll tell her she's wrong."

"I love it. I love Marina. She's my favorite singer. I saw my first Pop-Tartts concert when I was fourteen. I read she changed record companies and has a new album coming out."

"Yeah, it's finished. They're mixing it and shit and it'll be on sale in a couple months." Jason waited breathlessly for any more information. But Hank surprised him with a play-punch to his biceps and pivoted around to leave. "I gotta get back. It was nice to meet you, Jason. Tell you what—we'll have you over soon. I'm sure Marina would enjoy it."

"That'd be wonderful." It would be miraculous. It would be fucking heaven on earth. "Good night, Hank." Jason peeped and saw him cross the driveway and start to scale the landscaped bluff separating the two properties. Dazzled, Jason went into the kitchen and fixed himself a diet Coke with fresh lemon, then took it outside to the patio and sat.

The fragrant scent of expensive, night-blooming plants filled the air, which was cool and seemed infinitely cleaner here than it did south of Sunset. Marina Stetson. How had Andre been ignorant of such a famous neighbor? Jason had been collecting press clippings about her for years. The last he'd read, she lived in Malibu. And why no pictures of that massively sexy husband? She *had* been out of the public eye since her second solo album, *Rainwater Lullaby*, bombed. But to have her here, next door? It was incredible. Nothing had happened, yet it was the most exciting thing that had ever happened to him. *This* was what he had come to Hollywood for.

Violet, in bra and panties, applied the few products necessary for her to achieve great hair and broke open the lipstick locker. "So what do you think?"

"That you're flippin' white lightning in bed," Dave said from there, naked.

"I'm talking about the script, wise-ass," she told him. They'd been out a few times since the lemonade, and she'd resisted the sexual tension thick enough to drive a truck across until this afternoon. She'd known they were going to sleep together as soon as he picked her up for lunch and she smelled the Grey Flannel, barely perceptible around his neck, after he inserted a finger into her belt loop and drew her to him for a shamelessly raunchy hello kiss. Now she was about to run late for her "scene" at the Conan Carroll Agency.

Dave propped himself up on pillows and balanced the final draft of *Teenage Brides of Christ II* on his rough-hewn torso. "The script is pure shit. Nasty, too. Have to make sure I rent the movie."

"Can you believe my mother was mad at me for not going to the callback? I showed her the most disgusting part—where my character ties Sister Corky or whoever to the cross and eats her pussy, off-camera, right before stabbing her—and you know what she said?" Violet removed a short retro dress of ambiguous vintage from her closet and put it on. "That's how Mariel Hemingway got her start."

"Your mum just wants you to be a star," Dave said.

"She'd have let John Landis put me in the helicopter if she thought it would get my picture in *Casting Call* magazine."

"That's really shitty," Dave commented in an irritated tone she'd always hated.

"Well, I'm allowed," she snapped back. "She's my mother, not yours."

"Look, it's just that you're really hard on her all the fuckin' time—"

"Don't." She picked up her purse and waited a tense beat of silence before facing him and asking, "Do I look okay?"

He nodded. "You'll be a smash."

She made it to Century City exactly on time, and Tricia scuttled into the waiting room to tell her she was "marshaling the troops" to view the scene. Violet sat for twenty minutes, calmly reviewing the minor edits she'd implemented to transform one of her scenes from *Sunburnt* into a monologue. Then it was time to go in. Tricia showed her to a conference room. "I'd really hoped for a few more people," Tricia whispered stiffly as they went in. Violet scanned the room dubiously. Where did they expect her to perform? On the table? There *was* a small area of clear floor space in the corner. A long way from Broadway, she thought. A fuck of a long way.

"This is Ari Rosenblatt," Tricia said, introducing her to a young nebbish seated at the table. "Ari, Violet Cyr." They exchanged niceties while Tricia fretted. "Maybe I better see if Edgar—"

Edgar walked in. Christ, Violet thought, he's the trailer for *It Came from Palm Springs*. Suit by Bill Blass, loafers by Gucci, and hair transplants by whoever did Richard Simmons. He removed the sunglasses from his hand-tooled Corinthian face and flashed a set of shark teeth at her for exactly one second before sitting down heavily and summoning Tricia for a tense, whispered interlude. "That's unbelievable, Edgar," Tricia whined, dismayed. "I'll get right on it this afternoon."

"Why don't we get started?" Edgar asked abruptly. He laid his glasses and *Hollywood Reporter* on the table.

"Yes, we're all ready," Tricia said. "Violet, this is Edgar Black. Edgar, Violet Cyr."

"What do you have for us today, sweetheart?" Edgar asked her.

"I'm doing a monologue from the Broadway show I was in this spring called *Sunburnt*." She moved to the corner and began, surprised at how strange it felt to be saying the familiar lines out-of-context. Ari seemed to be enjoying the performance. Tricia was dividing her attention between Violet and Edgar's reaction to Violet. After hitting an emotional peak, Violet glanced toward Edgar and was appalled to see him leafing through his *Reporter*! She finished the scene without a hitch, and they applauded. She smiled beautifully and thanked them, anger and disappointment pulling her down like cartoon anvils.

"That was great, hon. We'll call you," Edgar said. Violet exited, exchanging brief eye contact with a visibly distraught Tricia. Violet left the office and hit the elevator button. That had been the most humiliating exercise in pointlessness she'd ever put herself through. The worst part was Edgar had been her only current prospect—none of the other agents she'd contacted had called. That smarmy prick couldn't even give her three minutes of his time? She jabbed the elevator button again. The doors opened and she stepped in. She hit Lobby and heard a voice cry, "Violet? Violet! Wait!"

The doors were closing, so she wedged herself in between and saw Tricia careen around the corner. "Violet! Thank God I caught you. I have an audition for you. It's in forty-five minutes for Barbara Claman. Here's the meeting slip." She handed Violet a photocopied form with the audition data meticulously completed in Tricia's too-decorous penmanship. "The role of Monique on *Leather & Lace*."

Jason took the empty video display boxes from the mustachioed blonde appliance salesman type and switched them for *Playboy's Wet & Wild* and *Body of Evidence*. He cast another glance toward the curly tressed beauty bopping around the horror section. She looked *really* familiar, but he was afraid he was becoming starstruck since the brief but oh-so-tantalizing intersection of Marina Stetson's world with his a few days before. Still, there was something. She caught him studying her and smiled. He gave her a little wave, then accepted the blonde guy's membership card. He zapped it with his retail stun gun and a late-charge flag flashed on the computer screen. Jason told him he owed $4.33.

"There's gotta be a mistake," the dude said.

"They were checked out on June twenty-ninth, due on the thirtieth, and returned in the night drop after we closed. So they're considered a day late."

"I really don't remember that," he insisted, fidgeting impatiently and folding and refolding the five-dollar bill he intended to trade for tonight's nudity-packed entertainment. "What were they?"

Jason hesitated a moment before saying, "A couple of adult videos."

The dude continued to shake his head. "Which ones?"

Jason kept his eyes on the screen as he read aloud. "*Lactating Lesbos* and *Fuck Me Hard, Please*."

"Oh." The customer hurriedly withdrew his wallet and charged the whole thing.

It was fairly dead tonight. Marilyn had been there when Jason came in at five. She gave him shit about some delinquent-account letters he was supposed to have printed out earlier, and then she became really pissy when he showed her the same completed letters stacked on her desk. Revenge for making her look like the stupid toad she was came later when she lowered the volume on the store's sound system to negligible Muzak levels two minutes after Jason had fired up *The Pop-Tarts Live at the Hollywood Bowl* on laserdisc. Then she conveniently made herself too busy to help during the afterwork rush. She left at eight with her son to gobble Extra-Value Meals at McDonald's after letting the butt-ugly, Metallica-loving teen have his pick of the new movie posters the store had just received.

Jason reset the Pop-Tartts disc and cranked it up. Even Marilyn's passive-aggressive nastiness couldn't poison the elation he'd felt since Hank's visit. He decided to invite him and Marina over for dinner by placing a clever note in their mailbox at the end of the week. Andre had homemade pizza crust in the freezer—add artichoke hearts, fresh basil, sweet peppers and mozzarella, and he'd have a suitable and easy gourmet presentation. Marina was a well-publicized recovering alcoholic (and vegetarian), so Jason wouldn't even have to worry about choosing the right wine.

He was mentally composing the invitation when the familiar female customer approached the counter with Coppola's *Dracula*. Suddenly he recognized her. "Oh, wow. Were you in a Stevie Nicks video? 'No Spoken Word'?"

She burst out laughing. "No one has ever, ever said that to me before. Yes! In 1985. I was eighteen. How the hell did you—wait, are you the world's biggest Stevie Nicks fan or something?"

"No, I mean—I like her, though. Especially that song. The video was great, too."

"I'm Violet Cyr. There should be a new membership card waiting for me." He checked a file box. "I don't even think they've shown that video in five or six years."

He zapped her card. Some lummox working another shift had mistyped all the member information. He started to revise Violet's file. "It plays on VH-1 every so often. Are you still acting?"

"Yeah. Amazingly. I got a job today as a guest star on *Leather & Lace*." She raised her eyebrows.

"I've never seen it," Jason admitted.

"Me neither. It's trash. I play an X-rated director who murders her porn star boyfriend when he cheats on her off-camera. They wanted a Julia Louis-Dreyfus lookalike. Don't ask me why. I've only been back here from New York for three weeks and I'm going to San Diego tomorrow for five days to shoot it."

"That's cool," Jason said. "I'll watch for it."

"Thank God for the hair," she said, flipping it with her fingers. "And from the looks of that waiting room, I was probably the only bimbo who could pronounce the word *obsequious* in the script. How much is this?" She opened her purse.

Jason handed her the tape. "On the house. Congratulations."

"Thanks, that's sweet of you. I'll see you when I get back. Jason," she said, reading his name tag.

The store closed at eleven. Jason had nothing to do but spray-

clean the counters and hope cute guys might come in and rent something that would authorize him to flirt. Why was it so damn hard to
find a boyfriend here? Was he just not trying? Of course, he was
smart enough to know the harder you looked for romance, the worse
your chances were. He'd started dating his sophomore year of college in Columbus, mostly guys he met at discos. But in the past
couple of years, the techno-pop Eurobeats of New Order, Erasure,
Bananarama, Pet Shop Boys, Dead or Alive and Depeche Mode that
had been the wantonly liberating soundtrack to his sexual awaken-
ing had been spun off the dance club turntable in favor of brain-
numbing, cacophonic hip-hop and the lazy sludge of industrial and
deep house, giving him an excuse to refrain from going out besides
that old standby, abject poverty.

A decent job that could possibly lead to an interesting career was
more important than meeting guys at this point, anyway, he told
himself driving home, relieved that the cool of the night and lack of
traffic congestion on Coldwater Canyon was keeping the Subaru's
temperature needle out of the orange *H* zone.

He'd write a couple letters to music video production companies
tonight (he'd copied down addresses from Tricia's Creative Directory) as soon as he took a swim, he decided, pulling up to the gate
and firing his remote at it. He enjoyed imagining the noisy, oil-
burning heap he drove was a blue Jaguar as he crested the mountainside and parked under the carport. He put on Voice of the
Beehive at an ambient volume and stripped, then wrapped a towel
around his waist and padded to the pool. It was a ravishing sight,
the tiny, inlaid underwater lights shimmering with *Estates Interna-
tionales* grandeur. He flung the towel onto a chaise and dove in. It
was freezing and delicious. He swam four laps freestyle, back and
forth under the glassed-in bridge, then bobbed to the surface. Shaking the water out of his ears, he heard a loud bark and turned toward
the sound with a messy, reflexive splash. Marina Stetson's pug was
trotting along the side of the pool, wagging his curly tail and panting.
It *had* to be the same dog. Jason climbed out and grabbed his towel.
"Nabisco?" He called experimentally, feeling slightly moronic.

The pug bolted toward him and began to lick pool water off
Jason's legs. "What are you doing down here, boy?" He quickly
swaddled his bare ass, half-expecting Hank to pop out from some-

where. But there was no way into the backyard except through the house, which he knew he'd locked. Nabisco must have squeezed under the hedge. Jason led the dog into the foyer, worried. Marina would certainly not be listed, but maybe Hank was. He dialed 411. They had only one Rietta, Vic and Helen, and they lived in Venice. Oh, well, he would just have to escort the wayward pup home in person. Marina probably won't even be there, he warned himself, dashing to his room to dry his hair and decide what to wear. He whipped off the towel and hopped nude into the closet. Underwear, jeans, socks. But what shirt? Silk? No, he might start to sweat. How about his Pop-Tartts *Kung Fu Grip* tour souvenir tee? What an inconceivably geeky notion. He decided on a long-sleeve, combed cotton Gap number and Andre's leather jacket.

Now for actually getting onto the Stetson-Rietta property. His best bet was the back route that Hank had taken the other day. Nabisco led the way, bounding up the bluff into a thicket of indeterminate foliage bisected by a reasonably well-beaten path that climbed uphill to a break in a clump of citrus trees. He hoped the backyard he found himself in belonged to Marina.

It was the garden of a Spanish villa, complete with double-tiered fountain and tiled patio surrounding a swimming pool and Jacuzzi. The huge house was creamy adobe, all turrets and French doors and balconies festooned with flowers. Nabisco seemed to know what he was doing. Jason followed him across the lawn to a wooden gate. Jason pushed it. On the other side was a circular driveway with a black Corvette parked by the heavy, oaken front door. That could be her car, Jason thought nervously, watching Nabisco take a leak on one of the rear tires. He called the dog to the marble and ceramic tile front steps, took a deep breath and pressed the buzzer. It was hard to say which surprise was more startling—the door immediately yanked open or Marina Stetson standing there, dabbing her face with a tissue, a cordless phone wedged between her ear and shoulder. She gave Jason a bewildered look, then collapsed against the door frame, spotting Nabisco, who darted past her into the house. "Oh, God, I just found him. Thanks." She clicked off and took Jason's hand. "Whoever you are, thank you so much. I've been looking for him for the past hour. I thought he got into the street and—shit, I'm . . ." She hastily wiped away a few fresh tears, then threw the Kleenex over her shoulder. "Hi." She was tiny, no more than five three, wearing jeans and a white sweater, her auburn hair longer than he'd ever seen it. When she asked him "Where was he?" Jason could barely stammer out a response.

"Down at the house. My house. I'm your neighbor, Jason. I met your dog earlier, I mean with your husband, like about a week ago, so when I found him, I figured I should . . ." Nabisco, apparently satisfied that everything was in order, had reappeared. Marina scooped him up and showered him with kisses.

"I've got to be more careful with him here. We moved in a whole year ago, but I was in New York and then working in France and then it was Hawaii and Australia and this is like only the third week in a row I've physically been *in* my house. I'm sorry. I'm Marina."

It was really, *really* her. "I know," Jason smiled. "I can't even tell you what a thrill this is for me . . . I'm just shocked. I have every song you ever released . . . Wow, honestly, this is like a dream come true for me. I—oh, God. I just can't believe it."

"Hank said I'd think you were cute."

Jason blushed. "So he told you I was . . ."

"Yeah. I was actually on the phone to the Beverly Hills police," she giggled, putting the receiver down. "Can I take you to dinner? I'm starving."

"Now? I mean, sure. I'd love to—"

"Just a sec." She stepped back inside. "Be good this time," she told Nabisco before emerging with her purse. She headed for the Corvette. "Hank said you were listening to my old stuff. What do you think's a better title for the new album, *Ghost in the Fog* or *Broken Mirror*?"

"I like *Broken Mirror*," Jason said, a little terrified. "Is that a song?"

"Yeah. It's *my* favorite. They want 'Ghost' to be the first single. That doesn't mean it has to be the name of the album, though. But what do I know?

"Hop in," Marina told him. *He was getting into Marina Stetson's car.* He barely had time to buckle the seat belt before she peeled out. The electronic gate swung open, and they were off. Marina hit a button and the top rolled down while the Gin Blossoms blasted from the finest car stereo Jason had ever heard and they sped downhill into the night.

"Is Kate Mantilini okay?" Marina shouted when they reached Sunset.

"Sure!" Jason said. He'd never heard of it. She made a left.

"Hank said you were in this huge empty house all by yourself. Doesn't it creep you out?"

He shook his head. "You should see where I came from. I'm just house-sitting. It's up for sale."

"Hopefully they won't list it with Syd Swann. We bought our house from him. He's *the* pissiest queen you ever met. Drives a fuckin' Rolls-Royce. So do you go to school or what?"

"I just graduated from college! Now I work at a video store on Ventura!" He hated admitting it.

"No shit! I worked at the first video store *ever* in Tarzana! I'd just dropped out of Cal Arts. My friends Wayne and Ernie used to come in all the time and I'd sneak them gay porno on Beta! *You're* gay, aren't you?" She put her hand on Jason's knee.

"Well, um, I guess—" he stammered, completely thrown.

Marina's tires squealed as she turned sharply onto Doheny. "Don't be shy! I can always tell." She laughed, then started singing along to "Until I Fall Away." Live. Jason nearly swooned.

The restaurant was full, but Marina was immediately and enthusiastically offered a choice table. "This is great," Jason told her, grinning.

"Order whatever you want," Marina advised before gnawing on a lump of fresh bread. Jason was determined to stay away from meat and poultry out of respect for Marina's vegetarianism, but he also had to worry about not getting anything that would be messy or embarrassing to eat in front of his idol. He settled on a seafood farfalle, still fretting about the high price and whether or not shrimp and crab were considered real animals. Marina got a large Caesar with fat-free dressing.

"You weren't working at that video store when The Pop-Tartts started, were you?" Jason asked.

"No. I got fired the night of our first rehearsal. It was the second and last job I ever had."

"What was the first one?"

"It was at this skanky resale boutique in Hollywood, in high school. I was having an affair with the owner, who was like this sexy Arab trash from Yemen. We'd do it in the dressing room," she confessed mischievously.

"No way! Just like your song 'Mr. Abdul'?" Jason wanted to know. He daintily tore a piece of bread between two fingers and ate it.

"Exactly. Our first album. God, you really know your trivia."

"I must have listened to that cassette three hundred times the summer of '83. My brother had just gotten his license and he'd let me hang out in the backseat while he and his friends cruised the Dayton Mall. And he took me to the concert you did in Columbus Thanksgiving. That did it. I was totally hooked."

"What's your brother doing now?"

"He's in med school. His last year. In Chicago."

"So we didn't totally fry his brain." Jason shook his head. "Or yours. You didn't move out here to schlep tapes at some video store. What's the deal?"

Jason couldn't tell her the truth. Not yet. She'd think he expected something from her. "I'm not exactly sure yet. I know I want to work in show business, though," Jason said. "I just got here, so I guess I have time."

"Take my advice. Decide what you want and go after it. Because if you wait, some other rotten little vulture's gonna grab it." A tough smile.

"I'll remember that," Jason said.

"Oh, 'scuse me a sec." Marina flagged down a waiter to ask if the mashed potatoes contained chicken stock. A nutritional discussion ensued during which Jason's gaze wandered around the place and stopped cold on an adorable young guy seated with six or seven friends at a center table. Curly brown hair just below his ears, killer smile, wearing a blazer and denim shorts and black leather sandals. His friends seemed to all be arguing about something, pointing at each other and exclaiming, but he was quiet, serene almost, his eyes, which Jason imagined to be blue and sparkly, sometimes closing for longer than a blink. He reached into the fray and retrieved an appetizer. Jason tried to decide if he had a problem.

The food came. Jason waited until Marina had taken a bite before beginning. He wanted to hear about her new album. "The street date is September twenty-ninth," Marina told him. "It's gonna be something different for me."

"Different from the other two solo albums?" Jason asked.

"They didn't exactly want the same thing after my last record bit the big one. You know, I changed labels."

"Yeah." He dabbed his mouth carefully. "Where'd you go?"

"I'm with Mermaid. New producer, too. It's supposed to be a more natural, acoustic, holistic kind of sound. And this is me. Suzanne Vega, look out," she laughed. "They've been real good to me. I'm lucky anyone's still interested."

"Oh, Marina," Jason interrupted, experiencing a tingly jolt that he was actually calling her that to her face. "Of course they're interested. The Pop-Tartts are a legend. They're a part of rock history." He glanced over to the adorable guy for a second. He caught him turning his head back to his friends. Abruptly, Jason thought. Could he have been looking over at Jason? He could have. Definitely.

"I know," Marina said, "but I'm not The Pop-Tartts. And *Rainwater Lullaby* proved it."

"*Rainwater Lullaby* was great. With three or four incredibly catchy singles your old label just did not push. These solo albums of yours are sweet, well crafted, romantic pop. Like the modern version of the Shangri-La's or Chiffons. They're wonderful." He self-consciously gulped down Pellegrino, stunned at his own shameless editorializing.

Marina melodramatically thumped her chest. "My my my. You should have been the publicist for that album."

"Yeah. I should have." He came within a syllable of spitting out his heart's desire, then a man desperately fighting off middle age with a goatee, designer duds and gold earring approached.

"Marina! You're looking fantastic!" She got up for hugs.

"How are you, Don?" Marina said. "Jason, this is Don Mann. He was The Pop-Tartts' lawyer. I'm sure you remember the whole Kellogg's brouhaha. Don bailed us out." Upon the immediate success of the first Pop-Tarts album, *Kittens with Whips*, the cereal giant had instigated legal action against the gals over the alleged theft of

Kellogg's registered trademark for their well-loved if nutritionally questionable breakfast pastries. The result had been a deluge of free publicity for the band, which petulantly appeased the disgruntled Battle Creek cornflakes empire by becoming The Pop-*Tartts*. The ironic conclusion to the saga came a year later, when Kellogg's paid the group an ungodly sum to appear in a commercial for their name-sake toaster treats, complete with a newly recorded, jingleized version of one of their biggest hit songs. "Now Don owns about thirty restaurants," Marina continued.

"Eleven," he corrected with schmoozy modesty.

"Don, this is my new friend, Jason." They shook hands, and Marina and Don began dishing Marina's former record company. Although keenly interested, Jason's attention was diverted—the waitress went over to the adorable guy's table, and he felt a weird twinge of panic that she was giving them the check, but instead she served dessert and trotted off, revealing Mr. Adorable looking full-on into Jason's eyes, smiling like a hologram by Caravaggio. Jason smiled back. The guy turned to his chocolate cake. Jason looked at Marina and Don to see if they'd noticed the exchange. Doubtful. Don gave Marina a card and left.

"I haven't seen him since I got out of detox," she remarked. "When I was in there, he sent me this big Easter basket to cheer me up. And it had a *giant* chocolate bunny in it. Anyway, this chick from the Eating Disorders floor started coming down and being really friendly to me and it turned out all she wanted was to binge on the bunny and later I walked in my room and she had the whole head in her mouth and bit it right the fuck off."

How could this conversation be happening? "Did that set your treatment program way back?" he said, laughing.

"Yes, it did!" she insisted, cracking up and batting his shoulder. She mimed going down on then chomping a giant object. "Imagine the horror." She filched Jason's discarded lemon wedge and squeezed it into her tea. "Thanks for bringing back Nabisco. And for coming out this late."

"You've got to be kidding. Thank *you* for being . . . you."

"So you're having fun?"

"More than you can imagine. I just wish I would have known

it was coming so I could have looked forward to it for years." A college-age girl was walking slowly by their table. She passed, then turned and retraced her steps to Marina.

"Excuse me, please, I do *not* want to bother you, but you're Marina Stetson and I am your *biggest* fan"—Marina winked at Jason—"and I'm just wondering if you could autograph this napkin for me?"

Marina was the soul of accommodation, allowing Jason to risk another peek at The Guy. He was talking to a woman across the table, then his gaze shifted over to Jason and their eyes intersected again and Adorable swiveled his body halfway around and they stared at each other for what seemed to Jason a ludicrous amount of time and the guy raised his thick eyebrows as if to say, Whatcha gonna do about it? and Jason felt woozy and helpless but also completely enervated to be trapped between his favorite Pop-Tartt and a flirtatious stud.

Then the waiter was asking Jason if he wanted dessert. Yes, please, I'd like that gentleman over there—yes, that's the one— naked, with a side of hot fudge dripping off his nipples. He shook his head and reattuned himself to Marina.

"So tell me about these friends of yours who bought a ten-million-dollar house, never moved in, and turned around and put it up for sale. In this market? That's nuts." He started to explain the twisted dynamics of the Fawn/Giles/Andre situation, although close to distraction over Mr. Adorable's proximity and obvious interest. Forget about him! a mental voice shouted. You're here with Marina Stetson! Focus!

But this is the first bite I've had from someone hot since I've been here, Jason's neediest self whined. *Shut up and focus.*

Marina had just made a joke about Fawn needing to take a Pia Zadora seminar. Jason agreed, then looked to the side and discovered to his dismay that Mr. Adorable's party had risen and was leaving the restaurant.

Not wanting to appear alarmed, Jason casually shifted his position for a clear view of the door. The Adorable Guy's friends were slowly shuffling out—the room was crowded, the exit bottlenecked —he was at the end of the procession, not really moving at all. Jason waited breathlessly for him to turn around. He did. Same smile, even more radiant as part of the full-length upright package—oh, God. Jason froze. The guy shrugged amiably and took a step backward, still looking into Jason's eyes with a magic kingdom of steamy, untold boyfriend possibilities. All Jason could do was stare helplessly as Mr. Adorable walked out of his life forever. There was no other way. He couldn't make Marina wait while he rushed over to chat up a total stranger—she'd think Jason was some kind of sleazy pickup artist.

"Do you know that guy?" Marina asked.

Jason looked at her, chagrined. "Yeah, he's a customer at the video store."

"I think he likes you. Do you have a boyfriend?" she continued, in front of the waiter returning her credit card. "Or are you dating anyone who makes you scream?" She got up to leave and he followed, exquisitely mortified.

"Uh, no. I just moved into town. Thanks for dinner. It was delic—"

"Don't change the subject. Do you *want* a man?"

"Sure, but—"

"You need to get out and meet people. You're too handsome not to, y'know? UCLA used to have these gay dances—we played one when we were first starting out—you should go to one of those. Or the beach! It's summer. Will Rogers Beach in Santa Monica—everyone calls it *Ginger* Rogers. All the studmuffins hang out there. I mean, they really hang out, too." She handed the ticket to the valet. Jason didn't know what to say.

Marina laughed. "I'm sorry. I'm embarrassing the hell out of you."

"No, you're not—I'm just not really used to—"

"Do you have a problem with your sexuality, Jason? Are you uncomfortable talking about it?"

Now he laughed. "No! It's fine. I swear."

" 'Cause you know I've slept with women a few times. You know, back when Nina Blackwood still worked for MTV. I'm just using that to set the scene for you—I didn't do *her*. It was no big deal. I just like boys a lot better."

"That makes two of us," Jason said, wondering if, as gossiped, she had done one of The Bangles. They got in the Corvette and headed for Vista Laguna Drive.

"Would you like to hear something off the new album?" she asked.

It was as if everything out of her mouth was specifically tailored to whip him into an emotional frenzy. "Are you kidding? I'd love to."

She fished a cassette out of her purse while simultaneously running a red light. It was blank except for a label that said BROKEN MIRROR and a date. "I don't *ever* play my own stuff in the car. But if you put it on, there wouldn't be anything I could do, right?"

Jason wasn't sure what she meant. "Go on, take it," she ordered. He did, ejecting *New Miserable Experience* and popped it in. The song was fab—darker than anything Marina had recorded since The Pop-Tartts' last album, with strong, outstanding vocals and a perfect hook. He loved it. It faded out just as Marina pulled into her driveway.

"So," Marina said. "Would you buy it?"

"At midnight on September twenty-eighth," Jason replied.

"Thanks. But I'm sure when the time comes, I can slip you a freebie," she said. "I had a nice time tonight. And I really appreciate you looking out for Nabisco."

Jason shrugged, knowing he could never communicate to her what the evening had meant to him. "It was great meeting you. Bye." He got out of the car.

"Hey, Jason. Give me your phone number." She reached behind her seat and pulled out a sheet of paper and wrote her number on the top. Then she wrote "Jason" on the bottom and he filled in his, tore the sheet in half and gave him the top.

"I'll call you. Bye, sweetie." She went into the house, and he stood rooted in place, holding the scrap of paper. The front was a take-and-track log from a studio recording session for "Untitled Marina Stetson Album" with various cryptic notes scribbled in a grid. On the back was of course Marina Stetson's home phone number.

In bed, he sighed contentedly. Marina Stetson *liked* him. Wow. And so did that adorable guy. He felt like a fool for not introducing himself. Remembering that last hopeful expression on the guy's face before he vanished into the city, Jason imagined himself springing up from Marina's table at the penultimate possible second, Mr. Adorable's eyes widening as Jason shook his hand and said something beguilingly clever . . .

You can't have everything, he thought, settling down to sleep, Marina's number already memorized.

Violet raised the pistol to shoulder level and backed onto the porn movie set. She lifted the mattress and withdrew a manila envelope, peeking in to verify the incendiary contents for a split second before Turk Marlowe grabbed her from behind, forced her gun hand over her head and pinned her down on the bed. They'd done four takes of this scene, and he'd had a hard-on for the last three. She could feel it like a length of pipe grinding into her stomach as they exchanged vicious cop-show dialogue and she prayed this would be the last angle the director had to cover it from.

It was her final scene on her final day on *Leather & Lace*, and Turk had been trying to get into her pants the entire shoot. His idea of welcome-to-the-set whimsy had been to strip *completely* naked in the scene where XXX video maven Monique (Violet) requires undercover cop Rip Lace (Turk) to disrobe as a preliminary porn audition.

Turk was supposed to keep bikini briefs on as he had in rehearsal, but at some point before the cameras rolled, the high-spirited star ditched his undies for the express purpose of wagging his hefty wang at guest lead Violet, who didn't bat an eyelash and continued unfazed until the crew cracked up and ruined the take. She'd gotten instant insight into Turk's personality when they'd been introduced and he asked if she wanted to borrow a few porn flicks from his personal library to help her "get into character."

Naturally, they ended up in adjoining trailers with nothing between them but a flimsy partition Turk kept unhooking to chat, usually, by coincidence, when Violet was changing. She was as friendly as possible, agreeing that a night on the town San Diego-style with Turk and some other show people would be a marvelous idea, and she knew she'd scored a major zing that night when she saw Turk's former-model's-face cloud with momentary hateful rage at the appearance of Dave, who'd driven down to spend the night with her as planned. Unfortunately, Dave left the next day, and Turk got her back by shoving his tongue down her throat during a kissing scene.

She tried to maintain a positive attitude—there was really quite a bundle to be joyful about. She had a job, San Diego was lovely, her wonderfully bitchy performance was much better than the crappy show deserved, there was no nudity involved. At least nothing scripted. She dropped a postcard expressing this to that cute video clerk, Jason, copying the address from her membership card.

The fourth night of the six-day shoot, Turk started phoning her hotel room. She ignored two messages from him, then returned the call after the third, afraid he'd show up at the Ramada if she didn't. He immediately started pitching his hot tub. She said, "Turk, I have a boyfriend, who you met, remember? I'm just not interested in being more than friends." He hung up.

The sordid script and upscale-slut costumes she wore in every scene made her feel like an accomplice to Turk's sexual harassment, which was standard procedure on the show, according to the sympathetic hairdresser (who was "insane" about Violet's hair and took every opportunity to fuss with it). "That spoiled rotten prettyboy motherfucker gets away with murder 'round this place," the Virginia Capers lookalike quietly revealed. "He did *her* and dumped her quick as you please," she whispered, nodding toward the bitter-looking makeup artist. "And he still sits in that chair every day and lets that poor thing slap makeup all over that glamourpuss of his. Mmhh-mmhh-mmhh."

"Cut! That's a wrap." Thank Christ.

"You can get off me, Turk. It's a buy," Violet said sweetly.

"I think we ought to try this a few more times," he opined to general amusement, giving Violet a wink. She waited to see if he'd try to adjust the conspicuous bone action at his crotch before facing the crew. He did. The second AD dismissed Violet. She said her goodbyes and promised to return for "Monique's Revenge." Her hotel room was booked another night, but she wanted to drive back to L.A. now.

Rush hour was over, the weather was cool, and she needed to rest up before she and Dave were due at her mother's for a home-cooked dinner/personal invasion session tomorrow night. Just in case she ran into Turk on the way out, she quickly changed into a sundress a Pasadena housewife might wear to Trader Joe's. She'd just laid out her costume on the shapeless, coffee-stained couch when the trailer rattled. Someone had just come in the other side. The upper right corner of the partition bent forward and Turk's head popped into view. "Hi," he said.

"Hello," she replied. "I was just leaving—" He disappeared and seconds later the partition was pushed away completely.

Turk ambled into her dressing room. "I guess we don't need that anymore. So, did you enjoy the show?"

"The show was great," she told him, emphasizing the second word only slightly.

"You know, I have a lot of clout with Stan and the other producers. I could see about you coming back . . . maybe for a four-episode arc or something." He came a little closer, toying with the costume she'd had on.

Violet gave him a Tricia smile. "No offense, Turk, but this casting couch business is so clichéd. The producers hired me, they've seen me act all week. If they want to use me again, they will. Now I gotta go, so—"

"In another life, we would have been married," Turk interrupted, turning on what she guessed to be his well-practiced smoldering routine.

"You can have any woman you want. This is ridiculous," she said, casual tone covering increasing apprehension.

"I want you, Violet. You felt how much in that last scene. And I could feel you responding to me." He was standing between her and the door. "You've seen it, Violet. You know how hard it is to keep a monster like that caged up?"

She started to get pissed. "What I know is that usually guys obsessed with their own dicks secretly want one right up the ass."

"Is that what you're into?" Turk asked coolly, taking a step toward her. " 'Cause I'm real versatile. And you are fucking gorgeous." His hand drifted through the air toward her.

"Don't touch me," she snapped, clamping her own hand on his advancing paw.

He made a pouty-lipped little-boy frowny face. "You are so sexy when you get mad," he purred. "It must be why you're such a good actress."

"I'm not acting now, Turk. Do you want everyone out there to hear me scream?"

"No, I want to be the only one to hear that," he whispered, snaking an arm around her waist.

She resisted. He backed her onto the couch. "Get away from me, you asshole!"

He emitted a noise between a laugh and a snort. "Oh, Jesus. I'm gonna cream in my jeans if you keep this up." She kicked him in the groin as savagely as possible. He immediately doubled up. A gasping groan came out of his mouth followed by a pint of whatever craft services had catered for lunch. Turk staggered around the tiny room, dropped to his knees, then his side. "You . . . *bitch!*"

She slung her backpack over her shoulder and left. Her hands shook on the steering wheel on the drive back to the hotel. Twenty minutes later she was in her room, sitting on the bed doing deep-breathing exercises. He had it coming—it's over—he had it coming, her brain whispered again and again like a mantra. The phone bleeped and she unthinkingly picked up.

"Hello, Violet?"

"Yes."

"It's Stan Sokol." The exec producer of *Leather & Lace.* "Are you all right? What the hell happened between you and Turk, honey?"

"He tried to rape me, *honey,* that's what happened." She felt equilibrium return and sat up straight, suddenly offended at being put up in this glorified LaQuinta for the past week. "I'm fine. Thanks for asking."

"Uh, Violet, Turk's on the way to the hospital. You racked him pretty hard."

"It couldn't have been hard enough. He's a real sick ticket, Stan. You know what I mean?"

"Honey—I mean, Vi, if there's anything I can do . . . we're all terribly sorry about this, uh, incident . . . I hope you won't hold it against the show. We all enjoyed working with you and it would be a shame to—"

"You want to know if I'm planning on suing? Or calling *The Star?* Is that it?"

"You know how it is, Violet. You're a pro. We hope we can sorta contain this mess where it is—"

"Contain this." She hung up. She listened to the phone ring and ring and ring as she gathered her things and walked out.

"What did you say, Dove Bar?"

Tricia forked goat cheese and pine nut salad into her mouth, exasperated. "Zach, you know I loathe pet names. And you're not paying attention. I was explaining to you what a ludicrous choice for *Exit to Eden* Garry Marshall is. I haven't read the novel, which I understand is quite torrid, but the *screenplay*—"

"Waiter, could we have some more bread?" Zach handed the empty basket to their server, who had blown a major soap audition that afternoon and was in no mood to refill this geek's focaccia every three minutes. "I'm sorry, Tricia. I'm just preoccupied about the summer schedule at work. They just sold a whole package to Tasmania, and Molly and I are practically inundated."

Tricia began to tensely dissect her calzone. Molly was a tan, blonde Pacific Palisades volleyball-type who worked with Zach editing out penetrations, erections, ejaculations and wide-open beavers from X-rated movies to "soften" them up for cable and Bible Belt video distribution. Tricia despised Zach's job but hated Molly even more. "I finally called your hairdresser Antonella, though," Zach said. "I'm going in at lunch tomorrow."

"Oh, good. Tell her to do something about those sideburns." She emptied another Equal packet into her iced tea.

"What's wrong with my sideburns?" Zach asked, hurt.

Why was he so bloody *sensitive?* "I didn't say there was anything *wrong* with them, Zach. It's just they're a little passé, aren't they? Why don't you try something like—"

He tossed his napkin onto the table. "Passé? Morrissey has the exact same sideburns and you think he's the hottest thing since sliced bread." A strand of cheese dangled from his chin and Tricia suppressed an urge to remove it.

"I said nothing of the sort. I find him *mildly* attractive and it certainly has nothing to do with those ridiculous sideburns." She couldn't *believe* Zach was on the verge of making a scene right here on the patio of Louise's Trattoria.

"Now I'm ridiculous? Why do neurotic women always give unsolicited advice? And let's talk about *your* hair."

She gasped. "I have *beautiful* hair! Antonella has told me dozens of times. Fine as silk and very healthy. *You* tell me what's wrong with it!"

"Nothing. If you want to look like Tipper Gore for eight years straight."

"How dare you call me neurotic!"

"You're right. I'm sorry. Someone who alphabetizes condoms in her nightstand drawer is *anal retentive,* not neurotic." Unbelievable. She did not have to sit here and take this abuse from the likes of Zachary J. Driscoll.

"If you had a problem with my hair, you should have *said* something!" She fumbled through her white purse and seized her wallet.

"You are not a stylist," Zach said, stuffing his face with tortellini. "You're an agent's assistant. And you have no business commenting on *my* hair. Save it for your actors."

Unbelievable! Thoroughly conditioned to go Dutch, she pulled out three fives and laid them next to her plate. "We're through," she announced frostily. Thank goodness they had chosen this restaurant, she thought as she got up and started walking west on Melrose. She'd be home in fifteen minutes. If Zach tried to follow her, she would utterly ignore him.

He didn't. He asked for more bread, finished his dinner, then started on hers.

Jason didn't want Violet to think he was hitting on her, so when he invited her up for a swim at the mansion, he told her she could bring a date. He was typically way too shy to instigate plans with people he hardly knew, but Violet *had* sent him a postcard from the set, and his confidence had been given a recent megaboost via Marina.

Less than a week after their dinner, she'd had him over for lunch in the garden, followed by a tour of her villa, including a built-in home gym featuring a shirtless Hank doing butterfly presses (he said Jason was welcome to work out there anytime) and a "rehearsal room" with a piano no one knew how to play and about twenty thousand dollars' worth of stereo equipment. While Jason was engrossed in a three-ring binder stamped LYRICS—UNTITLED MARINA

ALBUM, she disappeared into the closet and emerged with a cardboard box marked MISC CRAP.

"I told Hank to trash this stuff when we moved, but for some reason he didn't. Whatever you want, please take it . . . you know, if there *is* anything you want." There was nothing he didn't want. No childhood Christmas had ever been fraught with this kind of giddy euphoria. The "misc. crap" was a Pop-Tartts fan's wet dream—concert programs in Italian, Greek and Japanese, an entire press kit for their second album, a dozen folded posters spanning their whole career, British tabloids with paparazzi shots and headlines like "WHO SNAGGED MARINA'S NAUGHTY KNICKERS DURING KENTISH TOWN TARTT-TRAMPLE????" Marina left to take a phone call and came back near tears.

"Jason, the most awful thing just happened!" She sank onto a love seat. "Herb Ritts can't do my photo shoot!" She clasped her forehead and sighed miserably.

"At all?"

"He's booked through Halloween. Dammit, there goes the whole ad campaign. And I'm never gonna be in one of his books now, either. It's so unfair . . . how many times has he shot Tracy Chapman, for Christ's sake?" She dabbed a few tears away with her wrist.

"There are other good photographers, you know," Jason offered tentatively.

"Who?" She found a tissue and blew her nose.

"I could go through my CD's and come up with a list. And they'd probably be cheaper, too . . . Mermaid could spend the money they save on promotion."

"You are such a great kid," she said, rising and embracing him. He took his treasure box home and for the cover shoot recommended John Dugdale, who'd done gorgeous monochrome portraits of Book of Love for their new album, *Love Bubble*. Marina said she'd send for his portfolio right away and made kisses into the receiver.

Violet showed up at noon with a pitcher of sangria, a videocassette and Dave. "Hi, Jason. This is my male escort. Dave, this is Jason. He works at that video store where you returned *Dracula* several days late."

"I already erased the extra charges," Jason said.

"Thanks," said Dave.

"You better drop that nice-guy stuff if you want to own a place like this someday," Violet advised. "Thank God you invited us over, Jason. My life is hell right now."

"And by extension, so is mine," Dave added.

"What's going on?" Jason asked.

Violet shook her head and slouched against the wall. "I guess you didn't see *Hard Copy* on Monday." He hadn't. "Luckily I have it preserved forever right here."

"Let's check it out," Jason said. They went into the servants' quarters, where Jason's VCR was hooked to the giant-screen TV. "Does this need any introduction?" Jason asked Violet, popping in the tape. She shook her head. It began.

"*Leather & Lace*, the syndicated hit crime drama, went to the top of the ratings with hot-blooded tales of sin, vice and violence. In a bizarre case of life mirroring art, Turk Marlowe, sexy star of the series, was rushed to a San Diego hospital Friday after a mysterious incident which reportedly left his testicles swollen to the size of grapefruits," the ice blonde anchorwoman revealed. Jason looked at Violet, confused. "While the hospital would issue no statement regarding Marlowe's condition, his manager, Gail Ann Griffin, had this to say to *Hard Copy*."

Jason squeaked, "Oh, my God!" as they cut to a close-up of Gail, standing outside somewhere.

"This entire incident has been blown ridiculously out of proportion. Turk suffered some minor contusions in an accident on the set, but he's resting comfortably and will be back to work on schedule."

"While no one at *Leather & Lace* could confirm or deny this 'accident,'" the ice blonde commented suspiciously, "another alleged incident apparently took place that day." A photo of Violet appeared above Ice's shoulder. Jason gaped. Violet nodded. Dave, who had obviously seen this clip no less than a dozen times, reclined back on Jason's bed, leafing through the *Undergear* catalog.

"It has been reliably reported by several *L&L* insiders that an altercation between Marlowe and Violet Cyr, the beautiful Broadway actress guest starring on the current episode, took place in Cyr's trailer, where Marlowe was allegedly found collapsed in agony over an injury many believe to have been caused by a violent blow to the testicles. Cyr, who had completed work on the episode minutes before, had just left for her home in Bel-Air when Marlowe was discovered. Her mother spoke to *Hard Copy*."

Violet's mother was an attractive woman in her fifties helpfully labeled "Evelyn Cyr." "My daughter is a professional," she said. "She's been doing television and film for years and recently starred on Broadway. What happened in that trailer was self-defense—when a man attacks a woman, she has to protect herself."

INTERVIEWER: "So you're alleging that Turk Marlowe's injuries resulted from an attack, perhaps sexually motivated, he made upon your daughter Violet?"

EVELYN: "I'm alleging that that man is a filthy pig who should have left my daughter alone!"

Cut to Gail Ann Griffin.

INTERVIEWER: "How do you respond to the claim that Turk Marlowe sustained severe gonad trauma as a result of a kick in the groin by Violet Cyr, the guest star of *Leather & Lace*?"

Gail made a sickly attempt to smile and laugh. "That's preposterous." She hurried off-camera. Violet stopped and ejected the tape.

"I'm speechless," Jason said. "What happened?"

"Turk Marlowe harasses me all week, I kick him in the balls, I come home, my mother tells everyone on the planet about it."

Jason's mind was eating up the scandal like a pint of barely softened Ben & Jerry's. He looked at Violet with a deeper respect and admiration. "So where does this leave you?"

Dave sat up and encircled her torso with a tanned arm. "I keep telling her it'll blow over in a week or so."

She pretended to bite his hand. "Well, the *Leather & Lace* producers haven't said a word to me. They're waiting to see if I'm going to sue. And I haven't spoken to my mother, who I'm furious with. And Tricia, the assistant who's my quasi-agent at Carroll, is a complete wreck about the whole thing and is in no condition to talk to anybody."

"Tricia Cook? At the Conan Carroll Agency?" Jason retorted, amazed.

"Yeah," Violet said. "Do you know her?"

"She was one of my housemates before I moved in here."

"Go on!" Dave exclaimed.

"*And . . .*" Jason continued. "Gail Ann Griffin, Turk's manager, from the tape"—they nodded—"is the *ex-manager* of Fawn, the girl who owns this house. I got screwed into helping them put on this terrible showcase a few weeks ago."

"Was Turk in it?" Violet asked sarcastically.

"No. But get this. It was a total bust, of course, and Fawn was really mad at Gail, who spent thousands of dollars of Fawn's money putting it on, so Fawn went to Gail's house to fire her, and she walked in on Gail tied to her bed naked getting . . . worked over by *Turk* with this fifteen-inch dildo."

Violet gasped. Dave chuckled uproariously. "What a perverted fucker he is," Violet marveled. "Wait a minute. Why didn't you tell me this that night at the store? You knew I was going to do *Leather & Lace!*"

"We just met!" Jason protested. "For all I knew, you could have been a friend of Turk's or something."

"Thanks a lot," she mock-snipped.

"What a small, scummy world," Dave said. "How about a dip?" He cocked his thumb toward the pool.

Jason led them outside, where he had spread fresh towels on the chaises. He retrieved the sangria, along with some potato chips and Mrs. Fields cookies and set up a snack table under a red and white umbrella while Violet and Dave dropped their outerwear and got wet. Jason felt bronzed enough to be seen in his Speedo and joined them for a game of keep-away—he and Dave versus Violet. He called time-out to put on music—a rotating CD mix including the now omnipresent *Rainwater Lullaby* and the Stevie Nicks song Violet had so hauntingly interpreted on video in 1985.

They'd been frolicking and laughing for an hour before it hit Jason that for the first time since he moved to L.A. he was actually having a blast with people who might be considered friends. (The Marina rendezvous were still on another level—somewhere between *Song of Bernadette* and *Close Encounters of the Third Kind*.) Violet was frisky and clever, and Dave told deadpan hilarious anecdotes about grooming A-list pets. Jason didn't even dread the prospect of working a late shift at Video Xplosion that evening. Today was like a NKOTB video. Until now.

"Expecting anyone else?" Dave asked.

"Uh-uh. Why?" Jason replied, a tiny shiver inexplicably shooting up his spine.

"A big black Beemer just came up the drive."

The three of them were motionless in the pool, looking toward the house as if expecting something cataclysmic. "Excuse me a sec," Jason said. He sprang out of the water and dried himself with a towel on the way in. He'd stepped behind the bar and was two seconds from cranking down Bronski Beat when the front doors opened and a woman came in. Startled, he stopped the disc. A skinny guy appeared behind the woman. It could be no one but Giles Burke and his obscenely rich mother, Maggie.

"Hi," Jason said warily.

"Jason." That was all Giles said. Jason came out from behind the bar. They were moving toward him. He thought he saw a ripple of disapproval darken Maggie's wrinkle-free, blue-blooded hatchet face, probably at his skimpy swimwear. He glanced down momentarily to make sure nothing had slipped out, then quickly wrapped the towel around his waist.

Maggie was somewhere between forty-nine and eighty, with an expensively styled mane of chestnut hair, bony white fingers ending in a firetruck-colored manicure and a cardigan that matched her fingernails and hung off her scrawny, birdlike frame like a satanic lab coat. Heavy gold jewelry—chains and a gem-encrusted pendant— was draped around her neck and shimmered against her practically concave chest.

"Is this the boy?" she asked Giles.

"Yes. Jason, this is my mother, Maggie," Giles stiffly informed him. His eyes were bloodshot, and he nervously fiddled with his BMW-logo keychain.

"And who are they?" she demanded of her son, raising her chin toward Violet and Dave, who were drying off on the deck.

"They're . . . friends of mine," Jason weakly explained to Giles. Maggie glared at her son, as if addressing Jason directly was too gauche to consider. Maggie and Giles walked past Jason onto the patio. Jason followed, feeling his chest constrict with tension. Violet and Dave were dressing. They said hello. Maggie waved limply.

Violet looked at Jason and smelled trouble. He slashed a finger across his throat and made a face. "We were just leaving," she announced to no one in particular. Dave picked up their stuff, and they went into the house. Jason walked them to the door, cringing with embarrassment.

"Those are the owners. I mean, the guy, Giles, Fawn's husband, owns it, but that's his mother and I guess she owns him," he said quietly. "I'm really sorry. They seem pissed."

"You didn't do anything," Violet assured him. "They didn't tell you you couldn't have anyone over, did they?"

Jason shook his head. "Then piss on *them,*" Dave spat. "Goddamn snobs."

"We'll see you soon. Thanks." Violet kissed Jason's cheek.

"Good luck with everything," he told her. They left. Jason wanted to throw on a shirt and shorts, but Maggie was stonily staring at the patio snack table, so he went back out and started to clear everything away. Maggie squeezed Giles's arm.

He said, "Um, Jason . . . I'm sure you're doing a good job, and Andre told you what's expected, but you have to remember this isn't a party house."

"I know that," he said demurely. "It wasn't . . . a party. We were just swimming."

"Syd Swann is going to be showing the house," Giles continued shakily, Maggie evidently making him as nervous as she made Jason. "Everything's got to be perfect, 'cause there's a lot of money at stake," he added stupidly. Maggie picked up a towel by the pool and held it away from herself like a shitty diaper before flinging it onto one of the loungers. Jason carried the food and sangria into the kitchen. *Was* he not supposed to have any visitors? He didn't want to ask. He wanted to hide under the bed.

Giles came into the kitchen. "My mother's not mad at you," he began lamely. No, she's mad at the dirt, Jason thought loopily. "She's just anxious to sell the house. Is there a Pepsi or something I could have?"

"Sure. In the fridge," Jason said. "I'm going to change clothes if it's okay."

Giles shrugged and opened the refrigerator. Jason went to his room, closed the door and lay down on the twin bed. What had gone wrong? he asked himself dejectedly. Then he heard pumps clicking on the kitchen linoleum and Maggie say, "Where is Jason?"

He got up and hastily went back to the kitchen. Giles had fixed himself a glass of iced cola. With a kick, apparently, Jason noted, watching him surreptitiously stash a bottle of Bacardi in the cupboard behind Maggie's back. She stopped peering around the counter to speak to Jason. "Have you been flushing the commodes?" she wanted to know.

Oh, God. Had she found something vile in one of the toilets? "No," he said. "I only use the bathroom by my room."

"Well, they have to be flushed. Daily. All of them."

"They do?" Jason asked, looking to Giles for clarification. Giles appeared to be studying the toaster.

"Of course," Maggie sneered. "Otherwise, they'll get *rings.*" She strutted past him, out of the kitchen. Giles took a long sip of his "soda." Jason went to his room and heard Maggie flush eight toilets while he dressed for work.

Jason knew there wasn't one fucking thing wrong with the video-cassette of *Love Crimes* before he indulgently inserted it into the behind-the-counter VCR and hit Play. The membership computer screen flashed the warning "Do Not Give Credit for Tracking Problems—FSB," which proved that Fred, the manager, had already dealt with this customer, a geeky but smug asshole with witchy, sun-fried hair and matching Margaret Hamilton face. The movie began, clear as Andrew Shue's complexion. "There doesn't seem to be a problem," Jason said pleasantly. He stopped the tape and hit Fast Forward.

"Just because it plays on this machine doesn't mean it plays on mine," Witchie-Poo stated petulantly. He really thinks he's un-earthed the philosopher's stone for scamming free two-dollar video rentals, Jason thought, weariness suddenly replaced by a tinge of anger at this dipshit trying to make an ass out of him and his seven-buck-an-hour job.

Resuming play of the movie, Jason asked the customer exactly what the trouble had been. "I told you. The whole picture was streaked with snow," he snapped in an irritated nasal buzz.

"Like this?" Jason rotated the tracking knob and Sean Young, having a screaming fit while rubbing bloody fish guts into her bare breasts, deteriorated under an avalanche of jagged visual distortion. The guy held his tongue as Jason corrected the picture. "As you can see, sir, the tape is fine."

"Are you saying I'm lying?" the customer challenged him, poorly feigning outrage.

"If we can't find a defect on the tape, we can't give you credit. That's all I'm saying." You fuckhead. "In fact, I have a note on your membership from the manager—"

"Is there a problem here?" Marilyn had materialized from somewhere, presumably a cloud of cigarette smoke from the smell, and was jerkily shifting her pop-eyes from Jason to the customer to the computer screen.

Perhaps sensing an ally in ugliness, the customer blurted out, "Yeah, there's a problem. This tape wouldn't play on my machine and I'd like to get another movie."

"Of course. Jason, give him a rental credit," Marilyn huffed.

"Can I see you for a second?" Jason asked her, wondering how the hell she could have missed Fred's blinking message on the screen. He tried to lead Marilyn back behind the second rack of videocassettes—to discourage shoplifting, tapes were not kept on the "sales floor"—but she held her ground at the first rack, a whole ten feet from where the tracking bandit stood with arms crossed staring at the TV screen where *Love Crimes*, which he had doubtlessly viewed in its entirety, continued, torpid and unrated.

Jason took a step toward Marilyn and said in a low voice, "That guy does this all the time! There's a note on his screen from Fred saying not to credit him for 'tracking' problems."

"Well, Fred isn't acting manager anymore. I am," Marilyn announced in a voice plenty loud enough for Fuckhead to hear. "And customers are the reason we're in business. If you value your job, I suggest you start remembering that. Now why don't you cool down at the information terminal and enter the new stock on the computer while I help this gentleman." She pivoted on her gold pump and waddled back to the counter, where the "gentleman" was rocking to and fro on his heels and barely suppressing a smirk.

Jason ignored them both and calmly walked to the membership station. Lori, busy reassembling the Tot Town kiddie section in the wake of a recently departed tribe of rampaging six-year-olds, shook her head sympathetically at him. *Cool down?* That condescending sow, he fumed silently, slashing a UPS carton's sealed flaps with a scissors blade. *I'd like to cool her lazy ass down with*—images of vengeance and punishment vaporized when he opened the box and saw the top layer of new video packages. Jason's legs weakened and he collapsed from his crouched stance onto the carpet, staring at the glossy panoply of hot male flesh. *Carnaval in Rio. Island Fever. Manhattan Latin. Tropical Heatwave. Champs. Montreal Men.* Fred had casually mentioned he was planning to add gay XXX to the store's adult section, and he'd apparently ordered the whole line of Kristen Bjorn videos, which Jason had seen advertised in the few naked-boy mags he'd had the nerve to buy over the past couple years.

Jason's hand trembled as he removed the movies and stacked them on the floor beside him. *Oh, God, there must be at least thirty in here*, Jason panted to himself. *Powertool 2. Idol Worship. A Few Fresh Men. Laguna Beach Boy-B-Que.* Gleaming muscular bodies. Faces, not all stunningly handsome, but all promising single-minded surrender to a world of maxi-stuffed jocks, rippled stomachs and smooth, firm buttocks lightly misted with water droplets from a makeup artist's spray bottle.

As if in a trance, Jason gathered the bar codes, rewind stickers and clear plastic box sleeves and called up the stock-entry program on the terminal. By the time he finished typing in the first three titles, his erect penis had stretched through the leg opening of his briefs. He reached into his pocket to realign things but couldn't resist squeezing the head of his cock as he admired Ryan Idol, naked thighs wrapped around an enormous shiny bazooka. *This would have to be the first one Jason borrowed. No, no, no*—*Montreal Men* was the ticket. *Christ, look at those guys. Hard to believe they'd be all over each other for ninety minutes on Fawn's forty-five-inch giant-screen TV tonight.*

But could he smuggle the video out? Marilyn would be here when he punched out at seven, but she usually had a pizza delivered around that time and sat in the office gobbling while the rest of the staff handled the after-work rush. The times he'd absconded with those disappointing bisexual tapes, he'd been closing the store with the charmingly oblivious Lori and just popped them into his backpack, which he hadn't brought today. He could always check out a few innocuous normal movies, put them in a bag and covertly add the dick flicks. Why do you need more than one? He aggravatedly asked himself. You know damn well five minutes of this stuff and you'll cum your brains out. Maybe he could just hide the cassette in his pants, in the crotch of his underwear. He had his baggy khakis on—if he kept his hands in his pockets to flare out the front of his pants when he walked out, it might just work. Except he was so engorged, shoving anything down his Calvins might cause physical damage.

He worked as quickly as he could, mentally ranking and re-ranking the sizzling new arrivals in order of viewing preference, *Montreal Men* remaining at the top of the list despite stiff competition. Only an hour and fifteen minutes left and he was free. He could be naked in front of the TV by seven-thirty, shoot once, go for a swim, call Violet, flush all the toilets, then settle back for another pop or two with his French-Canadian friends before he went to sleep. He couldn't believe he was being left alone to complete this entirely pleasant task. But Marilyn hadn't said a word to him since the *Love Crimes* incident, and customer traffic had been light. He picked up the *Montreal Men* cover box, now appropriately encased in plastic and containing a styrofoam brick, and the actual videocassette, now appropriately encased in a durable plastic rental shell, and was about to store them under the membership counter for retrieval later when a faggy voice demanded, "Is that *Montreal Men?*"

Startled, Jason dropped the tape in question to the counter and turned to face Ronald, a mustachioed queen who often annoyed him by freely associating with Marilyn, who displayed true hipness by calling this guy "girlfriend" at particularly grating moments in their lengthy chats.

Jason pretended to check the title, then handed the cover box to the customer, saying through nearly clenched teeth, "Yes, we just got it in."

"I had no idea you carried all-male videos!" Ronald confessed loudly to Jason's chagrin, prompting a Helen Hunt-type in Drama to turn and regard them curiously. "Can I see those other ones? Oooooh!"

Jason helplessly handed over his primo picks for the evening as Marilyn sashayed over in those hideous gold heels. "Well, hello there, stranger," she warmly greeted her pal. His eyes remained trained on the back of *Davey and the Cruisers* long enough for her to shoot Jason a suspicious, dirty glance.

"Girl, this place is gonna be real crowded with these naughty things for rent!" He laid a hairy hand on her shoulder as she giggled conspiratorially, mirth rippling down from her shapeless bosom to the pot belly displayed so adorably in those navy blue stretch slacks.

"Jason, I didn't think this would take you this long. Lori needs help with the rush." Rush? There were three nonemployees in the store. "And you've got a *personal* phone call," she added.

He went behind the rental counter and picked up the blinking line. "Hello?"

"Jason, hi. This is Hank."

"Hank?"

"Yeah, Rietta. I live next door?"

Oh, my God. That Hank. Hot Hank. Marina's Hank. "Sure, of course. Hi. Working here kind of spaces a person out. How's Marina?" Oh, that's good. Treat him like an inanimate appendage of Marina's with no identity of his own.

"She's cool. What are you up to?"

"Working till seven. You know, unless I reach the end of my fuse and quit."

"Either way, I wanted to say you can come by and work out with me tonight if you want. Unless you've already joined a gym."

"No! I mean, I didn't. Yet. Is seven-thirty okay?" Jason realized he was mutilating the cardboard Winona Ryder on the countertop *Dracula* display with his fingernail and stopped before Marilyn noticed. Hank told him to come up the path. The exercise studio was at the back of the house. Jason thanked him and hung up. Now he *had* to figure out a way to sneak out one of the leftover gay pornos.

After watching Hank put those big hetero muscles of his through their paces, Jason would need fast, effective relief.

Jason walked through the open door and found Hank doing chin-ups. "Hey!" Hank called without missing a beat—he was wearing cutoff gray sweats, white socks, black Reeboks and nothing else. His eyes were squeezed shut with exertion so Jason thought it was safe to let his gaze linger over Hank's mind-bending body—he thought the best part was definitely the pectoral-biceps-underarm principality, Hank's silky-looking black chest hair dewy with a light sheen of sweat. That flat muscley expanse between Hank's navel and the cinched waist of his cutoffs also held considerable appeal . . . "Twenty-six!" Hank groaned, dropping to the mat. He crawled toward Jason, then bounced to his feet and put his arm around his shoulders. "How ya doin', guy?"

"I haven't worked out in a while," Jason explained, glad he'd worn a heavy-duty athletic supporter under his gym shorts. He gave Hank's back what he hoped was a buddy-buddy/shit's cool pat then ducked away, feigning sudden intense interest in one of Hank's Nautilus units. Hank was right behind him.

"You need to make sure you stretch and warm up or you can really fuck yourself up. Especially if you're rusty. Now do what I do." Hank began performing a series of stretches, which Jason imitated, certain he could feel the waves of body heat cascading off Hank.

Jason bent at the waist and touched the floor with his hands. Talking Heads' *Stop Making Sense* rumbled from six wall-mounted speakers. "Is Marina home?" he asked.

"No. She's been gone since this morning. At a photo shoot for the album cover. Should be back soon. Okay, let's start with bench presses. Spot me."

Hank lay back on the weight bench and seized the 150-pound barbell. Jason had no trouble focusing attention on Hank's reps and was in fact so absorbed by his duty he hadn't even realized they were supposed to trade places until Hank leaped up, replaced the barbell with a sixty pounder and invited Jason to take the bench. "Wait a sec," Hank said, grabbing a towel and wiping the black vinyl surface free of any Italian-American banker sweat. Like I really would have minded, Jason thought. He lay down and was staring straight up at Hank's substantial if undefined basket. God, this was hell and he hadn't even tried lifting the weight yet.

Without the snug jockstrap to confine him, Jason's erection would have surely tented up his flimsy shorts like a freshly chiseled Greek column. As it was, the cramp in his crotch was actually worse than the fiery pain in his chest and upper arms. "Come on, one more!" Hank urged. With a powerful burst of energy, Jason tried to expunge the alarmingly graphic image of Marina's husband, sweats crumpled around his ankles, lowering big balls and rock hard ass onto Jason's upturned face, and extended his arms completely vertical, grunting in agony as Hank gripped the barbell and set it down for him. "Two more sets left. I'm going to add ten more pounds."

"No!" Jason groaned, getting up to "walk it off" like a regular guy as Hank locked two additional five-pound plates in place.

They carried on this same routine—Hank demonstrating some new exercise and consequently flexing some new set of muscles to Jason's necessarily suppressed delight followed by Jason attempting three sets of twelve reps to readily expressed physical agony—for forty-five minutes and wound up on twin StairMasters, drenched in sweat.

With some gentle prodding, Jason was able to coax Hank into talking about himself. He was thirty-one years old and worked in downtown L.A. As the resident Boy Wonder in international finance, he was pretty much allowed by his more-conservative-than-God bosses to set his own hours at the bank and come and go as he pleased, which was often the middle of the night, since his job involved frequent phone calls to Japan, Australia and Hong Kong. During the past four years, he'd graduated in the top 10 percent of his Stanford M.B.A. class, married a beautiful rock star (her business manager introduced them at a party where Hank then accidentally doused the rehab-bound Marina with a full glass of champagne), was promoted to vice president and now made more money than his Long Island plumbing empire parents. Which put Hank just about even with his younger brother Cary Rietta, who'd been discovered at New York's High School of Performing Arts at age seventeen and was now the star of the TV soap *Hearts Crossing*. Hank told Jason his career goal was to put together foreign financing for a film studio or independent production company, but that the entry-level jobs had been much more lucrative in banking right out of Stanford. This led to a discussion of favorite movies. Hank's was *Brimstone & Treacle*, which Jason hadn't seen, although he owned the CD with music by The Police, Squeeze and the Go-Go's. Jason revealed his own favorite, *Desperately Seeking Susan*.

"Did you know Marina was up for that part?" Hank asked, blotting his sweaty, love-god's face with his towel.

"The Madonna part? Susan?" Jason stammered, completely out of breath and amazed at the existence of heretofore unknown Marina/ *DSS* trivia.

"Yeah. Of course, this was way before I knew her. She even did a screen test, but they gave it to Madonna. Marina didn't really expect to get cast. The whole time she had plans to go on a Pop-Tartts tour. You must get really sick of all that new-release crap working at a video store."

"It's the worst." Jason's thighs felt like burning saplings. "The preview tapes running over and over . . . the life-size Macaulay Culkin cardboard standees . . . posters and stickers and baseball caps . . . and all these customers acting like every dud that flopped at the theaters three months ago is suddenly the most exciting thing they've ever heard of because it's on VHS."

"So obviously the video industry isn't your lifelong ambition. What do you want to get into?"

Should he tell him? Should he say, "Your wife holds the key to my entire future and since she also happens to be my favorite celebrity and one of the only three friends I have in L.A., I'm a little sensitive about it." As it happened, Jason didn't have to say anything because Marina whirled into the room lip-synching and dancing to New Order's "Regret." Jason, eager for any excuse to get off the cardiovascular torture device, hopped down and started mopping himself with a towel, but Marina grabbed him and administered a smothering hug.

"Hi, you!" she giggled.

"I'm all sweaty!" he exclaimed, mortified that he was dampening his idol yet thrilled with this unprecedented display of affection.

Marina released him partway, then planted a juicy peck on his mouth. "I don't care if you just rolled in dogshit. You totally saved my life. That guy you sent me to, John, the photographer?"

"John Dugdale?" Jason asked, remembering.

"Yes! We had the most intense shoot today. He's brilliant and so are you!" She kissed him again and tried to pull him into a dance.

"You've been with him all this time? Usually you can't sit still for more than an hour," Hank commented, still trudging his way toward even more perfect buttocks.

Marina stuck her tongue out at him and wiggled it. "I had such a good time. Everything was perfect except the food. You say you're a vegetarian and they give you this crap that looks like it came from the bottom of a rabbit cage. Old bruised vegetables and carrot strips that tasted like someone should pack a box with them. And in L.A., the health food capital of the fuckin' universe? But I didn't even bitch. Until now. I'm starving. In fact, I want a big lobster. Let's go to Gladstone's. Come on, you two, mush!"

"I'm not real sure how being a vegetarian allows her to eat lobster," Hank said to Jason.

"I keep telling him. Lobsters are sea insects. It's like eating a cockroach." She reached into her Raymond Dragon shoulder bag for a thick, note-stuffed address book that looked like it had been tied to a mule's tail then dragged across Mexico. She dialed a handy cordless. "Hello, this is Marina Stetson . . . Is Damien there? . . . Okay, ask him please can I have a table for three on the water? . . . In an hour? . . . Great. Bye." She hung up. "Hit the showers, men. Jason, you can use the bathroom in here. Hank, loan Jason some clothes."

"I'll find you something. I think there's a crate with about a thousand *Rainwater Lullaby* concert T-shirts in a closet," Hank deadpanned, exiting.

Marina was swinging from the chin-up bar. "Jason, he is such a liar."

"I should really stop by the house—" Jason began.

"For what?" Marina interrupted, eyes twinkling.

"My wallet."

"Honey, it's my treat. Come on, I'll show you the locker room." There weren't any lockers or naked guys parading around, but it had everything else—sunken shower area with three heads, sauna, dressing room with full vanity, and a glassed-in Jacuzzi that was also part of the backyard garden, all done in exquisitely detailed Spanish tile. "Just hang your clothes on these hooks. Guadalupe will do laundry and get them back to you tomorrow. Hurry."

Jason peeled off his Ohio State T-shirt, shorts, jock, socks, and elderly Nikes, then went down into the showers. He adjusted the hard-pounding spray to the correct temperature as he scanned the shelf of fancy-pants shampoos, bath gels, conditioners and exfoliating scrubs that helped Hank achieve the heights of grooming success he obviously enjoyed. A large bar of spicy, rough-hewn soap was affixed with several heavy black hairs that could only have come from God-knew-where on Hank's body. Jason picked up the soap and was soon frosted with thick, fragrant lather. He listened to the techno-pulse of *Republic* on the bathroom speakers, the high-pressure tri-jets of hot water and the steam fogging the glass partition lulling him into a dreamy euphoria. He imagined Hank's soapy hand sliding between those thighs of steel and when Jason reached down to scrub his own crotch he found himself seriously erect. He backed against the tiled wall, the shower spray relentlessly pleasurable on the back of his neck, and ran his fist over his boner again and again, lather shooting off between his fingers.

"Hey, Jason!" It was Marina. He turned to the wall and cranked the cold on full blast. "I'll just leave the clothes on the bench. Do you need any help in there?" she asked teasingly.

"I'll be done in a sec," he spit out through chattering teeth. There was no way she could see him from around the corner, but Jesus Christ what had he been thinking? His penis, thwarted by the icy emergency rinse, hung at half-mast, refusing to admit defeat but deflating steadily.

After toweling off, Jason checked out the wardrobe they'd selected for him—faded blue jeans, a ribbed black cotton shirt and red mesh sweater, plus boxers and topsiders. Hank's Infiniti was sitting in the driveway, but Marina wanted to drive the Vette. Jason squeezed between the two of them so tightly all he could do was accept it. Marina pulled her seat belt around Jason and buckled it. His legs went over Hank's lap. One arm rested on Marina's shoulders, the other just above Hank's. Marina put on a John Wesley Harding tape and they were off.

Jason realized it was much more comfortable to let his arm rest at his side, where it brushed quite conspicuously against Hank's. But he seemed completely at ease with it and started asking Jason about the "fucked-up family" he was house-sitting for. Marina chimed in, wanting him to tell the Fawn-Gail-Turk-dildo story to Hank. He did, and they both started laughing uncontrollably, which worried Jason because Marina had only one hand on the wheel (the other was on Jason's knee) and was speeding down Sunset Boulevard with little regard for the propriety of Beverly Hills.

"So has the mother of the drunk guy—what's his name? Miles?" Hank began.

"Giles," Marina interjected.

"Has she been hanging around, giving you a hard time?"

"No, thank God," Jason said, wanting to shift positions because he had—surprise—a hard-on but was terrified of rubbing his leg against Hank's crotch. "I've only seen her three times the past two weeks. She really scares me, walking around with this *look* on her face . . ." He demonstrated.

"Like she's smelling shit?" Marina suggested.

"That's her all right. And she never like, addresses me directly unless she's complaining about something. The last time Maggie—"

"Short for magpie," Marina added.

"Or maggot," Hank said.

"Okay, the last time that *colossal bitch* came over, I was out by the pool wearing these really, um, modest swim trunks and she came in and started clattering around the house. So I stayed out there hoping she'd just leave, but she didn't. So when I came in, she was sitting at the bar, you know, right across from the front door, Hank?" Hank nodded, sending a posse of delightful cologne molecules up Jason's nose. "So she's there with about five hundred old black-and-white movie star photos and picture frames and scissors and matting, like this whole nursing home arts-and-crafts project, and she says 'I don't mind if you use the pool, but when Syd comes to show the house, please make sure you're not out there *on display.*' "

"So they *are* using Syd Swann? Yuccch!" Marina started coughing, then rolled down the window and actually spit something out. "Pardon me."

"Did Marina tell you we almost didn't buy our house because Syd was such an asshole?" Hank asked.

"He ought to be wearing one of those polyester Century Twenty-one jackets and showing condos in Reseda, but he makes such a killing selling every tacky, marked-up mansion from here to Brentwood, he's richer than most of his customers," said Marina. "Saul, my manager, was helping me look for a house and heard about this supposedly great deal, which turned out to be our house, but he couldn't get Syd Swann on the phone to make an appointment. And then, Saul hears from his facialist, who does all the gossipy bitches in BH, that Syd is trying to—I don't even know what the word is, *exclusify* his company by not selling to 'rock people.' Can you believe the balls? Anyway, Hank and I drive up one night and sneak over to the place, while these people are *home*—"

"We felt like the Manson Family," Hank said. "But she wouldn't be deterred. Once Marina gets an idea in her head . . . I had to hold her back from knocking on the door and demanding a tour."

"Jason, if you were trying to get rid of your house because you lost all your money opening this really hideous, over-the-top luxury hotel nobody wanted to stay in after a *Penthouse* Pet OD'd in the junior bridal suite while she was shacked up with a sixteen-year-old Mafia enforcer—no relation to Hank—and you really needed to sell it, wouldn't you want to know if your evil pissyfag realtor, no offense, Jason"—Oh, no! Did Hank know Jason had a problem? Marina had probably told him, but . . . Hank was *straightening* up in his seat. Now his arm wasn't touching Jason. Was Hank, beautiful, friendly Hank, homophobic? Hank settled back into his original position and Jason felt his hairy arm bristle into contact with his own smooth, nervous flesh. Thank God!—"was turning away potential buyers because they happened to be in the music business?"

Jason nodded emphatically. "Yes. I'd definitely want to know that."

"See, Hank? But Hank said we couldn't, so we snuck back out."

"I just wanted to get the hell out of there before we ran into some huge fuckin' dog," Hank protested. "So the next day I had one of the secretaries from the bank call for me, you know, real proper and official and Syd couldn't be sweeter and sets up an appointment right away and Marina and I went to see it together."

"Did he recognize you?" Jason asked Marina.

"Hell no. I went to Saks and bought this arch-twat business suit and then of course returned it immediately, and I had big Jackie O scarf and sunglasses action happening in my role as Mari, Hank's devoted, blasé ball-and-chain. Not that Syd would have spotted me anyway. You just know the youngest female singer he's even aware exists is Liza Minnelli. But he just ignores me anyway and starts being real flirty with *Hank,* taking him by the arm and pointing everything out, practically dancing with joy every time Hank says a word, doing everything but getting down on his knees to suck his dick."

"Marina!" Hank groaned, reaching over Jason to swat her on the arm.

"It's true!" she squealed. "That's the whole reason the chandelier thing happened."

"The house had this huge, wrought iron chandelier," Hank continued, "this great antique, and I asked Syd if it came with the place and he said he didn't know but he thought so and he was sure he could work something out."

"It's too late to make a long story short," Marina said, "but Syd said we could have the chandelier, and after the owners agreed to this really low offer we made, reducing the old queen's commission way down, he found out who I was and went ballistic."

"Or so we heard," Hank added.

"He was *furious,*" Marina insisted. "And at the closing, which I went to decked out like the biggest rock whore on earth, Hank mentioned the chandelier and the owners didn't know anything about including it with the place and we said Syd told us it was part of the deal and Syd stared right at me with the most hateful, pruney look I've ever seen and says, 'She is lying, Mr. and Mrs. Kramer.' So I freaked out and said the whole deal was off and walked out and Hank thought I was bluffing and followed me but I was totally serious. I didn't even want it anymore. And I bet Syd was really happy to get rid of us so he could massage the Kramers' price up and sell it to someone else, but they panicked and lost it and threw themselves in front of this very car"—she slapped the dashboard—

"and begged us to reconsider. Chandelier included. So we said okay. And we signed everything and that was that."

"Not quite. Marina stole the FOR SALE sign from the gate of the house and hung it in front of a gay bathhouse on Melrose," Hank said.

"Sounds like a harmless prank to me," Jason said.

Marina squeezed his hand in hers, causing Jason's heart to leap, partly because she was now steering one-handed down a treacherous mountainside. "It's not my fault a picture of it ended up in the *L.A. Weekly*," she concluded. "So what were you saying about Magpie?"

"Oh. That was the last time I saw her, until today. She made me check the oil in the Lexus and I was late for work. Thank God my poisonous toad of a manager, Marilyn, was delayed at the Jerry's Deli take-out counter and got in after I did."

"Do you have some kind of problem with female authority figures?" Marina teased.

"No!" Jason insisted. Then, playing distraught, he clasped a hand over his face and sobbed, "I don't know . . . maybe I do!"

"Maybe you just have a problem with bitches," Hank said.

Marina abruptly braked. They were at the end of Sunset Boulevard. Gladstone's blazed with light across Pacific Coast Highway. "That's what my last producer said *his* problem was," she chirped.

They got back to Marina's three hours later. Hank had to leave straight for a graveyard shift at the bank and she was "wrung out" from the events of the day and dragged the not-at-all-sleepy Nabisco to bed. Jason thanked them both and practically tumbled down the path to the Burkes', punch-drunk with the evening's overwhelming tastes (fried clams drizzled in lemon juice, brownies à la mode, Hank's neck—to be fair, the last was imaginary) and twists (Marina had told them they were adding another song to her new album and she asked Jason to compile a tape of old girl-group selections she might pick a cover from). Hank assured Jason he could keep the clothes as long as he wanted, and Marina said to call her as soon as he could get together RE: the extra song. He would help her make the perfect choice and she would introduce him to her producer, who would immediately hire him at five to six hundred dollars per week. He went into his bedroom and started culling his CD collection for

more obscure sixties girlpop. The answering machine was blinking
one message, but Jason didn't even notice it until he needed a pen
from the nightstand to start his song list. He was mildly astounded
to hear Andre's voice.

"Howdy howdy! It's Andre of course! We're in Texas and it's
hotter than Shawn Wayans' *ass,* but we're having the most delightful
time, aren't we, kitten?" Background noise of Fawn whooping.
"You go, girl. Anywho, doll, we just wanted to check in with you
and see how things were. We're about to hire musicians for Fawn's
demo and I'm utterly swamped designing the sleeve and writing liner
notes. We'll be in Austin, then Houston, then back here at the lake
I just don't know when, but we'll be in touch. TTFN. Ooooh! And
we heard through the grapevine that Maggie simply adores you. So
you're obviously doing a fab job. Bye, honey." What?!?! No phone
number? As it stood now, the only way he had to reach them was
Fawn's San Antonio voice mail, and Christ only knew when those
two fame hags would find time in their whirlwind spend-a-thon of
self-delusion to call him back. And what was this nonsense about
Maggie "adoring" him? She treated him like a hated stepchild home
for summer vacation, when she bothered to speak to him, that was.
Still, why would she tell anybody she liked him if she didn't? It was
probably just as well he hadn't talked to Fawn and Andre. Relaying
his exciting news about meeting and helping Marina could have
pierced the rosy bubble of Fawn's vanity recording project, with
toxic results.

He reset the answering machine then collected his Video Xplosion clothes from where he'd doffed them on the floor in his haste
to change into gym wear and join Hank. With all that had happened
that night, he'd actually forgotten about the porno movie he'd borrowed, carefully tucked into the waistband of his briefs, the sharp
edges of the plastic rental case pressing an angry red indentation just
below his navel before he'd reached the privacy of his car and
slipped it out. *Tropical Heatwave*—"six sizzling solos" by Brazil's
most deceptively wholesome-looking hunks, if the dreamboat on the
box was an indicator. Jason knew the production featured mastur-
bation only, as opposed to actual male-on-male sexual contact, but
it was still a giant step forward from the flaccid stripper videos that
had added scant sparks to his last two years of college. Besides, it

was merely an appetizer to the treasure trove of adult cinema they'd
welcomed to Video Xplosion that day, all of which he could enjoy
at his leisure.

He slid across the slate floor in his socks to the VCR and giant-
screen TV, *Heatwave* in his hand, penis already stiffening. He
clicked on the TV and inserted the tape. He had his dick out before
the FBI warning appeared. The first model came on and Jason's
stomach took a dip like he was on some violent, speedy amusement
park ride. His mouth was dry. Luckily he had a jar of Crabtree &
Evelyn's baby cream. He stripped nude very quickly to avoid stain-
ing any of Hank's clothing.

"Vi, it's Mom. I know you're still furious with me even though I
only talked to those reporters to protect you and your reputation. All
I can do is hope you haven't done something hotheaded like moved
back to New York, because I just got a call from a producer's office
and they want to see you right away for a new sitcom. So call me,
dear. B'bye." Violet replayed the message twice, trying to decide if
this was a hoax. She knew work was sacred to her mother, but Mom
might resort to desperate measures to get Violet to reopen the lines
of communication. It had been two weeks since the *Hard Copy*
broadcast, and they hadn't spoken once. Violet screened every call
and had luckily been out the two times her mother had dropped by
unannounced, leaving notes taped to the door and, once, a bag of
overpriced groceries from Chalet Gourmet.

In Violet's mind, her mother's complicity with the tele-tabloid
was to blame for the past wretched fourteen days. She hadn't heard
a word from Edgar Black, and Tricia had phoned exactly one time,
to ask for Dave's number. (Violet had mentioned the pet grooming
van at some point, and now Tricia had apparently been assigned the
task of finding someone to service her boss's two Airedales, Zelda
and Die Hard.) When Violet asked about when she might expect a
discussion of official representation—warranted, Violet felt, since
her *Leather & Lace* paycheck had been collected and commissioned
by the agency—Tricia became guarded and evasive, as if she remembered that Violet was trouble and Tricia had been told not to
promise her anything.

And now this message. She noticed how her mother had not

revealed an iota of information that might allow Violet to handle things herself sans a return call to Calabasas. Realizing how suicidal it would be to ignore even the possibility of another acting job that would move the *Leather & Lace* debacle a notch down on her résumé, Violet dialed her mother, resentment at this petty manipulation tactic simmering briskly by the time Mom breathlessly picked up on the seventh ring.

"Hello?"

"Mother."

"Oh, thank God, Vi! I was so afraid you'd miss this audition."

"Then why didn't you tell me where and when it was on my machine?" Violet asked.

"I wanted to speak to my own daughter in person. Is that so horrible? Never mind the attitude, Vi, please. And get a pen. Roxanne Morgenstern wants to read you as soon as possible for the role of Keisha in *Chillin' with Billy*. She's an executive producer whose credits include *It's a Living, Married . . . with Children* and *Dino & Muffin*. Are you writing this down?"

"Why are you calling me about this instead of my agent?" In spite of herself, Violet jotted down the information on leftover *One Life to Live* stationery.

"Violet, your so-called agent has apparently not signed you yet because SAG has nothing listed for you. And those nasty *Leather & Lace* people refused to talk about you at all and hung up on Roxanne's poor assistant. So she called *Hard Copy* and they gave her my number, so it's a damn good thing I talked to that show when I did."

"That was the most humiliating moment of my life, Mom, and don't think I've forgiven you for it!"

"Violet, do you really think yelling at your mother is going to help you get this sitcom?" she wearily and rhetorically asked.

"No, Mom. That's why I'm going to call my agent and have them set it up. Thank you. Bye." She clicked off before her mother could so much as groan one defensive syllable. It took forever to get Tricia on the phone, and then Violet had to listen to her insist that *Chillin' with Billy* was completely cast.

"Tricia, Roxanne Morgenstern is the executive producer, right?"

"I believe so."

"Well, if she tracked down my mother to get me to read for this part, they're probably still looking, don't you think?" Violet still had the pen in her hand and was using it to tensely color in Claudia Schiffer's face on the cover of a magazine. Why was Tricia being so fucking obtuse? She put Violet on hold for a second then told her she'd call Roxanne's office and "ring" Violet back. In the interim, Violet decided to gamble a costume change, which paid off when Tricia called ten minutes later with the meeting at Sunset/Gower Studios in Hollywood.

"But I think your mother must have been mistaken about Keisha being the role," Tricia said.

"My mother doesn't make mistakes that small," Violet responded, intending it as a joke but of course eliciting zero laughs from Tricia.

Instead she started reading the character breakdown issued by casting several months before. " 'Keisha Deauville. Mid to late twenties. African-American. She is Tremayne's younger sister, an intelligent, opinionated, very attractive television reporter who lives with the family. Initially skeptical about the existence of a talking goat, she soon grows fond of Billy and his salty sense of humor, and helps hide the loquacious goat from her colleagues at the local news.' I really don't understand this," Tricia sighed querulously.

"The show is about a talking goat?" Violet cut in.

"Yes. He goes through a meteor shower and develops anthropomorphic qualities. It's similar to a *Cosby* meets *ALF*, with a touch of *Baxter*, the French dark comedy. You did see *Baxter*, didn't you?" She pronounced it Bax-tair.

"Tricia, look. I'll just figure it out when I get there. But I have to leave now or I'll be late. Bye."

"Fine. I'll ring you later."

"Bye." Violet hung up. *Baxter* my ass, she thought, grabbing her bag, keys and hairbrush and dashing out the door.

Chillin' with Billy was located one floor above *Blossom*, the open door of which Violet passed on her way upstairs just in time to see Mayim Bialik skull-fry some assistant. "Fuck that! In case you were wondering, the name of the show is *Blossom*, not *Joey*! I don't ever want this shit to happen again, understand?!!!" Violet shuddered and hurried up to Suite 201.

She wanted to slip into a bathroom and check her makeup, but a cute black girl wearing what resembled a Sgt. Pepper's band uniform nearly collided with her in the hall and after saying "Excuse me" she grabbed Violet's arm and exclaimed, "Violet! Violet Cyr? Roxanne can't wait to see you! Come in here!" She guided her past Roxanne's nameplate into an anteroom decorated with an enormous framed photo of a crazed-looking goat, tongue lolling from between rubbery lips, an airbrushed twinkle in his eye. The black girl, Delicia—at least that's what the wooden alphabet blocks on her desk spelled out—entered the inner office and came right back out. "Roxanne will see you in just a minute. Can I get you some coffee or a soft drink? We also have white wine."

"I'm fine, thanks," Violet assured her. The phone bleeped and Delicia excused herself to pick it up. Violet was wondering if she could possibly ask to see a script when a loud altercation broke out across the hall.

"I'm telling you for the last time, Billy would never say that!" a nasal voice brayed.

"Billy's a fucking goat! He'd never *say* anything!" another man shot back.

"I am speaking of his character within the universe of the show!" the first voice whined. "Can we try to maintain some goddamn integrity here?"

At that, the door to Roxanne's office slammed open and a Nita Talbot-type with a severely lacquered hairdo resembling a Mayan temple stomped past Violet and into the adjacent fray. "For God's sake, people, calm the hell down!" she ordered in heavy Brooklynese.

"But Roxanne, the act break . . . ," the nasal guy protested.

"Billy's speech is fine the way it is," Roxanne said. "Now all this kvetching and screaming is working my nerves. So why don't you take a break and send the P.A.'s out for ice cream?"

Roxanne crossed the hall back into her office, ignoring the cries of "Frozen yogurt!" and "But I'm lactose intolerant!" now emanating from the writers' room.

"Sorry about that, dolly," Roxanne said. "It's great to meet you, Violet. Roxanne Morgenstern. Come on in. Delicia, no calls." Unemptied cartons spilled scripts, books, videocassettes onto the carpet. A StairMaster stood in the middle of the room and a TV/VCR unit was set up on an Italian coffee table consisting of a five-foot-wide circle of smoked glass atop what could have been a giant tarantula covered in molten iron. Sitting on the matching black sofa was a sixty-year-old broad in a bejeweled black sweater and pink bifocals. "Violet, this is Bertha Mueller, head of TV casting for the studio and the best friend a girl ever had. Bertha, Violet Cyr."

"It's my pleasure." Violet demurely offered her small smooth hand to Bertha's gnarled, beringed claw, expertly masking the shock that for some reason legendary casting maven Battle-ax Bertha was sitting in on her cold reading. Roxanne indicated Violet should sit on the couch, then joined her, bookending her between Roxanne and Bertha.

"Your tape is dynamite, honey," Bertha exclaimed in a basso nicotino voice. "Roxy and I just finished watching it."

Violet's eyes flicked to the table, and sure enough there was her demo reel. "But how did you get it? Did my agents send it?"

"Your mother messengered it over, Violet," said Roxanne.

"My mother!" Violet couldn't help blurting.

"Yeah, what a lovely woman. She was very helpful," Roxanne smiled. "Look, Violet, your acting's terrific and you're a very beautiful girl. But it's no secret you came to my attention on that *Hard Copy* piece."

Violet had her answer ready. "These things get blown so out of proportion and exaggerated. But you know what they say, any PR's better than no PR. It was really no big deal." She shrugged and tried to look as easy to get along with as possible.

"Bullshit," Roxanne replied, pointing a fingernail (the same chartreuse as her two-piece vinyl outfit) at Violet. "Honey, what you did, you did for every woman who's ever had to work with that piece of shit Turk Marlowe. I wish I would have racked him in the balls myself when I gave him his first acting job ten years ago."

"That son of a bitch is a sick ticket," Bertha croakingly concurred. "Did he whip it out on the set for you?"

"Yes, how did you know?" Violet was stunned and delighted she'd been called in to Turk-bash.

"It's his specialty," Bertha revealed, her face-lift pulled into a mask of disgust.

"I hope he can't ever get it up again," Roxanne added.

"If that happened, he'd have already killed himself," Bertha said. "And how about that schlepper manager of his? Gail Ann Griffin? That bitch is a nightmare! Ever met her, Violet?"

"No, but a friend of mine just told me this nasty gossip about her," Violet said, feeling that for some reason, dishing the dirt to these dames could only improve her chances of getting the part they hadn't once mentioned since she walked in.

Bertha put her hand on Violet's shoulder. "Tell me, doll. I'm dying to know. Roxanne?"

"God, yes! Does it have anything to do with Turk?"

Violet nodded. "This friend of my friend was a client of Gail's and she hadn't been able to get in touch with her so she went over to her house and found that Turk had tied her to the bed naked with scarves."

"Stop!" Bertha gasped.

"And he was about to . . . abuse her with this huge rubber . . . toy," Violet concluded with a guilty smirk.

"I guess that explains why he hasn't left that deadbeat manager," Bertha said. "He's getting a real deal for his fifteen percent."

"That fuckin' pig." Roxanne laughed ruefully. "Okay, let's cut to the chase. *Chillin' with Billy*. Black sitcom with a talking goat. Family show, eight o'clock, you get it. Well, a week before we're scheduled to start production, the network decides they want a nine o'clock show. Nine-thirty to be exact. With edge. I've been in this goddamn business twenty-two years and I still don't know what *edge* means."

"Nobody does," Bertha said.

"In this case, it means making Tremayne's sister white and giving the goat a few dick jokes. Which is where you come in, Violet. With the sister part, not the dick jokes. We need a new Keisha right away. And especially after seeing this tape, I think you're exactly what I'm looking for. So, I asked Bertha up here to read with you." Roxanne took out a couple of scripts and handed one to Violet.

What happened next was ridiculous. Roxanne turned to a scene in the first act of the script and told Violet to go ahead and read the part of Keisha while Bertha played all the other characters. No direction or prefatory remarks from author Roxanne. "Just try it on for size, honey." So she tried it out and got laughs from both of them on every joke, especially:

KEISHA: (TO TREMAYNE) The only thing you have in common with a genie is you live at the bottom of a bottle and you probably did Larry Hagman.

(In the show's nine-thirty incarnation, Tremayne was now apparently a recovering alcoholic who may or may not have been bisexual in the seventies.) They finished the scene and Roxanne said to Bertha, "Looks like we got ourselves a test deal."

"Who's your agent, doll?" Bertha asked, fishing a Gucci appointment book from her purse.

"Edgar Black," she stammered.

"Oh, yeah. We go way back," rasped Bertha.

"Since time's so tight, they'll probably want to do this tomorrow," Roxanne remarked, as if she were talking about getting a manicure instead of sending Violet in to audition for the network. "I'm sure you'll be fab." She got up and started leading Violet out.

"I'll be in touch. See you soon, dahling," Bertha promised.

Violet drove off the lot in a daze.

"I just don't get it," she told Dave later at La Salsa as they ladled exactly that into tiny plastic cups waiting for their Burrito Grandes to be served. "I've been through this series shit before and it usually takes three or four readings before they decide to test anyone. It was like Roxanne already decided I had the part."

The restaurant was a popular lunch place but was practically deserted at this hour, despite the late Beverly Hills rush hour traffic congesting on the street outside. She sat down with the food and Dave got them Cokes at the soda fountain. "Maybe the network is *letting* her have'r pick," he said, "you know, since they changed the whole bleedin' concept of her show on her at the last minute."

"Who knows? Twenty-four hours from now, it'll be all over." Violet had just beeped in and heard Tricia's message—the test deal was scheduled for three o'clock the next afternoon. She was supposed to stop by the agency around twelve to review it with Edgar.

When Dave heard this, he shook his head, dabbing tomatillo from his thin if well-formed lips. "Violet, you ought to tell those people to get fucked. They wouldn't even return your calls yesterday. You could go to any agent in town now."

"I know, but Tricia's been really supportive and I like her, even though if you stuck a lump of coal up her ass, you'd get back a diamond. And Conan Carroll is a really good agency."

"It's the principle of the thing, love. You ought to just keep the commission and worry about getting an agent when this job's over." Dave was trying to wrangle his hefty burrito with one hand and massage Violet's thigh with the other.

"Edgar already did the test deal," Violet pointed out, the first traces of sexual arousal joining anxiety over the audition to kill her appetite. She passed her food to the always-ravenous Dave.

"So if you get the part, send him one of those muffin baskets. Or better yet, I'll groom his dogs for free next week."

They went back to her apartment and he gave her an industrial-strength rubdown leading inevitably to sex. She set the alarm for seven to give herself plenty of time to prepare, then fell asleep with Dave's arm around her while he stayed up and read with morbid fascination the unutterably smarmy, completely awful Second Revised Table Draft of *Chillin' with Billy*.

When she woke up, she'd decided Dave was right about Edgar Black. How could she forget what an asshole he'd been at her "scene" for the agents a few weeks ago? Of course now that money was at stake, she warranted his full attention. Well he could forget it. She'd gotten this opportunity on her own and that was how she was going to get the series. She spent the morning memorizing the test scene and left for Century City an hour early to buy a new outfit at the mall before dropping in on Edgar.

Violet barely had time to announce herself to Misty, the underpaid, overchic receptionist, before Tricia appeared with a brief, passionless hug. "Congratulations. I'm terribly excited about this," Tricia said. If she gets any more excited, her body temperature might rise above forty degrees, Violet thought, suddenly distracted by the sight of an incredibly old woman with incredibly red hair wearing incredibly *Valley of the Dolls* hostess pajamas and four-inch heels putt-putting toward the receptionist with tiny, determined steps.

"Misty, dear, I'm going to fax, so just take messages. Sam's in a meeting." Her voice made Bertha Mueller sound like Didi Conn. Misty, fielding a sudden influx of calls, nodded at this directive and continued on the switchboard. Apparently miffed by this nonverbal response, the old broad swore under her breath and tottered off.

"That's Janice Twickenham, Sam Fein's assistant for the past thirty years. She is just unbelievable," Tricia whispered to Violet. "Anyway, you may not have been told *Chillin' with Billy*'s a summer replacement and it's going to be on the air very shortly. So you were really in the right place at the right time, as they say. Believe me, I was floored when I heard they had you cold read for Bertha Mueller. But apparently everything went extr—"

"Violet, my beauty!" Edgar cut off his assistant verbally and physically, stepping between them and scooping Violet into a very friendly embrace. He kissed both cheeks, narrowly missing her mouth. Christ, what an operator. He was making this real easy. "I don't want to keep you today of all days, so let's get you signed and outta here and onto a series." He pulled her toward his office. "Tricia, I put a priority fax on your desk."

Violet turned to give Tricia a wave or a wink or something, but she was already gone. From somewhere around the corner, Janice screamed, "Goddamn machine! I can't tell if—oh, fuck it!"

"Edgar, before we get anything started, I want to tell you I appreciate you handling this—" Violet began, but he interrupted her well before she got to *but.*

"Appreciate? Let's talk about appreciation after you see this test deal." He seated her on his leather love seat. A sheaf of contracts was fanned over the coffee table. "You'll get thirty thousand for the pilot or Episode One or whatever the hell they're calling it, then sixteen grand per show, all shows produced for the first thirteen. And they've already got a thirteen order. Did you know that?"

"Uh, I—I guess," Violet stammered, her brain a cash register wildly ringing up the huge figures Edgar had just quoted. Two hundred twenty-two *thousand* dollars?! That's what she stood to make from thirteen episodes of this crap? "Thanks for doing the deal," she said.

"That's what I'm here for, Violet." He stretched his Hugo Bossed legs, kicked off a loafer, revealing silk socks, and cracked his toes against the carpet. "By the way, your agency contracts are here with the test option papers. Sign everywhere there's a red *X*."

By the way, you and that jackpot wad are mine for a year, he meant. She couldn't figure out anything else to do but sign everything.

The network was headquartered in an immense complex full of humorless thirtyish types in ties and pumps droning around quietly, seemingly oblivious to the arctic-level air-conditioning as well as the many, many television monitors broadcasting the ultimate product of their labors, at this particular time a soap opera featuring a sniper taking aim at a wedding reception. Cut to a douche commercial. Violet checked in with the security guard and was sent up to casting. She emerged from the elevator just in time to see the five-tiered wedding cake blown apart as guests and extras ducked for cover under the gift table.

"Hi," she said to the young male assistant with braces unashamedly staring agape at the onscreen mayhem from the front desk.

"Shoot her, *please* shoot her!" he begged the TV. "Damn!" The scene had switched to a couple having dinner. "Sorry about that. This is my favorite soap."

"That's okay. I'm Violet Cyr, auditioning for *Chillin' with Billy*. I'm a little early."

The boy pulled a sharpened pencil from behind his ear and ran it down a clipboard. "Aha. Straight back, third door to the right. Just take a seat and they'll call you in. Break a leg." He smiled metallically and then she lost him to his daytime drama.

Violet found the appointed location, labeled Conference Room Two, and sat down outside the half-open door, hearing from inside, "Roxanne, I still got a big problem with the title. Why can't it be *Billy & Maurice*? Or better yet, *Maurice & Billy*? I didn't bust my ass in stand-up for the past fifteen years to be upstaged by a damn farm animal." It had to be Maurice Johnston, the star of the series. Why was he at her test? Did he have casting input, too? He was probably furious they were firing an African-American actress and replacing her with a white Keisha, "edge" or not. He'd hate Violet on sight. She breathed deeply, fighting off panic.

She heard Roxanne. "Maury? Honey? First, your character is named Tremayne. Second, *Chillin' with Billy* is the network's title. You really ought to discuss it with them. They'll be here in a second. Be my guest."

"That's cold, Roxanne."

"You know I love you, sweetie. We wouldn't have a show without you. You're who they're gonna keep tuning in to see. The goat is just a hook for the kids."

Sure he is. Violet got up and hid in the bathroom to do warm-up exercises. At precisely three o'clock, she entered Conference Room Two. There were about ten people already gathered, most of them in ties or pumps, none of them resembling prospective Keishas. Roxanne immediately stepped forward. "Violet! *Are you adorable.* Honey, I'd like you to meet Maurice Johnston, star of the show. He'll be reading with you today." The star was *reading* with her? The big-timery of this finally hit her.

"How nice of him," she smiled radiantly. "Didn't I see you on *Stand-Up Spotlight?*" she shot into the dark.

" 'Bout ten different times," he said in a "Yeah, I'm bad" tone that let her know she'd scored a bull's-eye.

She capped off the moment with, "You're hilarious."

Roxanne pulled Maurice away to show him something in the script. Violet spotted Bertha Mueller, who looked up from her conversation with a suit to blow her a kiss. Then a spiral-permed woman in leggings and a size twenty-six pinafore was putting her arm around Violet. "Hi, I'm Arielle Koblenz, casting VP for the network. I just wanted to shake the hand of the woman who nailed Turk Marlowe. Good work!"

"He's a really unpopular guy," Violet giggled nervously.

"I heard he lost a testicle," confided a willowy young woman with a blonde flip, garbed, like Arielle, in the executive-as-*Romper Room*-guest look. She introduced herself as manager of comedy development for the network. Violet good-naturedly denied the lost-testicle rumor.

"What did it feel like? Did he cry?" Arielle wanted to know, her chins rippling with excitement. "Oh, shoot, they're ready to start. Break a leg, Violet."

Violet found Roxanne and whispered, "Am I going first?"

"First? Doll, you're it. There's no one else testing. Knock 'em dead."

Arielle stepped forward and introduced Violet to everyone, then added, "And testing for the role of Tremayne, Maurice Johnston." Maurice looked momentarily annoyed, then flashed an immediate smile when everyone laughed at the little joke. "And as Billy the Goat, Bertha Mueller." Hearty applause.

Violet took her place at the front of the conference table. You're the only one up for the role and they start production in two days, she told herself. And everyone loves you. You're Sheena the Testicle Avenger. And you know this scene. So let's kick ass.

As it turned out, the ass she most wanted to kick was Maurice's. He was horrible! It was as if he'd never seen the goddamn script before, let alone rehearsed for five minutes. She still managed to get laughs despite amazingly ill-timed or bungled setups, such as Maurice mistaking *genie* for *genius* before her big "bottom of a bottle/ Larry Hagman" gutbuster.

"Obviously not. We'd need a genie for that," she ad-libbed. "And the only thing you have in common with a genie is . . . ," etc. They had to hold for laughs after that, and Violet caught Roxanne's eye and saw the extremely tense executive producer give her a thumbs-up.

Then it was over. She thanked everyone and made a quick escape. Roxanne followed her out. "Violet! That was great, honey. I'm so sorry about Maurice. It was the network's idea to bring him in. But if anything, it made you look better. You know you're my choice. They also want to test Jami Gertz, who I can't fuckin' stand but I don't know if it'll happen. I'll call you as soon as I hear anything. Bye!" She sped back down the hall and disappeared into Conference Room Two. Violet found a pay phone in the lobby and called Jason.

"Hi, it's Violet."

"Hey, what are you up to?" He sounded out of breath.

She told him. "I wanted to know if you had any interest in getting plowed."

"Plowed?" He suddenly sounded two inches tall. Did he think she meant—Oh, God!

She clarified quickly. "Yeah, you know, tanked, wasted, drunk. On margaritas. At Marix. Do you want to meet me there?"

"I'd love to, but I have to meet Maggie Burke at her hotel," he explained like he wasn't sure he believed it himself.

"Are you in trouble over something?" she asked.

"I don't think so. She sounded almost *pleasant* when she called me this morning. But I'm still scared." When the phone rang, he had actually been attempting to relax with the help of a video production entitled *Wheel of Foreskin*.

"Jason, you know she's on a power trip, but I doubt she'd summon you to her chambers to skull-fry you. She can do that at the house."

"Yeah, I agree," he said, stabbing a lotion-creamy finger onto the Pause button to avoid missing Marco Rossi's oral servicing by Tony Angelo and Ryan Block. "I'll call you when I get back. Leave me a message if you hear about the test."

He hung up, disappointed he had to pass up the margarita invitation even if he could barely afford an iced tea. The week had been lonely, hot and dull. Marina was in New York, doing preliminary press for the new album and meeting with her producer to decide on a sixties cover to record when she got back—she loved Jason's selections and took the tape he made with her—and Hank had gone with her.

Hank. Good lord. Jason's semiflaccid penis instantly returned to raging plump tumescence. He knew it was wrong to fantasize about his favorite singer's husband, especially when the two of them had been so nice to him. But Hank was straight and besides it wasn't exactly *fantasizing*—it was a purely natural physiological reaction to being around the guy. Jason hardly had to invent erotic scenarios when Hank was two feet from him performing exercises, muscular chest spilling out of tight undershirts with the sleeves torn off, unselfconsciously holding one of Jason's arms in the proper position while spotting him. Not to mention Hank's clean sweat (mingled with the musky spice of his twelve-dollar-a-bottle shower gel) evaporating inches from Jason's nose—that's what it must smell like to have sex with him, he would try not to think. But here alone in his bedroom behind a closed door in case Maggie should drop by (even though he was supposed to meet her at the Hotel Bel-Air in an hour), he could imagine sliding his fingers into the collar of Hank's damp T-shirt and tearing downward, then slowly lowering his face and lips and quivering tongue to that hairy expanse of muscle, the dark nipple always pointing at Jason through Hank's workout tops at last uncovered and rubbing stiffly against Jason's cheek . . . Jason scooped up another glob of lube with two fingers and disengaged Pause. How had he lived twenty-three years without porno? He upgraded his stroke to rapid friction and watched Ryan feast on Marco's ass. He was two seconds from climax when he realized he'd knocked the box of tissues onto the floor answering the phone, so he helplessly splattered across the TV. Holy fuck, look at the time! Still pulling his pants up, he staggered off to find the Windex.

The lush, storybook-romantic Hotel Bel-Air seemed an unlikely power base for Maggie Burke, but every enchanted fairytale kingdom needs a witch, Jason thought, as he walked through the front entrance after parking on an adjacent hilly street to avoid costly and embarrassing valet handling of his wheezing vehicular junkheap. He announced himself to the severe, silver-haired desk clerk-for-life, who discreetly rang Madam's room then asked Jason with just the slightest smutty inflection, "Have you visited Mrs. Burke here before?"

Jason shook his head, shuddering at being confused for a callboy ordered to satisfy Maggie's unspeakable Nancy Reaganite desires. A female employee was dispatched to guide Jason through the unbelievably exquisite and expensive hotel to Maggie's suite. The door was glass festooned with rich, elaborate draperies. Jason thanked the woman, who darted off obsequiously. He knocked. "It's open," Maggie called. Jason stepped in warily.

The place was like a Merchant Ivory set, but Maggie was certainly no Rupert Graves. She *was* perched on an antique divan, smiling for the first time Jason had ever witnessed. "Jason. Thank you so much for coming. Please have a seat. I ordered coffee and something to nibble on."

Jason was shocked to see an actual burnished serving cart against the wall, laden with cups, a golden espresso pot and a dessert tray.

Maggie wheeled the cart in front of Jason and really, truly, began pouring coffee. "I'm not sure what you kids like these days, so I got caffe mocha. It's Giles's favorite." Then hold the brandy, Jason mentally cracked. "Please try a scone. And the key lime pie here is heavenly."

Maggie selected the tiniest cookie on the tray and sat opposite Jason. "You're probably wondering why I asked you here," she began. Among other things, such as when Angela Lansbury wrested your personality from Leona Helmsley, Jason thought. "I don't think I've had the opportunity to thank you for helping us with the house. So here you go." She handed him a small white Hotel Bel-Air envelope.

He lifted the unsealed flap and stifled a quick intake of breath at the four fifty-dollar bills inside. "This really isn't necessary, Mrs. Burke."

"Maggie, please. We appreciate your efforts."

"I appreciate you letting me stay there," Jason said, nervously dumping Equal after Equal into his coffee. "Anything I can do for you is really no big deal."

"But it is a very big deal," Maggie insisted. "The house is an enormous investment for our family, of both time and money. And, to be quite frank, it's rapidly becoming a liability."

Jason couldn't figure out where this was heading, but it couldn't be anywhere good. "I'm sure you'll sell it soon. It's a beautiful house," he offered lamely.

"It's not my taste, but it is an impressive piece of property." She regarded the miniature cookie for a moment, then popped it whole into her mouth presumably to avoid crumbling. "Unfortunately, its value has been plummeting. We'll be lucky to get half what we paid for it in 1990, Syd Swann tells me. But Fawn just had to have it. Had to live in Beverly Hills. And why not? Giles was made of money!" She bitterly reached for an eclair, shaking her head at Jason, who was confused and intimidated by this unprecedented, unwanted candor, but felt he was expected to say something.

"I thought Fawn's family was very wealthy," he said.

"Well, I wouldn't call them *very* anything, except Texan," Maggie sneered. "Their so-called wealth is neither here nor there, since my husband and I gave Giles every dime for the Vista Laguna house ourselves. The way I understand it, the Farrars had no interest in further financing Fawn's attempts to enter show business. And that house was just another way to act like a movie star. How well do you know Fawn?"

"Not . . . well. I only know her through Andre, whose mom and my mom are best friends."

"Oh, yes. Andre. A very odd young man." Jason swallowed audibly. "But Giles is rather fond of him, too. That trip Andre's on with Fawn, I don't quite understand it, but I suppose she has to get on with her life. Is it just her and Andre, as far as you know?" she lightly interrogated.

The old bitch wants dirt on Fawn. Of course. You didn't have to be the head writer of *Falcon Crest* to figure it out. Jason put his half-eaten scone down, slightly queasy. There had to be a way to diplomatically detach himself from the situation—Fawn was a well-known slut, but it wasn't as if he knew any specifically juicy dish about her. "I haven't talked directly to either of them since they left. But I guess they're alone . . ."

"It seems to me Fawn would have a slew of men friends back there, wouldn't you say? Is she seeing anyone that you know of?" She leaned forward, eyes glinting manipulatively from beneath expertly tightened lids. "Not that there would be anything wrong with that. She and Giles *are* separated."

Jason tried not to squirm. "I honestly don't know. I thought she and Giles were getting back together."

Maggie set her coffee cup down hard enough to kill a small lizard. "What makes you say that?" she demanded, punctuating it with a ridiculously inappropriate peal of laughter.

"They've seen each other socially, I mean, lately . . ." Of course Maggie didn't want to hear this. But maybe this would put an end to the digging.

"Who told you? Andre?" Who else? He was in trouble now. End the conversation. She has to realize she can't *make* them go through with the divorce.

"Yeah . . . he mentioned that they'd been to this restaurant in Malibu."

Maggie rose stiffly and paced to the spun-glass French doors leading to the boudoir. "Jason, I understand you have a full-time job, but I imagine you might be able to use a bit of extra money."

"What do you mean?" he asked, alarmed.

"My family is extremely important to me, Jason. And I'm afraid Giles doesn't always make the best decisions where Fawn is concerned. He's been hurt enough by that . . . girl. I only want what's best for everyone. You understand, don't you?" She alighted on the arm of Jason's chair. Oh, yes, he understood quite well. Cash for details RE: Fawn's sexploits that Maggie could use to ensure no reconciliation occurred. Jason was so much more intimately connected not to mention less expensive than a private detective.

He felt like he was already in over his head and he'd told her next to nothing. He didn't know *anything,* for Christ's sake. How was he supposed to get out of this? He'd have to choose his words very carefully. "I wish I could be more help, but I don't have all that much contact with Fawn or Andre . . ."

"Yes, dear, I realize that. Making a record album takes so much time," she said condescendingly, "and so much money. You were part of that little theater project of Fawn's, weren't you? What was it called? A showing? Wouldn't you like to try a slice of this pie?" She got up, thank God, to fetch her coffee cup.

Jason discreetly slid the envelope with the bribe under his plate, then said, "No, thank you. Showcase. I just helped with the reservations and snacks and things." Whatever point he was trying to make, he wasn't succeeding.

"I saw the program for it at Giles's house. There were several young men involved, from the looks of those photos. Did Fawn choose the cast herself?"

Jason could only shake his head as the thin veneer of subtlety with which Maggie had coated their encounter thus far began to warp, crack and peel off. "They were all clients of the same manager."

Maggie was smiling again, her penciled eyebrows raised in a playful "oh-you-can-tell-me" configuration. "You're not keeping any secrets from me, are you, Jason? I want you to think of me as a friend." His genitals began to retract into his pelvic cavity. "I know Fawn rented a suite at the Peninsula. Giles seems to believe she needed a place to 'rehearse,' but I was hardly born yesterday and neither were you." She hadn't even been in town during the showcase. Was she getting her information from Giles? Doubtful. How, then? Credit card bills? Personal spies? What had she found out about Jason? "You know, dear, if Fawn has ever made certain . . . overtures toward you, please don't feel guilty or embarrassed about it. I certainly wouldn't blame *you* if anything were to have happened. She is after all an attractive, separated woman and you're a healthy young man . . ." Obviously, she'd found out nothing about Jason. He on the other hand had learned all he ever wanted to about Maggie, her family and her charming suggestion that he'd had sex with Fawn.

"Mrs. Burke, I barely know Fawn. And I'm sure she has no romantic interest in me. At all," he added quickly. "I'm sorry, but I really have to get to work." He debated standing, but her pissy new expression kept him nailed to his seat.

"I hadn't realized we were finished with our chat," she said coldly.

Why was he so scared of her? "I just don't think I can tell you what you want to hear. Because I don't know anything about it."

She didn't look at him as she walked toward the door. "Very well, Jason," she said evenly. He hurried to follow. "As long as you remember how *valuable* any information concerning my family is to me." She held open the door for him. "Thank you for coming." He exited, turning around to say something, anything to her, but she'd already closed the door.

Maggie went back to the divan and lay down, rubbing her temples. That slippery little moppet had given her a tension headache. And Giles and Fawn reconciling was a notion too gruesome to even consider. She'd deal with that situation later. Jason and his innocent act—he was a cagey one. But he'd taken the cash and he'd be back for more as soon as he realized the foolishness of protecting Fawn, that despicable whore.

She transferred the dishes from the coffee table to the serving cart, hating any sort of mess far too much to wait for room service, and reflecting confidently that even though Jason obviously knew more than he was telling, everyone had their price and she doubted Mr. Retail Clerk's would be much higher than— She dropped the saucer she was holding and ignored its fatal bounce off the table, anger flushing her sunken cheeks as she seized the cash-stuffed envelope Jason had folded into thirds and hidden under the dish.

Of course he didn't have the *balls* to tell her to go to hell to her face. And she'd spent most of her life breaking some of the biggest balls in America. That housesitter was toast points.

She wheeled the serving cart into the hall then paged Giancarlo. She needed a goddamn massage.

4:20 P.M.—Violet orders first house margarita (frozen, with salt) at Marix Tex-Mex, West Hollywood.

4:48 P.M.—Violet calls her machine. The only messages are two from her mother. She returns to find her waiter hitting on Dave. They order a pitcher of frozen kick-ass margaritas.

5:53 P.M.—After argument with Violet about parking regulations, Dave leaves to move van to avoid getting a ticket. Violet phones machine again and must listen to messages from her mother she forgot to erase before hearing new message from Edgar telling her she had the part and would start tomorrow.

5:54 P.M.—Happy Hour crowd toasts Violet, having been alerted to the situation by her tequila-lubed embrace/attack on passing restaurant host while screaming, "I booked a series!"

6:01 P.M.—Dave returns and disappoints vast majority of male customers and staff by planting torrid, deep-dish congratulatory kiss on Violet.

8:37 P.M.—Weird production assistant Benjie delivers to Violet Third Revised Table Draft of *Chillin' with Billy*.

8:38 P.M.—Dave commences derisive cracks about Third Revised Table Draft of *Chillin' with Billy*.

8:54 P.M.—Violet tells Dave to shut his face.

9:10 P.M.—Violet calls Jason at work with the good news, hoping "the answering cervix" (Marilyn) won't pick up.

12:05 A.M.—Violet calls her mother with the good news hoping the answering service *will* pick up.

1:05 A.M.—Violet finishes conversation with her mother.

9:06 A.M.—Violet's mother calls. Dave tells her she's in the bathroom preparing for the table read and will call her later.

9:19 A.M.—Violet leaves for the studio.

9:22 A.M.—Dave hangs up with Violet's mother.

9:51 A.M.—Violet parks in space labeled MS. CYR.

9:52 A.M.—Violet assembles breakfast plate (raisin bagel with fat-free cream cheese, orange juice, four strawberries) from craft services table.

9:53 A.M.—All but one strawberry launched from plate onto floor when Scottie, hyperactive seven-year-old cast member, caroms into her.

9:54 A.M.—Violet introduced to vice president of comedy for the studio while on her knees gathering spilled food.

10:08 A.M.—Cast introductions around the table by Roxanne Morgenstern. Stan, the famous comedian providing the voice of Billy, dons a pair of goat horns to great general amusement.

10:12 A.M.—Table read begins. First laugh.

10:15 A.M.—First dick joke.

10:16 A.M.—First mispronunciation of a word by cast member.

10:18 A.M.—8,439th sitcom script mention of something "from hell."

10:26 A.M.—First laugh by someone other than actors or writers.

10:29 A.M.—First objection to line in script by actor on religious grounds. ("I swear, you're so cheap your Sea-Monkeys are on food stamps.")

10:29 A.M.—First line-change by actor on religious grounds. ("I swan, you're so cheap, your Sea-Monkeys . . .")

10:33 A.M.—First whispered use of the word *shit* by executives to describe *Chillin' with Billy.*

By the time Jason realized Fawn and/or Andre were in no kind of hurry to respond to the brief message he left them the night of his tête-à-twat with Maggie, he'd come to the conclusion he was better off keeping quiet about the whole creepy visit for now, at least. Fawn's mother-in-law had never blatantly *requested* his services to undermine what was left of the marriage, and the bribe she'd tried to give him could easily be passed off as a house-sitting payment, since God knows he wasn't getting a nickel from anyone else. If Fawn had any trouble swallowing the magnitude of Maggie's hatred of her and put Jason on the defensive, he'd have no evidence. He was also worried about the negative repercussions of his having tipped Maggie off to Fawn and Giles's reconciliation, even though he'd only been trying to make Fawn sound like less of a tramp.

Fawn could certainly take care of herself, and she had her handmaiden Andre on a Gucci leash in case she needed any extra help. Jason was the one at Maggie's mercy, although it was now Tuesday and he hadn't had any contact with her since the Hotel Bel-Air one week ago. Sunday had been a close call—he'd seen Syd Swann's Rolls-Royce at the front gate and had just enough time to pull his sweats up, plunge barefoot into a pair of loafers and bolt out the door, shirtless and holding *Carnaval in Rio* on VHS in one hand. He dashed across the driveway and up the embankment to the path to Marina's house. He hid behind a bush and watched Maggie and Syd, a bony creature who favored Chinese pajama-suits and elaborate toupees, emerge from the Rolls (steering wheel on the right, naturally) and disappear into the house. They were joined shortly by a man in a burnoose who waddled out of a huge Mercedes with a veiled woman who followed him at ten paces through the front door.

In his haste to avoid Maggie, Jason had forgotten his watch but estimated it took everyone forty-five minutes to do their business and clear out of the house, by which time he'd sustained a cramp in his thigh from crouching too long and a scratched nipple from a stray twig.

Today Marilyn had him individually wiping down a thousand video box covers, but he didn't even care. He only had to work ten to two, and tonight was the first taping of Violet's new show. On the way home, he stopped by the supermarket at Coldwater and Ventura to pick up ingredients for Peanut Butter Marbled Brownies, a recipe of Marina's, along with a small basket to present the treats to his friend the series regular.

He must have been spreading peanut butter filling over the brownie batter when Maggie's rented Lexus slithered up the driveway, the sound of its faultlessly tuned engine obscured by the disco-pop warblings of Eighth Wonder, the delicious, tragically short-lived Brit group fronted by movie star blonde Patsy Kensit. In fact, Jason was unaware anything was wrong until Patsy was abruptly silenced in the middle of a paean to her baby's heartbeat. He put his mixing spoon down and jogged into the main foyer area.

Maggie stood at the wet bar, one red-nailed claw still on the stereo controls. "Obviously you didn't hear me knocking!" she snapped.

"I'm sorry," he said. "Your key wasn't working?"

"My *key* had been misplaced. It's a good thing I found it or I'd still be standing out there beating my fists bloody while you enjoyed your little heavy metal concert." Hmmm, he wondered with as much sarcasm as he could summon through the tightening grip of fear, maybe she's still mad at me. Rather than give Maggie the lecture on modern music she evidently required, Jason quickly apologized and hurried back to the kitchen. No sooner had he deposited the brownies in the oven than he heard her displeased, Endoraesque cadences: "Jason! I need to speak to you immediately!"

He returned to the foyer, shoulders involuntarily raised as if expecting a blow and unwittingly resembling Disney's Thumper on the first day of hunting season. He wasn't able to ask what the matter was—she just told him. "That answering machine of yours is driving me insane. Isn't there some way for it not to pick up so quickly?"

"No," he said, hoping she would soon fall out of the family helicopter into an active volcano while shopping for a Hawaiian island. "It has two settings. One ring and four rings."

"Sometimes I can't *get* to the phone in four rings." So carry a cellular, you cheap bitch.

"If the machine picks up, just go in the bedroom and push Stop. It will reset itself," he explained warily.

She looked at him as if the suggestion that she even enter the servants' quarters much less stoop to personally deal with the vexing technology of an answering machine ought to be punishable by crucifixion. "I don't understand why you need an answering machine here at all. Can't . . . *whoever* just call you at the pet shop?"

"Video store. And no, not really. I need to be able to get my messages because I'm looking for another job."

"Of course," she said nastily. "I'd forgotten how eager you were to improve your income."

Jason's eyes widened at the nakedness of this slam, but all he said was "Excuse me" because the phone started to ring. He answered it in his room.

"Hey, sweetie, it's Marina!"

"Hi, are you back?" he asked.

"No. I'll be in New York for about another week. I'll leave you my number here. I just wanted to tell you how much my producer loved your oldies tape."

"He did?"

"Shit, yeah! We're going to go with 'Tonight's the Night' or 'You Don't Know.' They're checking the rights and I'll probably demo them both right here at Electric Lady Studios in the next couple days. Thanks again. I'm so glad we met," she giggled.

"I am, too, Marina."

"When I get home, I want to—"

"Jason! What in hell has been going on in this kitchen!" Maggie screeched. "Hasn't it gotten through your thick skull by now—"

"I better go, Marina," he muttered hastily.

"Oh, my God, is that Maggot? Tell her to get bent," Marina advised. "I'll talk to you later. Hang in there, man."

She hung up as Maggie swept into the bedroom, furious. "The kitchen is a filthy mess! Chocolate splattered everywhere, dishes in the sink! I found *this* smeared on the range top!" She shoved a bony, batter-smudged fingertip in Jason's face.

"I was on my way in to clean up," he explained weakly.

"What if Syd walked in with a buyer? Do you have any idea how many millions of dollars are at stake here?" Her tiny fists clenched and unclenched, as if hungering for a small furry animal to throttle.

"I don't appreciate being screamed at, especially when I'm on the phone," he said quietly, replacing the receiver.

"And I don't *appreciate* lousy attitudes and sloppy work!" She trundled off down the hall. Jason sank down on the bed, too miserable and angry to even close the door. That rotten, evil old cunt. He heard her on the phone, her hateful voice resounding through the massive, empty foyer like she was on a bullhorn.

"Giles? . . . It's Mother . . . Well, what on earth are you still doing in bed at this hour? . . . I'm at the house and too upset to talk . . . I'm coming over!" She slammed down the phone, clattered across the slate floor and out the front door. Jason didn't move until he heard the gate at the bottom of the driveway clang shut.

He had the kitchen scrubbed within an inch of its life before the brownies were out of the oven. While they cooled, he gathered clothes, books, compact discs and toiletries and put as much as possible into his two tattered pieces of hand-me-down luggage. He packed his car, then repacked it so everything fit. He lined the basket he'd bought with wax paper and carefully cut and stacked the brownies. He put it in the passenger seat, slipped on his Ray-Bans and headed down the driveway. He could damn well return the gate remote and house keys in Giles's Bel-Air mailbox when it was convenient. He cranked up Quarterflash's "Harden My Heart" for courage and zapped the gate closed.

A brief but overwhelming sense of relief washed over him, replaced in a sizzle with a burst of rage at Maggie Burke. She had humiliated him in front of Marina Stetson! He should have left her a fuck-you note. Printed on the master bathroom mirror. Andre was bound to have a tube of Revlon ultra-frost somewhere in the servants' quarters. He smiled at the image of Maggie, cardigan sleeves rolled up past her knobby elbows, feverishly slathering on Windex and cold cream to remove a lengthy lipsticked kiss-off. Well, there was ample time to compose a poison-pen letter and leave it in the mailbox with the keys. Giles wouldn't dare open anything addressed to Mummy.

He made a left onto Sunset and was soon out of the Beverly Hills city limits. It wasn't officially rush hour yet, so he estimated it would only take ten to fifteen minutes to get home. Home. Orange Grove Avenue. Cramped, noisy, depressing. But at least there he wasn't subject to raids by megarich monsters and their asshole associates. He could fix up his room, insist upon improvements in the way Tricia and especially Wren handled things. One of those wooden gates for babies would keep Heathcliffe out. And if he couldn't find a Target in the Hollywood area to buy one, they probably carried them at The Pleasure Chest.

And he would definitely reveal everything about Maggie's meddling to Andre and Fawn, including the part about Jason and Fawn having sex, not resting until he'd convinced the singing showcase star that Maggie was out to destroy her. He took Fairfax to Santa Monica Boulevard, sweating profusely. Maybe he'd have time for a shower before the taping. Oh, God. He'd forgotten about his old shower with the tiny antique spigot and the water pressure of a co-

logne atomizer. Maybe Dave could fix it. He was the manly type—
Hello. Traffic had slowed to a stop, so Jason was not risking an
accident to gawk at the piece of work who'd just emerged from The
Eagle. Jason had of course never entered the neighborhood S-M bar,
but it nonetheless caused a speculative shudder each time he drove
past. The guy was built like the Paul Baressi-era John Travolta and
sported what looked like a malamute harness around his torso,
leather chaps and jockey shorts. Unfortunately, a toilet brush mus-
tache on an Ernest Borgnine face rendered the package more frightening than hot. He slid his mirrored sunglasses down his nose and
gave Jason a lewd stare, which he conveniently did not have to return
because traffic was flowing again.

Jason turned right on Orange Grove. Two cars were in the driveway, Wren's Escort and an old Saab in Jason's designated corner.
Tricia's VW Golf was naturally absent. Jason wondered if her boss
would let her attend the taping.

He parallel parked on the street and lugged an armful of things
up the cracked asphalt walk to the front porch. He used his key on
the bottom two locks, but the dead bolt was in place. Doubtful the
buzzer had been repaired in his absence, Jason rapped on the door
and got no answer. Schlepping everything over to the side entrance,
he got the door open, shoving aside a pile of crap someone had
stacked against it. Finding his bedroom door closed, he put down
the basket of brownies and opened it.

The blinds were drawn, so Jason didn't see the naked guy on
his air mattress until he had entered the room and turned on the
lamp. He took two startled steps backward, tripped and fell on his
ass on top of a tightly stuffed black duffel bag presumably containing the clothing the mystery guest felt more comfortable napping
without.

Expecting the man to wake up, Jason carefully got to his feet,
unable to keep his eyes off what the striped sheet barely covered.
His face, handsome and angular with a short black beard, was half-
hidden by a pillow, but he seemed to be in his late twenties. Jason's
gaze flicked in guilty amazement up and down a lanky, muscled
body, hairless except for the black bush surrounding an uncircumcised penis that could have been half-hard or just generally enor-

mous. Jason heard something down the hall and quickly snapped off the light before leaving the room.

Wren was coming from the direction of the kitchen, dressed in a miniskirt, white blouse and bouncy blonde wig. "Wren, what's going on?" Jason asked.

"Oh," she coughed. "I'm playing Sally Struthers from *All in the Family* at Ed Debevic's."

"What?"

"It's my new waitressing job. Gail, you know, my manager, helped me get it. I started yesterday." She slipped off one of her clogs and started examining it.

"Why is there a guy sleeping in my room?"

"Well, that's Stefan. He's living with us now."

"I need my room back. So tell him to crash somewhere else, okay?"

"You should talk to Andre. 'Cause he's the one who sublet the room to him."

"Wren! He sublet that room to *me*. It's mine."

"But—oh, man. Then I guess it's like a sub-sublet. Stefan said Andre said you moved into Fawn's place. Like, for good. But if you want to be back here, maybe I could house-sit for Fawn and you can have my room. You'd have to take care of Heathcliffe, but . . . Heathcliffe, what are you doing?"

Jason turned around. Somehow the dog had shambled by him and was now mindlessly consuming the contents of Violet's brownie basket. "No!" Jason screamed, lunging at the catatonic Doberman. He tried to push the basket away with his foot, but only succeeded in kicking the remaining brownies onto the grimy carpeting. "Fuck! Get away! Get away from me!" He shoved Heathcliffe toward Wren, but the animal just hung his head, unwilling or unable to budge.

Jason picked up his bags, scooped what was left of the brownies back into the basket, and awkwardly worked his way out the side door. "Hey, Jason," Wren called after him. "Can I get a ride to work?"

"No!"

"God. Jason, the Stefan thing is *so* not my fault—" He pulled the door shut with his foot, cutting her off.

He tossed everything in the backseat and got in the car. He had twenty minutes to be in his seat at the taping. He turned the key, heard a click and watched the idiot lights go on. He pumped the gas and tried again. Ditto. No, no, no . . . this couldn't be happening. He made himself wait five hellish, sweaty minutes, then tried again. It *was* happening. He started to cry. His head slumped to the steering wheel, honking the horn, which stuck.

Part II

T ricia pulled the memo from her Selectric and inspected it. The centering wasn't exactly right, but she blamed the incompetently photocopied memo forms. Misty could be trusted with absolutely nothing.

> To: All Personnel. From: Edgar Black/Tricia Cook. RE: Violet Cyr. Please try to catch Violet's guest appearance on *Leather & Lace*, Wednesday at 11:00 P.M. on Channel 5. Violet was just cast as a series regular on *Chillin' with Billy*.

She rang Hector's extension to ask the mailboy to copy and distribute the memo, but the call rolled over to Misty's desk. "He's out sick today," the bored receptionist reported.

"Fine," Tricia snapped, hanging up. How well did you have to be to operate a postage meter for pity's sake? She herself had missed only two days of work in the three and a half years she'd been with the agency. And both times she'd been so ill she could barely crawl out of bed to vomit. She went to the Xerox room and ran off eight copies, which she personally handed out to Misty and the agents via their assistants, saving Janice Twickenham for last. Good, she was on the phone. Tricia could leave her and her boss their memos and dash off sans conversation.

She was ordering from the market again. Lord. "Yes . . . now for meats and cold cuts . . . last week I asked for some deli frankfurters because I was having a friend to dinner . . . Yes, I know. Let me finish . . . one of the frankfurters had a blue spot on it . . . I don't know *what* it was. Who the hell do you think I am, Louis Pasteur? Anyway, it was very unappetizing . . . Of course I didn't eat it! . . . No, goddamnit, I will not hold . . . I left the frankfurters in a bag by my door and I would like them replaced when you deliver the order . . . I'll be there at precisely five-forty-five . . . And tell that fuckin' kid to wait for me this time . . . I can't carry those groceries in. I'm an old lady!" Tricia was halfway back to her desk when Janice bellowed, "Tricia, what the hell is this? Who is Violet Cyr?" She swiveled her chair around to face Tricia, a dangerous maneuver which, after one of Janice's regulation two-martini lunches, had more than once resulted in the octogenarian flying from her seat onto the mercifully deep-pile Karistan.

"Janice, she's a new client Edgar and I signed. She just got a series," Tricia explained patiently.

"Well, that's fine and good but what am I supposed to—" Tricia raised a small white hand, silencing her.

"Just give one to Sam."

"If you think I'm going to Xerox this, you are sadly—"

"Janice, I gave you two copies." Tricia spun around and marched back to her desk. She had to compile Edgar's expense report and submit it to Brenda, the nasty office manager, before four. She stacked the receipts in chronological order, approvingly scanning the invoice for Violet's first-taping gift. Tricia had calculated a formula whereby the agency would spend exactly one percent of the total commission for Violet's thirteen episodes. This amounted to $222, so Tricia ordered a Fancifull gift basket that, with tax and delivery, came to $178.65, then told the florist to send Violet the loveliest arrangement $44.35 would buy.

Edgar left that taping after seventy minutes, claiming a migraine, but Tricia stuck it out until the last pickup was completed at 1:20 A.M., making it the longest night she'd spent at a sitcom since that *Room for Two* episode in 1991, although to be fair, Gobbles the Goat had more of an excuse than Linda Lavin. Violet was by far the most talented and professional actor on the series, but Tricia had been appalled by what they'd done to her hair, putting it up in ponytails in every scene. It made her face look too thin. Tricia told Violet this after the taping, then had the most fascinating conversation with the episode's director about his London stage career. As for *Chillin' with Billy* itself, it was dreadful, but this network had made hits of such affronts to the intelligence as *Dino & Muffin* and *Fudge Factory*.

Tricia noted a receipt from Locanda Veneta with "Wendi Barash" scrawled across the top in Edgar's two-strokes-from-illegible chicken scratch. She supposed an eighty-dollar lunch with his close personal friend Wendi—a skinny, rich ex-Valley Girl with rhinoplasty so obvious the Jacksons would have had a problem with it—was an admissible business expense, since the apparently quite-successful-at-something Ms. Barash was now producing *Prying Eyes*, a feature Edgar claimed to be "packaging." Tricia had read the script, an erotic thriller that borrowed heavily from *Body Heat*, *Sliver* and *A Summer Place*, then submitted a list, which Edgar ignored, of suggestions for various roles. He wanted Marc Singer for the lead. Tricia had clenched her teeth and obediently messengered over the ex-Beastmaster's photo, bio and demo reel to Wendi's boyfriend, Igor, the director. It seemed to Tricia that Wendi should be treating *Edgar* to lunch, the way he constantly indulged her endless supply of starlet friends with "consultations," even signing a few of the "pet rocks with tits and hair extensions," as Zach derisively referred to Hollywood bimbos, his favorite topic.

She'd been sure Zach would contact her within forty-eight hours of their fight at Louise's, but when she didn't hear from him for an entire week, her resentment had built up like pus in an abscessed tooth. And his unapologetic, cavalier phone call a week later was just the clumsy dental drill to send that pus spewing out amid screams, shredded nerves and rarely used expletives. Tricia's mother would have referred her to Ann Landers's perennial question—are you better off with him or without him? Tricia, who'd personally favored Dear Abby as a youngster, would have answered a resounding "without him." Zach was cheap, petulant, and only mildly attractive. And their sex life could have been the subject of an entire agony column itself. Zach was a reasonably conventional lover, if you ignored such distasteful, obligatory detours as fellatio and his fondness for dumping baby oil in her cleavage, inserting himself and climaxing between her breasts. She suspected he'd gotten the latter urge from those adult videos he re-edited, which she also blamed for his obsession with her orgasm, or lack thereof, to be precise.

No matter how long he pumped away or what he did with his fingers or his mouth, it was the same as it had been with the two other men she'd slept with—she would not or could not cum. She enjoyed the closeness and friction and knew she had a nice body, trim, smooth and milky white, but believed nerve-frying tidal waves of pleasure centered around the clitoris were basically a psychoso-matic myth propagated by women who felt inadequate in other areas of their lives. Yet she found herself actually faking orgasms with Zach just to shut him up. Nothing obnoxious, just shallow breathing, accompanied by a little head-tossing. God, he was tiresome.

Her extension rang. "Edgar Black's office," she said.

"Hi. Tricia?"

"Speaking."

"It's Stefan." The new housemate? This was a surprise.

"Well, hi."

"I'm sorry to call you at work." But he didn't sound sorry. He had a deep voice that seemed to dance with sophisticated amusement.

"Don't be silly," she chided him pleasantly. "What can I do for you?"

"There's a guy here named Zach who says he wants his CDs back. I thought I'd call you before I let him go through your stuff."

How perfectly infantile of Zach to try something like this when she was at work. "Stefan, I'm so sorry you have to be troubled by this. I separated his CDs and put them on my vanity table. You can tell him I was going to return them this week."

"Would you like to speak with him? He's right here," Stefan said.

"No, that's really all right," she replied lightly. "I have no in-terest in speaking with Zachary again."

"I understand. See you later, Tricia," he said rather warmly. For Zach's benefit, she supposed. She said goodbye and hung up.

Paychecks were distributed just as she completed the expense report. She immediately pulled hers from the envelope (which was as always unsealed, so why did they bother?) to endorse and label with her checking account number and the words "for deposit only." Then it hit her, not as some great surprise or horrific discovery, but as if the lights had gone on momentarily in a crummy, windowless room she'd been sitting in for a long time but which felt substantially less dumpy and humiliating in the dark—Edgar's weekly expenses totaled more than her gross pay. It was a travesty. She'd gotten one raise all year, when what she really deserved was to be made a full agent.

Nobody was more efficient than she. She had a mental portrait of every client the agency repped and had memorized all their latest credits. She always knew which casting director was associated with what project *and* their most up-to-date phone numbers—every single person in the office asked her for those numbers, and that included *the* Conan Carroll and his useless pretty-pie assistant, Eric. And, unlike 90 percent of the staff here, she had the talent to read a script, understand what the writer and/or director were trying to say with the material, and submit only appropriate actors. And her level-headed, informed personal style made her an excellent negotiator. Or it would if they would give her one chance to be anything other than an unappreciated errand girl/message drone/(ugh!) enema nurse. And nobody could say she didn't have an eye for talent when she'd plucked Violet Cyr from a pile of mail-ins only to have her book a guest lead on her first audition and a series on the second. If she was going to capitalize on Violet's success, it needed to be while it was still fresh in her bosses' sievelike minds. Tomorrow. She would do it tomorrow after the staff meeting.

She spent the afternoon double-checking Edgar's phone log and submissions for the past week to make sure she'd left nothing hanging. At six-thirty she walked over to the Broadway in the Century City Shopping Center and purchased a new Liz Claiborne outfit. To take her mind off things, she decided to spend the evening catching up on new movies at the AMC 14. She bought tickets for a seven-twenty screening and a ten o'clock show. Walking into the second film without a ticket would have been easy enough, but since Tricia never purchased any of the high-end concession items (which were, she'd learned in her business of exhibition class at USC Film School, where theaters made the lion's share of their profits), she felt it would be unfair to bilk the multiplex out of a paid admission.

The next morning she sat in on the staff meeting as she sometimes did. She remained silent for the most part, occasionally supplying correct information when one of the agents was unsure of a name or project title. She fought the impulse to twist her hair around her index finger the entire time, until the meeting finally ended with a hysterical phone call from Andrea Cohen, driven to the brink of suicide yet again by her duties casting one guest role each on *Murphy Brown* and *Love & War*. Ari Rosenblatt left to handle her. "Conan," Tricia said, making a simultaneous hand signal to Edgar, "may I speak to you and Edgar, please?"

"Sure, honey. What's up?" Conan asked. He was boyish and glamorous and had risen to his prominent perch in the agency game at the tender age of thirty-two through an irresistible combination of charm, bitchiness, and aggressive plundering of clients, auditions and lines from *Mommie Dearest*, his favorite movie.

"Edgar, Conan," she began, "I've been thinking a lot about my responsibilities and my future here at the company, and I feel it would be in everyone's best interest if you would make me an agent as soon as possible."

Conan's eyes flicked from hers to Edgar's and back again in the space of one second before he burst into laughter. Tricia's thin lips parted in hurt dismay. She looked at Edgar, who seemed to be suppressing a smirk. Conan's giggles morphed into unconvincing coughs as he brought himself under control. "I'm so sorry, Tricia. I was up all night with Jean Smart and I guess I'm a little giddy."

"Tricia, I wish you'd discussed this with me first—" Edgar said, so effused with phony compassion he laid his hand on her shoulder.

"I had no idea you wanted to be an agent," Conan claimed. "Not that you aren't doing a beautiful job as an assistant. Edgar's always telling me how much he appreciates you, aren't you, Edgar?"

"Oh. Yeah. All the time," Edgar agreed. "But you're just not ready to be made an agent."

"But I think I *am,*" Tricia insisted, alarmed at how high-pitched her voice sounded. "And you need someone else. It's been three months since Steve Himber left for William Morris . . ." Conan's eyes widened in outrage. Oops.

"Haven't I asked everyone in this office never to mention that name again?" he demanded through clenched teeth.

"Yes, of course. I'm sorry," she quickly said. "But I feel I've shown my ability to cultivate talent. Violet Cyr, for example."

"Who?" Conan asked.

"She kicked Turk Marlowe in the nuts," Edgar prompted.

"She just booked a series regular role on *Chillin' with Billy.* I sent out a memo," Tricia added, unwilling to believe Conan did not know who he represented.

"Oh, yeah. The Julia Louis-Dreyfus hair. We love her. But honey, I gotta be honest with you. I've got eleven people on series. If you want to impress me, sign Keanu Reeves," said Conan.

"Tricia," Edgar smiled. He looked like a mongoose. "I'm not sure you really understand agenting. Being an agent isn't about keeping perfect files and typing Rolodex cards on the right friggin' side and memorizing the directors of everyone's TV episodes. It's shmoozing and stroking and getting anybody remotely right for a part in to audition 'cause that's what they're paying you for. And when I give you a script to read and ask for ideas, I don't want to hear 'Drew Barrymore is wrong for a Herbert Ross movie.' "

"But I only . . . ," she began, the words trailing off when she realized her voice was quavering on the verge of tears. What had happened here? Her arguments had seemed ironclad when she'd rehearsed them this morning on the way to work. But she certainly hadn't anticipated this kind of *attack.*

"We got enough problems with goddamn casting directors without you acting like one yourself. You understand what I'm saying, don't you, Trish?"

She nodded mutely.

"Sell'em, don't smell'em," Conan advised. "We'll talk later." He and Edgar walked out. If there had been a window in the conference room, Tricia would have gladly hurled herself through it. She collected her messages from Misty and went back to her desk, wincing with shame every time someone made eye contact with her, certain her humiliation had already been broadcast around the office.

She put herself on autopilot until Edgar left for lunch with a permed, microskirted Amazon whose chest resembled an FAA-approved flotation device. Then he had a meeting at Wendi Barash's house regarding "the feature" and would be out till mid-afternoon. He left without a word to her—she knew his schedule because she'd written it in his calendar for him last week.

Tricia went into the cubicle where Brenda, the office manager, sat surrounded on three sides by enough Precious Moments bric-a-brac to make Jeff Koons sterile, not to mention the Rear-View male buns appointment calendar, yellowing "Love Is . . ." cartoon clippings and a laminated Garfield poster shrieking, "You Want It WHEN???!!!!" As usual, Brenda was gossiping with Eric, who, on a $400-per-week salary somehow could afford to own more vests than Michael Damian.

"Excuse me, Brenda. I'm leaving for my appointment now," Tricia said.

"Appointment? What appointment?" Brenda replied, almost hostile.

"My doctor's appointment. I have to be there at twelve."

Brenda consulted Rear-View. "I don't have you down as having an appointment today."

Tricia sighed her most irritated sigh. "How many times have I forgotten to notify you about an appointment, Brenda?" Eric looked to Brenda for a response, enjoying this like the smirky little Gay Mafia stooge that he was.

"I guess this'll be the first time," Brenda snipped.

"The first time you forgot to mark it down at least," Tricia snipped back. "I'll be at the doctor's until later this afternoon." She left.

"Maybe he can surgically remove the stick from her ass," Brenda said to Eric. They cracked up.

Of course there was no appointment. She just needed to get the hell out of there. She decided to drive home, eat a salad and return this stupid outfit to the mall on her way back to the office. Maybe she'd even have time for a nap. As if she could sleep after the joke that had just been made of her nearly four years of service to that agency. The way Conan *laughed* at her. Laughed! The things Edgar had said—trivializing her top-notch office skills, acting like efficiency and intelligence were things to be ashamed of. And bringing up the Rolodex cards had been quite vicious. They *were* constantly being typed incorrectly. She wasn't crazy!

Her eyes burned with tears. She reached into the glove compartment and found a wad of In-N-Out Burger napkins Zach had stowed away months ago. She couldn't even listen to Enya or *Chariots of Fire* to soothe her nerves because when her parents bought her this car six years ago they purposely left out a tape player and radio. "It'll just get stolen with you living in that cesspit," her father grumbled while her mother pointed out that Tricia was much more likely to have an accident with station changing and cassette rewinding to worry about. Goddamn them all, she thought coldly, turning onto Orange Grove from Melrose.

The only car in the driveway was the Saab. Stefan was an assistant manager at Kinko's on Wilshire and worked odd shifts. He was probably asleep. Still, he might not be, and he didn't need to see her like this. She hadn't even properly thanked him for dealing with Zach yesterday, she remembered, applying Visene.

Her chance came as she was sitting at the kitchen table eating a pasta salad from Trader Joe's, reading yesterday's *Variety* and trying to ignore Heathcliffe and the way he smelled—the dog's fur had absorbed so much cigarette smoke, he might as well have been splayed out on the floor puffing on a Marlboro red himself. She heard Stefan's bedroom door open and close, footsteps up the back hallway, then he was at the kitchen door, looking surprised. "Hi, Tricia. I didn't think anyone was home." He smiled self-effacingly and pulled his short flannel robe closed across his bare chest.

"Just me, home for lunch," she sighed, expecting him to excuse himself to change into something less scanty and feeling an unexpected twinge of excitement when he instead came into the room, took a bottle of Calistoga from the refrigerator and joined her at the stained, periodical-strewn table. He *is* a strikingly handsome man, Tricia thought defensively. She let her eyes stray down his lean, well-defined body en route to her pasta. Well, why *not* look? He certainly wasn't overly concerned with concealing anything.

Stefan's leg brushed against hers as he lifted it onto the table's third chair. "I thought you worked in Century City."

"I do," she said. His eyes were rather arresting. Periwinkle. No, more of a cornflower.

"Isn't that quite a jaunt for Trader Joe's Pesto Primavera?" He playfully flicked the plastic salad container with a long, graceful finger.

"Yes, I suppose it is," she replied. "I just had to get away from that agency for a while." She wondered if she had anything green between her teeth.

He took a lengthy sip of water. "I don't know much about show business, but it seems like an incredibly consuming, stressful industry. Did you have a bad morning?" She must have been looking at him strangely because he grinned and raised one of those well-crafted hands. "Sorry. I'm prying."

"No, it's not you," she quickly answered, liking him even more. "Actually, I had a terrible morning. You don't want to hear about it, trust me."

"Are you an agent?" he asked. She laughed bitterly and shook her head. "Tricia, for whatever it's worth, what I've seen of talent agents is coarse and basic and greedy. Someone with your class and wit can't be properly appreciated by people like that."

"Thank you," she said, looking into his eyes again. He did not look away. Seconds passed.

"May I touch your breast?" She gasped, honestly believing she had hallucinated what she'd just heard him ask. She moved back in her chair, sliding it an inch or two across the warped linoleum. He stood up.

"I'll tell you what, Tricia. You don't have to give me permission. I can see that might be a problem. Just tell me when you want me to stop." Then his hand was under the Liz Claiborne jacket, over the Liz Claiborne blouse, cupping her right breast, fondling it. Nothing escaped her dry lips but ragged exhaled breaths. His fingers worked under the support wire of her bra and tweaked her nipple. Her thighs felt like two half-heated loaves of bread dough.

"You can touch my breast, too," Stefan said. But of course he didn't have breasts, just warm, hard planes of muscle. Tricia found herself reaching beneath his robe to stroke them with trembling fingers. She located his protuberant hairless nipple and slid it between her fingers, faster and faster.

Both of Stefan's hands were on her tits. He moved them up to her armpits and hoisted her out of the chair. With a couple of quick shoulder-shrugs, his robe fell to the floor. Before she could fully behold his nakedness, Stefan turned her around, grasping her wrists behind her. "Let's go into the bathroom," he breathed into her ear.

She had to put a stop to this. It was unbelievable, impossible and dangerous. A nude stranger had just molested her and was now forcing her into the bathroom. He was obviously a rapist. Kick him! Scream! Run out the front door! Tricia's mind shrilly commanded. You're not getting raped, you're getting *fucked,* a second mental voice hissed. You've wanted this from the moment you laid eyes on him, maybe even before then. That's ridiculous, the shrill voice argued—

They were in the bathroom, which it had been Wren's turn to clean for the past three weeks. Stefan positioned her in front of the commode and released her. She fell forward against the cracked tile wall, breathing hard. Her breasts felt hot, and she imagined that if she tore open her blouse and yanked off her bra, she'd be able to see glowing red trails where Stefan's fingers had been. This whole twisted episode reminded her of something, some disturbing world she'd visited once before, long ago. Now she remembered. It was that undergrad Japanese literature course where the creepy professor had forced them to read those Yukio Mishima novels. She was living a scene from Mishima, much more authentically than anything in Paul Schrader's terribly flatulent 1985 movie bio—

She heard the toilet seat crash down and then Stefan's hands were under her skirt, ripping down her short slip and Sheer Energy. Oh, God, he was spreading her legs with the width of his hand, rubbing and jabbing at her most private parts. She bit her forearm to muffle her cries of deeply ashamed delight. With her wrist still in her mouth, she peeked over her shoulder, her tastefully shadowed eyes bulging with shock.

He was sitting naked on the toilet (how unbelievably filthy!), her Liz Claiborne skirt gathered in his left hand. She watched him drool a pool of saliva into his right hand and lubricate the gigantic erect penis pointing up at her like a bludgeoning implement. She looked away and shut her eyes, jolts of terror clotted with a dirty, nameless craving tingling through her body. Stefan put both hands on her waist.

No, she couldn't have that huge male thing inside of her . . . how could she accommodate it? . . . it had to be a foot long—it rammed into her like an express train speeding nonstop to Pleasure-ville, over and over again. But he's not wearing a condom, Tricia's voice of reason, pushed to the brink of madness by this electrifying spontaneous sexual combustion, whimpered. "Plow my pussy, you bastard!" Tricia screamed, sending Heathcliffe clambering to his feet, terrified, and autistically twirling around the kitchen.

Stefan stood, bending her forward so that her hands were spread once more against the tile. She'd had two orgasms and was working on a third before she realized what they were. "Next time I'm going to fuck your lily white ass," Stefan said in a conversational tone that rendered the promise all the more erotic. What about the suit? You have to return the suit, Tricia's shrill inner voice sobbed just before Stefan withdrew and drenched the jacket with a sleet storm of semen.

Tricia collapsed to her knees, pantyhose in tatters, blouse still buttoned up to her chin. Tears she couldn't remember shedding stained her face. Every molecule seemed to vibrate with the abating ecstasy that had blown through her like a tropical monsoon. She tried to speak and could only gurgle.

"Pwetty wittle girl made a mess, didn't she?" Stefan asked in husky voiced baby talk. "Daddy's gonna have to give Baby a bath and make sure she's cwean aw over." He filled the tub with hot water as Tricia obediently removed the rest of her clothing.

"For the last time, Billy, you can't come with me when I interview the governor," Violet told the goat following her downstairs to the living room. "This is a really important assignment. I think I might catch him in a huge political scandal."

"So?" the stand-in reading Billy's lines fed from offstage. "I used to live in a barnyard. I'm very familiar with bull—"

"I told you to mind your mouth, Billy," Maurice, entering from the kitchen, sternly scolded the goat. "And don't say *anything* around Lucius."

"What about, 'Hey, Lu! I hear your noodle's too limp to doo-dle,' " the goat's vocal proxy read with a degree of expression and comic timing that made it clear why graduation to featured roles was a dim possibility at best.

Starla Brown, who played Maurice's lovely wife, Randee, entered. "Billy, that's rude," she said.

"But true," Violet confirmed. "I accidentally left my video camera running in Lucius's room last night. Not pretty."

She pulled a face and turned to exit. "What is he doing now? Cut!" the director intercommed. All attention shifted to Billy, whose face was buried between the sofa cushions.

"Gobbles!" the goat's trainer barked, understandably concerned that the all-too-appropriately named animal star's misbehavior was delaying production and causing the prop budget to escalate alarmingly.

Starla hurried over to Gobbles. "He's eating my script! How'd he know I stuffed it in the couch?"

"He's trying to tell you something, baby," Maurice laughed.

"Yeah," interrupted the popular singer stunt-cast as Maurice's suspicious but more intelligent, better-looking and well-acted older brother Lucius. "He's saying, girl, why the hell ain't you off book yet?"

Starla playfully smacked the singer on his fine fanny with the masticated script while everyone but a sour-faced Maurice laughed and laughed and laughed. The director called an early lunch break, and Violet watched Maurice strut off to his trailer, thoroughly pissed at being shown up again by the guest star. He'd been nasty since the Grammy nominee had scored much bigger laughs at the table reading. Maurice had actually called the network representatives aside and suggested the platinum recording artist be replaced immediately. The vice president of current programming, who personally okayed a network-funded increase of five thousand dollars to meet this guest star's price, had disagreed rather vehemently, according to reliable stage gossip.

Violet went to her dressing room and compulsively checked her hair. She had felt insecure about it since Tricia's comment after the first taping last week. Did her face look thin with her hair *down,* too? She doubted it—the video camera added fifteen pounds, anyway—but reached into the leftovers of one of her gift baskets and popped a couple of truffles just in case.

Someone knocked at her door. She hoped it wasn't Benjie the creepy P.A., who enjoyed calling her "Viola" and seemed the type who might have spent early adolescence crouched under a tract house playing with a naked Barbie and a cigarette lighter. "Violet honey, it's Emmiline. Can I come in?"

"Sure." Emmiline, who played Maurice and Violet's aunt, was a musical theater mainstay from way back who'd immediately bonded with Violet over their Broadway credits. She sailed into and immediately filled the modest dressing room, fanning herself with green script pages.

"Praise the Lord, but it's hot up here, Violet. Anyway, honey, have you seen these revised pages for today?" She displayed them for Violet.

"No, Emmiline, I haven't looked at mine yet. Is there a problem?" Violet asked, knowing there had to be.

"Mmmm-hmmm. They're a different color than Friday's, but other than that they're exactly the same. Identical. Even got Friday's date on them."

Violet checked them over. "Wow, you're right. I wonder if anyone else will notice."

"The only reason I did is because I told them to change this line," Emmiline said. She pointed it out to Violet—it was a joke in Aunt Petunia's B-story, which concerned the sixtyish character's romance with an unseen twenty-fiveish grocery bag boy, whose name she gets tattooed across her bottom (likewise unseen, thankfully). As she explains to a revolted Tremayne (Maurice): "Man, that tattoo hurt! Picture it: Laurence Cornelius O'Bannon."

TREMAYNE: "He's Irish?"
PETUNIA: "No! The O was already there, you damn fool!"

Violet, who had been simultaneously cringing at and enjoying the audacious vulgarity of this joke all week, said, "I know, Emmiline. That's really . . . awful."

"Mmmm-hmmm! I told Roxanne I wouldn't say *damn*. It's against my religion. She promised to change it to *darn,*" Emmiline complained, apparently having no moral conflict with direct dialogue references to her anus.

"Did you tell the stage manager about it?" Violet asked.

"Everyone left for lunch," Emmiline said.

"Well, let's go up to the production office and ask the writers' assistant what's going on."

"Honey, would you mind? I'm meeting my agent at Patina."

"No problem." Violet smiled. Actors were so damn needy. Oops, make that *darn* needy. She went down and walked through the stage, deserted except for grips hanging a drop depicting the quaint, bustling seaport of Bar Harbor, Maine, studio-chosen setting for *Chillin' with Billy*. Violet, who had performed and vacationed in northern New England numerous times, reckoned that a black family was only a fraction more likely to be found in midcoast Maine than a talking goat, but for this show, it was only appropriate.

The episode they were currently taping focused on whether or not Tremayne's obnoxious, overachieving brother Lucius would blow the whistle on Billy when he drops in on the Deauville family. It had been written months ago and recently "edged up" by making Lucius impotent (oooh! spicy!)—the only thing the insanely jealous and threatened Maurice approved of in the entire episode. Wednesday they would kick off Episode Three, in which Randee believes Billy has accidentally eaten a frozen embryo she accidentally brought home from her job at the hospital. Was it already tomorrow her mother was coming in for a taping? She prayed there wouldn't be lengthy pickup retakes after they released the audience—the idea of her mother loose on the stage with free access to castmates, executives, writers and God knew who else scared Violet. She'd have to press Dave into service to supervise her, which her mother surely would not object to. She adored Dave and would probably enjoy spending four hours reminding him he was too good for Violet.

She went up to the production office and found Delicia eating a chicken shawarma. Violet showed her the rewrite pages under suspicion and she whisked them away with an incredulous eye roll. Violet sat down to wait. She hadn't been up here since her first meeting with Roxanne. Since then, she'd earned $46,000 and her photo had been added to the full-color cast and logo display on the wall. What a world.

She could hear Roxanne on the phone arguing with someone. "No, that's impossible . . . *Why?* . . . Why do you think, Maurice?

For Chrissakes, you only have to work with him for another day and a half, max. . . . Let me spell it out for you, sweetie. We *cannot* have a stand-in play the guest lead during the taping, even if we've already pretaped every fuckin' minute of the show. . . . No matter how much you despise the man, Maurice . . . I know, doll, I know . . ." She laughed uproariously. "God, are you funny. . . . Bye, doll." She hung up. "Oy, is he sick."

Violet feared Roxanne would blitz out of her office and discover her eavesdropping, but instead Delicia returned with an armful of stapled green script sets. "I'm really, really sorry about this, Violet. But it's Benjie's fault. I guess he's too busy showing everyone your videotape."

"What tape is that?"

Dwayne, the freakishly nasal cosupervising producer walked by the open door and did a spazzy double take. "Hey, Violet! I didn't recognize you without your whips and chains! That *Leather & Lace* is one hot show. Is that porn producer you played gonna recur?"

That fucking Benjie could forget about a mention in her Golden Globe acceptance speech.

For the fortieth time, Jason punched in Fawn and Andre's lake house number, clenched his teeth and dispatched a virulent psychic command to Texas that one of those bubble-headed blondes pick up the goddamn phone. His hopes leaped when no machine interceded after four rings, but sure enough, on the seventh: "Hello, you've reached Aida Productions," Andre's recorded voice crisply announced, obviously quite pleased with itself for coming up with this overblown moniker. "Please leave messages for Fawn Farrar or Andre Nickerson at the sound of the tone and someone will get right back to you." Like hell they would.

Jason had received exactly one return call on his machine ("Sorry we missed you! We'll call you later, sugar!" Fawn, in Lorrie Morgan accent had chirped before babbling her number as an afterthought) in response to the messages he'd begun leaving over two weeks ago.

When his car had died on Orange Grove Avenue, he waited ninety-plus minutes for a tow truck, which had cost him, a non-AAA member, sixty dollars—to be added to the $329 billed by the mechanic for a new fuel pump and brake pads. Having missed Violet's taping, Jason had no choice but to ask for a lift back to Beverly Hills during which the leering 350-pound truck driver had stared at Jason like he was a breaded cutlet.

After trudging up the quarter-mile driveway, Jason immediately left Andre a message asking exactly what in God's name he thought he was doing sub-subletting Jason's room at the Orange Grove house to someone else and to please call him back and explain the situation tonight. Then Jason poured himself a rum and Diet Rite and called Violet's machine to apologize for not being there for her, remembering as he hung up that he'd left what was left of the brownies in the backseat of his worthless jalopy. He also realized that he had no way to get to work the next morning. He sucked down his drink, made himself another and went to bed, falling into a mercifully hastened sleep during the opening credits of *Too Big for His Britches*.

He woke up with a splitting headache and a mouth that tasted full of rancid cotton candy, and things got worse from there. Andre and Fawn did not call. Marina did not call but sent a postcard saying they'd decided to record the new song in New York and she'd be back "sometime sooner or later." Hank called to tell Jason he was back in town but extremely busy—Jason could stop by and use the gym by himself if he wanted to. Jason strongly suspected this indicated Hank didn't want to hang around alone with Jason because he had stared too much during their previous workouts. That had to be it. Hank knew Jason was gay, and it would have made him uncomfortable to interact so intimately with him, especially with the buffer of Marina three thousand miles away. How depressing.

Jason got his car back five days later, the whopping expense nullifying his sense of relief at no longer having to rely on rides to Video Xplosion from co-workers or, in one humiliating and pricey case, a taxi.

If he'd felt unhappy and unwanted in the mansion before, the removal of any possible escape route because of Andre's greedy treachery had rendered the house a ten-million-dollar detention center. He moved the stereo system into his room and only played it at wussy-pussy volumes so that he could hear Maggie Burke coming up the driveway in case of a raid. This could occur anytime between seven in the morning and ten at night, so the only time Jason dared use the kitchen was after eleven.

Sometimes Maggie came alone and spent hours fussing over her precious framed movie star pictures or tying up the phone line (her hushed conversations further muffled by the constant clicking of her Ferragamos on the slate as she paced) or actually getting down on her bony knees to measure something. Sometimes she came with Syd Swann, who built a career out of playing rich hags like violins—Maggie liked him—or a younger, Junior League type named Rochelle who was helping her with "interiors." One afternoon Maggie came in with a renowned decorator who found the exact, perfect location for a strikingly ugly black-metal-and-blue-glass floor lamp and was rewarded with a check for $360 for ten minutes' "work." Whatever the circumstances, Maggie would unsmilingly offer Jason a one-word greeting, "Hello" or "Jason," never both. Then she and whoever she was with would ignore him until her business was almost completed, at which point she would invariably address him as if it were the most wearying thing since the Great Depression and complain that the trash cans need to be rolled up the driveway *immediately* upon refuse collection or that new, hideous furniture was to be delivered and she would *greatly* appreciate it if he would make certain not to *use* any of it "until the rooms were finished" or that his answering machine was driving her *mad* with that four rings nonsense.

After Maggie's first grievance about the answering machine, Jason, fearful that she would unplug it in a fit of spiteful annoyance someday when he was at work, hid the thing in the storage cabinet below the giant-screen television in his room. He also turned the volume down to mute, which led to an interesting track on his message tape a few days before. "Lewis, hold on a moment! I think that damn machine's on!" Maggie said after the replay beep.

"What? You mean it's taping us?" a flat male midwestern voice brusquely demanded.

"I don't know! What if it is?" Maggie snapped at her husband.

"Wouldn't we hear something on the line? A clicking? Yeah, I think you definitely hear clicking if a call's being taped."

"I don't know what you're talking about, Lewis. I'm going to find that machine and turn it off." Maggie's heels clicked down the hall as she carried the cordless phone into Jason's room. "Lewis, I can't find the machine!" Her irritation was escalating into uncharacteristic hysteria.

"Isn't it next to the phone?" Lewis was losing patience.

"No!"

"Look, Maggie, the friggin' machine probably shuts off as soon as someone picks up the phone. Now forget about it. I told you there'd be *clicking* if . . ."

"Lewis, I'm calling you back." Click.

Jason wondered what would happen if he told Maggie he'd been digging up dirt on Fawn and was preparing a list of male names she'd been naughty with. It might actually be a good strategy to keep on Maggie's good side while he was trapped at the mansion, if he could somehow string her along with no real payoff. But if Fawn or Andre got wind of it, he'd be out on his ass with no place to go, and he couldn't afford the monthly rent on a divey studio apartment, much less an exorbitant L.A. move-in. Not that there was any guarantee Andre would evict that horrible, hunky Stefan and give Jason back his crummy room when they got back from Texas. What a shitty mess.

He had already zapped the gate closed behind him and was chugging down Vista Laguna Drive on the way to Video Xplosion when he remembered the "movies" he'd borrowed a few days ago. He'd seen them both and wanted to trade them out for some new releases that had arrived yesterday. The "Adult Male" section was an unqualified success (although Jason had yet to see anyone remotely cute rent one) and would be expanded through the summer, thank God, since those videos were the only things Jason really had to look forward to. He had a few extra minutes, so he opened the gate, went back up and retrieved them from under his bed.

The store was swarming with activity—Saturday afternoon crowd, new Disney sell-through items, Marilyn presiding over employee training of the store's latest staff member. Jason deposited his backpack under the counter, punched in on Marilyn's latest fascist innovation, the time clock, and quickly checked the shelves for the Buckshot videos—featuring the men of Colt Studios in "heavy contact, remastered masculine excitement"—that had arrived just as

he was leaving yesterday. There they were! Lori had dutifully prepared them for immediate rental during the late shift. Now he just
had to get a couple of the choicest Buckshot cover boxes from the
gay section and slide them into place on the shelf next to their corresponding, precious cassettes, which he could then spirit into his
backpack at a convenient moment. Damnit! There was Ronald, that
big fag customer/pal of Marilyn's who was always scooping Jason's
video picks.

"Jason, man, can you watch the register for me while I take a
piss?" Tigger, an aspiring Sunset Strip guitarist with black stripes
dyed into his orange mane, asked, before dashing toward the rest
room with one hand already unzipping the khaki pants that clung to
his spaghetti legs like a second skin.

"Sure," Jason said to the air. Perfect, actually. Nobody was
ready to check out. Marilyn and Ronald were embroiled in some
conversation that evidently required more hand gestures than American Sign Language. The trainee was restocking cover boxes in Tot
Town. Jason dropped to his knees and opened the cupboard directly
beneath the cash register. He withdrew his Jansport and unzipped it,
furtively looking to his left. His hand was inside the backpack gripping the tapes when a nervous glance right revealed Marilyn behind
the counter, her bulging eyes glaring at him.

"What are you doing?" she demanded.

Jason's mouth opened to form words that were simply not there.
His fingers released the forbidden videos and encountered something
at the bottom of the bag. "Getting my chapstick," he said, pulling
it out and innocently applying the waxy grape flavor to his pert lips.

Marilyn rolled her bullfrog eyes and compulsively tried to pull
her blouse into a more flattering shape. "Personal belongings go in
the break room," she informed Jason crossly.

He yanked the zipper closed with a "God-you're-a-bitch" smile,
hoisted the backpack on his shoulder and got up to cart it to the
walk-in supply closet Marilyn referred to as the break room, counting
on replacing the videos on the shelf on his way back.

"Give it to me. I'll do it for you. You've got a customer," Marilyn said, holding out a small chubby hand for the bag while cocking
her head toward a teenage girl slouching near the register holding

the cover boxes for *American Anthem* starring Mitch Gaylord and *Mystic Pizza.*

"S'okay, I'm waiting for my brothers," the teen helpfully responded, giving Jason license to waltz past Marilyn with the backpack. He did but was unable to get rid of the tapes because Tigger emerged from the bathroom and glazedly shuffled down the hall, perhaps reflecting on his good fortune that the store so far had no mandatory drug-testing policy. Jason hung the backpack on a nail in the "break room" wall, wishing he had a jacket or anything else to throw over it. He had to get those movies out—he felt like they were broadcasting an incriminating ultra-frequency signal only sows could hear directly into Marilyn's brain. He began to unzip the backpack—

"Ja-ason! Might we have some assistance here!" Marilyn sang. Shit! He gave the backpack a final helpless look then hurried to the front counter. Every transaction took twice as long because the new trainee was pulling tapes and was unsurprisingly unfamiliar with the alphabetical layout of the library shelves. Jason and Tigger each manned a register while Marilyn put the videos in bags and waylaid the customers with idle chitchat and film recommendations. After twenty minutes that seemed like nine hours, the store was quiet. Marilyn had one hefty hip leaning against the counter, trying to decide on which preview tape to torment them with. Jason took a couple of preliminary steps backward, then turned tail and scurried up the short hallway to the break room.

"Jason! Where are you going now?" Marilyn called.

Jesus H. Baldheaded Christ. What was her fuckin' problem today? "To the rest room, Marilyn. If that's okay," he added, the thin wall that normally concealed his hatred for her nearing total collapse.

He darted into the bathroom and locked the door behind him. He made himself wait, but not long enough for the others to think he was defecating, then flushed and came out. The break room was right across the hall. And Marilyn was in it! She was seated at the card table with the trainee, explaining how to fill out income tax forms. Was her own office too full of pizza boxes and chicken bones to use for official tasks? "Did you want to come in here and take your break?" Marilyn asked in a nice tone Jason instantly distrusted.

"No," he said.

"Good. Because you've only been here an hour and there's plenty of work to do up front," she snorted.

There was no civil retort to this, so Jason went back to the counter, where Tigger was applying eyedrops, picked up an armful of cover boxes and started restocking the display shelves. You've got to relax, he told himself, purposely ignoring Marilyn's Macaulay Culkin section in Comedy and shoving *Home Alone* in with the *H*'s. Forget about returning those damn tapes today. Just sneak out some more and bring them all back when she's not here. He worked his way around to Adult Male and spotted the Buckshot collection conveniently stacked together. He checked the counter. Tigger was on the phone and the coast was clear. Now would it be *Fort Muscle, USA* or *Rodeo Rump Ranchers* . . . ?

"Oh, hi, Jason!" Damnit, what the hell was Ronald still doing here? Jason regarded his blow-dried hair, Jordache jeans and medallions visible in the forever-tan V of his half-unbuttoned rayon shirt and shuddered at what might be waiting for himself on the other side of forty.

"Hello," he said politely, spinning on his heel for a quick getaway.

"Where is that Miss Marilyn?" Ronald asked.

"She's in the back doing paperwork. Can I help you with something?" Jason replied, hoping to get him rung up and out the door ASAP.

"Oh, there she is! Yoo-hoo, madame!" Ronald began flamboyantly signaling for Marilyn, who was now waddling past the counter toward them.

She put a flabby arm around Ronald's shoulders. "How's it hangin', hon?" she quipped saucily. Jason shuddered again.

"Marilyn!" Ronald gasped. "You naughty thing. I'm looking for a special boy-boy tape I thought I saw here a while back. *Loads A' Leaping*," Ronald said without batting an eyelash.

"*Loads A' Leaping*," Marilyn repeated thoughtfully. "Does that sound familiar, Jason?"

Yes, very. Because that exact video presentation, starring Zak Spears as a blessedly insatiable college track hero, was one of the cassettes currently burning a hole through Jason's Jansport. "I know we carry it," he said, hoping his face wasn't flushing a hot, panicked pink. "It's probably checked out."

"Well, there's one way to find out," Marilyn said. Jason's eyes were across the aisle on normal, heterosexual Adult, so it took a few seconds for him to realize Marilyn and Ronald were both staring at him.

He backed away, mumbling, "I'll check the computer." They both followed him to the counter so he had to actually go through with a title-status check, revealing of course that the "film" was in. He was about to lie and tell Ronald it was checked out and due tomorrow, when he felt Marilyn behind him, her polyester potbelly pressing against his ass ever so slightly and sickeningly.

"According to this, it's in," Marilyn announced. She flounced into the storage racks and returned with the cover box, depicting Zak in a well-stuffed jockstrap, running shoes and white tank top, which he was lifting over one nipple all the better to pinch it.

Ronald snatched it out of her hand. "That's it!" he whined.

"Apparently it's been rented but not checked out on the computer," Marilyn huffed.

"Oh, damn," Ronald said.

"I need a cigarette break," she told everyone. Like you need a cheddar and sausage omelette, Jason wanted to reply, but if it would get her out of the store, he'd buy her a carton himself. Luckily, Tigger had a fresh pack from which he obligingly dispensed a Camel each to Marilyn and Ronald. They made a beeline for the front door. Jason made a beeline for the break room. He would put the tapes in the basket under the counter, as if they'd just been checked in but not put back on the shelf yet. Let Marilyn and her horny "girlfriend" Ronald figure it out.

He unzipped the backpack, reached in and grabbed a videotape. One videotape. Where was the other one? It had to be in here. They had both been in here before. Hadn't they? It wasn't in here. What if—thank God, he felt it. He'd shoved it in the inner compartment when Marilyn—

"What the hell are you doing?" A strangled cry of surprise escaped Jason's throat as he whirled around, violently startled, his right hand still in the backpack. The bag flew onto the floor, leaving Jason with a tape in each hand and jettisoning a stack of full-color eight-by-ten gayporn ad slicks (which Jason had swiped out of a discarded UPS box the day before) at Marilyn's feet. He looked up her dumpy body very slowly, as if dreading making eye contact. She didn't disappoint. Her normally bulging eyes were sticking out so far they seemed to hover half an inch in front of her face, and her nostrils flared with porcine rage. Her lips, however, remained set in their standard smug sneer, making her look like a bloodthirsty farm animal too constipated to charge. "I won't even ask what you're doing with these promos," she said, kicking them with her gold flat. "I'm much more interested in what else you've been stealing from here."

"I haven't *stolen* anything in my life!" he protested.

"We'll see about that!" With that, she advanced on him and reached for the videocassette in his left hand. He instinctively raised it over his head. Instead of jumping for it, Marilyn snagged the tape in his right. "*Loads A' Leaping*. I should have known. I don't suppose this is checked out to you by any chance?"

"No, but—" His chest felt like it was inexorably compressing over his frantically pounding heart. There had to be an explanation. What would Andre have said? Like Andre would ever have a job, he argued madly with himself. Well, if he did!!!? Andre would have checked the goddamn things out on the computer and tough tittie to whoever knew it.

Marilyn took a step closer. "Give me that or you're fired." He handed her the other movie. "*I Luv Foreskin*. That figures."

If there had been a mirror in the room, Jason would have been stunned at how wide his mouth could actually open. Any shame or humiliation was evaporated by a sudden, brutal bolt of rage. "I quit!"

He realized he'd screamed this at a considerable volume and quickly gathered his backpack and the few nonporno items that had spilled out of it. "Resignation accepted!" Marilyn chirped. "And if you cool down and change your mind, Jason, don't come crawling back, because we don't want you here."

He looked into her evil troll face for what he knew would be the last time. "Fuck. You." He marched past her, past a shocked and eavesdropping Tigger, past the counter and past Ronald. He was leaving this hellhole the way Violet had left that psycho actor's trailer in San Diego. Like a man. He was halfway to the door when

he heard Marilyn say: "You'll never guess where I found *Loads A'
Leaping*, Ronald. Jason was trying to steal it."

"That's *awful!*" Ronald moaned. "Closet cases are so uptight!
I had Missy pegged from Day One. It's eating you up, honey! Go
with it!" he shrieked at Jason before bursting into giggles with Marilyn. Jason had a horrible psychic flash of Ronald, baby-oiled up in
French bikini briefs drooling over the confiscated videos as he imagined what Jason must have been doing to himself while watching
the exact same filthy scenes.

The first thing he had to do was tell Violet. And right away before
she or Dave asked for him at Video Xplosion and got the whole
sordid scoop from whoever was manning the register. So he left a
message on her voice mail at the studio saying that he'd gotten into
a terrible fight with Marilyn, told her to fuck off and got fired.

She reacted much as he thought she would. "Good for you! To
hell with that place. I'm never going in there again," she proclaimed
in her dressing room the next day to Jason's relief. She'd invited
him to spend the day on the set—they were taping the frozen embryo
episode that night—and he was grateful for a place to hide out from
Maggie and for the abundance of free food. The mansion's cupboard
was bare, and a chilling personal financial analysis had indicated to
Jason that a trip to the grocery store would be ill-advised at best
until further notice. He had to find something fast, preferably something that paid better than Video Xplosion, which, to make things
even more difficult, he would be unable to mention on future job
applications.

Violet had just finished re-pretaping a scene in which she awak-
ens from a sexy dream to discover Billy enthusiastically licking her
neck. "That goat's tongue is like sandpaper. And there's cake mix
between my tits," she complained, scrubbing at herself with a
makeup sponge. Gobbles's favorite food was Duncan Hines batter,
which had to be strategically daubed on the actors (yellow or white
cake for Violet, chocolate for everybody else) before taping any intimate scenes. Between this and the caramels the goat was continually fed—they stuck in his back teeth so his protracted chewing
would provide lip movement for voice-over dubbing—Jason worried
that the creature's career would be sabotaged by tooth decay much

the same way human performers often succumbed to drug addiction and alcoholism. "I asked our line producer if there were any jobs available here on the show. For you."

"You did?" Jason asked, feeling simultaneously special and pathetic. "Thanks. I guess there wouldn't be much for a deposed video store jockey, though."

Violet sat down and lightly slapped his wrist. "The shitty attitude has got to go. Erase the video store from your résumé and your memory. What you are is a recent college graduate exploring your many options in the entertainment industry. And no, there's nothing on *Chillin' with Billy* right now."

He sighed and let his head fall back against the vintage seventies-insurance-agency couch, smiling. "As I predicted."

"Not exactly. You know that obnoxious production assistant that I'm always complaining about? Benjie?"

"The one who showed your *Leather & Lace* episode to everyone?"

"*And* asked to use my home phone to call his horoscope when he was dropping off a script at midnight *and* took a bite out of a tortilla chip and put it back in the bowl at the craft services table—I saw him! Anyway, Roxanne's assistant has had it in for him since she caught him faxing copies of the confidential cast and crew address list, and I told her before they hire anyone else to let me know. It only pays three-fifty a week, but you get overtime and plenty to eat and can mingle with really fabulous stars like myself," she said.

Jason picked up *The Hollywood Reporter* and involuntarily flipped to the want ads. "But this guy has to get fired first?" he asked.

"I'm working on it," she hissed, making him laugh.

"Here's something," he said. "Do you think I can sound enough like a German female to do 'adult fantasy phone recordings'? 'Comfortable Santa Monica location'?"

"Look, maybe you don't want to do this, but have you thought of asking Marina Stetson for help? The music business is what you're really interested in, isn't it?"

"Violet, I've tormented myself with that since I found out she lived next door. It's *exactly* what I want. To be in A&R, maybe even produce records someday. Somebody has to write the liner notes for

The Pop-Tartts' Greatest Hits, I mean, when they finally release it. Why can't it be me?"

"So do it! Ask her! Tell her! She's in New York right now recording a song *you* found for her, right?" she demanded, excitedly whapping him on the shoulder.

"Yeah. I haven't heard anything for, like, over a week," he said.

"She's making an album. She's busy! But she'll get back. And when she does, you're gonna do it, do it, do it!" She put her arms around him from the back and shook him like a stuffed animal to punctuate the command. There's no way she'd do this if she thought I was straight, he sighed to himself. She did give good advice—he debated spilling his guts and seeing if she had any tips on finding a boyfriend.

The horseplay stopped when they heard a knock. "Yes?" Violet called.

Benjie barged in. "Am I interrupting anything, Viola?" he smirked.

"Well, that's pretty irrelevant at this point," Violet said, smiling back, no trace of bitchiness in her voice. Benjie had a coil of plastic ID bracelets commonly used at clubs to separate legal drinkers from underage, cover-paying teens. The show used them to tag personnel authorized to attend the catered meal on tape night. Benjie lumbered in and tied one around Violet's wrist. "Will your friend be joining you?" he asked in an attempted French accent. She nodded wearily. He approached Jason. "Are you over twenty-one?" he demanded playfully, holding the orange bracelet out of Jason's reach when he presented his hand.

"No, Benjie, he's fourteen, like all the boys I bring in here to molest," Violet finally snapped. "Now just cuff him for God's sake so we can go eat."

"Pardonnay-moi, Vi-o-lay," Benjie replied. He left, miffed.

"Jesus. Could he be a little more annoying?" Violet fumed. "The worst part is he really makes me act like a bitch."

"I thought he was cool. Can't we ask him to dinner?" Jason begged.

"You are *so* mindlessly impressed by anyone in show business," Violet admonished in mock disgust.

Jason peeked out into the hall to make sure Benjie wasn't lurking in the area, then he and Violet left the building to walk over to the vacant soundstage where dinner was served. Jason had been warned by her to be on the lookout for cast members from *Blossom* and *Saved by the Bell* wandering around the lot, but Violet was the one who went ballistic upon sighting an empty parking space labeled MR. SPACKLE.

Jason knew the name from the video store. Aldo Spackle was a young director whose two features, the ultraviolent *Scab-Picker* and the coffeehouse love triangle thriller *Sodom & Cremora* were constantly rented by jaded, postmod twentysomethings as well as the thirty-five- to forty-five-year-olds still in denial about being displaced from the cutting edge by Generation X. Marilyn had been a big (make that HUGE) Aldo Spackle fan. Jason had seen *Scab-Picker* at a midnight show with his roommate Oscar in college but remembered very little but the pulverizing anxiety of whether or not the sexy, half-Cuban Oscar would try to hold his hand or press his thigh against Jason's. (He didn't.)

Violet had seen neither of Aldo's films. "But I just read this incredible interview with him in *Movieline*. He's only twenty-six. Everyone says he's the next David Lynch or Coen Brothers. Oh, my God, Jason, there he is!" She pulled Jason between a parked Mercedes and Jag and squatted down. Through the car windows she pointed out a short guy with black jeans, a red cowboy shirt, curly blonde hair and wraparound shades strolling up to a nearby office door and unlocking it.

"What should I do?" Violet whispered.

"About what?"

"About meeting him! He's got a two-picture deal with the studio. John Waters had Divine, Aldo Spackle can have me." Aldo was in the office moving around. The door was open.

"Um, yeah, Violet. But Divine was with John Waters from the very beginning. Aldo's already made two movies. And don't you have this TV series to do for, like, the rest of the year?"

She stood up. "Jason, in case you haven't noticed, this is the worst fucking show ever conceived. If we get thirteen episodes of *Chillin' with Billy* in the can, *I'll* eat dogshit myself. Now how can I meet Aldo?"

"Uh—wrap yourself up in a welcome basket and have Benjie drop you off at his door?"

"You're a genius!"

When Jason beheld the lobster ravioli, grilled lemon-herb breast of chicken, whipped potatoes, hot sourdough bread and dessert tray glittering with cheesecake wedges and big fat tollhouse cookies, his body forgot he'd been snacking all day and instantly became ravenous. Luckily, Violet spared him from acting like a glutton in front of servers, cast and crew by loading up a carryout tray with heaping portions of everything. "Do you mind eating up in my room? I know you were probably really looking forward to shmoozing with Maurice Johnston and his *entourage,* but I don't have much time before I have to get into costume." Jason readily acquiesced but was unable to resist chomping down a coconut-encrusted fudge bar as he followed Violet out of the soundstage.

Back in the dressing room, Jason began attacking dinner as Violet gathered the remnants of gift baskets from Roxanne, the studio and Edgar's office (there wasn't much left of that puny thing) along with a recent unopened arrival from the network. "The *Movieline* article said that he loves coffee. He's obsessed with it. He wrote the screenplay for *Sodom & Cremora* while he was working at a coffeehouse. And he only applied for the job so he could drink coffee all day." She had emptied out one of the baskets and was now filling it with an assortment of leftover items to create her own specially themed presentation. "Raspberry roast coffee, Parisian vanilla mint coffee, hazelnut torte coffee, an espresso crunch chocolate bar all the way from Switzerland, mocha-chip muffin—wait, I want that— Bavarian coffee cake in a lovely decorator tin, and a handful of delicious truffles." She tossed them in, then grabbed an extra one and lobbed it at Jason. It bounced off his shoulder, and he dropped his plastic fork in his potatoes, startled. "Sorry to interrupt the feeding frenzy."

He looked so chastened, defensively dabbing his lips with a napkin, she had to laugh. "Kidding. Now please evaluate these head shots and decide which one Aldo gets."

She fanned out three very similar photos which she respectively referred to as "Laura Ashley sexual compulsive," "Smart-ass ex-girlfriend" and "Feenamint commercial." Jason chose Laura Ashley.

"That's my favorite, too," she confessed. "Oh, no. The only paper I have is this." It was the newly printed official show stationery featuring the title logo, with a cartoon goat kicking the *y* in *Billy* crooked.

"I think it's perfect," Jason said. "You can make a joke about him directing an episode or something."

"That's good." She started writing. "How's this? 'Dear Aldo, As a devoted admirer of your work, I'd like to welcome you to Sunset/Gower Studios on behalf of everyone at *Chillin' with Billy*, the African-American sitcom with a talking goat. If you'd care to direct an episode, please let me know and I'll submit your reel for consideration. Let's have coffee. Violet Cyr."

"I like it. It makes you sound respectfully irreverent."

She slipped the photo and résumé into an envelope and scribbled Aldo's name on it in fancy mock calligraphy. Jason went back to his dinner as she orchestrated ribbons, bows and shrink-wrap into her creation. "You didn't know I worked as a gift wrapper at the Glendale Galleria for two years in high school, did you?" she asked, displaying the finished product, which Jason appreciatively inspected. "But you probably know what I'm going to ask you to do with this."

"Walk it over to Aldo's office as soon as possible?"

"Do you mind? Look, you can wear this baseball cap the studio gave me. No, turn it around backward. Okay, here's the key to my dressing room. I have to go down to get into makeup. Do you want to watch the show in the green room with the network people and agents and Emmiline's minister, or sit in the actual studio audience?"

"I think the audience. Is that okay?"

"Yeah, as long as you're not wearing gang colors."

He found his way back to Aldo's door with minimum difficulty. It was still open, he noted with simultaneous relief and apprehension. Hey, you're a close personal acquaintance of Marina Stetson, he told himself. Some flavor-of-the-month director was hardly worth a dry mouth. Think bored, jaded messenger boy. He knocked.

"Come in," Aldo muttered. Jason did and found the *Buzz* magazine coverboy trying to make a pyramid of seventies lunch boxes on a shelf in the outer office of his suite. He made minute adjustments to the *Sigmund & The Sea Monster* at the top of the structure, then muttered "Motherfuckers" as everything came clanging down —*Scooby-Doo*, *Josie & The Pussycats*, *Adam-12*, *Dark Shadows* and the 1976 *King Kong*. Jason experienced a pang of regret for his late, lamented Pop-Tartts lunch box, unforgivably sold at a garage sale by his clueless mother.

He proffered the basket to Aldo at arm's length, then pulled it back slightly, remembering how bored he was supposed to be. "Delivery for Aldo Spackle."

Aldo took it and regarded it through his apparently omnipresent hipster shades. "Coffee. Cool. Do I have to sign for this?"

"Uh, no. Sir. You don't." That sounded *real* jaded.

Aldo placed the basket on the floor next to the lunch box wreckage, then pulled a rattlesnake wallet from his hip pocket. "All I got's a ten."

"You don't need to . . . ," Jason began, but Aldo had already taken out the cash and was trying to hand it to him.

"Thanks a million," Aldo said. Jason took the bill and stuck it in his jeans. What the hell. He needed gas. He thanked Aldo and turned to go.

"Have you seen that?" Aldo asked. He was pointing to the enormous framed movie poster that hung over the sofa and took up most of one wall. It was a French banner for something called *The Naked Kiss*, "*un film de Samuel Fuller.*" Jason shook his head.

Aldo sighed and picked up two of the lunch boxes. "Rent it. It's really the nuts."

Jason got home at eleven that night. Factoring in the free food and cash tip, the day had been quite a success. The taping *had* been excruciating, though. Sitting through scene after botched, insipid scene, Jason thought that there was no way *Andre* could have come up with a worse episode and should perhaps pursue sitcom writing a bit more enthusiastically. Violet was one of the very few cast members who had apparently memorized her lines, but even she was constantly undermined by miscues and Gobbles the Goat's disruptive behavior, including literal scenery chewing, flagrant disregard for his blocking, and propping his front legs on the kitchen table, revealing to the audience an extremely conspicuous erection. Jason stayed through it all and was finally escorted by Violet out of the studio audience, which appeared to consist equally of busloads from reform schools and homes for the retarded, down onto the floor for the final scene. During pickups, Violet introduced him to the show's line producer with an unsubtle "I'd like you to meet your next production assistant." The very agreeable man automatically asked for Jason's résumé then proceeded to keep his arm around Violet until she was needed on-camera for a reprisal of the hilarious climax in which the missing frozen embryo, mistakenly labeled AUNT PETUNIA'S SPAGHETTI SAUCE, is nearly microwaved by the littlest Deauville.

Jason had been awake since seven-thirty that morning on Maggie-watch and was exhausted, too exhausted to even turn on the light in his room. He took off his clothes and tossed them on a chair, hesitating before removing his underwear. What if Maggie showed up at the crack of dawn and ordered him out of bed? Since his room was technically servants' quarters, he wasn't surprised there was no lock. Giving the maid or houseboy that much privacy and dignity could only be seen by Maggie and her ilk as an incitement to illicit behavior. Fuck her, he mentally snorted, kicking the door closed.

He shed his Jockeys and crawled into bed. The monolithic outline of the forty-five-inch television set took shape in the darkness, his former private adult cinema, now closed indefinitely. He still had his memories, though. Marilyn couldn't take those away from him. Memories of Randy Mixer's brilliantly whorish performance in *Bang the Gang Slowly*, of mega-hung Johnny Davenport and his jet-propelled cum shots in hit after video hit. Jason's hand made a quick pass over his nipples before venturing down his taut stomach to discover his own, unfamous penis was ripe for reminiscing as well.

His casual, lazy stroking quickened as he did a brain-rewind to a particularly unshakable moment from *976-HUNK*—a scene with built-like-a-brick-shithouse Alex Stone. Handsome Alex was kneeling on white satin sheets, naked, a red telephone cord wrapped around his beefy thigh, snaking under his balls and between his scrumptious buttocks before encircling his torso en route to the receiver he was using to carry on a nasty conversation with j/o buddy Hunter Scott while doing exactly that with his free hand. Then

Hunter, who coincidentally lived in the building, came through Alex's coincidentally unlocked door and surprised his phone pal with a big throbbing—damn, I forgot to check my messages, Jason remembered, the porn reenactment fizzling out as he hopped from his bed and opened the cabinet below the TV where he kept the answering machine hidden behind some blank videotapes of Andre's. The digital readout said 3. He knelt on the utterly neutral gray-blue carpet, his erect penis wagging stubbornly in front of him, and hit Play. "Yes, this is Mrs. Burke," Maggie said irritatedly. "That was someone's answering machine. I do apologize."

"Did you want to reschedule your massage, madam?" a British voice politely asked.

"Eeeuh, yes, that'll be fine," Maggie replied.

"Will you be coming by or shall I schedule an outcall for the Hotel Bel-Air?"

"An outcall, please. This evening around nine. And I *don't* want the same one I had last week. He was much too rough."

"Yes, madam. I'm going to send Loek. He's just in from Amsterdam and has been very well received by all our clientele."

An interesting way to put it, Jason thought, more amused by Maggie's continual besting by the answering machine than the excellent possibility that she was paying to get porked by rent-a-studs. The cavalcade of unlikeliness went on—the next message was from Andre. "*Como estas, pobrecita?* Do you hate me? I'm so sorry about the whole Stefan situation . . . I guess I just assumed that when I stopped collecting rent from you on the house, our agreement was *temporarily* suspended . . . Um, if you're really miserable, we can talk to Fawn about you maybe staying in *her* apartment . . . she's just way too busy for me to bother her *this* week—we're about to start recording. It's very exciting. I'll send you some of the proofs from the photo shoot. And I'm so tan I look like Shari Belafonte before the skin bleaching. Call me!" There were so many offensive things in this message he'd have to listen to it again to enumerate them all. On to number three. "Hi, Jason. This is Hank Rietta." Oh, God. Jason reflexively covered his now-relaxed genitalia. "I'm home and I'll be here till around eleven-thirty tonight. So please give me a call as soon as you can."

Jason reset the machine, then almost gave himself whiplash looking over his shoulder at his clock radio. 11:29. He dove for the phone and dialed Marina's number, knowing he was probably too late. It rang only twice before Hank picked up. "Hello."

"Hi. It's Jason, Hank."

"Hey, bud. Where've you been?"

"At a taping of my friend Violet's new show."

"Cool. A sitcom?"

"That's one way to put it." Hank laughed. "How about you?"

"Me? Busy keeping the world safe for capitalism. We just wrapped up this leveraged buyout and they're flying me to Bangkok in the morning. Can you stop over for a minute?"

Now? "Now?"

"Yeah. Marina wanted me to discuss something with you," he said in the tone Jason thought he must use doing international banking.

"I'll be over in ten—five minutes," Jason said. They hung up. What the hell could it be? Besides incredibly important—it was almost midnight. He turned the light on and picked out a fresh shirt to go with the jeans he'd cast off. He went into his adjoining bathroom, one-fourth the size of the smallest powder room anywhere else in the mansion, and brushed his hair.

Oh, no. What if Hank was going to tell him it was over between Jason and Marina? The record company had hated her sixties cover and she flipped out and blamed Jason. Or she'd decided he was a dangerous, obsessive fan with stalker tendencies and had to be cut off completely. He gripped the sink for support and splashed a handful of cold water onto his face. He had to get up there now or he'd become too afraid and spend the night imploding under the synth-fill comforter over his twin bed. He snatched up his keys and jogged across the driveway and onto the path to Marina's.

Hank was standing on the terrace outside the upstairs master bedroom when Jason emerged from the thicket into the villa's backyard. He waved, a tiny figure bathed in the warm glow of wrought iron electric lanterns and myriad pinpoints of light strung through the balcony railing like jeweled buds suspended on an invisible vine. Jason waved back. "Back door's unlocked. Come on up," Hank called.

REM's *Automatic for the People* softly filled the dark corners of the house. Jason went through the gym and upstairs, the surreal sensation of actually being inside Marina Stetson's home—surrounded exclusively by things she had chosen, bought, touched—as powerful as it had ever been. He wasn't sure which bedroom was the right one. As if to guide him, Nabisco appeared in a doorway at the end of the hall and came toward Jason. "Hi, puppy," Jason said, crouching down to pet the pug. Nabisco's curly tail bobbed back and forth as he attempted to cuddle with Jason, who noticed a new tag on the dog's collar. It was a small silver heart engraved with "NABISCO, M & H Rietta" and their phone number. Apparently Marina was taking drastic precautions in case of another escape. Jason picked up Nabisco and carried him into the bedroom.

Hank was sitting at an umbrellaed table on the terrace opening a bottle of wine. "Bisco must have smelled you coming through the trees," he said. "He started prancing around like a crazy dog, didn't you, baby?" Nabisco jumped into Hank's lap. "I hope you like zinfandel," he told Jason, filling two glasses.

"Oh, yeah, it's great," Jason replied, not exactly sure what it was but naturally eager to please Hank, who looked fantastic in a semi-unbuttoned teal henley and smelled even better.

Jason sat down and banged his knees against the tabletop, causing everything to shake but thank God no spillage. "Maybe you already had some wine tonight," Hank remarked.

Jason reddened. "Sorry. I'm a total klutz."

"Shit, I was just joking." He smiled and slid Jason's glass across the table toward him, then raised his own. "Okay, what should this be to? I know. To the *Ghost in the Fog* preview concert."

"Marina's doing a preview concert? When?" Jason asked excitedly.

Hank clinked their glasses together. "Tomorrow night."

Jason took a long sip of wine, afraid of spazzing out and dropping it. "You're kidding," was the only response he could come up with on short notice.

"No. She's been in Vegas this week rehearsing for a special show at Caesar's Palace. She wanted to surprise you."

"Me?" Jason stammered.

Hank handed him a long envelope with the Mermaid Records logo on it. It wasn't sealed. Jason pulled out an American Airlines ticket—first-class from LAX to Las Vegas. 10:30 A.M. Tomorrow morning. Jason Dallin. Returning the next night. "I told her to check with you before she had the ticket delivered, but she said it had to be a surprise. She didn't even want to tell you about the concert till you got there, but I said that for you, I thought anticipating it would be almost as good as actually going to it. So she relented."

"I'm glad you told me," Jason said.

"Good. The record company's sending a car to take you to the airport tomorrow at nine. I okayed the whole thing earlier tonight, which I hope you don't mind. See, I went by the video store looking for you, and some girl, Lori was her name, told me you didn't work there anymore. That you'd quit sometime last week."

Lori had said that he'd *quit?* Well, she *was* the type to buy that freakishly overpriced charity candy from underprivileged tots who came into the store in blatant defiance of the NO SOLICITING window sticker. He'd better just be grateful for it. "Yeah, I'd had enough of that place. I'm really hoping to expand my résumé beyond retail."

Hank nodded. "Sure. What kind of work are you looking for?"

Now. Tell him. Do it! "Something in entertainment. But not in-home, rented entertainment."

"Marina's been telling me she thinks you'd be perfect for the record industry. Has that ever crossed your mind?"

"Uh . . . Yeah. I'd really enjoy that."

"Enjoy it? You'd be great at it. You're the most enthusiastic person she's ever met."

"She said that?"

Hank nodded and refilled the wineglasses. Jason was feeling lightheaded but knew the zinfandel was not primarily responsible. He drank more. "Jason, getting to know you has really meant a lot to Marina. I think it's helped her confidence in a big way. Knowing someone appreciates what she did before makes it so much easier for her to move on."

"But of course people appreciate her. She's a big star. She still gets all those fan letters. The Pop-Tartts' albums are in print, the videos are on TV . . . ," Jason protested.

"It's not real, though," Hank said. He got up and ambled over to the balcony. Jason had been so apprehensive about everything he hadn't even noticed the jaw-droppingly beautiful nighttime cityscape glittering hotly before them like a decadent, hacked-open treasure chest. "There's this built-in alienation from your fans. I mean, that's what she tells me. You're perfect. For her. It's so rare she would get the chance to know someone like you."

"Hank, I'm the one who's lucked-out here. How many people get to be friends with their idol? And this?" He waved the ticket. "I still can't believe it. She's the best."

Hank did a weird kind of knee bend so that he was cradling his head in his arms over that twenty-four-karat chest and said, "She's really very sweet. I worry about her. And I can't even be there on this really important night. But I'm glad you're going to be."

Jason nodded, not knowing what to say. He scratched behind Nabisco's ears and tucked the envelope into his breast pocket, where it protruded ridiculously. He took it out. "I should probably go. Back. I mean, if I have to get up for the airport and all." He stood up and everything was momentarily, drunkenly askew before swiveling back into place around Hank, who was walking toward Jason, twirling his empty wineglass between his fingers.

"I'll walk you out. Come on, Bisco," Hank said, tapping his denimed thigh.

Jason was careful not to fall down the stairs, although he did nearly trip over Nabisco stepping down from the butler's pantry into the gym. Luckily Hank didn't notice. He was lamenting all the workouts he'd been skipping the past few weeks. Although this seemed like George Kennedy complaining that he hadn't done enough *Airport* sequels, Jason kept the observation to himself. "Thanks again, Hank." But before he could step onto the path home, Hank came closer and put his arms around him in an unexpected, manly hug.

"Have a great time," he said softly, his breath warm exquisite torture on Jason's ear. Jason allowed himself to reciprocate the embrace. He would not allow his penis to get hard, but of course it did anyway. How could it not? Hank was rippling, fragrant and hot, not to mention the first male to initiate physical contact with him since he fell asleep in Beau Teasdale's private dorm room at Ohio State and woke up to find himself fellated by inebriated study partner Beau last November. Jason moved back a step, before Hank could be grossed out by seismic activity in Jason's basket.

"I'll try to call you guys from Thailand. And tell Marina she can pick this one up"—he gave Nabisco a vigorous rubbing—"at my brother's place whenever she gets in. You have a good night." One last tap on the shoulder and he was walking back toward the house. Jason was still, unable to move, until Hank turned around and waved. He waved back and plunged into the trees, skidding and clambering down the path, the envelope clutched in his hand, his ticket to paradise, his boarding pass out of this pathetic, penniless fringe existence. Gaining momentum, he spilled off the embankment into a run across the driveway. He unlocked the front door and danced into the main hall, suddenly loving the mansion and finding it an entirely appropriate setting for his dreams to materialize. He went to his room and put on *Rainwater Lullaby* as loud as he dared, then flushed all the toilets and tried to inspect the kitchen through Maggie's malevolent eyes. All he could find amiss was a quart of milk, nearly empty but stamped with today's expiration date. He poured it down the sink and tossed the carton.

Now—packing. He had nothing suitable for the flight and limo to the hotel, much less the concert. Luckily, Texas in summer was one of the most overbroiled spots on earth, so Andre had left a great deal of his relatively lavish wardrobe behind. "If you *absolutely* have to wear my clothes, don't do it," he'd quipped to Jason just before Fawn had picked him up for the airport. And stranded Jason while Andre rented out his room and let Maggie Burke run Imelda-shod over his defenseless white ass. He selected a DKNY leather vest, Calvin Klein pants, a tercel/rayon Armani dress shirt, Guess blazer and Italian loafers that fit beautifully with one or two extra pairs of socks.

He set his alarm for seven and undressed, thought of calling Violet, but decided to shock her with a postcard from Vegas. He'd never been but was familiar with the city from films such as *Viva Las Vegas* and the William Higgins porno *Route 69*. He wanted to see the plane ticket again, touch it to make sure it was real before he fell asleep. He'd propped up the AA envelope on the small mahogany bureau in the corner of the bedroom, balancing it against the metal sunburst frame that held a snapshot Hank had taken of him and Marina on the deck of Gladstone's several weeks ago.

Holy fuck. That embrace up on Marina's lawn came bursting forth from whatever memory holding tank he'd temporarily filed it.

He fell back onto the bed, arm-wrestling his rigid cock. Since Hank was obviously completely straight not to mention married to Marina, Jason had arrived at the rationale that sexual fantasies about his brooding, swarthy, unbelievably attractive neighbor were as harmless and acceptable as whack-off scenarios involving the Soloflex info-mercial boy or anyone similarly unattainable. Jason's newfound knowledge of what it felt like to actually touch Hank (although he knew it was only a simple friendly hug and nothing else) merely injected a bonus note of virtual reality into his current masturbatory mindtrip, exploring in nut-clenching detail what might have tran-spired had Hank's arms found their way around Jason's waist and up under his shirt prior to tossing him down to the grass for poolside ravishing. Jason fell asleep happy, envisioning the hunky *Caligula*-extra types he might get lucky with at Caesar's Palace.

He woke up at seven and leapt out of bed, utterly energized at the realization that the day would end in a luxurious hotel theater watching his *friend* Marina Stetson perform a private concert. He was scrubbed, shampooed and fully packed in forty-five minutes, so decided to log onto Andre's Macintosh and tinker with his résumé — it would be insane not to be prepared for shmoozing with the record executives he'd almost surely be meeting. He deleted Video Xplosion from the document with only the slightest hiccup of trep-idation. So what if he supposedly hadn't worked since moving to L.A.? He'd only graduated from college in May, for Christ's sake. With Marina as a reference, it shouldn't be a problem. He added her name and management number to the bottom of the résumé, along with Violet, and then, just so there would be three entries under References, "Fawn Farrar and Andre Nickerson, Aida Productions," plus their all-but-worthless San Antonio phone number. The laser printer Andre had insisted Fawn furnish him with before agreeing to house-sit spat forth five résumés, which Jason tucked into a folder he packed in his duffel bag.

He wrote Maggie a polite note explaining that he'd be away overnight, realized this was brazenly asking for trouble, and had just finished ripping it up when he heard a car in the driveway. He flung the shreds into a wastebasket in the breakfast nook, which presently offered a dismaying view of Maggie's Lexus creeping around the bend. He decided the best strategy was to hide in his room and hope she left quickly. It wasn't that he was doing something wrong, it was just . . . okay, it wasn't anything but that she was a snotty bitch. He closed the bedroom door seconds before he heard her heels on the foyer floor. She can't do a goddamn thing to sabotage this Vegas trip, so calm down, he snapped at himself. The old fossil would probably be happy to have Jason out of her way for a day or two. She knocked on his door then opened it before he could respond. What if he had been asleep naked with a boner prodding up the sheet? Or, just as likely, whacking it to something by Matt Sterling on the forty-five-inch TV screen?

"Jason," she said.

"Yes?" He involuntarily glanced at the duffel and garment bags, as if expecting them to blurt out something incriminating.

Maggie looked different somehow. What was it? Ah. She had traded in the red cardigan for a green one. "The movers will be here this morning with the furniture. If you're not going in to the toy store today, I need you to help me here. Naturally, you'll be paid."

"I'm not working at the toy store anymore," Jason replied with a straight face. "And I'm sorry, but I already have plans today. I'll be back sometime tomorrow."

She stared at him with undisguised annoyance. "I see." She pivoted and marched in the direction of the wet bar phone, which had begun ringing. "Yes, hello, Maggie Burke speaking," echoed back. "One moment. Jason."

He hurried down the hall into the main area, apprehensive. Maggie was holding the receiver at arm's length, her face a tightly pulled mask of confusion and disapproval. "There's a *driver* on the line who says he's at the gate with the car you ordered?" Jason checked his watch. Eight-fifty. He took the phone from Maggie.

"Thanks. Excuse me. Hi, this is Jason. I'll open the gate. Bye." He hung up, went to the switch panel by the front door and pressed the gate button. Then he got his luggage from his room and brought it to the entryway just in time to witness a white limousine pull up, eclipsing Maggie's Lexus. He covered his surprise much more successfully than Maggie managed to conceal hers when he looked back at her to say goodbye.

This ought to put a big fat monkey wrench in the way she perceives Jason the lowly shit-boy, he thought with delicious smugness as the chauffeur loaded his bags into the trunk and opened Jason's door for him, and he imagined Maggie bitterly twisting a Kleenex in the pocket of her sweater to tatters and hoped he had a few extra bucks in his wallet to tip the driver.

The flight to Vegas lasted less than an hour. Jason, who'd flown a total of four times and never first-class, felt like he was in a day care center for incredibly pampered alcoholics. Before takeoff, a mimosa. After takeoff, a "late breakfast platter" consisting of a snow crab omelette, fresh fruit and toasted sun-dried tomato bread and a mimosa, consumed while the passengers enjoyed recent *Seinfeld* episodes via big-screen TV and free headphones. After this feast was cleared away, there was just enough time to serve fresh-baked cookies and a final drink. Jason could think of no reason to deny himself mimosa number three, didn't, and landed enjoying his second buzz in twelve hours.

Even more startling than the slot machines in the airline terminal was his own name printed on a white paper sign held waist high by yet another limo driver. This guy was a strapping muchacho with a ponytail dangling from under his cap and made Jason momentarily wistful for the days when he had a full shelf of Kristen Bjorn videos to pilfer. He immediately snapped back to the heady unreality of the day, introduced himself to the driver and followed him to baggage claim. Flying first-class meant first off the plane and resulted in a prime spot in front of the luggage carousel, so in minutes the muchacho had his duffel bag slung over one massive shoulder and was leading him outside, where a breeze the equivalent of a nine-thousand-watt hot-air blower had already chapped Jason's lips by the time he crawled into the tinted, leathered interior of the air-conditioned black stretch Cadillac.

"Been here before?" the driver asked, slipping on Terminator sunglasses.

Jason, proving himself a quick study when it came to the glamorous life, opened the minifridge and extracted a diet Coke. "No, never."

Las Vegas resembled nothing so much as some giant toddler's collection of glitzy toy buildings that had been arranged and abandoned in an equally titanic sandbox.

At the hotel's front entrance, Jason gave the guy three bucks and carried his own bag into the main lobby, across the red carpet emblazoned with Caesar's trademark laurel wreaths, past circular red couches surmounted by Roman statuary, to the registration desk. The shortest line placed him behind a middle-aged couple whose garish vacation outfits seemed to perfectly match their luggage. Jason studied the patterns intently, trying to decide if this was intentional rather than some horrific accessorizing accident, but became distracted by their conversation.

"I didn't just fly a thousand miles to see a dirty show," barked the woman, whose hyperteased salt-and-pepper hairdo was so large it had a slenderizing effect on her chunky body.

Her big-butted husband irritatedly rubbed the back of his unshaven neck. "*Nudes on Ice* is a classy show. It's at Bally's! And that girl from *Diff'rent Strokes* is in it."

"The one who posed for that girlie book before she robbed the dry cleaners?" his wife squawked. "Skating around bare-assed? Why isn't she in jail?"

"I never heard about her robbing no dry cleaners. What's her name, Dana something?"

"No, Marc, I got it all frigged up," she exclaimed, slapping his meaty shoulder. "She *worked* at the dry cleaners. She robbed a video store. And those other kids are up to no good, too. One's a drug dealer and that gal who played their mother ended up on *Designing Women*. Now that was a dirty show."

"Dana Delany. That's her name," the man said.

"Oh, it is not. It was Dixie something," she insisted. They moved to the front of the line and refocused their bickering on which room rate they had been quoted and how Marc absolutely needed a king-size bed because of his "bad back." Finally, a settlement was reached, and they and their hideous luggage were swallowed up by the casino, which cleverly stood between all hotel guests and the room elevators.

Jason gave the seen-it-all desk clerk his and Marina's names and was given a key marked 1159. He signed a registration form and went into the casino, where roulette wheels spun under a giant domed chandelier ceiling, and the dinging and ringing of slot and video poker machines was constantly punctuated by the elusive jangle of cascading jackpot coins.

He was the only one left on the elevator when it reached the eleventh floor. Stepping out onto green and black marble, he saw small numbered signs directing guests to the appropriate corridor, all framed by ornate black columns topped with elaborately scrolled if fake gold.

The door to 1159 was one step up from the hall carpet. Jason unlocked it and was almost knocked on his ass by what he saw on the other side. Facing him across marble steps and a sunken living area was a twenty-foot mirrored wall decorated with gold geometric patterns. The room was furnished with black leather couches, leopard carpeting and a baby grand piano. Except for the giant-screen television, the room was perfectly, fabulously 1967. Jason half-expected to see Ann-Margret or Sharon Tate come sliding down the silver banister of one of the twin staircases (also leopard) that whooshed up to a second-story balcony.

Wait a minute. Someone was obviously already staying here. A pair of Capri pants was draped over one sofa and breakfast remnants littered the black and green dinette set. Jason stepped down into the room and saw a familiar leather shoulder bag overflowing onto the wet bar that separated the dining area from the small but fully equipped kitchen. He began to sift through the spillover—headphones, a plastic *Aladdin* doll, antifur pamphlets, battle-scarred address book, enormous key chain anchored by a Lucite-enclosed photo of Nabisco. Jason picked up the phone and dialed the front desk. "Hi, this is Jason Dallin, Room one one five nine?"

"How may we help you, sir?"

"I think I was given the wrong key. Somebody already has this room. I think it's Marina Stetson." He absently fingered the contents of her bag, realized that was snooping, and pulled his hand back, guilt reddening his cheeks despite the fact that it was only natural for a boy to be curious when left alone with the open purse of his celebrity goddess.

The desk clerk came back on the line. "Sir, that suite *is* occupied by Marina Stetson, but I have a notation here that she requested you share it with her. There are two bedrooms upstairs. I can check on vacancies if you'd like a room to yourself."

"No! I mean, this is fine. It's great. Sorry to bother you." He hung up, dazed. Marina wanted him here, in her ultraluxurious rock star suite. He bounded up the stairs to check the bedrooms. The one on the right was in absolute chaos, unmistakably Marina's. He entered the identical room on the left and found a handwritten note on the round bed surrounded by draperies on a dais.

Jason my love,
    We're down rehearsing in Circus Maximus, off the casino. Come! Hope you had a good flight. Thanks for being here.
                                   Love, M.

Clipped to this note was a laminated pass bearing the Mermaid Records logo and his name laser-printed in bold above the fabled words ALL ACCESS. I'm halfway there, he thought giddily, fastening the pass to Andre's shirt as soon as he'd changed into Borrowed Outfit Number One.

He picked up the folder containing his résumés, then made a pit stop in his adjoining bathroom. It wasn't as spectacular as most of those in Fawn's house, but was of course far nicer than the utilitarian servants' crapper adjacent to his room at the mansion. Best of all was the array of free Caesar's products displayed on a pedestal by the sink—bath oil, shower gel, shampoo, bubble bath, cologne and moisturizer all in little Roman column-shaped bottles. He peed in the black Art Deco toilet, marveled at the matching bidet and left.

The Circus Maximus was back toward the registration area. Jason stepped over some velvet ropes and trotted up a low staircase to the entrance of Caesar's grandest showplace. From inside, he heard a song from Marina's first solo album, minus vocals. A security guard was cooling his heels and unispherical stomach in a folding chair by the closed doors, shooting the shit on a cell phone. He waved Jason through without even looking him in the face.

Jason estimated there were 1,500 seats and wondered who would fill them. Fans? Vegas show-goers? Friends and record company people? Three guitar players, a keyboardist and a drummer were rocking onstage for about a dozen people in the first few rows, Marina not among them. They wound up the number, and several roadies leaped up to take care of the equipment.

"Let's take twenty everybody," a man in the front row called. "And try to regroup, like the happy family I need." Uh-oh. Jason went down the aisle and approached the guy, who was somewhere in his thirties with Michael Bolton hair and a blazer over a black Oingo-Boingo T-shirt. He was talking to a handsome, younger, suit-and-tie guy with a goatee and six rings in his left ear. "Her manager called and he's 'en route'! Can you imagine driving here in this fuckin' heat? I'm going to try to talk to her again."

"She sounds fine. I don't know what she's—" The earring guy stopped talking and regarded Jason skeptically. "Hi. Can I help you?"

"I'm Jason. Marina's friend."

"Oh, that's great," Earring said. "Perfect."

"Thank Christ," Bolton Hair echoed. "I'm Terry Davidson, Marina's producer. This is Chip Reeves, A&R for Mermaid." Handshakes.

"Marina's a little freaked out right now," Chip explained lightly, placing a hand on Jason's shoulder as Terry guided him by the arm toward the stage.

"What's the matter?" Jason asked, unreasonably fearing the problem was somehow his fault.

"We're hoping you can find out and solve it. She doesn't want to talk to us," said Terry. "I think it's stage fright. She hasn't performed since Johnny Carson in '91. But this isn't a real intimidating show."

They were walking across the stage into the wings. "But this place is huge," Jason argued. "The Pop-Tartts played smaller places than this when they were at their peak."

"Oh, Marina's not playing *this* room," Chip said in a vaguely condescending tone. "She's in Cleopatra's Barge on the other side of the casino. It's more like a nightclub—a couple hundred people *max.*"

"We're just rehearsing here because it's more private," Terry added. "Jesus, she goes on in eight hours." They were outside a dressing room door marked NO ADMITTANCE. "Marina, it's Terry." He knocked and tried the knob.

"Give me a fuckin' break, okay, Terry?" Marina demanded in a miserable voice.

"Jason's here," Terry said hopefully.

Something was unbolted. "He can come in. Alone," she said through the door.

Chip patted Jason on the back. "Good luck," he whispered. Unnerved at the responsibility that had been inexplicably thrust upon him but thrilled at being of assistance to actual record industry big shots, Jason hesitantly opened the door and went into the dressing room.

Marina was sitting in near darkness at a makeup table. The only light came from the vanity bulbs surrounding the mirror. Jason closed the door, locked it and said, "Hi."

"I'm so screwed. This was such a rotten idea. I just want to cancel it and, like, control the damage before it gets any worse. A comeback for *me*—what a fuckin' laugh," she sighed bitterly, then spun around in her chair to face Jason. Her look of despair softened into a tight-lipped smile. "Thank you for coming, though," she got out before breaking into tears.

Jason's mouth popped open with panic. "God, Marina, don't cry. What's the matter?" He went to her and took her hand. "Out there they told me everything was going great. That you were terrific." He looked around for some tissues and found a dispenser at the corner of the table. He pulled out some and gave them to Marina, who took the whole wad and shoved her face in it, blowing her nose.

"They think I'm a joke," she said, tossing the tissues over her shoulder. "Untalented, unprofessional, undeserving. And they're right. Look at the way I'm acting. I just can't—"

"Marina, you've played me most of the new album and it's great. Terry knows it, that's why he wants you to do this show tonight. And Mermaid believes in you. They know the whole *Rainwater Lullaby* flop was your old label's problem, not yours." He was afraid of squeezing her hand too hard so released it. She immediately grabbed his hand even harder.

"Jason, I haven't had a hit since I got detoxed. Whatever career I was *meant* to have, it was with The Pop-Tartts. That first album by myself—those couple of songs did well because everyone was still totally obsessed with Sherry dying. And when I got off the drinking and the pills and the blow and the rest of that shit and was living in reality for the first time in eight years, it was real clear that it was over, but I couldn't accept it then. And now . . . can I have some more Kleenex?"

Jason got her more then dragged a chair beside hers and sat. "Look, I don't think you can jump to those conclusions until you've at least offered what you've been working so hard on to the public. You know, there are millions of people buying records today who were too young or too out-of-it to even remember The Pop-Tartts. And their first exposure to you is going to be this new album. So maybe your old career *is* over. But this new one can be anything you want it to be. Does that make any sense?"

Still holding his hand, she swiveled in the chair till she was facing the mirror again. "What if there's nothing to reinvent?"

"There is," Jason immediately replied. "What was it that made you want to perform in the first place? When you were doing shows in L.A. and San Francisco in 1981? When you worked at that video store? When you were a little kid jumping on the bed pretending to be Cher in your cousin's wig?"

A tiny giggle escaped her. "How do you know about that?"

"My favorite Pop-Tartts interview. It was in *Rock Video* magazine. It had these great color photos of everybody and these boxes with all your biographical data. And whoever wrote it was obviously as huge a fan as I was 'cause they were asking all the right questions. And I think you were saying that when The Pop-Tartts started, you sort of imagined yourself as this hostess throwing a party up onstage. For some reason, I could really relate to that."

"Your memory is so damn scary. But that is what it was. Like I was making up for being such an unpopular loser in junior high and high school. I had no friends until I discovered this group of kids that was obsessed with the B-52's. And three of us ended up as The Pop-Tartts. I always told myself I wasn't going to glamorize those years, and believe me, I hated being broke and desperate and sneaking food off the Perry's Pizza buffet, but those shows we did . . ." She trailed off, thinking, and Jason studied her still-reddish gray eyes, hoping he wasn't making things worse.

"I still want to go to the party," he said.

"What pa— Oh. That's sweet." She smiled a little, and Jason was afraid she might cry again.

"It'll be fun. I promise. And now you know how to sing." She twisted the chair and faced him with an appalled look so exaggerated he knew the well-intentioned barb had been a direct hit. "Hey," he said, holding up a hand. "You've come a long way. You have to admit."

"This is supposed to cheer my sorry ass up?" she demanded. "Huh? Is that it?"

"It's tough love," Jason explained.

She nodded agreeably, then bit his hand. He yelped. "So what did those guys tell you to come in here and do? Slap me around?" He told her. "Terry's okay, and I guess I have been kind of a nightmare for Chip. I told them you were the terrible infant of pop music and deserved a job at Mermaid Records pronto."

His heart lurched. "You did?"

"That's what you want, right?"

"Well, yeah, I mean . . ."

"I know you didn't want to come out and ask me to help you. I *don't* know if it's because you didn't want me to think that you were using me, which I'm sure you're not, or because you were too polite or chickenshit to bring it up, but now that it's out in the open, I hope you'll, like, go with it."

"Actually, I brought some résumés."

"You little whore!" Now it was his turn to look deeply offended, which Marina found inordinately amusing.

"So are you going to be okay?" Jason asked, getting up, unsure as to what if anything had exactly been resolved.

"Yeah. I always pull this before every concert. I do. Oh, you poor thing. I'm kidding," she said. "You must think I'm crazier than a shithouse rat. Now that's what we should have called the album." His laugh was stifled by a kiss on the mouth. The surprise must have registered big on his face, because when she drew back—it had only been a slightly moist peck—she covered her own mouth, her eyes flashing guiltily, before apologizing. "God, I'm sorry! I just had this urge to do that. I'm not hitting on you, I swear."

"I know," he quickly insisted.

"Not that I might not be if you were single and I was straight —I mean . . . you know what I mean."

"Yeah."

She hugged him and felt tiny and frail, and the smell was the same Marina fragrance she'd had on when he'd brought Nabisco home that first night commingled with some inoffensive sweat—she *had* been rehearsing, after all. "Okay, Jason, go out and tell my pimps I'll be right there. Since you're a guy, they'll probably try to give you credit for 'handling' me. Do you know what to do if that happens?"

Uh-oh, this is a fuck-myself op, he realized. "Not exactly . . ."

"You take it! They already think I'm a very spacey broad. You might as well make the most of it. Tell them I was paralyzed with stage fright and you put it all in perspective for me. That's not even a lie, really. You did help. A lot. Thanks, for you know. Caring."

He could only nod and say, "This . . . whole thing is the biggest thrill of my life."

"I'm going to be good for you tonight. But later we have to talk about you getting a life, babe. Now go be a hero. I'm going to call Hank."

"But he said he was flying to Bangkok today," Jason said and immediately wished he hadn't when he saw her face drop.

"Oh, yeah. I forgot."

"He said he'd try to call when he got in tonight," he added brightly.

"I've been there. Twelve-year-old strippers who shoot fire out of their butts they got. Overseas phone lines, forget it." They heard a knock at the door. "I'm going to the can. Good luck," she whispered.

Jason waited until the bathroom door was closed, then answered to Terry. "Hey, Jason. What's happening?"

Jason let himself out, shut the door behind him and briefed the producer in a confidential tone. "You guys were right. It's stage fright. She's afraid of screwing up and not being able to do the album justice. She doesn't want to make you look bad." This was a complete improv which, once said, Jason was rather proud of. "I kind of helped her put it all in perspective. She's coming. I think she'll be okay."

"I keep telling her she's gonna be aces," Terry sighed. "Have you heard any cuts from *Ghost in the Fog*?"

"Yes! It's wonderful. I mean, this puts her on a whole new level. With Sophie Hawkins or Aimee Mann."

"Actually, I'm a huge fan of The Pop-Tartts, especially their last album, *Kung Fu Grip*. It seemed like they were evolving into an excellent rock band when the shit hit the fan, they broke up and Marina went bubblegum."

"But the champagne of bubblegum," Jason agreed. "Those records were like drinking a really frosty can of Big Red on a hot summer night."

"Oh, my God, that's brilliant!" Jason turned around and there was Chip Reeves, displaying a gap-toothed grin and now radiating warmth and friendliness. "I love Big Red! And have you tried Diet? I've *begged* grocery stores in L.A. to carry the stuff but no one will. Are you from Texas?"

"No, but in high school our neighbor was a truck driver," Jason explained, "and he'd bring home these cases—"

"What's up with Marina?" Chip interrupted, suddenly remembering the crisis.

"Jason said she's fine. A minor panic attack," Terry quickly assured him. "He talked her through it."

"Thanks," Chip said. "But the band just left for lunch."

They went onto the stage and Jason sat at the keyboard, thumbing through the sheet music for what looked like mostly new, intriguing material from *Ghost in the Fog*, as well as a terrific sampling of Marina's solo and Pop-Tartt highlights, all of which were included on his own personal Greatest Hits tape.

"Okay, where is everybody?" Marina had entered and stood center stage, hands defiantly on hips, facing Terry and Chip.

"Dismissed. The hotel's already replaced you with Romeo Void," Terry deadpanned.

"Fuck you," Marina cheerfully replied. "Chip, I'm really sorry. If I promise to be a good girl the rest of the day, will you not tell Mermaid how desperately I don't want to blow it with them?"

"Deal," Chip said. "Should I order lunch?"

"No, let's go to Spago," Marina said. "Terry, wanna come?"

"Actually, if this is our break, I need to go over to the Sands and talk to Tom Jones. I'm supposed to do an Unplugged album with him. I'll be back in ninety." He left and Marina led Jason and Chip across the casino and into the Forum, an adjacent shopping

mall that simulated the streets of ancient Rome with fountains, ani-
matronic larger-than-life gods and goddesses who put on a badly
dubbed, self-congratulatory floor show every hour on the hour, and
a fake blue sky over it all. But instead of market stalls and public
baths, there were Gucci and Structure. And the beggars and street
performers that could have added a touch of historical accuracy to
the piazze had been shrewdly supplanted by slots and video poker
machines.

Marina had perked up considerably and was prancing from store
window to store window like an effervescent little girl on her first
Christmas shopping trip. "I love it here . . . it's better than Disney-
land. I'd love to do a video right in this mall. But of course, my
new album is far too *mature*. Right, Chip? Oh, goody, there's
Spago!"

The restaurant was less than a quarter full, and, Jason reflected,
owed its livelihood to the same midwestern tourist types in QVC
sportswear who would be laughed out the door if they attempted to
get a table at the Spago on Sunset Strip. Interestingly, the Spago
celebrity experience was now being simulated to at least a partial
degree with the arrival of Marina, but because of her John Lennon
sunglasses/Pucci scarf disguise, even diners with rudimentary pop
culture skills were denied a thrilling brush with fame as they came
to the conclusion that the only thing glamorous about the restaurant
were the prices.

Jason, however, was so giddy with excitement his stomach
seemed to have clenched up to the size of a nectarine, and he could
only graze at the three-miniature-pizza appetizers Marina immediately ordered then declined to taste. "No dairy before the show,"
she sensibly explained to Chip and Jason. "But you boys please eat
up. And Jason, get whatever you want. Mermaid's paying for lunch,
right, Chip?" She asked like a ballbuster testing a subordinate.

Chip turned to Jason. "This one's worse than Mariah Carey,"
he complained, shaking his head incredulously and passing the test
as Marina pealed laughter and told them a Mariah Carey story involving a televised awards show and innocent production assistants
being abused.

"And it was hardly worth the shitstorm," Marina concluded between gulps of mineral water. "She hit that fuckin' high note and my IUD cracked."

Whatever mental demons had been sabotaging her back in the dressing room had apparently been sent back to Rock and Roll Comeback Hell because Jason had never seen her as charmingly together. Part of it had to be a show put on for Chip's benefit, but Jason allowed himself a dollop of credit. This was definitely the closest he'd felt to her—she'd seated him literally at her right hand with Chip across, and continually tapped his arm, affectionately pressed her head against his shoulder and nonsexually squeezed his leg under the table—and he tried to be a worthy escort by actively participating in the conversation, which she kept shifting back to A&R at Mermaid, allowing him to ask Chip many intelligent questions about his job.

Unused to the spotlight inverted upon him during interaction with an artist, Chip started to thrive under the attention and soon was regaling them with his past as a Freddy DeMann intern, his new wife, their honeymoon and his Saturn. Jason picked at the modestly priced pasta entrée he had selected, not wanting to appear either extravagant or ungrateful, but luckily this was California cuisine (read: supermodel serving sizes), so after a few bites, he was able to arrange the remaining food on the plate so it looked like he'd eaten almost everything. There hadn't been exactly the right moment to specifically ask about a job for himself at Mermaid, and Marina hadn't overtly suggested it either, so Jason planned to discuss it with Chip before the concert. Hopefully Marina could arrange for them to sit together. Wait, what if Chip had to be backstage the whole time—?

"—have any résumés with you?"

Jesus! Chip was talking to him and he had just said the word *résumé*. Hadn't he? Jason turned to Marina and smiled, hoping she'd repeat or give some indication of what Chip had said so Jason wouldn't have to ask "What was that?" like an idiot. Instead, she just smiled back. Jason looked at Chip and quickly blurted, "Yes!"

"Great," he said. "Let me have one. There might be something opening up in A&R in the next month or so. I'll have you drop by for an interview."

Could it actually be this easy? The waiter cleared Chip's and Jason's dishes as Marina continued to nibble her baby greens and shrimp salad and ordered a dessert sampler she resisted until Chip had signed the check and they were getting up to go. "I think brownies with chocolate icing contain dairy, Marina," Chip told her.

"Screw it," she said. "You know what I used to put away every night of the *Kung Fu Grip* tour? Three vodka Super Slurpees. And that was during the show. Let's blow this cannoli stand."

The rest of the afternoon shimmered by like some insane behind-the-scenes rockumentary projected at double speed. Marina rehearsed with the band till six, when they had to break to reset at Cleopatra's Barge. Jason sat with his new pal Chip, watching Marina perform —quite well—mostly new songs under Terry's low-key guidance, and exchanging Pop-Tartts reminiscences with the affable A&R exec. They met Marina's manager, Saul, a hulking Jewish gangster type in damp Versace brandishing a constantly bleeping cellular phone in one hand and a can of Solarcaine in the other, which he kept inserting under his collar to spray what must have been one bitch of a sunburn.

During the reset, Marina was supposed to have a brief meeting with Terry and Saul, but first she found Jason and pulled him aside. "This is where it starts to get really nuts, but I'm okay. The sound check's at seven, then I get dressed, and hair and makeup work me over and I go on at nine. Anyway, Mermaid's got this hospitality suite set up on the eleventh floor near our room, you know, for all the people invited to the concert, and you can go up there and eat and mingle and shmooze with whoever Mermaid and Saul convinced to drag their ass up here."

"Didn't you invite anyone?" Jason asked.

"Just you. And Betty Fonseca." The rhythm guitarist/backup singer for The Pop-Tartts who'd since founded the cult band Bubonic Pest?! "Because even if I sucked, you guys would be nice to me."

"You're going to be great," he said, knowing it was the truth.

"See you at the show," Marina said. She kissed him on the cheek and went to get handled.

Jason went up to the insanely luxurious suite and changed into the Calvin slacks, white shirt and leather vest. He put on his own tube socks first, then a pair of Andre's silk dress ones and tried on the loafers, wondering why he'd never noticed what huge feet Andre had. It should be okay if he didn't walk around too much. But he had to go do something because Chip told him the Mermaid party wouldn't be for another forty-five minutes, and Jason wanted to leave their suite to Marina so she and her beauty technicians could prepare for the concert in private.

He opted for a self-guided tour of the hotel casino and lobby area and was soon somewhere in Caesar's gift shop wing staring at an exact replica of Michelangelo's *David*. What societal, religious or personal pressures had driven the brilliant artist to equip the staggeringly hunky sculpture with such a ludicrous, tiny penis? The uncircumcised nonendowment looked even smaller next to David's elaborate pubic hairdo, which, from Jason's angle, seemed to have been curled with hot rollers.

Realizing he was obstructing an Asian family who wanted to snap each other's photos in front of the statue, Jason moved on to something even more jolting than an eighteen-foot naked man. It was a store called The Fashion Accent, and the window display was very *Eyes of Laura Mars*—mannequins in gold-flecked fishnets, lamé pumps and other Roman hooker-wear cavorted alongside *Bonanza* dominatrices in fringed cowhide belts and zebra-striped cowboy boots. Rents at Caesar's Palace must be fairly steep, Jason supposed, so The Fashion Accent must actually *sell* this astonishing froufrou to real women (or abnormally petite drag queens) at rather high prices.

He found tamer souvenirs at a store around the corner, which featured T-shirts, bathrobes, boxers, key chains, refrigerator magnets, shot glasses and Kleenex dispensers displaying the Caesar's logo in varying shades of metallic gold, as well as a rack of postcards from which Jason selected a particularly dated color shot of the hotel's exterior, shelled out thirty cents, found a seat on a bench and began to write:

Dear Violet,

Since I saw you last night, I got invited to Marina Stetson's preview concert, flown first-class to Las Vegas and put up in a hotel room that looks like a hideout for a *Leather & Lace* villainess. Coming home tomorrow. Will tell you everything. Hope things are going well RE: Aldo the Coffee Man.

Love, Jason.

Cradling the cordless phone between her ear and shoulder, Violet put her arms around Dave from behind, giving him a quick squeeze before grasping a stray wooden spoon and dipping it into the marinara he'd been slaving over for an hour. "It's not ready yet, you booger!" he exclaimed indignantly, trying to intercept the sauce before it reached her lips and failing.

"Dave, please. I'm on the phone," she scolded. When he turned his attention back to the stove, she tossed the spoon into the sink. "Hi, Misty . . . Yes, it's Violet . . . Edgar or Tricia . . . 'Kay . . . Oh, wait, Misty, that's my other line. Just put me on hold. Hello? . . . Hi, Greg. What's up? . . . you're kidding—I see . . . Yeah, I'll be there. Bye. Dave, that was the second AD. I have to go in early tomorrow to get fitted for a giant kangaroo costume per today's rewrite. Hello . . . hello?"

"Violet?" Tricia was now on the line.

"Yes, it's me, Tricia. I was on with my AD. Sorry."

Tricia sighed like an impatient suburban matron whose children kept talking during *Oprah*. "I thought I lost you. So, how's tricks?"

How's tricks? She must have been dipping into the David Mamet again. "Everything's okay. I mean, the show is a steaming pile of horsecrap, but I'm fine. Is Edgar in?"

"No, he's left for the day. Can I help you with something?"

Violet suppressed a sigh of her own. "Yes. Can you please leave him a message to try and call me tonight? I'm going to be working all day tomorrow, so it might be hard to get hold of me."

"I'll put in a call, but I'm not sure he'll check his messages this evening," Tricia said. Since Edgar was on a yacht in Newport with Wendi Barash and an "actress" named Brianna, Tricia would have bet her signed Anne Tylor collection that he would definitely not be beeping in to his home machine tonight. "Are you sure there's nothing I can do?" she asked again, wondering why Violet seemed to distrust her.

"It's not technically an emergency," Violet began, wondering why Tricia was compelled to be so controlling. "But Aldo Spackle the director is on my lot, right across from the stage where we tape, actually, and I'd really like it if Edgar could get me a meeting with him."

"I don't think Aldo Spackle is casting anything right now," Tricia told her. "There's certainly been nothing about it in breakdowns. And I'm sure I would have noticed, because I think he's quite iconoclastic, rather heavy-handed, yes, but—"

"He's got a two-picture deal with the studio," Violet interrupted, regretting this call like nobody's business. "So he must have something in the works. I only want to meet him on a general."

"Well, I'll see what we can do. So *Chillin' with Billy* premieres when, exactly?"

"A week from tonight. But since you did sit through the entire pilot taping, Tricia, please don't feel like you have to tune in," Violet assured her.

"Well, I print up a weekly calendar of all our clients' film openings, TV and stage appearances for the agents here," she said. *Great,* Violet thought. And while you're at it, send a tape to every television critic in the country so I'll never be taken seriously again after this piece of swill is canceled.

"Okay, thanks," Violet said. "And just tell Edgar I'd really like to talk to him." She clicked off and turned to Dave, who was plopping tortelloni into boiling water. "Next time you groom Edgar's mutts, can you leave him a note asking if he could possibly call me?"

Tricia hung up, initialing an entry in Edgar's phone log. There was really no need to call him at home; she knew he wasn't there, and besides, she was in a hurry. Her crotch itched maddeningly. Stefan had shaved it completely smooth two nights ago before carrying her into her bedroom and driving her into a spasm of cunnilingual bliss, her involuntary squeals of abandon muffled between her pillow sham and comforter.

She had begun to realize how much she resented her time with Zach. How on earth had she put up with him for two days much less two *years*? If Stefan hadn't entered her life, how long would she have gone on believing her ex-boyfriend in any way represented the male race? she wondered, unconsciously shaking her head as she slid some filing that could certainly wait until tomorrow into her lower left desk drawer and switched on the voice mail. She spontaneously elected to deviate from routine and exit via the back door. As she approached Conan Carroll's office, she noticed his evil assistant, Eric, facing away from her, tilted precariously back in his chair, Doc Martens planted on his cluttered desktop, perusing the phone sex ads in *Edge* magazine. "Naughty, naughty," she clucked with a smirk as she strolled by.

"Tricia!" he shrieked, nearly capsizing, the smutty newsrag fluttering out of his hands.

"Good night, Eric," she called sweetly.

On the way to the elevator, Tricia couldn't help imagining Zach and Stefan as Goofus and Gallant from *Highlights for Children* magazine. Goofus whines endlessly about the stagnation of his career and the insensitivity of the film industry to intelligent, original screenplays like his own. Gallant speaks in low, sensual tones that often assume a tantalizingly menacing edge. Goofus frequently snacks in bed and falls asleep with cookie crumbs in his stomach hair. Gallant never brings food into the bedroom that he doesn't intend to incorporate into sex play.

Tricia knew her relationship with Stefan was unconventional to say the least. But wasn't she entitled to it? If this was how two responsible, mature, attractive adults chose to relate, where was the harm? Stefan was HIV-negative—he had shown her recent written test results—and she was on The Pill. Since that first apocalyptic afternoon by the toilet bowl, he had stalked, teased and taken her according to some indecipherably perverse personal schedule, ignoring her for two or three days at a time, then appearing by her side while she was making her morning tea and wordlessly placing her small white hand on the rigid bulge in his boxer shorts. Passing her in the driveway with a disinterested wave and then phoning at 2 A.M. from his room, whispering for her to come in and do things with him. Mounting her on the dingy, dog-haired hall carpet by the back door (while Wren was *home,* veged-out in front of *Montel Williams*) for a fast fuck and then walking out the door for a shift at Kinko's, necktie askew and his penis still wet.

She reached the parking garage and got into her VW Golf. She casually glanced through the rear and side windows to ascertain that no one was nearby, then put her hand under her skirt and slip and attempted to soothe the scratchiness of her shaven pubis through her pink cotton panties. Her body responded to her touch with a jolt of pleasure, her knees reflexively spreading wider, left hand seizing the steering wheel. This was Stefan's night off, and she prayed she'd find him at home. She envisioned what he might be wearing and how quickly he might take it all off. His body had opened up new worlds of desire for her—the erotic appeal of a man's nipples, the dusting of hair just below the second joint of his long, powerful fingers, the smooth, secret place under his scrotum . . . Tricia scooped her keys off the floormat, started the car and, ignoring the 5 MPH directive painted on the wall, sped out of the garage.

Cleopatra's Barge was just that, a replica of an Egyptian cruising vessel. The venue was just off the casino and came complete with fiberglass sphinxes flanking the entrance, a huge figurehead with pro-portionally massive knockers jutting from the prow into the corridor, a mast and sail under which the band had set up, and a carpeted gangplank across the wishing well in which the whole Disneylandish contraption floated, bordered on three sides by cabaret-style seating. The VIP section was of course on the boat itself, on a raised platform covered by a pagoda-esque canopy under which the Queen of the Nile would presumably ride if she were to suddenly materialize in Vegas, and were the Barge not attached to the back wall of the nightclub, its stern sacrificed for table space.

Jason was seated in a primo spot, as close to the tiny rectangular performance space as possible. His tablemates were Chip Reeves, ex-Pop Tartt Betty Fonseca, and Marina's manager, Saul, who dressed considerably better than Joey Buttafuoco but had the same hairdo. Jason sipped a cappuccino, trying to counteract the three goblets of champagne he'd had upstairs at the hospitality suite before they'd descended en masse to Cleo's. He had to keep reminding himself that nobody here knew him as anything but Marina Stetson's cute young friend from L.A. As far as they were concerned, he had never house-sat for nasty zillionaires who hated him, never mastur-bated to smuggled porno, and never been fired from a crummy retail job while attempting to sneak back said porno. He'd given his re-sume to Chip (who carefully filed it in his black leather briefcase while promising to keep in touch with Jason "till something works out"), introduced himself to Betty and chatted knowledgeably about her band Bubonic Pest, and flirted quite successfully with a hot young Puerto Rican publicist until the guy's boyfriend showed up and started proprietarily patting his fine PR ass.

Chip finished a Sinead O'Connor anecdote, and Jason laughed harder than necessary because it was getting loud in there and he really, really wanted Chip to help him get a job. Jason estimated that twenty-five or thirty people out of the hundred Mermaid had invited had shown up, and with the additional smattering of clueless hotel guests and casino patrons lured in by the sign next to one of the sphinxes (LIVE MUSIC—9:00, inked on fake papyrus decorated with pseudo-hieroglyphs), there were a fair number of empty tables. He hoped Marina wouldn't feel rejected and blow the performance. If Jason had been Chip, he would have ensured every seat was full, perhaps by renting a few extra hotel rooms and inviting members of Marina's fan club from neighboring states.

Oh, God. The musicians were crossing the gangplank onto the barge. The concert was about to start! No one else seemed overpowered with anticipation—Saul was giving Betty his business card. Chip was signaling the waitress, whose sole concession to the venue's theme was her eyeliner. The preshow music (uncoincidentally a sampler of Mermaid's summer catalog) faded down, the house dimmed and suddenly the small stage area was flooded with light, a hanging silver disco ball flinging shards of glamour everywhere. Terry Davidson stepped onstage and adjusted the microphone.

"Good evening, everyone. Thanks for, uh, cruising with us tonight on Cleopatra's Barge. Now it's time to welcome, direct from recording her new album, *Ghost in the Fog* for Mermaid, exclusively previewing at Caesar's Palace, one night only . . . Marina Stetson!" Enthusiastic applause was immediately overpowered by the band breaking into a raucous intro to "Walk Like an Egyptian." Terry waved his hand toward the back wall of the nightclub, and everyone's head turned to decorative double doors, framed by two gold pillars, at the end of an aisle of red carpet that cut through the VIP tables directly down to the stage. Two hunky, oiled extras dressed in slave loincloths appeared out of nowhere and yanked open the doors. Marina stood in an alcove, arms crossed over her chest, head turned to one side. She was in a short and slinky black dress, calf-high *Quo Vadis* sandals Jason swore he'd seen displayed at The Fashion Accent only hours before, and most spectacularly, a shimmering beaded headdress in the shape of a phoenix on top of a shoulder-length Cleopatra wig. Jason had to yell to make his voice heard above the cheers of the audience.

Marina jerked her head forward and extended her arm. The slave boy on her right handed her a microphone. She stepped out and began to sing, making her way down the aisle with playful confidence. When she passed Jason she gave him a big wink. She finished the number onstage, employing appropriate dance moves and hand gestures. As he clapped, Jason looked toward the club's entrance and saw a dozen or more new people being plugged into the remaining empty tables. Marina curtsied, then seized the gold plastic bird's head crowning her costume and doffed it, wig and all. She shook out her hair and traded the headdress for a bottle of Arrowhead from one of the slave boys. "Is this fuckin' thing moving, or am I just really, really nervous?" She asked the audience. The barge *was* actually bobbing up and down in the wishing well via some hydraulic wizardry. Marina turned to confer with her lead guitarist. "Oh, so it actually does move," she said. "Okay," she told the crowd, "I'll be Carol Lynley in *The Poseidon Adventure*. If you're wondering why I chose to open with that song, like it's not obvious"—she spread her arms and looked around—"it's a little-known fact that The Pop-Tartts were supposed to record 'Walk Like an Egyptian' on our third album, but we all decided it was *too* pop. So those other tramps did it and made about fifty million bucks. Oh, well . . . speaking of the eighties, remember The Pop-Tartts?" Massive cheering. "I know some of you do . . ." Marina blew a kiss to Betty as the band fired up the Tartts classic "Sick of You," which Marina proceeded to perform the hell out of.

"Wow," Betty said into Jason's ear, "she never sounded better." Absolutely transported, Jason could only nod.

An hour later, Marina had done more Pop-Tartts standards and five new songs from *Ghost in the Fog*, which all sounded like solid rock hits to Jason. Chip also seemed profoundly impressed; between his rapt, slightly goofy expression while Marina sang, and his obvious appreciation that not only was the room now packed to capacity, but a crowd was watching the concert from the corridor, clustered around the fiberglass sphinxes and applauding as excitedly as those on the barge, Jason was certain he would recommend that Mermaid partially back at least a moderately extensive tour.

Jason didn't realize anything was amiss until the second verse of "Ain't Exactly a Secret," the second single from *Marina Stetson.* Marina sang the chorus, the band went into the bridge, Marina danced, the band came out of the bridge, Marina danced, kept dancing, didn't sing. To their credit, the band seamlessly continued with an instrumental verse, but Marina was acting a little odd. She looked Jason in the eye, tapped her forehead and held her hand up as if to ask, What the hell am I doing? all while bopping and swaying in a generic New Wave shimmy.

Shit, she forgot the words! Jason had to hold himself in his seat and fight panic. Now what the hell were the lyrics? He'd only listened to that album two thousand times since high school! The music was so loud he couldn't think. He shut his eyes. This could ruin the whole show. He had to do something—Oh, God, wait. It's gotta be so obvious/When I'm standing next to you/There's no sense in tryin' to hide/All the things I'd like to do . . . That was it. He snapped his eyes open and she was staring at him imploringly. She better read lips, he thought madly as he leaned forward and mouthed the words at her. She danced closer and he did it again, nakedly aware that everyone at his table was watching him. "What? She forgot the song?" he heard Saul say just before comprehension dawned on Marina's face and she nodded one time.

"I think she's okay now," Jason said in Chip's ear. Marina had turned to face the band and presumably cued them to repeat the verse, because that's exactly what they were doing. She zestily attacked the troublesome stanza, and to Jason's immense relief sailed through it straight to the chorus.

Chip put his arm around Jason. "You saved her ass," he said. But the song was not over. There was a very short verse before the final chorus and Marina must have had no idea what it was, because she had bopped up to Jason during the refrain and now was pointing the mike at him. Somehow the terror he should have felt was swept away on a wave of giddy exhibitionism, and he made all those years of singing along to Marina in traffic pay off by crooning into the microphone with a respectable level of competence, "Tonight you're gonna know everything I feel . . ." Marina smiled, the sweat on her face making her even more radiant, then completed the couplet, "And when the morning light splashes your sheets, baby, it'll be so real!" She held Jason's arm up, and the crowd applauded lustily. Marina finished the song, introduced the band and announced that she'd be taking a short break. She darted offstage to a roped-off bar area where the cocktail waitresses picked up drink orders. Chip pulled Jason up with him and followed her.

They found her dabbing her face with a towel while a hairdresser furiously brushed, gelled and teased. She tossed the towel aside and spread her arms for a three-way hug. "Shit on toast!" she laughingly groaned. "Thanks so much, cutie. I totally blanked on that song. Can you fuckin' believe it? And I told Terry I didn't even want to sing it—I kind of hate it—but he reminded me it was my last *hit*, which is truly sad, and anyway you bailed me out."

"Marina, this concert is fantastic," Jason practically squealed. "You sound amazing, and the energy is bouncing off the walls. Thank you so much for inviting me!"

"It's been a great show," Chip added in a more professional tone. "And Jason's right about your voice. I can't wait to hear the rest. There is more, right?" he asked somewhat nervously.

"No, Chip. I'm going to sneak out a back exit, check into Treasure Island and O.D.," she said. Marina got off the stool and kissed Chip's cheek. "Go sit down, you guys." As they returned to their table, Jason noticed that the room had filled to SRO capacity, and the throng gathered at the entrance was seriously impeding traffic in the corridor. Thunderous applause greeted Marina's re-entrance.

"I really got to play Vegas more," Betty said.

"These are from my new album, *Ghost in the Fog*," Marina prefaced the set. "Please buy it or I'll never work again." She did three songs: "Delusions of Glamour," an upbeat, guitar-driven number reminiscent of latter-day Pop-Tartts, the title tune, and as a finale, "You're Everywhere," a well-crafted ballad she'd written with Patrick Leonard that left Marina wet-eyed and Jason's hair standing on end. She got a standing ovation during which one of the hunky slave boys presented her with a bouquet of roses. Marina continued to bow and blow kisses until the noise quieted enough for her to say, "Encores are really a load of crap, don't you think? I mean, the band goes off, they know they're coming back, you know they're coming back. What's the point? Besides, there's nowhere for me to go." This was the band's cue to strike up one last classic Pop-Tartts hit, "Stop! You Tease Me," spiced up by Marina with some strategically placed vulgar language, to overwhelming popular approval. "That's it! Good night and thank you all so much!" Marina told everyone as the lights came up.

Terry appeared and took Marina's arm. Jason, Chip, Betty and Saul met them at the edge of the stage in a frenzy of congratulations, hugs, and forecasts of imminent success. People were screaming "Marina!" from the dispersing audience and from the crowd by the sphinxes that did not appear to be going anywhere. She waved to the fans, realizing for the first time the amount of attention she'd generated.

"Look in the corridor. This place is mobbed," she said to Chip and Jason, amazed.

"How are you going to get out of here?" Betty asked.

"Betty!" someone yelled.

"I'm going to use you as a human shield," Marina told her.

Terry called security while Chip and Saul positioned themselves at the Barge's gangplank and back stairs to prevent any admirers from rushing the ex Pop Tartts. Marina held tightly onto Betty's and Jason's hands but seemed fairly unruffled. Jason estimated about thirty people were clustered around the entrance. Some of them shouted questions at Marina, which she politely attempted to answer.

"Are you touring this fall?"

"Yes. I mean, I'd like to."

"Are you doing more shows here?"

"Maybe. There's nothing planned yet. I'd really like to."

"Will the surviving Pop-Tartts get back together?"

Betty and Marina looked at each other, then violently shook their heads. Everyone laughed.

"Can we get an autograph?"

"I don't have a pen. Sorry . . ."

"Why wasn't this concert advertised anywhere?"

"It was just supposed to be a surprise preview . . ."

Terry and a phalanx of guards arrived and began to cordon off the crowd, creating an aisle at the edge of the corridor. "Can ev-

eryone please stand back?" Terry commanded nicely. "We're sorry
if you missed the concert, but Marina will be on tour this fall so
you'll get your chance, I promise."

"Come on, Jason. Let's make a run for it," Marina urged. They
crossed the gangplank, assumed formation and started down the
steps. Marina had Jason on her left, Betty on her right, Chip and a
couple of security guards running interference in front and the rather
hulking Saul covering the rear. They headed for the elevator at a fast
trot, accompanied by cries of "Marina! Marina!" and a few
"Betty!"s. A guard was holding the door and stepped aside so they
could dash in. The door was sliding shut when Terry inserted his
arm, wedged himself in and lifted Marina up in a jubilant embrace.
She laughed and locked her legs around his waist.

"You did it!" Terry hollered as they sped toward the eleventh
floor.

Saul agreed heartily. "You still got it, baby. Next time you're
headlining in the Circus Maximus, right, Reeves?"

"Oh, she's gonna play Vegas again," Chip assured everybody.
"Saul, you and I should talk about a twenty-city tour."

The elevator stopped, and they spilled into the hallway, which
echoed with Blondie. Marina held Jason back a bit and said, "I'm
not going to be able to take much party shit, Jason. I'm about two
inches from plotzing on this carpet."

"Do you just want to go to the room? I can tell them you're
wiped out," Jason offered.

"Oh, no. That would be way too Stevie Nicks of me," Marina
drily replied.

They ended up staying twenty minutes. Marina played obligatory
kissy-face with Chip and the other Mermaid execs (who thought the
show was "electrifying" and "really rocked!") then worked her way
around the party, the nuclei being Terry and Tom Jones—the latter
swept Marina up into a torrid fake smooch. Sniffing a possible duet
on someone's next record, Saul lumbered over and started glad-
handing everyone.

Jason stepped back and observed. Betty Fonseca caught his eye
and waved. "I gotta get to the airport. My son's in preschool and
it's my turn to carpool in the morning. If Bubonic Pest ever books
another gig in L.A., I'll call you." She went off to say goodbye to

Marina. Jason scanned the room and decided every single person there made more money than he did (before being fired from Video Xplosion, that was), including the wait staff and bartender.

But Marina liked him best. She came up and slipped her arm around his waist and he got goose bumps. "Jason—I gotta get out of here," she whispered. "Do you mind?" He wondered briefly if anyone assumed he and Marina were lovers. A reminder glance at Andre's outfit suggested this was highly doubtful.

"No, it's okay. I'll be fine by myself. I'm having a great time here," he insisted.

"But I want you to come with me."

ABBA was blasting from Marina's CD boombox and they were well into the truckload of room service Marina had impulsively ordered when Jason realized what was going on. Yes, it was nine years after the entry deadline—scheduled to coincide with the release of The Pop-Tartts' second album, *Pandora's Box*—and he was three Tartts short, but that didn't matter. The grand prize of MTV's Pajama Party with The Pop-Tartts Contest was at long last his. He told this to Marina, who had changed into bike shorts and a Rough Trade Records sweatshirt postshower and was now sprawled across her bed, wet hair wrapped in a thirsty, gold-trimmed Caesar's towel, poring over the reams of prostitution ads in the Vegas phone book with giggly amazement.

"Fuck! That contest was a disaster. The winner was this rotten little bitch," Marina said.

"Diane Sykes," Jason immediately replied.

She dropped her spoon into her mashed potatoes. "Yes! How in hell do you remember that?"

"Please! I entered that contest like, at least fifty times. I drove everybody in my family crazy asking for stamps. I was so determined to win that when Martha Quinn drew Diane's postcard out of that giant Pandora's Box, I actually cried. And then, to have to see her on MTV with all of you at the Chateau Marmont. It just about killed me," Jason groaned. He fished a Fresca out of the ice bucket.

"Okay, first of all, the pajama party was supposed to be at this house I was renting in West Hollywood, but our manager nixed it 'cause he thought this kid Diane might find something there like drugs or photos or a vibrator and, you know, blackmail us or ruin our career or some shit. Anyway, we all get packed into this suite at the Chateau with a camera crew and this horrible snot-nosed little cooze from Tustin. Diane's like, seventeen and really over us, especially because she thought it would be this big party with all these rock stars, and so here she is stuck with just The Pop-Tartts and these MTV guys who are begging us, no booze, no drugs, she's a minor, blah blah blah. And they want to shoot us playing Twister and doing a dance routine to the fuckin' *Footloose* soundtrack and it's a Friday night and we're all miserable. Except Angela, who has the hots for the sound guy and takes him into the bathroom where we've hidden coke and a bong and a big jug of Absolut and blows him."

Jason sighed wistfully. "So did the MTV crew stay with you all night?"

"It seemed like it. I mean, us girls were getting progressively trashed and Diane kept getting pissier, so it was really hard for them to get tape they could actually use. So finally around one a.m., I call my current boyfriend who was in a frat at UCLA and he came over with like ten friends."

"Well, it's not a real pajama party unless boys crash it," Jason said.

"Right? So Betty and I are wondering why we haven't heard Diane bitch in a while, and we find out she's boffing like four of the guys. Too bad MTV had already left," she laughed.

"That's unbelievable."

"No. What's unbelievable is that I even remember any of that. Jason, you have to realize most of the eighties are *gone*." She tapped her middle finger against her forehead. "Do you think they can dredge up those kind of memories by hypnotizing you or something?"

"I wish they could *implant* them. I'd go in and get myself an actual life to look back on," Jason said.

"Come on! Your life couldn't have been that boring. What about all those midwestern farm boys?"

"What about them?" he laughed.

"Didn't you do a lot of skinny-dipping and circle jerks and fooling around in cornfields and stuff?" she asked with a straight face.

"Jeez, I wish!" he stammered, reddening. "I don't think things like that go on in Kettering, Ohio. Or if they do, they sure didn't invite me to any of them. Nobody laid a finger on me until I was in college."

Marina reached into the ice bucket and pulled out a chocolate milkshake. She dipped a finger into the glass then inserted it between her lips. "Awesome. Try yours." As Jason sampled his vanilla, she pressed on. "So what was your wildest sexual experience in college?"

"Marina, this is embarrassing," he said, trying not to smirk like an idiot.

"But this is really interesting to me," she mock-pouted. "I'll tell you mine . . . It was at an orgy in London the night of the BPI Awards. In Dead or Alive's hotel suite. I don't remember *exactly* how it happened, but a sandwich was made and Stacey Q and I were the deviled ham."

He stared at her a moment, the evening's surrealism coming to a sudden, almost overpowering head. "Well, I'd say having my roommate's cousin Skippy give me a hot-oil massage followed by oral sex in his aunt's Winnebago beats your story."

"I'm not sure," she frowned. "Define oral sex."

"We sucked each other's dicks! There! Are you happy now?" Jason squawked.

Marina burst into giggles. "Yes!"

Jason shoved his face into a pillow. Marina put her milkshake on the nightstand and tossed herself down next to him. He felt her tiny hands on his shoulders. "There. Don't you feel free now?" she said in a teasy voice that reminded him of the nurse she'd played in The Pop-Tartts' "What Are You, Nuts?" video.

"Oh, yeah. That had really been weighing on me. Dying to get out." He peeked up from the pillow and saw that she had lost the towel-turban.

"Of course," she remarked, thoughtfully twisting her damp, unmoussed hair around one finger, "now that I've heard your darkest sex secret and it turns out to be sixty-nining in a motor home, I totally agree with you. Your life has been duller than Amy Grant."

"Told you," he smiled.

"Not that there's anything wrong with living a decent, clean life. I think it's really sweet that you're . . . saving yourself."

"You know, I never thought of it quite that way. Saving myself. For death. I like it." He dove back into the pillow and emitted a fake sob. Through "Fernando" they heard a sharp rap on the door.

"Shit!" Marina grimaced. "I begged Saul and Chip to leave me alone till morning. Could you go out and tell them I'm asleep?" She cranked down the ABBA and actually clambered under the covers, as if whoever was at the door was going to verify Jason's story by barging into the bedroom. He went into the living area and peeked through the peephole. A small person further dwarfed by a monstrous arrangement of red, white and pink roses stood on the doorstep. Jason quickly answered, and then had to shell out five of the last fifteen dollars in his wallet for a tip because he didn't have any singles and Junaid the delivery midget certainly had no idea that Jason was broke and unemployed and just happened to be staying in an eight-hundred-buck-a-night hotel room.

Jason brought the roses to Marina. "Oh, my God! Who are those from?" she squealed, catapulting out of bed. Jason handed her the envelope. She tore it open, glanced at the card and threw her arms around Jason. "Thank you!"

Confused, he picked up the card, which had fluttered onto the bed. "Congratulations and all our love, Hank & Jason," it read. Jason had known nothing about the flowers, but it was nice of Hank to include him. Marina had replaced ABBA with the B-52's and was tossing roses onto the bed.

"I know Hank really wanted to be here tonight," he told her.

"I'm sort of glad he wasn't. I think I would have been a lot more nervous. If that was possible. The only time he's ever seen me perform in front of an audience besides that *Tonight Show*-why-bother thing was at a Pop-Tartts concert when he was in college," she said. "I guess it's real important for me to show him that be-lieving in me wasn't, you know, for nothing. That sounds so sappy. But do you know what I mean?"

Jason nodded. He knew they had met just before Marina's career had dipped to its nadir. Hank had seen her through rehab and they'd gotten married just in time for *Rainwater Lullaby* to bomb across the globe. "As great as Chip and Terry have been through this whole new album thing, what's been the best for me is really feeling like I'm doing it *for* somebody. For Hank. And lately, for you. I don't wanna disappoint you guys, so the pressure's kind of on, you know?"

"Marina . . . I don't know what to say." She had just validated his entire life. He needed another Fresca.

"Say that you'll consider becoming my personal assistant."

What?!! This had to be a dream, an exceptionally vivid, cruel dream. Jason glanced past Marina at the blazing Vegas midway lit up through the window and knew tonight was real—there was no way he could dream a detail like "44 OZ. BLOODY MARY 99 CENTS, ONLY AT THE GOLD COAST" flashing on the side of a passing blimp.

"You don't have to give me an answer right away," she said. "I know it's not exactly what you want for a career or anything. But maybe we can talk about it next week."

"Okay. Sure. I mean, thanks." "Planet Claire" was playing, and he was very close to letting loose with a wild dance to it. He shoved his hands into the pockets of Andre's pants and tried to stop moving. Marina retrieved a rose from the bed and slid it behind his ear.

"Hank's probably not going to be able to call, so maybe we should go to bed," Marina said. Jason agreed, but on the way to his room discovered a gift basket from Mermaid full of brownies, Toll House cookie bars and chocolate-covered strawberries, all of it so rich they could only manage a few exploratory nibbles before collapsing onto Marina's pillows, groaning.

"One thing that always bent my mind was that if I actually ate everything the record company sent me before an album got released, I'd be so fuckin' fat they'd have to shoot the videos in Panavision-seventy," she sighed. "Oh, look. The Morgan Brittany infomercial. Did you know they offered The Pop-Tartts tons of money to pose naked together in *Playboy* back in the good ole days?"

"Yeah."

"That figures."

Ten minutes of Morgan's assurances that it was possible to make love to the same person for the rest of one's life crept by without a word or snicker from Marina. Jason turned toward her. Her eyes remained closed. He sat up slowly and began to slide toward the edge of the bed.

"Jason?" Marina's hand lightly squeezed his calf.

"Huh?"

"This probably sounds so dorky and tragic," said Marina softly, "but do you mind staying until I fall asleep?"

"No problem." He lay back down, wanting to hug her and thank her and gush about how wonderful she'd been that night. But that of course would have disrupted a moment so indescribably perfect he refused to permit anything to endanger it, least of all a newly surfaced, completely ludicrous brainfart suggesting that Jason had somehow taken over Andre's life.

"This is my favorite line," Violet said, wiping her fingers on a napkin and picking up the new *Entertainment Weekly*. "Unfunny, unoriginal and unbearable, *Chillin' with Billy* belongs in a barnyard with the rest of the manure."

Jason winced, dipping a french fry into a cup of poppy seed dressing. Violet had invited him to lunch at Chik-A-Boom in West Hollywood and had brought with her the first national review of the show, scheduled to premiere in two days, Thursday night at nine-thirty Eastern/Pacific. Jason took the magazine, featuring Sam Neill and a herd of *Jurassic Park* critters on the cover. "I'd've thought your favorite line would be this one: 'The shrill cast boasts only two bright spots—beloved Broadway staple Emmiline Willis and sassy newcomer Violet Cyr.' "

"Well, as the token white girl, I do sort of appreciate being called sassy." She rolled salsa and strips of grilled chicken breast into a tortilla. "My mother had the same reaction you did. She calls me at eight-thirty this morning—the mail comes really early in Calabasas—to babble about this 'rave review' I got. So *my* copy comes just before I'm supposed to leave to meet you and I notice Mom neglected to mention a few things, like they despised the show and gave it a D-plus. Not that I really care. It *is* a piece of shit. I mean, you've seen it live." She shuddered.

"It could still be a hit," Jason supportively asserted.

Violet moved over to the soda fountain and refilled her Coke.

"Oh, I *know*. With *Dino & Muffin* as a lead-in, the ratings could be right up there." The network had scheduled *Chillin' with Billy* directly after this embarrassingly popular top-ten hit about a precocious biracial six-year-old adopted by a rowdy fraternity house full of wisecracking hunks in various states of undress. "Anyway," she continued, "the reason I wanted to talk to you is there's a job open on the show. Benjie the P.A. was fired last night."

"What happened?"

"Well, Roxanne's assistant Delicia, you know the really gorgeous black girl?"

"Delicia?" Jason asked, eyebrows slightly elevated.

"Yeah. Like Alicia, only tastier. So she's been out to get Benjie for a while and she noticed a discrepancy in the cost of the dinner orders. The show has to buy dinner for everyone whenever the writers work late, which on this show is apparently every night. Anyway, Delicia investigated and found out Benjie has been ordering extra dinners from restaurants, on the show's dime, and delivering them to his loser friends at the convenience store across the street from the studio. So the line producer confronted him and bang, he was fired," she said, shrugging. "And since I'm Roxanne's favorite person in the world—next to Barbra—she said my friend could have Benjie's job. You just have to interview with the line producer and production coordinator, like as a formality."

"Violet, that's great. Thanks!"

"I know it's not your ideal career stepping-stone or anything," she quickly qualified.

He stopped her. "You know, I'm hearing that kind of often lately, and it's okay. I just need to shove my foot in the door, and this is perfect because now I have an excuse not to become Marina's assistant."

Violet struggled to swallow the rest of her lunch, eyes popping at this detail Jason had omitted from his account of last week's fantasy getaway to Vegas. "She asked you to be her assistant? And you don't want to do it?"

"Well, yeah, of course, but our friendship is so . . . amazing to me, I don't want it to change. Like that," he haltingly explained. "I do want to work with her, but I don't think it should be like the whole *thing* is some big favor she's doing 'cause I need to make money. She really doesn't *need* an assistant. With the album coming out, her manager and the record company will be taking care of everything for her. And that's where I want to be. Working at Mermaid. That way I can have it all. Dealing with her and her music but when we're just hanging out together, it'll be because we're friends. At least that's what I'm hoping."

"Cool. You can keep chipping away at what's-his-name? Oh, yeah. Chip. With Marina's help, it shouldn't take too long. And when they make the offer, you can quit the show. No one'll hold it against you, believe me." He smiled. "You know, I think you're making the right decision, but I'm still floored that you're turning down the chance to spend every minute with your idol and get paid for it."

"Yeah, me too. But I've seen this situation sort of, like, happening before my eyes, with Andre, the guy who sublet his mansion-sitting job to me."

She nodded. "With that girl, Fawn, the actress?"

"You're probably the only person who's ever called her that besides her manager, but yes. She and Andre are best buddies and travel all over the place and have *so* much fun, but he's totally dependent on her for everything. I mean, I know *my* millionairess is like a legitimate big deal and hopefully I'm on the way to something a little more exciting than Andre is, but it would still give me the creeps. I told you Fawn went back to Texas to supposedly record an album, right?"

"God, that *is* creepy. Now I see." She stacked the lunch debris on the plastic tray and remanded it to an adjacent table. "So what's up with the evil mother-in-law?"

"They moved all this hideously expensive mod furniture into the house while I was in Vegas, so she's been abusing these uppercrust-faggy decorators all day, every day, trying to get it all perfect. You and Dave will have to come over late some night and check it out. This morning they delivered these huge—I mean, like eight-by-ten-foot—amazingly ugly framed posters that I guess are like French advertisements from the eighteen hundreds or something. Maggie's taste is pretty mind-boggling."

"If you don't want to go back there, you can help me with my lines for this week's script. Now I've only skimmed it, mind you, but I think it's about Aunt Petunia volunteering Billy for the petting zoo at the church bazaar."

"And hilarity ensues?" Jason guessed.

They got up for a final soda refill. Violet regarded him suspiciously. "Wow. Are you sure you've never executive-produced a sitcom before?"

Despite the universally bad reviews amassing like a bank of dark clouds over *Chillin' with Billy*'s imminent premiere, Violet thought the cast had their best Wednesday morning table-read ever, due in no small part to Maurice Johnston's conspicuously minor role in the church bazaar episode. The show's human star pouted his way through Wednesday's rehearsal, sulkily noting his blocking as he obsessively pored over *The Hollywood Reporter*'s pan (*"Good Times* meets *ALF* as viewers' index fingers doubtlessly meet the channel-change button") and made various cellular phone calls regarding the premiere party he was throwing at Aunt Kizzy's Back Porch, a trendy soul food institution in Marina del Rey.

By Thursday, Maurice had ascended into serious divahood. Just as rehearsal for the day's studio run-through commenced, he laid eyes on *Variety*'s review of the show—comparatively mild but unfortunately containing the sentence "With the exception of nonactor Johnston, cast is far more energetic, fresh and likeable than their material." The director was able to stroke him away from a major freakout, but Maurice insisted on immediately canceling his subscription via a loudly indignant public cell phone call.

Violet glanced at her watch. She couldn't believe lunch had only been an hour ago. Why was this day dragging so much? At this rate, they'd have to put crack on the craft services table if there was going to be any energy at the run-through. She was standing outside the back door of the Deauville kitchen/living room set waiting for Maurice to report to the stage. The scene required Violet to enter with Scottie Taylor, the alarmingly queeny seven-year-old who played the precocious youngest Deauville.

"Violet, you got pretty hair. Can I play with it?"

"Okay, Scottie. But don't pull." She squatted down on the fake back stoop, stifling a sigh as Scottie's small manicured hands plunged into her luxuriant tresses. He gathered them into a large ponytail and giggled. "I got a karaoke machine for my birthday. Do you like the song 'Finally'?"

"Uh, sure. Honey, watch it. That's a barrette—"

"All right, I's here!" Maurice brayed in the politically incorrect slave dialect he employed when put upon. "Sorry, y'all, but I forgot I was in this week's episode." Light, forced laughter from everyone. Maurice hit his mark.

"Very quiet backstage! This is rehearsal. Here we go," the stage manager called.

"Wait, Maurice! Here's your newspaper," the propmaster said, darting onto the set.

"I already *have* a newspaper. Open your damn eyes," Maurice snapped. "Can we get on with this?"

The director cued them, and Violet and Scottie entered the kitchen, where Maurice was reading the paper and doing schtick with a coffee cup.

"How'd it go with your new producer, Keisha?" Maurice asked Violet. The episode's B-story dealt with Keisha the TV reporter and her conservative new family-values boss, who naturally assigns the saucy gal to cover Aunt Petunia's church bazaar, where Billy causes on-camera hilarity to ensue from the petting zoo.

"It went *heavenly,*" Scottie chirped with a smirk at Violet.

"Tremayne, it was awful!" Violet complained. "He makes Pat Robertson look like Rick James."

"How come he—I mean, what did he think of your outfit?" Maurice barely got out.

"Luckily, I had some of Petunia's dry-cleaning in my car," said Violet, miming opening her coat to reveal the enormous, garish caftan she'd have on during the taping.

Scottie began his next line but was interrupted by a yell from Maurice. "I'm gonna kick this motherfucker's ass!" He slammed the newspaper down on the counter. "Why didn't somebody show this shit to me!? Huh?!!" he loudly demanded, sending Scottie running in tears to the child welfare representative assigned to the program. "I want Roxanne down here right now!"

The script supervisor hurried to the phone as the director, Violet, Starla Brown and Emmiline warily approached Maurice, who was once again fixated on the *Los Angeles Times*. Violet heard the prop-master insist to the stage manager, "I *tried* to give him the business section!" and then she saw what had set Maurice off—Howard Rosenberg's *Chillin' with Billy* review.

Starla attempted to rub Maurice's shoulders while the director assured Maurice that Rosenberg was an elitist prick who hated everything. But he really, *really* hated this show, Violet thought, glancing at the review. "In another inexplicable example of a randomly marginal stand-up comic awarded a television series, charisma-free Maurice Johnston proves that even playing second banana to a talking goat is beyond the scope of his barely discernible talents. Chillin' indeed." Yikes.

Roxanne arrived, dressed like a Patsy mannequin at an *AbFab* boutique. She went into the kitchen and took Maurice's hand. "What's the trouble, dahling?"

He yanked his hand away and snatched up the paper. "This is, goddamnit!"

"Howard Rosenberg? He's a prick," Roxanne stated drily. "You make more in one month than he does in two years. Who gives a shit? Do you think the *Dino & Muffin* audience reads TV reviews? Please."

"Roxanne, this show is making me look like a chump. Working with that goat is bad enough, but can't you come up with some decent scripts?" Uh-oh.

"Excuse me?" Roxanne asked.

"I'm the anchor character, so y'all think you don't have to give me any jokes," Maurice said, obviously having had a recent chat with his manager. "How can I be funny if I'm not even in the motherfuckin' show? All I got's two or three scenes this week. Nobody gives a frog's fat ass about Aunt Petunia. I'm the star, not her!"

With that, Emmiline let out an operatic sob and fled the set, wailing. Starla and the stage manager went after her, and Violet supposed she should, too, but was somehow rooted to the floor as Roxanne finally lost it. "Great, Maurice. That's just adorable. Now that you've completely fucked up today, I'm going to have to cancel the studio run-through."

"Go ahead!" Maurice shouted. "I'm canceling the premiere party!" He gestured wildly to those left onstage. "Y'all can watch this piece of shit anywhere you like, and buy your own fuckin' dinner and drinks!" He stomped to his personalized director's chair and grabbed his monogrammed cellular phone holster.

"John, send everybody home," Roxanne told the director. "And Maurice?" The star jerked his head toward her, glaring. Roxanne casually picked up the *Los Angeles Times* Calendar section. "You've heard the expression 'Don't believe everything you read'?" He nodded condescendingly. "Well, believe some of it." Maurice flipped the bird at her back as she exited. Violet discreetly escaped through the kitchen door and locked herself in her dressing room. She hopped onto the couch and dialed Dave's van.

"Pet Spa."

"Hi."

"I'm going through the canyon, love. If I lose you, can I ring back?"

"Yeah, I'm in my dressing room. Maurice just threw a huge fit and canceled the premiere party. Isn't that great?"

"So we don't have to go anywhere tonight?"

"No. They released the cast. I've got some stuff to do, gym, Beverly Center, et cetera. I shouldn't be home too late."

"I'm actually off to groom Edgar Black's dogs. Bleedin' little neurotics."

"Send them my love."

"All right. Cheers then."

"Bye."

She hung up just as someone knocked on the door. Shit. It was probably Emmiline. She really should have stopped by the poor lady's dressing room to console her. Violet opened the door.

Aldo Spackle was exactly her height and resembled a blonder Willie Aames. It took her several seconds to recognize him, partly because the baby-blue service station attendant's uniform shirt he wore with Levi's and engineer boots bore the name tag RED.

"Hi, Violet," he said, smiling, hands clasped together in front of him like he was about to wring them.

"Aldo Spackle," she simultaneously realized/replied. "Hi! It's so nice to meet you. Please come in. This is really a surprise. Would you like something to drink? I don't know what I've got up here . . ." She crossed to the minifridge, giving her look a quick once-over in the mirror on the way. Not optimal, but it didn't suck. She opened the fridge.

"I'll take a Cappio," Aldo said excitedly. She handed him the bottle, wondering if she should have twisted the top off for him. Get a grip, Missy, she warned herself. He's probably only here to thank you for the basket.

Aldo gave the Cappio a couple of brisk shakes, opened it and flicked the top into the wastebasket all with one hand. "I wanted to stop by and thank you for the basket you sent me," he told her. Damn! But he *was* here in person. He could have sent a note. "It was really the nuts. I've been spinning on that raspberry roast for days. Where did you find it?"

She couldn't tell him she'd recycled her own baskets to create his. "That I think came from a store my mom took me to . . . In Topanga a couple weeks ago."

"Could you get me the name of the place? I'll order about fifty pounds. We had unlimited coffee of my choice put in my contract," he said, slugging back the rest of the Cappio.

Actually, trying to locate fifty pounds of that exact coffee would be a perfect task for her mother, who naturally would do anything to get her in good with a director who had a studio deal and a prize from the Berlin Film Festival. Plus Mom still hadn't been punished for the *Hard Copy* stunt.

"Not a problem," Violet chirped. "So what's new, Aldo?" She sat on the arm of the couch and did her best PJ Soles, although she felt more like Margaux Hemingway.

He shrugged. "I've never seen them do a sitcom before. I guess I thought it would be like *The Dick Van Dyke Show.* I watched that after school. I never really liked or thought about Mary Tyler Moore very much. And then *Ordinary People* came out when I was thirteen and I was sexually attracted to her. That's weird, huh?"

"A little," she agreed pleasantly. He was just what she expected after renting (thank God) both his movies last weekend. She started to relax. "I'd invite you to stay for the studio run-through, but it's canceled. Besides, the goat doesn't come in till Fridays."

"I have this weird feeling that it wouldn't be as interesting as what I was watching for the past half-hour downstairs," Aldo said.

"You were here? On our stage?" Violet asked, involuntarily springing up from the sofa.

"Yeah. I just walked in and sat up in the audience seats. That guy Maurice is some kind of bastard, isn't he? Was this like a typical day on your show?" He seemed genuinely curious.

Violet's brain rewound furiously as she scanned the past hour to determine whether or not she'd done anything embarrassing in front of Aldo. As if being a series regular on *Chillin' with Billy* wasn't mortifying enough. "The tragedy is that it's a very special day," she confided facetiously. "We premiere tonight."

"I'm sorry."

"*You* are."

"And your party got canceled."

"To add insult to injury," she smiled.

"It's weird to eat dinner this early, but you want to come with me? We can talk about stuff."

Stuff? Her digestive tract lurched momentarily and she had to force her mouth to refrain from popping open in delight. "Let me pack up my bag and I'm good to go," said Violet.

Tricia sealed the last envelope and wrote the actor's name in the center with a Sharpie. She considered the packages for a moment, judged them a tad unprofessional, typed the names on five separate agency mailing labels and affixed them over the handwritten names. All five of the young actors were auditioning for the same small part in the new Tim Robbins film. The sides were only two pages and she probably could have gotten by with just photocopying *them,* but Tricia felt it was important for clients to read an entire screenplay to truly understand how their prospective roles, however brief, fit into the filmmakers' overall vision.

The phone rang. "Edgar Black's office," she answered.

"I'm sending you a fax and I suggest you be at the machine when it comes through," said Stefan, his cruelly masculine voice instantly quickening her pulse. One breathy syllable escaped Tricia's throat before she heard the click of him hanging up and forgot what she was going to say anyway. She headed toward the fax machine, which was already ringing. It began to receive. Slowly. Very, very slowly. Stefan was transmitting on the extra-fine setting, usually reserved for photographs. As the fax rolled out millimeter by millimeter, Tricia noticed a dark, conical shape in the right hand corner of the page. She bent over for a closer look and realized the bulbous object was the head of Stefan's penis.

A prickly crimson flush crept up from the collar of her blouse from The Limited, inflaming her porcelain neck and cheeks. She bolted upright and checked over her shoulder. Oh, my God! Janice was teetering down the hall with a handful of papers, doubtlessly intending to fax them. Panic seized Tricia. Should she unplug the fax machine? No. If his transmission didn't go through, Stefan would just send it again. Besides, there would be no way to discreetly remove the X-rated semifax from the machine. She was screwed! Tricia turned to face Janice, simultaneously taking a step backward to shield the incriminating document with her buttocks.

"Are you using this?" Janice crossly demanded. "Because if not, I need to fax."

"Yes, Edgar's getting something very important," Tricia told her. "If you'd like, Janice, just leave those with me and I'll fax them for you."

"Thank you, but I'll wait. I need the confirmations." As if I'm incapable of collecting a paper slip and bringing it to your desk, you crotchety old bat, Tricia thought exasperatedly, repositioning herself between Janice and the machine, from which Stefan's ten-inch erect cock was emerging with fascinating, nightmarish slowness. He must have Xeroxed himself right there at Kinko's while he was on his shift. That man was an *animal.*

"Tricia, you have a call on line two," Misty the receptionist announced over the intercom.

"Take a message!" Tricia responded.

"She can't hear you," Janice growled. "That fuckin' kid's always dumping calls on me when I'm too busy to take 'em." This brought on a hacking bout of smoker's cough which gave Tricia the opportunity to step away from the fax and pick up line two. "This is Tricia."

"Hello, it's Dave. Violet's mate?"

"Yes, Dave. What can I do for you?" Tricia hurriedly asked. Janice's coughs were tapering off. She was turning toward the fax! Tricia tried to move over to protect it, but the phone cord was too short.

"Well, you know, Violet's show starts tonight and since there's not going to be any sort of party or anything"—Janice seemed oblivious, thank God. She turned away from the machine and started blowing her nose—"I thought I'd surprise Violet and invite a few people over to watch it on telly and have a spot of food," Dave went on. "Are you free? Around eight-thirty, then? At Violet's flat?"

"Yes, thanks, that'll be lovely. See you then." Tricia hung up. Janice was staring at the still-incomplete fax.

"What the hell is that thing?"

"It's a map," Tricia said without missing a beat. "Edgar's going on a rafting trip."

Janice rolled her eyes. "I can't stand around here all day. I'm going down for a cigarette. Send these through for me, dear. And don't forget the confirmations." She passed the letters to Tricia and hobbled off.

Tricia's heart hammered at her chest, and not just because of the close call. Stefan's squat, brutal handwriting was visible on the fax now—TO TRICIA COOK, REQUESTED MATERIAL. The fax was coming out even more slowly now, probably because the dark blob of Stefan's scrotum at the upper left-hand corner required denser printing by the machine's image sensors.

"Where the hell have you been?" Edgar wanted to know from behind her. She lunged for the dangling fax and whipped it out, sliding it between Janice's things.

She turned to Edgar, her expression innocent yet concerned. "I was just sending these faxes for Janice. She's not feeling well."

"Then she should have retired when she was supposed to. The week Sputnik was launched." Edgar cracked his komodo dragon smile, amusing himself. Then, "I need you to send Faith Ford's TV movie reel to Jim Cameron on a rush. And I put my bills on your desk."

"I'll take care of it," she promised. As soon as he was gone, she put Janice's letters in the fax and snuck peeks at what Stefan had sent her. She had never much cared for penises before, but there

was something *about* this one. It was more than just visually stunning—quite apart from Stefan's extremely skilled if admittedly off-
beat manipulations of the organ, his penis seemed to have a life force
of its own, a *mind* that knew every private thought and secret place
she'd ever—

Her phone was ringing when she got back from Janice's desk.
"Hello? I mean, Edgar Black's office."

"So what did you think?"

"Stefan, you can't send me things like this at the office," she
said.

"And why is that?" he asked, with just the slightest tinge of
mockery.

How can a voice be so bloody sexy? "What if someone saw
that? With my name on it?" she insisted weakly.

"They'd never believe you had anything to do with it. They'd
certainly never believe pretty, perfect Tricia wanted that big nasty
cock inside her right this second. And that *is* what you want, isn't
it, baby girl?"

His words were like a sinfully hot breeze lapping at her ear. She
glanced down to her lap where the fax was hidden under the desktop.
"Yes."

"Yes what?"

"Yes . . . , Daddy." Edgar had somehow appeared at her desk,
and was looking at her strangely. "Daddy, I told you Mother doesn't
like angora sweaters. Your best bet is cashmere." She rolled her eyes
at Edgar. He shrugged and handed her another bill, then went back
in his office.

"Very clever, Tricia. Was that Edgar?" Stefan asked.

"Yes. But I don't think he heard anything."

"What is that idiot putting you through today?"

"Right now I'm mailing his bills for him."

"Which bills?"

"Cable, Bullock's, pet grooming, cellular phone . . ."

"Yes. Where would Mr. Bigpants Agent be without his cellular
phone?" Stefan sneered.

"Whenever he's out at a meeting he calls me on it just to impress
whoever there," Tricia said.

"Trash it."

"What?"

"Rip it up. Take that phone bill and tear it into a hundred pieces and dump it in the garbage."

"Stefan, I can't . . ."

"Put your hand under your skirt. Put it inside your panties."

She made sure she was alone, then scooted her chair as close to her desk as possible. Her hand casually dropped below the desk and was presently beneath her slip, tugging at the crotch of the black satin underpants Stefan had given her last week. As he graphically described ravishing her in the agency foyer during peak business hours, she brought herself to a discreet, shattering climax without so much as a moan.

"That was good," he purred. "Now rip up that phone bill. And bring the pieces to my room tonight." He hung up.

Tricia replaced the receiver and slowly withdrew her hand from beneath her skirt. She dried it on the cushion of her desk chair, then picked up the cellular phone bill, sealed, check enclosed, ready to be run through the office postal meter (a powerful agent like Edgar couldn't be buying his own stamps, heavens no). If the payment (probably due tomorrow or the next day, if she knew Edgar) somehow never made it to the phone company, and the final notice somehow got lost en route from her desk to Edgar's, his cellular telephone privileges would be quickly revoked. That would make Edgar angry. Bewildered, aggravated, furious. She pulled the envelope out of sight and carefully ripped it in halves, quarters, eighths, sixteenths, thirty-seconds, sixty-fourths. The handful of shreds went into her purse. For some reason her panties were freshly soaked.

Edgar left early to meet with his client Ione Skye, whose recent rumored lunch with CAA indicated probable dissatisfaction with her current representation and warranted an immediate dinner at The Ivy. Tricia, who had predicted Ione would be a major star after *Say Anything*, couldn't really blame the actress—the last thing Edgar had gotten her was a pernicious modern remake of *Gun Crazy* with Drew Barrymore and Joe Dallesandro.

Tricia had debated returning to the house and changing before driving over to Violet's, but if she left the agency at six-forty-five and didn't hit traffic, that would have left her only a maximum of forty minutes at home before she had to drive back the way she'd come and beyond to Beverly Glen Canyon. Even if Stefan was going to be home (and he was working till midnight—she'd checked), forty minutes would barely afford them a quickie. So she remained at the office, catching up on filing and typing all the agency contract renewals for the next three months for Edgar's A–G clients. Stefan's brazen fax she put into a manila folder next to her Selectric for easy access.

She still knew next to nothing about him. He rarely revealed information about himself, and when he did it was in offhanded fragments—he was thirty-two, he had grown up in Boston, he preferred Kids in the Hall to Monty Python. Tricia privately dabbled at sketching in the rest: He had been hurt very badly in a relationship in the not-too-distant past, his ambition to be a genetic engineer or concert pianist crushed, his will to live almost completely snuffed out, leaving him with no way to express the tortured feelings locked inside but through savagely intense sexual acts. And only by shattering every taboo with him could she share the long, dark night of his soul and lead him back to a place of trust, love and commitment. It was all very *Last Tango in Paris.* Although the things she and Stefan had done together made Marlon Brando's buttered finger look like something from *The Umbrellas of Cherbourg.*

It wasn't as if she never had conversations with Stefan. It was just that they were always about her. She realized Zach's neurotic self-absorption had left her unsure of how to deal with a man's attention. Because it had been so long since anyone actually listened to what she had to say, Stefan's probing questions caught her as much off guard as his sexual advances. Not only did he find her endlessly desirable, but he respected her intelligence and self-possession. He was outraged at the way the agency treated her and kept urging her to quit. She agreed that she was being wasted in the position of assistant but assured him that their recent denial of her request to be made an agent was only a temporary setback. Stefan had developed an intense, rather cute dislike of Edgar—based solely on Tricia's daily reports—and insisted her boss was holding her down.

She packed up her things, making certain the phallic fax was tucked into her shoulder bag. She supposed she really ought to bring something to Violet's party, but it was already ten past eight, and by the time she drove to the Gelson's in the Century City mall and parked and tried to pick out a decent wine within her very narrow price range and stood in line and got out of the garage and onto Beverly Glen, she'd definitely be late. Passing Edgar's office on the way out, she had an idea. She unlocked it with her key, went in and closed the door, although she knew she was the only one left at the agency at this hour. Edgar's minifridge sat back in the corner, under his Nagel print. She opened it and took out one of four bottles of Veuve Clicquot. He'd never miss it, and after all, Violet *was* his client. The bottle fit perfectly in her bag.

Traffic had thinned out nicely, and she was able to sail across Wilshire and Sunset into the canyon in less than ten minutes. She felt terribly flattered to have been invited to a soirée at Violet's and wondered if any of the other cast members would be present. Conan would certainly be impressed if she handed him Maurice Johnston or Emmiline Willis on a silver platter. If only the show weren't so dreadful. The trades had not been kind, and that Howard Rosenberg piece was nothing short of annihilating. At least Violet had gotten some favorable notices. Tricia imagined Violet had a healthy, cynical attitude about the quality (or lack thereof) of *Chillin' with Billy*, but since this *was* the premiere, it wouldn't hurt to come up with a few complimentary comments during the broadcast. If she remembered correctly, the costumes had been rather festive . . .

Tricia had never been to Violet's but had memorized her address weeks ago. She pulled up and parked on Beverly Glen. It was a lovely street, but the constantly speeding traffic rendered it, to Tricia's taste, an unappealing residential area. The shabby white Subaru directly behind her car looked oddly familiar, but Tricia didn't figure out it was Jason's until she went inside and saw him serving a drink to an attractive fifty-five-year-old woman she recognized from *Hard Copy* as Violet's mother.

"Hi, Tricia," he said.

"Jason. What are you doing here?"

"Dave invited me. I'm a friend of Violet's," he explained, heading toward the kitchen. "Would you like a soda or some wine?"

"Something caffeine free, preferably," she said, wondering what embarrassing facts he might have revealed about her to Violet. She followed him into the kitchen, where Dave was removing a tray of miniature toasted sourdough slices from the broiler. He deposited it on a cooling rack and turned toward Tricia.

Jason, en route to the fridge, said, "Dave, this is Tricia. Tricia, Violet's boyfriend, Dave." Dave was extremely handsome in an Aidan Quinn sort of way but of course couldn't hold a candle to Stefan. He stuck out an oven-mitted hand and Tricia shook it.

"We've spoken on the phone a few times, about Zelda and Die Hard," he said, smiling quite dazzlingly. What was he—oh, of course, Edgar's dogs. "It's a pleasure to meet you."

"Likewise," she replied. "Thank you for inviting me. I thought we could toast our star," she added, handing over the champagne. "Is Violet in the powder room?"

"She's not back yet," Dave said, dumping bruschetta from a Cuisinart into a ceramic bowl. "But I expect her any time now."

"She's probably out shopping, no idea of what time it is. It's a good thing the malls close at nine." Violet's mother had joined them, a piece of Dave's pesto-and-sundried-tomato pizza in one beringed hand. "Hi, I'm Violet's mom, Evelyn Cyr."

"Hello. Tricia Cook. One of Violet's agents."

"Oh . . . Edgar's assistant," Evelyn smiled.

Tricia nodded, lips pressed tightly over clenched teeth. Stefan was right. She had to rise above that job if she was going to establish any credibility in the business. Tricia made a conscious effort to relax her facial muscles and openly admired Mrs. Cyr's glitzy, diamond-encrusted locket (naturally containing a tiny Violet head shot), then accepted a glass of bubbly from Jason.

"So, are you enjoying your new place?" she asked him, thinking, Not half as much as I'm enjoying your old place, I'll bet.

"It's okay," he said. "House-sitting a mansion isn't exactly the same as living in one."

"I didn't know you were house-sitting. Whose mansion is it?"

"Fawn Farrar's. You know, that friend of Andre's. From the Gail Ann Griffin showcase?"

She stared at him blankly, before assuming a pissy expression. "Oh, yes. I thought Andre was her house sitter."

"Well, yeah. I'm kind of doing him a favor. Actually, two favors, 'cause while I'm substitute house-sitting for him, he's subletting my room at your house. It's kind of complicated, but I think

I'm getting screwed." She smiled perfunctorily. "I hope the guy who took my room isn't like a nightmare or anything. But it's only supposed to be temporary."

Tricia had been putting an olive into her mouth with her fingers and when she heard the word *temporary* she bit down on said fingers, causing her to simultaneously yelp with pain and spew the olive onto the floor. "Are you okay?" Jason asked.

"Yes, fine. Excuse me," she coughed, humiliated. "You were saying?" He looked unsure. "Something about your living situation being temporary?"

"Well, it's just that Fawn and Andre will eventually come back to L.A. and then supposedly I'll be moving back to my old room at Orange Grove Avenue," Jason said, as if this was of absolutely no consequence whatsoever and would in no way fuck up and ruin and destroy the most precious and exciting summer of her life. There had to be a way to keep Andre out of town. She wouldn't give up Stefan. There was no way in hell. She had to—"Gather 'round, everyone!" Mrs. Cyr called. "I brought my Violet scrapbooks, and I think we have time for the first two before the show starts. Dave, can I turn this music down?"

Dave, wondering where the hell Violet was and why she was the only actress on television without a beeper, turned the music down himself.

From what she knew of Aldo and his affinity for kitschy retro, Violet half-expected him to escort her to Roscoe's Chicken and Waffles (or worse, Ship's) in a 1973 Buick Impala. Instead, like every other guy under thirty in Hollywood, he drove a Jeep. They went to Cha Cha Cha, a Caribbean restaurant that seemed even more hip and colorful than it actually was because of the atrocious, Silverlake-adjacent neighborhood. Over sangria they discovered they'd had the same childhood.

She'd grown up on a sunny, tree-lined street in Altadena with no brothers or sisters, a father who died when she was eight, and her own subscription to *TV Guide* so she'd never miss an episode of *Happy Days, Laverne & Shirley, Three's Company, Soap, Charlie's Angels, The Love Boat,* or *Fantasy Island.* He was raised on a sunny, tree-lined street in Phoenix with no brothers or sisters, a father who left when he was nine, and his own bedroom TV tuned without fail to ABC Tuesday, Wednesday and Saturday nights. She read her mother's Judith Krantz and Sidney Sheldon books on the sly, then transcribed them into crude scripts on her typewriter, forcing Douglas, the cousin who had a crush on her, to play all the male parts in scenes with her in the backyard. Aldo got his first video camera when he was in eighth grade and proceeded to turn the family reunions and birthday parties he was forced to tape into weird, upsetting psychodramas. They both skipped their proms, she because she was appearing in *Steel Magnolias* at the Pasadena Playhouse, he because he was a geek who couldn't get a date to save his life. And they'd both been irrevocably corrupted by multiple late-night cable screenings of *Mandingo*.

"I think it's still my favorite seventies movie," Aldo revealed, shucking a tamale from a gargantuan appetizer plate. "The scene where James Mason's trying to 'drain the rheumatiz' out of his feet by propping them up on those little black boys? That's just the nuts."

"And all that naked interracial 'pestering,' " Violet recalled fondly. "It's gotta be the dirtiest R-rated movie of all time. You know, I think Perry King's was the first penis I ever saw."

"Yeah, it was my second. I have the movie poster framed at home and everybody's always giving me shit about how un-p.c. it is. Well, I was leafing through that jack-off Writers Guild directory, and guess what? It was nominated for an NAACP Image Award in 1975. I'm totally vindicated." He tapped out a victory rhythm on the tabletop.

Sultry young muchachos kept refilling the sangria pitcher, and by the time she was supposed to order dinner, Violet was feeling a smidge lightheaded, to coin her mother's preferred expression for getting totally shitfaced. She quickly asked for a double cappuccino. Aldo saved her the trouble of navigating the menu by ordering five different entrées for them to split. Then he began to pitch her his latest screenplay, *You Lucky Bastard*, a black comedy about Tommy, a wiz-kid syndicate assassin who falls desperately in love with Lucy, the fraudulent hotline psychic whose reading he thinks saved his life.

Violet found it bizarre and refreshing to be effortlessly, genuinely laughing at something. The character she'd played for six months on Broadway had required her to perfect the display of phony

mirth, a skill she was able to put to good use during every *Chillin'*
with Billy table-read and rehearsal. Aldo's hilarious storytelling was
insanely fast paced but never confusing, despite frequent and elaborate detours for dialogue samples, directorial observations and character impersonations. Violet would definitely have green-lighted the
film if she'd been a studio executive. But she was an actress, so after
applauding the wrap-up immediately asked who'd been cast.

"Adrian Pasdar's going to be Tommy. You know who he is?
The lead from *Near Dark*? A fucking amazing vampire movie. I
wanted Bill Paxton for another part, but he's booked. Who else is
set?" he asked himself. "Fred Ward. Ann Magnuson. This new
young guy named Max Parrish. Alexis and Patricia Arquette."

Okay. Question answered. Patricia had to be playing the psychic.
Violet made certain not to let even a glimmer of disappointment
darken her enthusiastically rapt expression. There might still be other
roles available. The waiter piled platters of jerk chicken, paella and
camarónes negros onto their table. Violet needed to say something
approving fast. "I think Patricia Arquette will be great opposite
Adrian Pasdar. I really liked her in *True Romance.*"

"Best thing in the movie. But she's not playing opposite Adrian.
She was my first choice, but she's doing this big Tim Burton thing
about the life of Ed Wood, the transvestite Z-flick movie director
from the fifties. So Patricia's going to play Adrian's girlfriend at the
very beginning. I have her for two days. Is that the nuts or what?"
He began to create messy sampler plates for both of them as Violet
felt the pendulum of her expectations swing the other way. "I
haven't cast Lucy yet," Aldo continued. "You should see the fuckin'
'suggestions' the studio's trying to force-feed me. Uma Thurman.
Cindy Crawford. Julia Roberts! Jesus Christ, I'd sooner hire *Tanya*
Roberts, you know?" Fearing bad karma from bashing the more
famous and talentless, Violet simply smiled and ate a forkful of
dinner, which was delicious. "So you know why you're here."

The fork hit the plate with a clang. "Sorry. Um, no. I mean, you
think I'd be . . . for Lucy?" Brilliant, honey. She quickly brought
her napkin to her mouth, as if trying to wipe away what she'd just
said.

He nodded seriously. "I think we should pursue it. Your tape
kicks ass. I saw it yesterday."

"God, please tell me my mother didn't send it to you."

"I got it from your agent. I called and told them it was for a Danielle Steel miniseries this fall. They sent it right over. I used to just tell agents who I was, but they tend to freak out and start acting even more like desperate assholes than usual. You don't mind, do you?"

"No! I mean I'm really flattered, Aldo. I'd love to read for you. Whatever you need, it's just fine," she said, thrilled.

"I know you've got that sitcom to do, but if things worked out, we might be able to do it around your schedule. Most of it'll be shot here. With three weeks of location in Chicago," he muttered to himself, lost in thought as he distractedly yanked the tail off a shrimp.

"I *hope* the series wouldn't keep me from working for you," she said. "But you saw what we're dealing with. It might not ever be on again after tonight," she said, laughing. Jeez, what time was it? Her watch must be in her gym bag. Had she missed the premiere? Not that she really cared. She'd seen it on video weeks ago, trying to find the least humiliating snippets to edit onto her demo reel.

"It's not *totally* my decision. But we can audition the hell out of you, right?" he grinned.

"Absolutely. Maybe you can give me the script, like, tonight." She prayed she wasn't being too pushy.

"Yeah, sure. Actually, I should probably wait until the final polish is ready. About a week. I'll send it to your agent."

"*You Lucky Bastard*, by Danielle Steel. I'll look for it."

They had espresso and Violet waited for the mass in her stomach to shift or depressurize itself or something as she talked about her career and, after prodding, let slip a few hideously stupid *Chillin' with Billy* anecdotes that sent Aldo into paroxysms of incredulous laughter.

Although he hadn't seen her episode, Aldo was a big fan of *Leather & Lace*, which he aptly described as "easily the scummiest thing on TV. Very Farrah-era *Angels*, don't you think? But without the Aaron Spelling gloss. I always imagine they shoot extra splattery gore scenes and raunchy sex to cut in when they sell it to Europe," he said as they drove back to the studio, listening to *Bat Out of Hell* on CD.

"That's not too far from reality," Violet replied, not wanting to elaborate on her adventures on the program in case Aldo played pool with or frequented the same motorcycle dealership as Turk Marlowe.

Hers was the only car left in the *Chillin' with Billy* section of the parking structure. Aldo pulled up next to the del Sol, keeping the Jeep's motor running. "So thanks again for the coffee, Violet," he said, looking past her at the glove compartment.

"God, you're welcome. Thank you for dinner. I had the best time. I can't wait to read your script."

His eyes darted over and met hers and he nodded and shrugged at the same time. Smiling, she reached for the seat belt clasp and didn't find it. Okay, there it was. She pressed her thumb down and it wouldn't release. She tried again. "Aldo, I think this is stuck."

He put his hand on the clasp, hesitantly covering hers as he unfastened the catch. The seat belt slithered off Violet, and they drew their hands away from each other with self-conscious casualness. For some reason Violet was reminded of the mammoth seventies crush she's had on Willie Aames. "Well, good night," she said in a much softer voice than intended.

"Night," Aldo said. He raised his right hand, as if he were uncertain what to do with it then ran it through his springy blonde curls before placing it on Violet's left upper arm, leaning over and giving her a brief, closed-mouth kiss.

Violet was startled but certainly not offended by this chaste gesture. Aldo was just being friendly. She looked into his long-lashed blue eyes for reassurance, and realized what a boo-boo this was when those eyes languidly drifted shut and he was kissing her again with considerably less restraint. She put her hands on his shoulders, meaning to push him away, but his arms gently encircled her and she opened her mouth to say hold it, buddy, and that was a mistake, too, because he apparently construed it as a welcome mat for Mr. Tongue, and she just had to wrench her face off his in what she was sure was a very awkward and hurtful manner.

"Aldo, I can't."

"I know. I'm sorry. I don't know what—"

"It's not you, I swear. You're the coolest. But I'm in a relationship."

"Oh, Jesus Christ, I'm such a douchebag."

"Aldo, it's really okay—"

"You've gotta believe me . . . you getting that part is not contingent on us having sex or—what is that word, petting? Or—God, how embarrassing. I never should have listened to my shrink."

"Hey, I don't think you're that kind of guy. So let's just forget this. It's not a big deal. Okay?"

"*Please* forget it if you can. Everything I said still holds, okay? 'Cause I think you're really the nuts."

"Thanks, Aldo. Then we'll be in touch?"

"I promise." He made a weird finger gesture she loosely translated to be some kind of scout's honor signal. She disembarked and he peeled out at around sixty.

She unlocked her car and just sat in it, shell-shocked. She'd never hear from Aldo again. Whether he just wanted to get laid or really thought she'd be right for his film, that excruciating moment in the Jeep had sealed her fate. Surely. Well, probably. Stop it! She hissed at herself. It ain't gonna happen and if it does it'll be a fucking miracle now so don't expect one goddamn thing from him easy come easy go Uma Thurman Cindy Crawford Julia Roberts fuck fuck FUCK!

It was her fault. She should have mentioned Dave on the ride to the restaurant. But she'd always found setting up little boundaries like that such a narcissistic, sorority-bitch device. Did she have to assume every straight man in the universe wanted to get into her pants? Apparently, the answer was yes.

Traffic on Sunset Boulevard was moving like an arthritic stegosaurus. Who did all these cars belong to and where the Christ were they going at ten-nineteen on a Thursday night? She saw some hookers strutting by the Saharan motel and felt such kinship she nearly honked. She thought about tomorrow and how impossible it would be to pull the current *Chillin' with Billy* together before the network run-through. She wondered if Maurice would show up and figured seeing his top billing on a nationally televised sitcom would be enough of an ego boost for him to *drag* his pompous ass back to work. She dreaded the ratings. On one hand, for the sake of her bank account and Roxanne's career, she didn't want the show to bomb. Conversely, if they somehow tapped into the vast and easy-to-please segment of television viewers who'd made hits of *Full House*, *Martin* and *Dino & Muffin*, Violet could easily be spending the next three to seven years letting a goat lick cake mix from her flesh.

She braked for a derelict shambling across the street, headlights glinting off his crammed-to-capacity shopping cart, and immediately felt guilty for hating her obscenely high-paying job. This commute was ridiculous, however. She had to move to Studio City or West Hollywood. After which she'd doubtlessly be cast in something at 20th Century-Fox, the only lot remotely convenient to Beverly Glen.

Her apartment windows were dark when she pulled into the carport, but she knew Dave was there because his van was parked on the street. The door was un-Daveishly unlocked. She went in and flicked on the kitchen light. It looked as if every piece of cookware she owned had been employed in some epic culinary campaign, the leftover results of which could be seen on her chipped-tile dinette table. Bruschetta, stuffed olives, half a pizza. Empty champagne bottles and glasses, one smeared with lipstick, stood clustered on the counter. What the hell had gone on here? Oh, shit.

Dave was sitting in the dark in the living room amid more dishes, cups and, she discovered when she snapped on her lamp, a small frilly chocolate cake still in the box from Sweet Lady Jane, her favorite bakery. "You're back, then," he said, not looking at her.

"Dave, what is all this?" But she knew. She also knew she was really in for it, and consequently stopped halfway to the couch, arms folded and lips already tensed defensively.

"It was meant to be a party for you while the first episode of your show was on. But since that was an hour and a half ago, it looks like the answer is . . . a huge waste of time that made me look like a goddamn idiot." He gathered a few stray dishes and stacked them on a plate. "Tricia and Jason send you their best."

"I'm sorry I wasn't here, Dave," she said carefully. "Who else did you have over?"

"Your mother."

"I'm *really* sorry."

"Don't make a bloody joke out of this, Violet. I'm warning you." He got up and angrily transported the dishes to the kitchen.

"Dave, we'd both seen the pilot. And I don't remember making plans to watch it again tonight." The clatter he was making in the sink was beginning to overpower her well-worked nerves.

"What you did actually was call me at four o'clock to say you'd be home *soon.*"

"I said I had errands to do. Then something came up."

"For six hours."

"Yes! Am I supposed to check in with you every hour now or something? I'm a busy girl, Dave. Stop cleaning. I told you, something really important came up."

"Well, pardon the crap out of me for figuring that the premiere of your first sodding series was 'important' as well. Do you have any idea how much trouble I went to tonight?"

"For Chrissake. I said I was sorry!"

"Well, it wasn't one of your more effective line readings."

"Nobody asked you to do all this. Just remember that." She headed for the bedroom, anticipating a juicy slam before recalling that there was no door.

"Could you at least pretend that I mean something to you? Anything at all?"

Why was he being so fucking needy? Well, she'd had enough. "Yeah, Dave. I really don't care at all," she spat sarcastically. "FYI: If I didn't feel compelled to come home to you, I could have spent the rest of the evening with the hottest new director in this town *and* ended up with the lead in his next movie. But here I am. How's that for devotion?"

"Brilliant. Charming. I must be completely fucking mental. Why in hell should you be any different than you've always been?"

"What are you talking about?" She watched him toss a few unwashed kitchen implements into a Trader Joe's bag. He charged past her into the bedroom.

"Your precious career." He flung a pair of his jeans into the bag. "I guess I just imagined success might help you relax a bit. Stupid me." He peeked under the bedspread and withdrew a pair of boxers and an overly squeezed tube of water-soluble lubricant. The underwear went into the bag. "Work's all you want. And apparently all you need. Well, far be it for me to come between you, darling."

"Now who's the drama queen?" she barked as he collected his

things from the bathroom. He ignored her and proceeded to the door.

"So this is it?" she asked dubiously.

He made a disgusted scoffing noise. "You honestly expect me to wait around while you fuck your way to the top?"

"Blow it out your ass, Dave!" Furious, she snatched the cake from the box and prepared to heave it at his back as he exited. She stopped herself. There was no need to match his childish theatrics. She pistoned into the couch, grabbed a fork from the coffee table, and dug in.

"What do Michael Jackson and Kmart have in common?" Ari Rosenblatt asked, smearing a two-day supply of fat grams onto a leftover bagel via apple-walnut whipped cream cheese.

"I have no idea," gay Eric tittered.

"Little boys' pants, half-off."

"I don't get it," Janice complained, tapping her unlit after-lunch cigarette on the employee lounge table. Eric explained it to her because Tricia was laughing too hard.

"That is *hilarious,* Ari!" she gasped, nearly spilling her lime-flavored mineral water. Janice grumbled something and hobbled out to smoke. Tricia continued to nibble her sea legs salad and listened to Eric and Ari chatter on about *Melrose Place.* They'd certainly find Heather Locklear's antics a bit tepid if they had any earthly idea how Tricia had spent the rest of her evening after leaving Violet's last night. (For the record, being taken from behind by Stefan as she lay nude on a bedspread strewn with the shreds of Edgar's cellular bill.) Misty paged her with a call from Violet, and she excused herself, leaving Ari to remark how much more pleasant it had been to be around Tricia lately.

At her desk, she buzzed reception. "Hello, Misty. Put her through." She did.

"Hi, Tricia. Is Edgar there?"

"No, he isn't, Violet." Shouldn't she be apologizing for skipping her own party? "Can I help you with something?" Tricia asked, somewhat peeved.

Violet sighed. "My show is off the air."

"That's unbelievable. After one broadcast? Violet, did this just happen?" She shifted uncomfortably on her sore bottom.

"Yup. The network called and canceled our run-through, which was supposed to be at six. They're shutting down production in the middle of this episode and putting the series 'on hiatus' indefinitely," Violet stonily reported.

"But why? I don't understand," Tricia whined.

"I guess you haven't seen the ratings. We dropped five and a half points from *Dino & Muffin* and lost nine shares. It's supposedly the worst dip in that time slot since 1982. Roxanne says the network was ready to drop the axe this morning when they saw the Nielsen overnights, but they had to wait for the nationals, which were even worse."

"I'm so sorry, Violet. You know of course that you were the best thing on that show. I'm sure it won't do much damage to your career."

"Uh . . . thanks, Tricia. I guess I'm going to pack up my dressing room and get the hell out of here. The network's going to be running 'Double *Dino*s' starting next Thursday."

"Here's a bit of good news," Tricia interjected. "Edgar and I suggested you for a key role in a new Danielle Steel miniseries. They're looking at your tape."

"That's great, Tricia. I'll call you later." She clicked off. Tricia replaced the receiver, silently damning the rotten luck Violet had been having this summer. First, Nicole Kidman nabbing her Broadway role in that film, then the whole ugly *Leather & Lace* imbroglio, now this. She reached for the TV submissions binder, fully intending to review the most recent episodic breakdowns for any guest leads the newly available Violet might be right for, but was interrupted by the telephone ringing.

"Stefan for you," Misty intercommed, bored.

"Okay. Hello?"

"Yes, I have a message from Daddy's big cock for Baby Girl's asshole. Can you help me with that?"

"Yes, sir," Tricia responded primly. "I'll relay the message."

"Right now my cock is harder than your clit was last night." She blushed to her Jhirmacked roots. "It's harder than your little pink nips got when I fucked those pretty butt-cheeks." Her anus involuntarily contracted, shooting delicate, exquisite pain into her bowels. The phone suddenly felt slippery, and she realized her palms were slick with sweat. "Baby Girl was very naughty yesterday," Stefan growled. She envisioned him fondling his enormous penis with both hands, the receiver jammed between his ear and shoulder. She remembered the electric sensation of his beard between her bare shoulder blades as he invaded her most private orifice—"Naughty at work and very naughty at home. I like it when you're naughty. Will you please be naughty again? Pretty please with sugar on top?" Now he was a coyly manipulative prepubescent boy. She glanced down at her chest—her nipples were protruding through the green silk of her blouse. She pinched the fabric away from her breasts just in time for Ari Rosenblatt to pass by her desk. He waved and smiled. She wiggled her fingers back in response.

As soon as Ari was out of sight, she quietly said into the receiver, "What naughty things would you like me to do?"

"Oh, I think you can figure that out," he whispered mockingly. "And tonight when you fingerfuck yourself for me—"

"Tricia, Edgar's holding for you!" Misty squealed over the intercom.

"Stefan, I have to take this," she began before hearing the click of his disconnection. Damnit—she hit the other line. "Edgar, hi."

A burst of static, then, "Christ on a crutch, Tricia, I'm on the goddamn car phone! What took you so long?"

"Misty just this second told me you were on the line! Edgar, the most dreadful thing has happened. *Chillin' with Billy* has been canceled!"

"Fuck! Already? How many times' it been on? Three? Four?"

"Edgar. Once. Last night was the premiere. Violet just called and apparently the network claims the drop off in the Nielsens was just atrocious, so—"

"How was Violet?"

"Well, depressed, rather stunned, I'd say. Should I send her flowers or a gift basket?"

"Why? She's out of a job. She should be sending *me* the goddamn gift basket. I'm the one who's going to have to sell her canceled ass to someone else. Christ. Do me a favor, honey. Send Javier to Gelson's for a jumbo jar of Rolaids."

"Hector," she corrected.

"What did I say? I'll be back in an hour. I'll need coffee. Two pots. See ya." He hung up.

Not even the repulsive imagery of Edgar's imminent caffeine enema could squelch the sexual excitement she felt as she took Edgar's actor file floppy disk from his desk drawer, inserted it into the office computer, and began to randomly amend and delete addresses and phone numbers.

"The worst part is you're out of a job."

"Violet, don't even think about that," Jason told her, hoping his Chipper & Supportive tone was enough to cover the bladder-shriveling disappointment wrought by this phone call.

"Maybe working for Marina a while wouldn't be so bad," she suggested hesitantly. But that was impossible. Jason had already explained to Marina why he couldn't take the job. She told him that maybe four people had been that honest with her in thirteen years of show business and how much she respected him, basically admitting that the assistant position was nothing but a mercy fuck.

"I'll work something out," Jason said to Violet. "What are you going to do?"

"I think I'll start with convincing my mother not to picket the network with her bridge club for canceling the show. She's already launched a letter-writing campaign. Then I'll be starring in Aldo Spackle's new movie. Not." She'd told him what had happened the night before. "Do you ever feel like the universe is just out to fuck you for the fun of it? That we're all just sex toys of the gods?"

"Oh, yes. Look, I bet Aldo's thought about it and realizes it was just a misunderstanding," Jason said. "He could still call you in. I think he will."

She sighed. "At least I got five episodes out of the piece of shit, right? I won't starve."

Jason, who quite conceivably could starve unless he supplemented the $186 in his checking account with a cash advance from his credit card at 19.8% interest, felt suddenly so unable to sustain Chipper & Supportive he had no idea what to say. Thankfully at that moment call-waiting bleeped in his ear.

"That's your other line. I'll let you go," said Violet. "Jason, I'm really sorry you got your chain yanked about the P.A. job. I'll take you to dinner later this week."

"Thanks, Violet. I'd really like that." I'll probably need a nutritional boost after selling plasma all day. "Bye." He clicked over. "Hello?"

"Jason?" A woman's voice he didn't recognize.

"Yes. Who's this, please?"

"Gail Ann Griffin. How *are* you, sweetheart?"

Jesus. What could she want? Something with Fawn, obviously. "Uh, Gail, Fawn's out of town, like, indefinitely, and right now I don't know exactly how to reach her."

"Oh, yes, I know. I think it's great that Fawn is pursuing a music career. She has such a wonderful singing voice," Gail purred, as if her last meeting with her ex-client had not ended with Fawn both firing and slapping her naked, bound personal manager across the face. "I'm sure you know that Fawn and I had some creative differences after the showcase, but hopefully we'll work together again someday. Actually, though, this call isn't about Fawn," she segued brightly. "You're who I want to talk to."

"I am?"

"Mm-hm. I have a little business proposition for you."

He couldn't help it. He was curious. "What would that be?"

"Are you still looking for a job in The Industry?"

"Yes," he replied warily, then was inspired to add, "I was hired on a sitcom but it just got canceled today."

"Then the timing on this is perfect! You see, I have this friend who's a vice president at this specialty film company. Exercise tapes, music videos, that sort of thing. Very upscale and artsy. He's in charge of marketing and can't seem to find an associate for the department."

"An associate?" Jason asked, knowing the word was Hollywoodese for *secretary*.

"Someone to work with him writing the catalog—they do a lot of mail order—planning, packaging, press releases, that type of thing. He said it pays around three thousand a month before taxes. Would you be interested in a job like that?"

Thirty-six thousand dollar a year? "Yeah, it sounds great." Uh-oh. "What's your proposition?"

"Oh, it's very simple. I recommend you for the job and see you get an interview, and you let me host a little dinner party for a few business people some evening next week."

"Here? At the man—at Fawn's house?"

"Well, yes. You are house-sitting, aren't you?"

"Yes, but—"

"It would be very small, and I would *of course* provide and clean up everything. You'd be there the whole time. And I give you my word all of the furniture would be treated with extreme care." How did she know about the furniture? For that matter, how did she even know he was house-sitting? Not that any of it made a bit of difference. He could just imagine Maggie and Syd Swann walking in on a dinner party. And that would only be a moderate explosion compared to the total core meltdown guaranteed to take place when Fawn found out Jason was doing favors for Gail, who he was 100 percent certain Fawn still despised more than Sinead O'Connor hated the pope.

"I don't think that'd be such a good idea, Gail. Fawn's in-laws are in town trying to sell the house, and they're—"

"Well, I won't tell if you won't," Gail tittered confidentially.

"It's not that I don't trust you. I just wouldn't feel comfortable with it. Personally," he said, half wondering if she would understand and do the decent thing and offer to get him the interview anyway. She didn't. The bitch.

"Darling, can you just think it over for me? I don't need an answer for, let's say, forty-eight hours?"

Did she not understand English? "Gail, I—"

"I won't say another word about it, Jason. Just write down my phone number, okay? Here it is . . ." Jason scribbled it down just to shut her up, realizing the absurdity of this as call-waiting heralded someone on the other line he statistically stood a very slim chance of actually wanting to speak with. He bade Gail a brief, civil goodbye and clicked over.

"Hello?"

"Hi, Jason. It's Giles Burke, man." And we're off!

"Hi, Giles."

"Is my mother over there yet?"

Fabulous. "Not that I know of . . ."

"Uh, could we talk?" Giles blurted abruptly. "Over here?" Oh, goddamnit. What now?

"Is something wrong?" Jason asked as lightly as possible.

"It's—I can't get into it over the phone. It's personal. Do you mind?" Giles practically whined.

"Okay. Now?"

"Yes. Let me give you the directions." Jason retrieved the notebook he'd dropped onto the floor and flipped Gail Ann Griffin's phone number over to a new page. After some initial incoherence, Giles was able to explain how to get to his house in Bel-Air. Jason made sure the kitchen held no evidence of the pizza he'd reheated for breakfast then left. He had no idea what the fuck Giles was up to, but a command performance for this apron-stringed lush was substantially less terrifying then being summoned to his mother's hotel suite. At least he'd missed running into Maggie today. Giles had said she was on her way over, and sure enough, there was the Lexus, gliding up the hill, Maggie at the wheel, oblivious to Jason as he passed her, face pinched into a pissy scowl about whatever at the moment was plaguing her busy, productive life.

By the time he'd driven through Bel-Air's overblown West Gate, he'd decided all Giles probably wanted was for Jason to do a few errands for him. Andre had always been popping over to Giles's house to take the cats to the vet or go to the liquor store or the post office or the cleaners or Chalet Gourmet, invariably receiving hefty cash tips as well as helping himself to free stamps, dry cleaning, groceries and liquor. Sometimes Andre even drove Giles's BMW. *I could sure use fifty bucks*, Jason thought, checking under the seat for tapes to play on the BMW's incredible stereo. He had been up here once with Andre (who excitedly revealed they were mere *seconds* from Sammy Davis and Kim Novak's top-secret former love nest) and recognized the place even though no house number was visible on the curb or near the front door. Probably a security measure—after all, he was still legally married to superstar Fawn Farrar.

Giles looked like shit—barefoot, unshaven, longish blonde hair slicked back with mousse, SilverTabs hanging off his bony ass. Despite the ninety-five-degree heat, he wore a Cleveland Indians hooded sweatshirt, perhaps because the house's air-conditioning cur-

rently simulated Christmas in Siberia. "Jason. Hi. Come in," he said.
"Sorry about the mess. I really need to call The Maid. She hasn't
been here in a while." Obviously. In fact, it looked like her brother
The Drug Dealer might have recently ransacked the place, Jason
snorted to himself.

The entryway was clotted with a small forest's worth of news-
papers, presumably unread, if several lashed-together Sunday edi-
tions were any indication. Jason stepped in and winced at the stale,
sour smell of the house, an amalgam of burnt toaster pastries and
cat piss. The living room stereo blared the Beatles at an offensive
volume. Giles shuffled off to lower it after directing Jason toward
the kitchen area, a riot of dirty dishes, pizza boxes and food delivery
cartons. The only conceivable place to sit was the triangular glass
dining table, but the three chairs were stacked with messy piles of
books, file folders and mail. A laptop computer sat on the table, its
Tasmanian Devil screen saver endlessly repeating destructive cartoon
vignettes. Jason took a step back and peeked into the laundry room.
Three litter boxes mounded high with soiled Johnny Cat blocked
access to the appliances and explained most of the smell.

"Sorry, Jason. Here, take a seat," Giles told him, clearing off
one of the dinette chairs. Jason sat, felt paper sliding under his ass
and discovered a stray financial statement from some mutual fund
indicating Giles's account balance was now $118,768.12. And he
still can't figure out what the recycling bins next to his garage are
for, Jason thought, quickly shoving the statement under *The Celes-
tine Prophecy.*

Giles went into the kitchen, where, Jason now noticed, a full
blender was camouflaged amid the counter clutter. "Want a piña
colada?" Giles asked, adding, "it's really hot out," as if they were
actually outside instead of in what felt like an ice-fishing hut. But
what the hell. Jason said, yes please, Giles threw in a few pineapple
chunks, blended, poured and served.

Jason thanked him, took a sip and recoiled. It was like a crushed
Popsicle made with Bacardi instead of water. Giles slurped down a
third of his drink, topped it off from the blender and leaned against
the counter, twisting one of his hood drawstrings with his free hand.
"I really need your help, man."

"What's up, Giles?" Jason noticed his fists were clenched with anxiety and relaxed them. He attempted a calm, curious expression.

"You're pretty good friends with Fawn, aren't you?" Oh, no. It couldn't be. There was no way this was happening again. "I mean, she talks to you about her . . . personal life. Right?" Jason just could not believe it. It was like he was a rat trundling through an ever-expanding maze with every possible escape route controlled by the Burkes.

Jason took a swig of piña colada. "Uh, Giles. I haven't talked to Fawn in person since she left for Texas. I don't really know what's happening with her."

"But Andre's like, your best friend, isn't he? And Fawn's his best friend, so you must have heard something. Jason, I gotta have her. And I'll do anything to get her back." He drained the blender into his *Batman Returns* souvenir cup. "She's not seeing anyone else, is she?"

"Not that I know of," Jason replied truthfully.

"What a relief. What a fuckin' relief." Giles tossed aside the contents of the chair next to Jason and sat down heavily. He was quite drunk. "I couldn't believe she'd be sleeping around. Not after those nights we had right before she left. You heard about that, right?"

"I think so," Jason agreed. What the hell was he supposed to tell him? His only hope was that Giles would pass out.

"It was just like old times," Giles lamented. "Then she got freaked out about the showcase and that lying-scum manager of hers. That Gail Ann Griffin. Goddamn her! And now Fawn's gone. And I'm—I'm—" About ready for another pitcher, it looked like.

"I'm sure she and Andre will be back in L.A. soon," Jason offered weakly.

"And then what? What does she want to do?" Giles grabbed Jason's arm and stared at him in desperation. "Jason, I don't want to go through with the divorce. I know what you've heard. That Fawn cheated on me. But it wasn't all her fault. I was having a lot of arousal problems and shit. You know how that is?" Mortified, Jason could only nod. "And my mother. Man, she always gave Fawn a hard time. Never made her feel welcome. She practically made me break up with her. Fuck, is my mother mean. Well, it's none of her goddamn business!" He grabbed the Westside yellow pages and hurled it against the wall. Okay. This was getting really hideous.

"Giles, please. Don't get upset," Jason said, standing up and removing the *Batman* cup before Giles spilled the small amount of remaining piña colada onto the computer keyboard.

"There's no reason why Fawn and me can't stay married," Giles proclaimed.

Well, if you don't count your mother's at-any-cost meddling and the fact that your wife is probably getting it on with everything in Wranglers right this minute, then, yes, there's no reason at all, Jason thought, but said, "What exactly do you want to do about it?"

"I already started. I told that sleazebag hotshit divorce lawyer my mother hired to take a fuckin' hike." Jason was impressed. That had taken guts. "I mean, I didn't actually say the words 'take a fuckin' hike.' I told him I didn't want to file until Fawn was back in L.A. And that I was too upset to talk about it at all until then."

"That was . . . smart," Jason said.

Giles nodded sagely, cocking a finger toward Jason. "See how Mr. Legal Eagle likes it when I never call him back. And that's not all. Wait till you see this!" He got up, banging his knees against the glass tabletop, and took off in a slightly staggering jog for the bedroom.

Jason sat down again, the buzz from the cocktail radiating not unpleasantly from his empty stomach. It was amazing that Fawn could generate such drama in real life and still be unable to land so much as a supporting role in a Fred Olen Ray shocker. Giles came back with something in hand. A Tiffany box. He thrust it at Jason, who removed the lid and withdrew a black jewelry case. Giles took it and flicked back the lid, revealing a diamond ring that resembled a prop from *The Flintstones*. "Twenty carats," Giles announced. "Now how do you think Fawn would like me to pop the question?"

"You're going to ask Fawn to remarry you?" Jason said, hoping for Giles's sake he hadn't drunkenly misplaced the receipt.

"No. We're still married," Giles replied testily. "I'm going to ask her to . . ." He trailed off, confused.

"Not divorce you?" Jason prompted.

"Yeah. Something like that," he mumbled, snapping the box

closed on the chunk of ice. "I've gotta figure out the best way to approach this. I've got these numbers in Texas, but do you have any idea how hard it is to get her and Andre on the phone?"

"Actually, yes. Andre tells me she's really busy with her demo. Hiring musicians, rehearsing, photo shoots, you know, so maybe you should just—"

"God, she's got a beautiful voice," Giles sighed, staring past Jason with a wounded, slack-jawed expression. "She used to sing to me when we made love," he said to Jason's great discomfort, the information even less welcome with "Yesterday" playing ridiculously in the background. Giles closed his eyes and began to croon something by Sade. Oh, good Christ.

"Uh, Giles?" He opened his eyes and looked at Jason as if he'd appeared out of nowhere. "I just really, you know, don't think you want to get into all this over the phone. With Fawn. If you can wait until you two are face-to-face—"

"Holy shit. That's it!" Giles exclaimed. "Why didn't I think of that? Man, you are brilliant!"

"What do you—" Jason began, bewildered, but Giles was up and spinning around, overcome with inspiration.

"I gotta go to Texas! I'm going to show up at that lake house with this ring and I'm not leaving until everything's okay between us. How could I have waited this long? Jason, you saved my life, dude." He smacked him on the shoulder. "Shit, I need to pack. Jason, can you do me a favor and call my travel agent right now?"

Oh, why not? "Sure. Do you know the number? Or just give me the name of the place."

"Oh, I don't . . . know that. Andre put it on speed-dial." He waved at the wall-mounted kitchen phone, then exited toward the bedroom. Jason went to the fingerprint-besmirched AT&T and checked the memory pad. All of the speed-dial slots were blank.

"Giles, there isn't anything listed on this phone," Jason called down the hall.

"Yeah, I lost the card. Try number four!"

Jason dutifully hit four. Seven rapid beeps, ringing, then, "Good afternoon, Vendome Liquors."

"Sorry, wrong number," Jason said, disconnecting. "Four's not right!"

"Try five!"

Jason did and was extremely surprised to hear "Gunderson Travel, can you please hold?"

He agreed to, then yelled to Giles, "I've got them on the line. What do you need?"

"Um . . . San Antonio. Today. First-class. And I'll need a car. See if they can get me a Porsche. And a limo to the airport!" Jason followed these instructions, charging it all to Mr. Burke's American Express, then proceeded to Giles's spectacularly unkempt bedroom, dominated by a TV identical to that at the mansion and an enormous round bed upon which Giles was now filling a black leather suitcase with clothes tossed from his closet.

"It's all taken care of. Your plane leaves at five-twenty. The limo will be here at four. They're messengering your tickets and itinerary and rental car confirmation within the hour," Jason said.

"Thanks a lot, Jason. And thanks for the great idea. Oh, here you go. For gas driving over here." He opened his wallet, fingered the bills therein and handed them all to Jason, who smiled, thanked Giles and slid the cash into his pocket without unfolding it. Charity gladly accepted. In fact, we could look into an adoption through Save the Children.

Giles dug some long-sleeved shirts and sweatpants out of the suitcase. "What the fuck am I doing? It's Texas. I can't wear this. Shit, there's no way I can concentrate on packing. I'll just buy new stuff when I get there." He shoved the suitcase onto the floor. "Oh. Jason. Sorry, man. You don't need to stick around. You helped me enough already, dude."

"Okay. No problem. Have a nice trip. And, I guess, good luck." Jason waved and headed down the hall to the front door.

"Hey, Jason. Please do me just one more favor," Giles said, hanging off the bedroom door frame.

"Uh . . . what is it?"

"Don't mention any of this to my mother, okay? Like if she asks if you've seen me or know where I am or anything, just say no."

"Sure. That's fine."

"Cool."

The furnace-bake of Jason's car was a relief after the chilly house. For about forty-five seconds at least. He took the money Giles gave him out of his pocket and counted it. Two fives, two ones. So much for a shopping spree at Pavilions. He cranked up Scandal's *The Warrior* on cassette and decided to hang out at the Century City mall. He hadn't seen a movie since Andre took off.

He bought a ticket to an adults-only comedy called *Hold Me, Thrill Me, Kiss Me*. It was set in a trailer park and concerned the feud between an ingenuous, perky animal-lover and her evil stripper sister. More importantly, the male lead was a steamy, underdressed hunk and the theater was comfortably air-conditioned. Jason enjoyed the film thoroughly, and since it was still too early to return to the mansion, when it was over he snuck into *Coneheads* and quickly wished he'd opted for Brentano's next door and ninety minutes of beefcake coffee-table volume perusal.

It was still light when he got out. Starving by this time but unwilling to go into further debt to purchase something at the concession or the mall's notoriously overpriced food court, he took the long way home and stopped by Taco Bell on Beverly for a four-buck face-filling. He could see the mansion lights blazing behind the landscaping when he pulled up to the gate on Vista Laguna, but that didn't mean she was still there, he insisted to himself. Halfway up the drive, he almost backed right down to kill another hour at Tower Records. But that would have been stupid. Instead, he killed the lights, quietly loped up the driveway and crept around the corner of the house. The carport was empty.

Relieved, he sprinted back to the car. He parked, went in, turned on the nighttime lights and checked the answering machine. Two messages! He hit Play and unlaced his sneakers.

"Hi, cutie, it's Marina. I *think* today's your big interview with that TV show and I know you'll do great, so break a leg. I'm red-eyeing to New York tonight to be interviewed by, like, everyone in town, and listen to all the remixed, remastered tracks from the new album. I'll only be gone a few days and Chip's going to be with me so I'll keep bugging him about your job. I'm staying at the Paramount in New York. Hank's got the number. But if you get back before nine, call me, sweetie. Later." Damn. It was nine-forty. Not that he had anything to tell her that wasn't completely depressing.

Another beep. "I'm telling you how I know, Lewis," Maggie

snapped. "He left the travel agency receipt right on the dining room table!"

"He's a grown man, Maggie. If he wants to fly to San Antonio without telling anyone, it's his business."

"Well, I think it's our business if that little slut ran out of money for that idiotic album of hers and called him to bail her out. Why else would he go to *Texas*?" she spat.

"Maybe he just wanted to see her," Lewis replied, sounding bored. "They *are* married."

Long silence. "They are *separated*, Lewis. And getting divorced. Now I don't know what kind of nonsense is going on down there but I intend to find out. I'm flying to San Antonio tomorrow. And I expect you to join me there this weekend. We must do something about Giles. Lewis, you would not believe the condition of his house. It looks like a serial killer lives there. And the stench! I spent half an hour cleaning out cat boxes!" Jason laughed. "No wonder he'd never let me past the front door."

"How'd you get in? Break a window?" Jason decided he sort of liked Lewis Burke.

"Of course not. I had a key made months ago. And it's a good thing I did or we'd have no idea where he is right now."

"He's twenty-eight years old."

"And it's high time he started acting like it. Shall I book you a flight for Saturday?"

"No, Maggie. I'm playing golf this weekend in Shaker Heights. It's business."

"Damnit! Monday morning, then. I'll call you from there tomorrow. Goodbye, Lewis."

Jason rewound and replayed the conversation to ensure he had the details straight. Maggie was out of town, effective tomorrow until at least Tuesday of next week. Awesome. As he pondered the sweetness of this development, his eyes fell upon Gail Ann Griffin's number scrawled across a notebook page. Before he tried to convince himself to do otherwise, Jason picked up the phone and dialed.

On the first ring: "It's about time. I was ready to trade Moët et Chandon in for Black and Decker," Gail said sultrily.

"Hi, Gail. This is Jason Dallin."

"Oh, Jason, excuse me. I was expecting someone else." Obviously. "Do tell me you've reconsidered?"

"Actually, I have. If you want to hold a dinner here, you can do it this weekend."

"Wonderful. I think I can pull it all together for Sunday night. How would that be?"

"Fine. The job's still available, isn't it?"

"What job, dear?"

Jesus Christ. "The video company? The interview you were going to get me?"

"Oh, of course. I'm sure it is. I'll call Bryce first thing in the morning. Jason, I'm so glad we could work this out. And I hope you'll join us for dinner. It should be delish. Patina's catering. I'll be in touch. B'bye."

She called him at nine-thirty the next morning with the fax number of Bryce Barger at Aquarius Images and to reconfirm directions to the mansion so she could fax maps to her dinner guests. Jason took off for a copy shop to fax Bryce his résumé and a brief cover note, returning just in time to welcome Gail to the house for a "look-see."

"Sweet baby Jesus! This is *beautiful!*" she gasped, stepping in and whisking off silver-flecked cat-eye sunglasses. "What a difference the furniture makes!"

She hungrily ran a hand over the yellow marble dining table. "And I love the art," she added, wandering into the living room to stare at a wall covered with an antique French advertisement for what Jason guessed to be poodle soap. Gail hopped onto the white sectional sofa and kicked up her heels, beaming at the coup de grace she obviously felt she'd scored.

"The decor is sensational. What is it, Japanese?" she asked Jason.

Tokyo S–M bordello, he thought of saying, but instead replied, "I guess so." Next Gail wanted a tour. Jason cheerfully obliged, leaving out his own quarters. When they got to the master bedroom, Gail demanded to know who had "done" the house.

"Fawn's mother-in-law, actually," Jason sighed.

"She's very talented," Gail pronounced, turning down a corner of the king-size, leather-trimmed bed to admire sheets no one in their right mind could afford. "She must be a professional decorator," Gail said. "These rooms are brilliant."

Jason wanted to remark that if Maggie happened to catch Gail throwing a dinner party in her house, Mrs. Brilliantly Talented Professional would not hesitate to chew a new hole in Gail's lipo-sucked ass, but he merely shrugged. They were back in the foyer/dining hall, and the personal manager was verbally incorporating the wet bar into her dinner plans. She asked Jason if he wanted to be bartender for forty-five dollars.

"I don't know that much about making drinks," he admitted reluctantly, unhappy about passing up not only desperately needed cash but a perfect opportunity to oversee the dinner party without having to socially participate in it.

"Don't worry, honey. I'll get someone else," Gail assured him with a pat. "Now tell me. What is this showplace selling for?"

"They're asking eight-point-five million, furnished," Jason told her.

"A few more clients on series and I might just put in a bid myself," she commented with a straight face.

Unable to think of an appropriate segue, Jason waited a few seconds, then said, "I faxed my résumé over to Bryce around ten. Do you think you'll talk to him today?"

"Absolutely. In fact, let's call right now." She whipped an electronic Rolodex from her purse and typed in Bryce's name. She dialed the bar phone. "Yes, hello? . . . Gail Ann Griffin for Bryce, please . . . Sure . . . Bryce-Baby? . . . How *are* you, sugar? . . . Oh, my sinuses are killing me, too . . . Honey, I'm here with Jason Dallin . . . oh, it's right in front of you? . . . Yes, fresh out of school and cute as a bug's ear . . . Uh-oh, I think I'm embarrassing him," she giggled. Jason, indeed embarrassed but displaying no outward sign or expression that this was the case, noncommittally lowered his eyes to the floor. "Six today?" Jason looked up. Gail was holding up six fingers, eyebrows raised questioningly. He nodded. "That'll be fine, hon. Let me take down the address . . . 'Kay. B'bye." She hung up and triumphantly handed the slip of paper to Jason. "Break a leg, darling."

"Thanks, Gail. I really appreciate it."

She promised to be back Sunday by five-thirty for the preparations. He walked her out to her sport utility vehicle. "Jason, I realize this dinner party would put you in an awkward position with Fawn, so let me give you my *word* that she won't hear about it from me. And I'm not going to tell any of my guests whose house this is. We'll just say you're sitting it for friends. How's that?"

"Fine. I'm really not worried about it," he said truthfully, but as soon as she drove off, he went inside, called the Hotel Bel-Air and asked for Maggie Burke's room, holding his breath until, instead of a ring, a snooty voice came on the line.

"Mrs. Burke has temporarily checked out of the hotel. She's asked us to forward her messages to San Antonio, Texas."

"No message," Jason said, hanging up. So she was really gone. However Jason might be affected by the repercussions of the hideous family mega-crisis bound to erupt when Giles, Fawn, Andre, the Burkes, and a twenty-carat diamond all came together in 100 percent Texas humidity, it would be worth this weekend of tranquility. He reinstalled Andre's CD system under the wet bar—Gail would probably want some light music during her soiree, anyway—squeezed into his Speedo and did laps to randomly selected cuts from all three Pop-Tartts albums.

Aquarius Images was located in Century City in one of the twin towers adjacent to the Shubert Theater on Century Park East. Gail hadn't mentioned whether they validated parking, so he played it safe and drove to the nearby mall garage. He got out and touched the hood and yanked his hand back, scalded. The engine always threatened to boil over when he ran the air conditioner, an absolute necessity on this scorching afternoon to avoid shvitzing up his hairdo and the Andre outfit he'd borrowed. If he somehow got this job and it actually paid three thousand a month, the Subaru would be euthanized pronto, after some minor surgery to remove the stereo, he decided on the walk to Aquarius Images.

He arrived ten minutes early and only slightly damp. The office was on the eighteenth floor. When he opened the door, he heard Army of Lovers' "Crucified," which he took to be a good sign. A large framed Hippolyte Flandrin print hung over a reception desk occupied by a girl with good bone structure in a Catholic school uniform and purple ringlets. She was on a headset. "Is this to place an order? . . . Let me transfer you." She hit a button on her console and looked up at Jason with a smile. "Hi. Can I help you?"

"I've got an appointment with Bryce Barger," he said.

Bryce was on a call at the moment; the receptionist would notify him as soon as she could. Jason sat down next to a table with *Vanity Fair*, *Premiere* and several copies of the Aquarius Images summer catalog. Jason grabbed one, his curiosity piqued by the arty cover photo of a nude male turning his firm tush toward the camera, chiseled arms resting on elbows on a stone balcony railing, a starscape bleeding into a white streak across the night sky over his head.

Arty, *nude* and *male* proved to be operative words, Jason discovered as he leafed through the catalog in disbelief. Aquarius, it seemed, specialized in videos featuring very, very attractive young men cavorting in a variety of locales, from the naked beaches of Hawaii to clothing-optional tropical jungles to tasteful, pajama-free boudoirs. The odd thing was that these productions did not appear to be sex films in the traditional sense—no popular adult stars were involved, the subtly crafted descriptions made no mention of hungry holes or throbbing manmeat, and even the "explicit" safer-sex instructional series had the endorsements of Gay Men's Health Crisis and Dr. Ruth. Pretty, upscale, shame-free gay soft porn? It was certainly a long way from those tacky male-strip videos he'd ordered from a *Playgirl* ad back at Ohio State.

Jason continued through the catalog. Nude workout tapes, a clothed workout tape starring Bob and Rod Paris-Jackson, movies by Derek Jarman, Pedro Almodovar and John Waters. He flipped back to the sexier stuff at the beginning. The photos really were gorgeous, and much steamier than the stiff, airbrushed and over-photostyled box covers that had led to his downfall at Video Xplosion. He made mental notes to omit the store from his discussion with Bryce and to get on this catalog's mailing list (under Andre's name) as soon as he got back home.

"Hi, Jason. I'm Bryce," a voice said, startling him into spasmodically batting the catalog to the floor when all he wanted to do was close it discreetly in his lap. "Did I scare you?" he laughed as Jason stood and shook hands.

"I shouldn't have had that second Polar Swirl at Arby's," Jason shocked himself by deadpanning out of nowhere. Bryce laughed again. He was on the short side, very cute, bald with a goatee, in jeans and a flannel shirt. He led Jason back into the suite, to an office whose small size was offset by the breathtaking view that, on this exceptionally clear day, spanned Beverly Hills all the way to the Griffith Park Observatory and beyond. Jason took the guest seat beneath an equally breathtaking Skrebneski monochrome of a naked, hung beauty.

Bryce tilted back in his chair, bracing his he-man boots on the cluttered desktop, and scanned Jason's fax-copied résumé. They chatted about Jason's college career for a few minutes, moved on to a cleansed and abbreviated version of Jason's recent relocation to L.A., then Bryce began describing Aquarius Images and its attitude toward hunk-filled entertainment.

"Basically, we wanted to take the sleaze out of gay erotica," he explained. "You know, to create the kind of product people don't have to be ashamed to rent or buy. Not that I think there's anything wrong with hardcore porn, it's just that our market research showed there was an audience eager for more artistic, sensual videos with models they'd never seen before, great production values and classier packaging. Our safer-sex series does contain some explicit stuff, but there aren't cumshots or anything." He looked momentarily abashed, and asked, "You wouldn't have a problem working with homoerotic material, would you?"

Keeping a straight face, Jason shook his head. "I'm very open-minded."

"Great." Bryce handed Jason a glossy color slick. "This is *Waterfall*, our number one selling title. Eight stunning guys splashing around bare-ass for forty-seven minutes," he said, smiling. "Some kissing, some massage, a couple of erections. Nothing we can't ship to all fifty states. We've got some great new releases this fall. More highbrow stuff. A Tom of Finland documentary—want a press kit?" He handed Jason a folder, the cover of which depicted several maxi-buff leathermen and the blonde sailor boy they were doubtlessly about to ravish six ways to Sunday dinner. "Also, a music video collection with Cocteau Twins. Tower Records and Virgin Mega-stores are both carrying our line now," he added proudly.

"That's terrific." Jason wondered how enthusiastic it was appropriate to sound. "I really like your catalog. It's the kind of thing people would tend not to throw out."

"Exactly!" Bryce agreed, removing his feet from the desk and rolling up his chair. "We want them to keep the catalogs on their coffee tables and nightstands and keep flipping through them until they break down and order something. Do you do any writing?"

"Well, some. I was the music critic for my college paper for two years," Jason said, thinking that if Bryce wanted to see a writing sample, Jason's rave review of Bananarama's *Please Yourself* probably wouldn't cut it.

"The job wouldn't really involve that much writing. I mean, you'd be welcome to try a little. Mostly it's helping me keep all this"—he waved his hand in a dismissive arc—"organized. The Christmas edition of the catalog goes to press in about six weeks, so that's sort of a priority. And tracking our print campaigns, working with ad reps at magazines, figuring out new and inventive ways to describe naked guys. So, do you have any questions?"

Jason hated to mention it, mostly because he was afraid Gail had been mistaken or lied about the amount and Bryce would tell him the job paid $275 a week, but knew this was the time for a salary discussion. He asked Bryce about the money. "It's what I told Gail," he replied lightly. "Three thousand a month. We get paid every other week here. And after ninety days, there's full medical and dental. Plus of course wholesale rates on any of the videos." He stood up. "So it was great to meet you, Jason. I appreciate you coming down." He offered his hand, which Jason shook, hopes plummeting at Bryce's kiss-of-death last sentences. Don't stop smiling, he ordered himself as Bryce scanned his appointment calendar, probably to see when the next applicant was due in.

"I'm going to be out of the office most of Monday afternoon, so can you come in Tuesday morning?" he asked Jason.

A callback? Just like that? "Sure. Will I be meeting other people?"

"Yeah," Bryce said, giving him a slightly confused look. "You'll be meeting everybody. You're not going to spend every day caged up in here for eight hours." He laughed. "Just get a ticket and park in the garage downstairs. They'll give you a parking card when you fill out your paperwork and I-9's."

"Sorry. Wait a minute," Jason said, having obviously missed something crucial. "You're telling me I have the job?"

"Uh-huh. If you want it." Bryce sounded surprised.

"Oh, God, yes! I guess I never expected it to be this easy," Jason tried to explain, as relief flooded through him in warm, wonderful jets.

"Hey, you're fresh, you're qualified, you're bright. And you seem like a really nice person with a great energy. That's good enough for me," Bryce said, clapping him on the shoulder. He loaded Jason up with some more catalogs, promotional materials and videotapes, and escorted him back down the hall. Bryce introduced Jason to Doreen, the purple-haired receptionist who was unable to stem the unrelenting influx of calls, but waved and grinned politely.

Jason agreed to be in at nine-thirty Tuesday morning and before he left asked how Bryce knew Gail Ann Griffin.

"We met at Guru Mayi's Intensive at the Siddha Yoga Center," his new boss explained. "Gail was sitting next to me during meditation and started screaming and convulsing. Everyone thought her yoga position made her slip a disc, but it turned out to just be her sex chakra opening. See you Tuesday!"

Jason rode the elevator down and walked out of the building into the still-sizzling early evening, happier than he'd been since Las Vegas and maybe even before. Finally, he was assuming some control over his life, banishing helplessness and dependence on those both beloved and despised. He would still actively pursue Mermaid Records, but in the meantime he'd be earning the first decent money he'd ever seen, paying off bills, renting his own apartment (maybe he could take Violet's—she was planning on moving out soon) and expanding his résumé with a legitimate (yes, legitimate—tasteful homoeroticism did not render this job sleazy *or* shameful) entertainment position that would make it that much easier to attain the showbiz career he most wanted. And a company like Aquarius was the perfect setting in which one might meet a buttload of successful, creative, fun, sexy, assuredly gay guys and perhaps obtain a boyfriend before one hit the age of thirty.

Jason headed back to the mall, intending to splurge on a chicken sandwich and fries at Brentwood BBQ and then maybe hit the used CD store on Pico. He relished every second of the upcoming weekend, even Gail's dinner party. He was employed and out of Maggie's grasp for days. He couldn't wait to get home and listen to lots of Stock-Aitken-Waterman artists.

"Jason?"

He was so awash in his own good fortune he barely heard let alone saw Hank Rietta. But Hank called his name again and Jason turned and saw him a few feet away, in a sharp suit carrying a black briefcase. "What are you up to over here?"

"I had a job interview at a video company."

"How'd it go?"

"I got it. I start Tuesday."

"Congratulations! Jason, that's fantastic. But Marina said you were starting a job on a sitcom."

"It got canceled. But this is better. A lot more money, normal hours. It seems like a really cool company."

"What's the name?" Hank asked.

Missing only half a beat, Jason replied, "Aquarius Images."

Hank frowned behind his Matsuda sunglasses. "That sounds familiar . . ."

"They're kind of new," Jason said, eager to change topics. "What brings you to this side of town?"

"Bank shit. Which I'm finished with. I got a great idea. Dinner. To celebrate your job. How 'bout it?"

"Sure. I'd love to. Do you just want to meet up somewhere later?"

"I'm parked right here under the towers. Why don't we just leave from here?"

"Well, my car's over at the mall——"

"I'll drop you back here. Come on. You like Italian, right?"

Hank drove them to Chianti on Melrose in the air-conditioned, baby-smooth comfort of his Infiniti, Jason's bag of Aquarius hunkery discreetly stowed in the trunk. The restaurant was probably the darkest Jason had ever been in and only got darker as summer evening faded into night outside and two hours somehow went by without the conversation flagging any longer than it took for them to chew and swallow mouthfuls of the most delicious Italian food Jason had ever tasted.

Surprisingly, Marina hardly came up at all. Instead, they talked about Giles, Fawn and Maggie, and Hank's impressions of growing up nouveau riche with all the suburban Long Island trimmings—plastic slipcovers, Cadillacs, lawn fountains, and next-door neighbors who frequently had John Gotti over to barbeque. After they'd split a bottle of red wine, Hank revealed that his real name was Henry, but he had insisted on a permanent change to Hank at age eight after deciding "Henry Rietta" sounded too much like X the Owl's treemate Henrietta Pussycat from *Mr. Rogers' Neighborhood.*

Hank ordered an unspeakably rich chocolate dessert not on the menu for them to share. Jason was grateful for the sugar, since he had a hell of a wine buzz and would have to drive home as soon as he was dropped back at the mall. Hank classily, nearly invisibly took care of the check, and they headed back to Century City listening to the new Cyndi Lauper CD. Hank pulled up to the Bullock's entrance.

"Thanks again for dinner. It was fantastic," Jason said. "Can you pop the trunk for me?"

"Sure. Hey, what do you got going on tonight?"

"Not a damn thing." Jason smiled, flattered and surprised Hank was apparently okay enough with him as a friend to want to hang out on a Friday night.

"Maybe we should do something," Hank suggested. "Why don't I meet you back at your house? I'd like to see what Maggie did to the place."

"Okay. See you there." Jason took out his bag, shut the trunk and hurried up the stairs to the open-air shopping center, passing shuttered stores and people on their way to the AMC until he found the right escalator to the parking garage. It had been over three hours and he had to pay to exit the mall, but he didn't even care. His new life was starting today. He dug through the dash and located a Kim Wilde remix tape, which had never sounded better than it did that hot evening as he cut behind the Beverly Hilton and took Whittier Drive up to Sunset, joining the weekend party traffic moving east toward Hollywood.

The Infiniti wasn't around when he turned onto Laguna Vista and stopped at the mansion gate. Hank probably had to drop by his house first, Jason guessed, hitting the remote and leaving the gate open. He checked for nonexistent answering machine messages and took The Pop-Tartts out of the CD changer and replaced them with more Girls, Indigo and Everything But The.

When he saw the headlights shining through the windows and moving across the breakfast nook wall, his heart reflexively lurched into his throat, but of course it was only Hank. Jason opened the door. Hank had lost his jacket and loosened his tie and carried a champagne bottle with a curly red ribbon around it. He passed it to Jason. "For you."

"Dom Pérignon? Are you crazy? For what?" Jason laughed.

"Your new job, what do you think?" Hank said in a goombah voice, giving Jason a light tap on the back of the head. He stepped in. "It sure ain't to celebrate Mrs. Burke's taste in home furnishings. Jesus Christ, this is amazing." Jason carried the champagne to the bar and stuck it in the fridge as Hank continued to the living room. "It's like every hideous, overpriced piece of chichi junk you see when you drive by Robertson and Melrose that you can't imagine anyone actually going, 'Yeah, this for me!' and buying, she bought," Hank marveled. "Look at this lamp! I *resent* that somebody can create something this ugly and then expect people to pay for it."

"And Maggie certainly didn't disappoint them," said Jason.

"I can't take it. Let's go outside." Hank looked through the glass wall at the shimmering lights of the city splashed beyond the pool and lawn. Jason opened the sliding glass doors behind the bar, and they went out on the patio, which had recently been stocked with a shipment of rattan and bamboo furniture festooned with garish South Seas "throws" Jason was expressly forbidden to touch unless in-clement weather threatened, in which case he was to immediately stow them inside.

Hank strolled to the edge of the pool and squatted down, dipping his fingers in the water. "This water's nice and cold. Mine's like a bathtub."

"The pool guy just filled it this morning. I was in there all af-ternoon. It felt great," Jason said, brazenly leaning against a throw-covered chaise.

"Want to take a swim?" Hank asked, flicking water from his fingers toward Jason.

"Sure. I'll go get towels," Jason said. He went to his room and located a couple of clean Fieldcrests, then tossed off his clothes and donned his Speedo, fresh from the dryer. Andre would have taken all his swimsuits to the lake house, so Jason selected a pair of his own madras shorts from The Gap for Hank to wear.

But when he got outside, Hank was already in the pool. He must have decided to take the plunge in his underwear. Hold on—there they were, piled with the rest of Hank's clothes on one of the chaise throws. Calvin Klein boxer-briefs. On the chaise. He was skinny-dipping. Naked. As if to verify this rather jolting deduction, Hank swam toward Jason, his bare buttocks breaking the surface as he dove down to the black marble bottom, then came bobbing up at the edge of the pool, raising himself out of the water, crossing his muscular arms on the deck and looking up at Jason. "This really kicks ass. Coming in?"

"Yeah!" Jason exclaimed, trying to appear utterly relaxed about if not completely oblivious to Hank's nudity. But the Speedo suddenly seemed to be very tight and there would be no way to hide the boner currently under construction and he wanted to slip the Gap shorts on over the Speedo but that would have looked ridiculous and suspicious, so he crumpled them up and pitched them over his shoulder and leaped into the water.

It was still cold, but not cold enough to freeze Jason's penis into flaccidity. Thank God the underwater lights were off. Oh, for fuck's sake, chill! he ordered himself. A, he's not going to be checking out your crotch and B, he couldn't see anything in here anyway, so if your dick feels like getting hard, who gives a shit? He resolved not to think about it and promptly schwinged into full erection while treading water.

Hank glided over. "When you were a kid, did they tell you not to piss in the pool because there was some chemical in it that'd turn the water red and everyone'd know what you did?"

"It was a rumor at the municipal pool," Jason said. "But I think it was supposed to turn our water purple. I never felt the slightest urge to test it out."

"Right? We got a pool when I was twelve, and my old man was obsessed with me and my brothers or our friends pissing in it. 'I'm tellin' youse, that water's gonna go red, and the wise-ass in the middle of it's outta there for the summah!' " Hank bellowed. Jason laughed. "I just wanted to tell him, 'Believe it or not, Pop, we're not exactly dying to splash around in our own piss.' " He paddled backward and seated himself on one of the large marble steps descending into the shallow end. The water came to just below his wide, round pecs, lapping at his dark, very pointy nipples. Everything below the chest was a barely perceptible blur. If Aquarius Images put Hank on a video cover just like this, it would outsell all their other tapes combined.

" 'Course he had no idea what I was doing alone in the Jacuzzi every night," Hank continued with a smutty nod to Jason. "Lucky for me there wasn't a chemical that turned jism purple."

Jason's astonishment at this candid (and yes, horrifically sexy) revelation must have been obvious on his face because Hank self-consciously submerged up to his neck and said, "Sorry. Am I grossing you out?"

"No. I've done the same thing myself," Jason heard his own voice confessing. "At this Howard Johnson's on a vacation with my parents. I told my mother I'd pulled a muscle in my back and spent a three-day weekend in the hot tub."

"Felt great, huh?" Hank asked. He'd drifted close enough for Jason to see the droplets glistening in his thick eyebrows. Jason nodded, acutely aware of his own heart beating in time to the pulse in his erect cock.

"Kids today!" Hank squawked à la his dad, backhanding a splat of water at Jason's face. "I'll race you to the end and back. Go!" And Hank took off in a ragged butterfly. Jason took his first breath in about three minutes and kicked off after him. They were in a dead heat passing under the enclosed bridge connecting the living room and master bedroom, but at the far wall Hank gave him a playful, sabotaging shove and lunged into a headstart as Jason screamed no fair and watched Hank's naked body propel itself back toward the steps.

When Jason reached them, Hank was sitting on the second step again, arms folded across his shins, knees pressed against his chest. "I cheated," he said.

"I demand a rematch," Jason replied.

"I'm freezing my balls off here. Let's get out and crack open the Dom."

"Okay. Let me get out the towels," Jason quickly offered. He paddled to the edge of the pool and hoisted himself out, butt to Hank to shield his swollen basket. He hurried, dripping, to the chaise and secured a towel around his waist. He grabbed the other one and turned around. There was a splash and Hank was striding nude across the patio. He stopped twelve feet from Jason and held out his arms. Jason threw the towel. Hank caught it and began to leisurely dry himself.

"I'll get the champagne," Jason said, his voice actually cracking into a squeak on the last syllable. He raised each foot for a fast swipe with the hem of the towel and walked briskly to the kitchen, not daring to look back, the image burned into his retinas forever, the image of Hank and his big swinging dick. At least it looked big. He'd only beheld it for less than five seconds. It hadn't been hard (that he would have noticed in *one* second) but it was definitely big. And that story about the Jacuzzi. Jason couldn't believe he'd admitted doing the same thing. Didn't Hank realize or care what kind of effect he had on guys With a Problem?

Obviously not, you idiot, he chastised himself, taking two crystal flutes from the cupboard. He's straight. He doesn't care who sees him naked. You work out together. If it was at a public gym, instead of his house, you would have been naked together lots of times. Hank was treating Jason like one of the guys, and if Jason didn't want him to start feeling weird about the whole thing, he had better quit fixating on Hank's perfectly muscled, mouth-watering nude physique. Jason got the Dom Pérignon from the bar and went back outside.

Hank had not dressed. The snowy white Fieldcrest was tied around his waist, and he was sitting at the rattan umbrella table, his legs comfortably stretched across to the opposite chair. Jason deposited the bottle and glasses on the glass-topped table and sat down in the chair next to Hank. "I wish you hadn't been so extravagant," Jason began as Hank stripped it down to the cork and twisted. "It's not that great of a job—"

The cork ejected with a loud, sound-FX record pop and rocketed into the night. They heard a splash. Champagne foamed over Hank's hand and forearm. "It's just the beginning for you," he said, slurping wine off himself before filling the glasses. Jason imagined the entire bottle cascading onto Hank's bare chest. And how it would taste to lick it all up.

"To all the success you have coming to you," Hank said. Jason clinked his glass to Hank's outstretched one, then took a sip. Fizzy and decadent. Hank downed his entire flute in three swallows, then suppressed a belch, laughing as Jason attempted to quickly empty his glass, resulting in facial contortions and an involuntary shudder.

"Hank, you gotta remember I'm a lightweight," he insisted, certain he could feel each bubble zipping up to pixillate his brain.

"You're in Beverly Hills now, bud. This stuff is like Nestlé's Quik up here." He refilled the flutes. "It's your turn, Jason. What are we toasting?"

"Can't think. Too drunk."

"All right. I got one. To the Burkes. For making you our neighbor."

"God bless those Burkes," Jason snickered. Their glasses smashed together. "Careful. These are their glasses." Jason took a long draught, sighed contentedly and extended his legs under the table to the opposite chair. There was enough room for both himself and Hank, but they were touching, just barely, enough for Jason to feel the hair on Hank's calf against Jason's left foot. A prickly sensation tingled through this foot up past Jason's ankle. He blamed it on the wine. "I'm sure I would have met Marina someday," Jason said. "It had to be my destiny, house-sitting gig or not."

"I think your destiny was to be right here this summer, in Queen Bitch Maggie's mansion," Hank said after a moment's pause.

"And why is that?"

"Well . . . because if you'd met Marina a little later down the line, I probably never would have gotten to know you," Hank said in a voice that might have been inaudible if the CD changer hadn't been between tracks, shuffling. Hank was looking away from him, at the city lights, but his leg was pressing firmly against Jason's foot. Hank's right hand released his empty champagne flute, and as Everything But the Girl's gorgeous cover of "Time After Time" chimed forth on the cooling, fragrant, hillside air, Hank turned to face him with a look that rendered all else that had taken place in Jason's life momentarily meaningless, vague and forgotten, a black-and-white drive-in movie glimpsed through fitful sleep in the backseat.

Hank's foot grazed across Jason's, then moved up Jason's leg, past his knee, under the towel. His right hand dropped to Jason's hip then spread out as his fingers slid up Jason's stomach. When he had Jason's left pectoral firmly cupped, his wildly pounding heart-beat literally in the palm of his hand, Hank leaned forward and kissed him.

Jason, stricken with paralysis everywhere but the groin, neither closed nor opened his mouth. This was insane. The expensive champagne was making him hallucinate. Hank Rietta *could not be* doing this—Hank stood, his towel fluttering to the patio. His left arm encircled Jason and gently pulled him to his feet, their mouths still pressed hotly, tentatively together. Hank broke the kiss and trailed his fingers up Jason's back and neck, raking them slowly through his damp hair. Jason looked down and found himself staring at Hank's penis arcing skyward. Oh, Jesus. He looked up and into Hank's eyes. Even worse. "Hank, what are you—I don't understand," Jason stammered. "Marina—"

Hank laid his fingers against Jason's lips. "It's okay. I can't be with her anymore. I'm gay, Jason. And I've wanted you for so long. If you feel anything at all, don't fight it, buddy. Please . . ." Hank slid his fingertips down so they were between Jason's lips. Jason closed his eyes and allowed Hank's fingers into his mouth. Then he was suckling them. He felt the towel around his waist unfastened and pulled aside. Still he felt frozen, his limbs rigidly suspended between the realization of how *wrong* this was and the insanity of denying the most incendiary mutual attraction he would certainly ever feel.

The fingers of Hank's other hand were hooked into the side of the Speedo. Jason opened his eyes and Hank withdrew his wet fingers from Jason's mouth, bringing them down to Jason's nipple, moistening and tweaking and teasing it. "Oh, fuck. Come here, Jason." Then Hank's hands were on his ass and their dicks were mashed together with only the thinnest sheath of nylon between them and Hank was kissing his shoulders and the side of his neck. Warm breath and a flicking tongue and the unbearably erotic scrape of five o'clock shadow below his ear eroded resistance until it was impossible to do anything but melt into Hank's arms.

The master bedroom had the biggest bed (king as opposed to Jason's twin) and the best view, but its selection had been based entirely on its sliding glass doors, which happened to be two feet from where Hank had yanked off Jason's swimsuit. The hour since then had been a continuous surrender to Hank's tireless sexual passion—he was ravenous, every movement and caress burning with a feverish, near-desperate intensity, yet hyperaware of Jason and sensitive to his smallest actions and responses, Hank constantly whispering in his ear, wanting to know if something was okay to try or felt good or just calling him "baby" and "beautiful" and "dicksucker."

Now, however, Hank wasn't saying much of anything, since his mouth was otherwise occupied. Sprawled on his back diagonally across the bed, fists clenched around the pillow under his head, Jason looked in dumbstruck awe at Hank lying between his legs, languidly stroking the lower two-thirds of Jason's engorged cock, swallowing the rest, swirling his tongue around the corona, forcing the head against the roof of his mouth.

Hank went down on the entire length, his hands massaging the insides of Jason's thighs, then slowly came up and off the penis, which maintained its rigid ninety-degree angle no-handed, harder than it had been before Jason shot his first load twenty minutes ago. Hank tightened his fist around it again, then with the other hand squeezed a single drop of lubricant from a handy tube and slicked it down the shaft. Apparently there was a stockpile of accessories of which Jason had been unaware, because Hank was now fitting a condom over Jason's dick. He rolled it down to the base then drizzled it with lube. What the hell was this? Surely Hank didn't expect him to f—

Hank got on his knees and straddled him, wielding Jason's erection in his slippery hand. He was facing him, so Jason could not actually see his penis disappearing between Hank's firm, white buttocks. But Hank's tensed muscles and turning-Japanese face and stiff cock wagging above Jason's stomach were the most heart-stoppingly erotic vision ever, matched by the never-before-experienced sensation of jamming his dick inch by torturously delicious inch into another guy's actual, honest-to-God butthole.

He thought he would die before Hank was able to get it all the way in, then when he did and started to move, Jason realized exactly what the big deal about fucking was. Hank took his hand, and Jason reached up and stroked his beautiful chest, the silky black hair dewy with sweat, down his stomach until he had Hank's penis in his hand. "Yeah . . . squeeze it. Ohhh, Jason, you feel so good inside me . . . Shit . . . wait . . . I'm really close." He gently moved Jason from his cock.

Jason's hands traveled up Hank's sides to his shoulders and held tight as he locked his legs around Hank's hips and sat up, their bodies still one, mouths hungrily devouring each other, Hank's tongue slithering between Jason's lips in frenzied counterpoint to Jason's thrusts.

"Jesus, Jason, I'm gonna cum," Hank moaned, his lips hot against Jason's ear, his chin digging rough little barbs of pleasure into Jason's neck. Jason held him tighter, rocking forward farther and farther till Hank's back hit the mattress, his legs were in the air, and his hands were on Jason's ass. Jason pumped faster and rubbed his face on Hank's chest and grabbed Hank's dick, which splattered Jason's hand and stomach and Hank's whole torso with a torrent of cum. Jason rammed into him as he felt his own orgasm begin and then somehow suspend itself so that instead of just ejaculating a second time he was being drained of every tension that had ever troubled his mind or body and he lay trembling on top of Hank, the guidelines for prompt withdrawal and condom disposal from the safer-sex seminar he'd taken for extra credit his third year of college completely escaping him.

Hank dispelled another stereotype about big, butch he-men by not dropping off to sleep. He lay there, arm hooked around Jason's waist, and told him everything—how Hank had ignored the high school fantasies about guys that had gradually become more vivid and persistent, how he had spent college sublimating his attractions to his male classmates and frat brothers and Rupert Everett by dating and screwing and dumping a bevy of fun-loving coeds. After graduation, he gladly became a workaholic, leaving no room in his life for anything but international finance and four weekly workouts at the straightest East Side gym he could find. When he met Marina shortly after being transferred to L.A., he thought the problem had been licked, so to speak. She was the best lover he'd ever known, but as he later reflected, much more importantly, she needed friendship, emotional support and stability far more than sex.

He called his first "phone fantasy hunk" from a scrap of paper he'd torn out of the yellow section of *Frontiers* magazine two months after Marina left rehab. That had proven the single thread that unraveled the carefully woven cloak of rationalizations and denial in which his secret self had been so cozily bundled since his first wet dream. Hank found himself powerless to resist feeding the priapic beast he'd awakened—stealthily stashed copies of *Freshmen* and *Inches*, 1-900 car phone jack-off sessions in deserted parking garages, covert cybersex with on-line pals named ButtSlut and LongNThik. When he realized he could no longer make love to Marina without elaborate homoerotic fantasizing both before and during, he knew the marriage had to end. He would tell her after *Ghost in the Fog* was released and she'd had some successful concerts. He loved her and still wanted to be part of her life but knew that might not be possible.

Jason had been basically silent through this entire confession, but he had at least one question. "This wasn't the first time you ever . . . were with a guy, was it?"

Hank said nothing for a long beat. "No. The first time was just after Christmas. I was in a hotel in New York and I ordered a massage. Like I needed to pretend it was something else right up until the guy put my cock in his mouth. I don't want to lie to you. I've done it maybe once a month since then. People I pick up at Spike or the Sports Connection, sometimes through sex ads. The last time was when I was in Bangkok. A threeway with this Eurasian model and his boyfriend from Norway or Sweden or something. Nothing too heavy, all really, really safe. That sounds so shitty, but I'm not a whore. I felt like I was going out of my mind and it was like a short-term solution. But it's all over. I swear to you. Tonight was the first time anyone's fucked me. And it was the first time I was with anyone I cared about. And it was incredible, Jason." He rolled on top of Jason for a soft, deep kiss.

"I loved it, too, Hank. But Marina—I just . . ." He couldn't say it, not with Hank on top of him, playing with his hair.

"Jason, I've been thinking about this for weeks. Wanting us to be together. I know Marina means so much more to you than just a friend, but she and I can't work. She's going to have a tough time, but if you and I are miserable, too, what good does that do anybody?"

"I don't know," Jason murmured, suddenly too tired to think about any of it. And Hank felt so warm . . . Jason fell asleep thinking he should stay awake all night just to memorize what every minute of being there felt like.

He woke up, disoriented by the unfamiliar bed and the expanse of bright midmorning sunshine via the uncurtained glass wall facing the pool. Hank was out there putting on his clothes. Oh, Christ. Last night. Hank was coming back across the patio. Jason snapped his eyes shut, pretending to sleep. He couldn't deal with this yet. He heard the sliding door click shut and kept his face blank and his breathing slow and even. Nothing happened for at least a minute, then he felt a hand settle gently on his shoulder and Hank's soft lips kissing his for the briefest moment.

Jason lay frozen until he heard the Infiniti start in the driveway, then jumped out of bed. In the center of the blue-gray carpet was a small square of paper. It was a note written on the back of a dry-cleaning receipt.

Hi—Had to go to work. I'll call you tonight, buddy. Miss you.
                                                                    Hank.

Buddy? Could anything be sexier? And "miss you"? He folded the note and sank back to the bed, pulling the rumpled sheets around him. He inhaled the pillow, pressing it against him. It smelled exactly like Hank. His mind spun backward, needing to arrange the previous night's developments into some kind of sensible order. Oh, God, was that a car coming up the drive?

It was. Hank probably forgot something. And here he was, naked, with bed hair and bad breath. Holy shit. What if it was Maggie, back from Texas and out for blood? Look at this bedroom! He bolted into the kitchen and sprang onto the counter, fingers, toes and balls crossed. It was a Federal Express van. He streaked to his room and hopped into a pair of boxer shorts, which received barely a first let alone second glance from the kd lang fan who traded Jason's signature for an envelope with Mermaid Records' New York office in the Sender block.

He zipped it open and discovered a cassette tape wrapped in a piece of Paramount hotel stationery upon which Marina had scribbled a note.

Dearest Jason
I'll be home Monday night but could not wait to get this to you. Hope you like it. It's really "your song."
Love & Kisses, Marina.

He inspected the tape. MARINA STETSON—YOU DON'T KNOW—3:13. This was the sixties cover they had added—1965, to be exact. Originally recorded by Ellie Greenwich, the composer who pioneered the girl group sound with such all-time classics as "Leader of the Pack" and "Chapel of Love" with husband Jeff Barry and George "Shadow" Morton for Red Bird Records, "You Don't Know" was a very obscure nonhit that tenth-grader Jason had found in a box of his aunt's old 45's. He hadn't included it on the tape he'd made Marina, but it was on a supplemental list he'd attached of other recommended songs. And it was the one they'd picked.

He warily inserted it into the cassette deck and hit Play. "You . . . don't . . . know . . . what I've been going through," Marina huskily crooned, "since the day I laid eyes on you/And you . . . don't . . . know . . . how hard it is to hide/All my love, baby, deep inside." He remembered the words but was unprepared for the chill that pervaded his entire body at Marina singing them.

"And I'll pray that's the way it's gonna stay," Marina confessed to acoustic guitar and some dynamic percussion, "And day by day I'll just pretend/'Cause she's my friend/And I can't let her know/I really love you so/Won't somebody help me/Oh, help me/Please help me . . ." She might as well have sent him a fax saying "How dare you fuck my husband!?!"

He reread Marina's note. Oh, it was his song, all right. This one goes out to Hank Rietta from your wife's Number One Fan! "And I'll try not to cry/When you walk by/'Cause she's just like a sister

to me/And she is so in love with you/I don't know what to do/Won't
somebody help me/Please help me/I love you . . ." If he hadn't spent
the night getting it on with Hank in every possible way, Jason knew
he would have found the song delightful. As things were, he could
barely peck out Violet's number on the cordless phone. There. It was
ringing. *Won't somebody help me . . . Please help me . . .* He mindlessly wandered into the master bedroom, the scene of the crime.
Violet's machine answered. Damn! He left a message, asking her to
call back soon, it was important.

After examining the linens for offensive stains, he set about making the bed in a guilt-wracked daze. How could he have done this
to Marina? *But Hank seduced me . . .* What bullshit. But it's not like
Marina hadn't crossed his mind . . . Jason had been uncomfortable
about it from the moment he caught Hank skinny-dipping. Oh, yes,
he taunted himself bitterly. *So* uncomfortable you just rolled that man
over and fucked him up the ass. And loved it! How the hell had
those pillows been? He approximated the arrangement, then reached
out to adjust one of the big ones. Was it the one Hank had slept on?
He sat on the leathered bed rail and lowered his face to the pillow.
God, yes. It was wonderful. And he said he missed me—

Jason recoiled and fled the room. He had to clean up the pool
area. His Speedo, which Hank had thoughtfully folded and placed
on a chaise. *Yeah, after he ripped it off with his teeth.* The glasses,
the Dom Pérignon bottle. *That was the answer: you were drunk.* All
that wine at dinner, then half a bottle of champagne? Okay, maybe
he could live with that. For now. He'd just gathered up an armful
of stray towels when the phone rang. He ran in and answered it.

"Hi, what's wrong?" Violet. Thank God.

"Um . . . I just really have to talk to you about something that
sort of, uh . . . happened to me last night."

"Are you okay? What is it?"

"Yeah, I'm fine. Are you busy, like, now?"

"I just got back from aerobics. I need to take a shower . . ."

"Me, too. But in like an hour?"

"Sure. No plans. Should I come over?"

"No." He wanted to get out and stay out and never come back.
"How 'bout your place?"

"Sure . . . Jason, are you all right? You sound a little nuts."

"I am, a little. But I can't go into it over the phone."

"Okay, now I feel like I'm back on *One Life to Live*."

"Just wait."

He felt better as soon as he saw the mansion gate close behind him in his rearview mirror. Violet was the perfect person to discuss this with. He could be completely honest with her and she would be helpful, sympathetic and, above all, nonjudgmental.

"Twisted, filthy and wrong, *that's* what I think. Jason, how could you?" Violet demanded, incredulous, after he'd spilled his guts. His face crumbled and she grabbed his hand. "Sorry, kid. But you said you wanted my unvarnished opinion."

"I know you're right," he sighed miserably, sectioning off a wedge of the omelette she'd made him. "But what am I supposed to do?"

"Break it off. Clean and fast. Preferably before Marina gets back from New York."

"How can this be my life?" he bitched, exasperated. "Nobody displays, like, a fraction of romantic interest in me since I moved here. I meet a guy who's really nice and incredibly sexy and *straight*, so I get this big, harmless crush on him, which is fine, until he says, 'Hello. I want you. Take me.' So now I have to choose between the most perfect boyfriend I could ever dream up and Marina Stetson? I refuse to accept that."

"Accept it. And what do you mean, *choose*? There is no choice," Violet argued. "You may not believe it now, but trust me, there are plenty of perfect boyfriends out there for you. There is one Marina Stetson. She's your idol. And she considers you a trusted friend."

"I can't believe I actually had sex with him," Jason said. He finished the eggs and brought his plate to the sink. "What a mistake. It was a complete betrayal of Marina. And now I know exactly what I'm missing. Jesus Christ."

"We can't change what happened. Regrets are wasted energy. Let's concentrate on the present. Marina is already nervous about the new album, right?" He nodded. "Her whole career is basically on the line. Not the best moment to find out she's married to a gay guy who wants a divorce. She's going to need your support to get through this."

"What was Hank thinking? How could he expect me to—" Jason went to the couch and beat his head against a cushion.

"Look, I'm sure he was feeling scared and desperate and trapped. And you can't blame him for liking you. You're adorable." She sat next to him and pulled his head to her shoulder. "But aren't you a little curious about what Hank might have been doing with God-knows-how-many cute young studs before he got up the nerve to make his move with you?"

In an instinctive urge to protect him, Jason had omitted Hank's confession of his recent all-male sexploits. "He said he just wanted to be with me. Besides, I wore a condom."

"I would have worn two," Violet said.

Eager to change the subject, Jason asked her what was happening with her career. "Oh, haven't I told you? It's over."

"Come on. You've only been out of work a few days."

"Yeah, and my agent hasn't bothered to call me once," she snorted.

"If he's such a turd, you should get rid of him," Jason said.

"Probably. But you can't break your contract if you've worked within ninety days. And don't think it'd be that easy for me to waltz into a good agency and get signed. *Chillin' with Billy* is the joke of the whole damn town. I need to get something decent, like a movie, really soon."

"So no word from Aldo?"

Violet shook her head. "Nothin'. I've been checking the trades every day for anything about *You Lucky Bastard*, but if they've cast the lead, it hasn't been announced."

"Tricia can't help you at all?" Jason asked.

"She has been acting so weird. Like really nice and friendly and chatty? I mean, normally she has this very *superior* tone," Violet said, imitating her, "not exactly condescending but very 'Don't be stupid, of course I know what's best.' " Jason nodded, familiar with it. "And now she's . . . relaxed, somehow. But she's not focusing on *me,* that's for sure. Yesterday, she sent me on a *Murder, She Wrote* audition. Bad enough, right? But I would have gladly done a guest lead. So I drive all the way to Universal—you know how fucking hot it was—and get the sides right before I'm supposed to read for the producers and it's literally four lines. I was shocked."

"Did you audition?"

"No way. I very politely explained to the casting director that I had been under the impression it was a more substantial role and I felt it was best for my career to take only guest leads. Which is so humiliating because you know they're thinking, 'Who the hell are *you* and why are you wasting everyone's time?' and that I'm some kind of schmuck for having an agent stupid enough to submit me for bit parts. So I called Tricia—Edgar had left for the day, conveniently—and she apologized and said Edgar thought I needed some dramatic TV credits." She took a Crystal Geyser from the fridge and roughly yanked off the bottle cap.

"What was *Leather & Lace*?" asked Jason.

Violet shrugged, rolling her eyes. "What was touring in a David Mamet play? What was the soap I did? And two Broadway shows? Thank Christ I saved all my *Chillin'* money."

"You've got enough to live for a while?"

"The rest of the year, easy," Violet said. "In fact, let's go to the mall and spend some of it. I want to buy you a new outfit for your first day of work."

He protested but was actually relieved she wanted to spend time together. He knew he'd start to suffer renewed Hank-xiety before the day was over and, sure enough, when Jason retrieved messages late that afternoon from the Westside Pavilion, Hank's voice on the machine made Jason's heart ache and his guts clench.

"Hi, buddy, it's Hank. I'm going to be here at the office the whole goddamn day but maybe we can get together for a late dinner." He left his private number at the bank. Jason replayed the message for Violet and felt an overpowering sense of dread.

She thought for only a moment. "Okay. Here's what you do. Call him back and say you're spending tonight cheering up your friend who just broke up with her boyfriend. Which isn't even a lie. And tonight we're going to forget about this, go have dinner and see this hilarious late show I heard about. Tomorrow you can talk to Hank in person and tell him whatever you're going to tell him."

Relieved and grateful, Jason managed a weak smile. "Thanks, Violet. Will you come stay at the house tonight? Slumber party?"

She considered cracking a joke about seducing Jason into anal sex but wisely decided against it. "Sure." She handed him the pay phone receiver.

He dialed Hank's number, hoping for voice mail. Hank picked up. The conversation was brief, untraumatic, as rehearsed. Hank would call him the next morning. Jason hung up quickly, before Hank could say anything sexy or adorable. "All right. That's officially postponed until tomorrow."

"Good. We can work on your dumping speech later," Violet promised. "Hopefully you can tell him before that dinner party tomorrow night."

Jason winced, moaning. "I forgot about that. I'm praying that wasn't another colossal error."

"I don't think so! You got the job, Jason."

"Yeah, I did, didn't I? I'm just worried about the furniture. I wish I knew they were going to stay out of the living room."

"Jason, you are in control here. You have what you want out of the deal already. Lay down the law with GAG Management and don't take any shit," Violet insisted. "I'm sure everything'll be fine. Wait a sec. What if that pissy old realtor queen drops by to show the place to somebody?"

The thought had never crossed his mind. "Fuck! You're right. What can I do?"

"Hmmm." She put her shopping bags down and folded her arms over her breasts, wheels spinning. "What if Maggie Burke called Syd and told him not to bring anyone by?"

"But why would she—?" he began. Violet was already on the phone. She dialed 411 and requested the number of Syd Swann. Five seconds later she plunked in two dimes and dialed again.

"Yes, hello?" Suddenly Violet was channeling Maggie. "Maggie Burke for Syd, please . . ." Jason stood by gape-mouthed. "Oh, he isn't? . . . I see . . . Yes, I am . . . Texas . . . He doesn't need my number. I won't wish to be disturbed . . . Just let him know I do *not* want the house shown tomorrow . . . The decorators will be there all day and evening . . . Any appointments can wait until Monday . . . That's right. And to whom am I speaking? Thank you, Yoram." She hung up triumphantly. "I *won't* wish to be disturbed!"

she repeated, twisting her hand into a claw and tightening it around Jason's shirt before cracking up.

"How did you do that?" he demanded.

"I'm an actress, Jason. I bring characters to life. As if by magic. I remember Maggie quite well, thank you. The bitch threw me out of her pool, remember?"

They killed a couple more hours in Westwood Village, then headed back up to Violet's to freshen up. She had her heart set on Marix for dinner, a near-suicidal choice on a Saturday night, but they bravely checked in with the host and staked out a few square feet by the bar to pass the projected hour-long wait drinking expensive, lethal margaritas and checking out the grade-A West Hollywood beefcake packing the hellaciously popular patio café from top to aggressive bottom.

Violet and Jason split a second pitcher over dinner, which only enhanced their enjoyment of the show Violet had selected, conveniently located next door at the Coast Playhouse. Titled *Little Darling Dykes*, it was a brilliant Sapphic spoof of the 1980 teen classic about summer camp rivals engaged in a contest to see who can lose her virginity first. The Tatum O'Neal role, a petulant, spoiled, lonely rich girl, was spectacularly portrayed by Jackie Beat, an enormous and enormously talented drag diva. Alexis Arquette was hilarious in a winged wig as Kristy McNichol's petulant, street-smart tomboy. The petulant, bitchy brat who goads the gals into their cherry-popping competition was played by a glamorous, deadpan gender-bender identified in the program as Candy Ass.

They got back to the mansion around twelve-thirty, changed into their jammies and baked frozen Pillsbury cookie dough. Jason asked about the breakup with Dave. Violet said they hadn't spoken since the night of the ill-fated *Billy* premiere. As far as she was concerned, he could take his dog clippers and shove them up his ass. "Okay, so maybe this whole thing isn't all his fault," she conceded, flipping the sizzling disks of dough onto a plate. "But he's way too controlling for me. We shouldn't be together. I haven't decided if I'm going to break this to my mother at lunch tomorrow or not. Her meddling engines will already be in overdrive about my career now that the show's canceled."

She asked to hear the tape Marina sent him. He swallowed the knot of tension that instantly formed at the mention of the song and led her into the foyer/dining area. The cassette was still in the deck. They listened to it in the dark, leaning against the bar. "You know I don't believe in any of that New Age bullshit, Jason," Violet said after the song had faded into grim, pregnant silence, "but that is a horrific signal from the universe that your karma is in real danger."

"I'll tell him tomorrow," said Jason dully.

Violet gave him a hug and went into the servants' bathroom to get ready for bed. Jason stripped to underwear and got into his bed, reflecting, as he turned the sheets down, that the last time he'd slept there he'd had neither a job nor Hank. How could his life have veered off into such an orbit in forty-eight hours? Violet entered in a network T-shirt and panties and slid into the other twin bed. "You're thinking that the last time you were in a bed it was with him, aren't you?" she asked.

Uncanny. So where the hell was she last night at the pool when he *really* needed her?

The phone started jangling at ten the next morning with call after call. Jason felt more of his nerves fray with each successive ring, none of which heralded the call from Hank he was simultaneously hoping for and dreading. Gail phoned no less than six times, asking if she could come at four instead of five-thirty, if he had a corkscrew (yes) and wineglasses she could use (no) or should she bring her own (yes), if Jason could call Ryan Olstrum (the bartender) and give him directions—Gail was out of maps. Patina called to confirm that they were catering dinner and dessert for eleven and asked for directions, which Jason patiently repeated three times, mildly curious about how Gail intended to fit eleven people at a dining table that seated eight. Ryan Olstrum returned Jason's call, wondering what to wear.

Hank did not call and Jason did not call Hank, a tiny, stubbornly deluded mental voice insisting that there was an excellent chance the whole situation would just evaporate if left untouched for a little while. Basically Jason was scared shitless, and the more he tried to rehearse what he was going to say to Hank, the worse he felt.

Obsessing over Hank consumed Jason's every available brain

cell, leaving no room to worry about Gail Ann Griffin's soiree. The hostess showed up just after four, loaded down with a box of candles, glassware, napkins, shoes and what looked like the entire MAC and Aveda product lines, as well as a hanger from which billowed some designer atrocity. She asked if there was a room she could use to get ready in later and got a little frosty when Jason directed her to his room and adjoining, no-frills *salle de bain.* Well, fuck her. Violet was so right—now that he had the Aquarius Images job (which, God forbid Gail should feign enough consideration to actually ask about), Jason had the upper hand.

"Just to make sure everything's sort of clear between us," Jason began saying to Gail, who was intensely creating a centerpiece for the dining table, "we should get a couple things straight."

"Sure, honey," she chirped, jerking her head in his direction as if it were attached to a marionette string. "Is there a problem?"

"No . . . but we're agreeing to keep this dinner a secret, right? Fawn and her family and Andre can't ever know about it." Gail pantomimed zipping her lips. "And there can't be any smoking anywhere. Not even outside. There aren't any ashtrays," Jason continued, feeling fairly assertive but still expecting attitude from Gail any second.

Instead, she enthusiastically concurred. "Oh, I would never dream of letting anyone smoke in this gorgeous house. Please don't worry, Jason. This is going to be an elegant, low-key affair." This pronouncement coincided with the arrival of Ryan Olstrum, his truck doing sixty to zero as he slammed on the brakes outside the door after barreling up the driveway, Nirvana blaring from the pickup's cab.

"And Gail, I've really got to ask you to do your, uh . . . entertaining in this area right here and, you know, the kitchen. The furniture is really expensive, so I keep hearing, and they don't even want *me* in the other rooms, so . . ."

"Jason, I personally guarantee everything in this house will be left in the exact condition it's in right now," she said on her way to open the door. "Try to relax and enjoy the party. We'll have Ryan fix you a drinkie."

The caterers showed up next, annexing the kitchen, making lots of noise Jason hoped was not generated by any activity likely to cause a stain. Why the hell wasn't Hank calling? Jason checked both phones' ringers. On. He was momentarily distracted by the appearance of Wren, who looked remarkably healthy and cute despite the fact that she was wearing what seemed to be a fairy princess costume minus the conical pointy hat. She and Gail were exchanging hugs, Wren's drugged-out truancy from the final night of the showcase obviously forgiven. Way to keep this discreet, Gail. Invite Andre's ex- and possibly future roommate. It turned out Wren was not precisely *invited*, though—Gail had hired her to amuse the guests by doing psychic readings before dinner.

It was time for Gail to gussy herself up, so she vanished into Jason's quarters, leaving him nowhere to be but loitering in the dining/foyer/bar area, nursing a wine spritzer, forced to participate in an insipid and pathetic conversation with Ryan and Wren RE: their careers as deadbeat starlets.

"I had *so* many auditions last week I had to quit Ed Debevic's," Wren told them. "I'm going to get offered this student film at USC. The director showed me his reel and he is a *genius*, man. He's going to be the next Roberto Rodriguez."

"Thursday I had a callback for *Red Shoe Diaries*," Ryan boasted. "What are you up to, Jason?"

"I just got a job with a video production and distribution company," he replied, not elaborating even though Ryan really needed work and the Aquarius Images casting department would doubtlessly be quite interested in getting the dishy blonde Minnesotan out of his clothes. Jason asked them if they knew who was coming to dinner tonight.

Wren naturally had no idea, but Ryan said, "This comedian Gail wants to sign. I think her name's Doll Babcock. She's from Nashville. She's probably gonna get her own TV series soon. Some kind of deal with Walt Disney. Do they do TV, too?"

"Uh-huh," Jason nodded without a trace of condescension.

"Oh, and Turk Marlowe. From *Leather & Lace*?"

"Cool!" Wren giggled. "I hope he lets me do a reading." With the right props, he'll probably let you do a lot more than that, Jason thought.

Gail finally emerged, swathed in black harem pants decorated with rhinestones swirling up from the cuffs, and more appallingly, a sheer black top that left shoulders bare and a strapless bra completely visible beneath a wild pattern of puckered black shapes that made it look like Siouxsie of the Banshees had just kissed every inch of the garment.

Jason went to his room to change. While he was deciding between two of Andre's jackets, he heard a car in the driveway and felt a conditioned cardio-gastric palpitation, but he ignored it. He knew it was one of Gail's guests, but so what if it *was* Maggie? Let her throw him out. He had a job now, and he could always bunk on Violet's couch while he looked for his own place. He'd start checking the papers this week, so as soon as Maggie did park her broomstick back at the Hotel Bel-Air, he could blow out of here for good.

When he got back, Gail was nibbling hors d'oeuvres with Edgar Black while Ryan mixed drinks for a leggy, blonde Azzedine Alaia'd vixen; a gangly, frizzy-haired gal whose plastic surgery was evident from twenty feet away; and swarthy male Eurotrash marinated in Halston for Men. Gail introduced Jason to the newcomers, who proved to be, respectively, Kendra, Edgar's date; "producer" Wendi Barash; and her boyfriend Igor, who was directing *Prying Eyes*, the new movie Edgar was packaging.

Jason squeezed in beside Ryan and loaded the CD changer with Harry Connick Jr., the *Maurice* soundtrack, and *Sensual Classics*, all from Andre's collection. He eavesdropped on Edgar and Igor. ". . . so it looks like the Ione Skye thing is all sewn up. I talked to her Friday. We'll take care of the details tomorrow. You'll be able to start on time," Edgar said, smiling wolfishly before devouring a miniquiche.

"Excellent," Igor rasped in a Slavic accent. "I want her up there right away. We rehearse. Next week we shoot. But I worry about Marc Singer. He flew in last Wednesday, and we have had some strange conversations about character and script and emotional centers. Bullshit, do you know?"

Edgar slid an arm around Igor's dandruff-dusted shoulders. "Marc's just concerned about his craft. He's one of the most talented actors I rep. And he's a dream to work with. You can ask the *Body Chemistry* people."

"What part am *I* going to play?" Kendra pouted, putting her arm around Igor, too.

"For you—aerobicising murder victim. Big scene on balcony," Igor promised.

"Awesome! That's perfect 'cause I used to teach aerobics."

Edgar clapped her on the back and slid his hand down to rest on her hip by way of her ass. "I'll have Tricia get the contract over to you tomorrow."

"Where is the Bionic Assistant tonight?" Wendi elbowed Edgar. "Although I have to admit, the last few weeks she's been a lot friendlier."

"Haven't noticed," Edgar said, motioning Ryan for a refill.

"You don't have that poor thing slaving away for you as we speak, do you?" Gail teased Edgar.

"Yeah. I told her she had to work Sunday nights. We run a tight ship over there, but I got bills to pay. She's back at the office doing Conan Carroll's nails right this minute," Edgar deadpanned.

"Oh, Edgar, you're so wicked!" Kendra squealed.

"And this one knows wicked. Trust me," Wendi added, pinching Kendra's apparently irresistible butt. Jason made an hors d'oeuvres sweep then hid in the breakfast nook to devour his shamefully over-loaded plate.

Edgar had of course absolutely no idea that Tricia was indeed hard at work at his office that very moment. She'd also been in for several hours on Saturday, finding the solitude and quiet—any phone calls were automatically forwarded to the answering service—ideal for her tasks. One of her chief tasks Saturday afternoon had been a call to Ione Skye during which Tricia had confessed that Edgar did not seem to have the actress's best interests at heart and that Tricia, who respected Ione's talent and was fond of her as a person, wouldn't feel right about letting her take the role in Wendi Barash's produc-tion of *Prying Eyes* without informing Ms. Skye that the part had been turned down by all the other "A" names on Edgar's list, in-cluding Drew Barrymore and Lara Flynn Boyle, and that Edgar's primary concern was locking in the final piece to complete the pack-age before shooting commenced, that in fact he was quite desperate to do so. Ione, fresh from being pampered by Edgar at a recent ego-stroking lunch at The Ivy, had been unaware Edgar represented any other movie actresses in her category and listened to Tricia's revelations with much alarm, which quickly turned to anger when Ione received several breakdown pages with her name buried in laundry lists of Edgar's clients (in his own handwriting) next to corresponding film roles she'd never met on. Tricia had removed these pages from Edgar's movie submission file and faxed them to Ione's home just in time for the actress to type out a letter terminating her representation by Edgar and get it to the post office to send to the agency via registered mail.

It had been a busy week for Tricia. Late Wednesday, at Stefan's suggestion, she'd compiled a list of Edgar's top twenty-five clients, their addresses, private phone and fax numbers. (List A, Tricia mentally christened it.) She then assembled a list of ten rival agents from firms equally prestigious or more powerful than Conan Carroll. (Or List B.) After a walk to the mall for Edgar's yogurt shake and prescription refill, she typed out ten different lists of five randomly selected entries from List A and anonymously placed one list each in ten different envelopes, each addressed to a different person from List B. Imagining the rampant plundering and counterplundering that would take place when this irresistible bait reached its ever-greedy, sharklike addressees made her nipples throb with each zap of the postal meter.

Thursday morning, the jiggling ben-wa balls Stefan had implanted in her vagina during *Live with Regis and Kathie Lee* rendering each step she took a delicious masturbatory assault, Tricia typed a complete set of breakdowns per Edgar's notes, pulled the appropriate photos and résumés for each submission, stuffed and addressed the delivery envelopes, deposited photocopies of all seven cover sheets in Edgar's box for filing after lunch, then sent all seven envelopes sailing down the hallway garbage chute next to the janitors' closet.

But Friday had been best of all. Edgar had finagled a meeting with Cicely Tyson, who was disenchanted with her current representation. Ms. Tyson was concerned about discretion, so eschewed a restaurant luncheon for an informal morning meeting at Edgar's office. Tricia greeted the multi–award-winning star with a freshly brewed cup of rose hips tea and a sincere statement of admiration for her many fine performances. "And Edgar will do a wonderful job representing you," Tricia said, leaning in to murmur this confidentially, eliciting an annoyed "as-if-I-could-care-less-about-anything-you-could-possibly-think-you-have-to-keep-secret" snort from Misty the receptionist.

"He specializes in handling actresses and is quite well known for his rapport with them. In fact, he just spent nearly two hours with this talented newcomer, developing strategies for launching her career." Tricia handed Ms. Tyson an especially slutty photo of Debbra, a vacant-eyed blonde and her cleavage Tricia had plucked from Edgar's mail the day before. She allowed the star to dubiously regard the head shot for only a moment before whisking it away. "Edgar's just freshening up and he'll be with you in one minute," Tricia assured Ms. Tyson.

Edgar was in fact winding up a meeting with all the other agents and a personal management team in Conan's office and had never laid eyes on the slutty blonde or her head shot, which Tricia crumpled into a wad and deposited in her deskside wastebasket. From her purse, she then withdrew a sealed Ziploc freezer bag, which she slid between two three-ring submission binders and carried to Edgar's office.

Once inside, she opened the Ziploc and removed its contents, a pair of her black underwear, still rather wet with the semen Stefan had shot into them that morning during a little game they often played before work called Baby Nastypanties. Tricia wedged the sticky satin beneath the arm and cushion of Edgar's comfiest guest chair, leaving about an inch of lacy material visible at the very edge of the seat. She adjusted the panties slightly, then bopped back to reception to fetch Ms. Tyson.

"Edgar will be with you directly," she smiled, indicating the comfy chair. Ms. Tyson sat, thanking her, apparently oblivious to the surprise Tricia had planted. Oh, well . . . a minute or so and she was bound to notice what "Debbra" had left behind, and then what would Edgar's chances of signing her be? Absolutely—

"Cicely!" Edgar exclaimed. "What a pleasure to see you again. Tricia, hold all calls," he winked, placing his hands on her waist and turning her toward the door.

Damnit! Why had Edgar picked today of all times to be on top of his schedule? She had planned on giving Cicely a moment alone before buzzing him that she'd arrived. Maybe it didn't matter. It actually might be better for the discovery to be made in front of Edgar. All Tricia had to do was sit at her desk and wait. So she waited. And waited. Twenty minutes had gone by, Tricia noted with exasperation after curtly taking yet another message for Edgar. What if the panties festered there undiscovered while he shmoozed a major star into changing agencies, throwing all of her meticulous under-mining of the past weeks horribly out of balance?

There was an excellent chance Cicely had noticed something odd lodged under her seat cushion, Tricia reasoned, but felt inhibited about tugging it out for examination with Edgar sitting right across from her. Tricia's only hope was to get her boss out of his office. The phone rang, solving the problem. It was a prominent and wacko feature casting director unaffectionately dubbed "Morticia" by most of The Business. Tricia had been ignoring progressively frantic mes-sages from Morticia's assistants since Wednesday as part of Tricia's plan to completely shut Edgar out of the tiresome would-be block-buster Morticia was now casting, but Cicely Tyson was an emer-gency.

Tricia put Morticia on hold and knocked on Edgar's door. "It's Tricia!"

"Come in," Edgar called with obviously far less irritation than he felt.

Tricia opened the door and smiled at Cicely while simultane-ously checking for the panties. They hadn't moved. Tricia turned to Edgar and told him who was on the line. "Sorry to interrupt, Edgar, but she said it was urgent and she has to talk to you right now."

Edgar's hand went to his forehead as he struggled to stay on his best behavior in front of a prospective client. "Fine," was all he said. He reached for the phone.

"Uh, Edgar?" Tricia interjected, beckoning with her index finger when he looked at her.

"Excuse me," he said to Cicely. "I'll only be a minute." He exited the office, pulling Tricia by the arm and shutting the door behind him.

"What the hell is going on?" he hissed.

"Edgar, it's like she's gone crazy. Insisting she's been trying to get hold of you all week, saying she was washing her hands of this agency! I swear I haven't heard a peep out of them since we submitted that breakdown last month," Tricia babbled fretfully.

"I'll take care of it," he said, clenching his jaw. He propped his ass on the corner of her desk. "Which line?"

"The blinking one. Oh, by the way, how's it going?"

"Christ, it's in the bag," he boasted. "She'll be ours by Tuesday. I guarantee it. She never stops working. We'll make a fortune." He hit the line. "How *are* you?" he asked, warm as honey. "Mmmhmm . . . Yeah, he's available . . . oh, really?" He looked at Tricia and spun his finger at his ear in the universal sign for crazy. "We'll make sure that doesn't happen again . . ."

Tricia heard a noise and whirled toward Edgar's office. Her heart leaped as his door was flung open and Cicely Tyson marched out, a fatally grim expression on her face. "Cicely? Is something . . . ," Edgar began, but she blew past them without so much as a glance and was out the door to reception before Edgar could move.

"Cicely, wait!" He remembered he was on the phone. "Something's come up here. I'll have to call you back," he said, hanging up. Edgar vaulted off the desk after his fleeing prize. Tricia followed him, already feeling sexual desire reawakening low in her belly. They dashed through the reception area and careened down the corridor, turning the corner before the elevators in time to see Cicely get into one.

"Cicely! I don't understand! Wait, please!" Edgar shouted. She fixed him with a look of death and began jabbing a button. The doors closed. "Shit!" Edgar cursed. "I don't get it! I only stepped out for a goddamn second. Jesus Christ. I gotta take a piss."

Tricia gave him her best sympathetic face. He stomped into the men's room and she skipped back to the agency, now abuzz about the incident. Tricia's panties were on the floor in front of Edgar's desk, where Ms. Tyson had doubtlessly flung them in disgust before making her exit. Tricia scooped them up and resealed them in the Ziploc. She had to do a load of darks tonight.

Edgar returned and was immediately summoned to Conan's office for a screaming fight about how and why Edgar had fucked up the Tyson acquisition. When Eric, who'd been eavesdropping, scuttled over to Tricia's desk to spill the details of the royal reaming, she became so aroused she drove home and spent her lunch hour sitting on Stefan's face.

When she got back to the office, Misty told her Edgar had left for the day and to cancel his appointments. Tricia ignored this directive and proceeded to open the day's mail which included a final notice for Edgar's car phone bill. Delightful! She tossed it into her wastebasket without even tearing it up. Why bother? When a soap actor and a hip, influential publicist arrived for their respective meetings, Tricia gave truly inspired twin performances, first badly covering for Edgar's absence, then admitting with great distress that her boss's personal problems were making it difficult for him to concentrate on business and would they please not hold it against him? She remembered Edgar had asked her to get Morticia back for him and set up as many auditions as possible. Tricia had no intention of calling her but did fill out a phone slip to Edgar from Morticia and wrote in the message space, "Very angry—doesn't want to deal with our office anymore." She delivered the slip to Misty's desk and dropped it in Conan's message mailbox, an easy mistake to make since the boxes were alphabetical and Conan Carroll was right next to Edgar Black. Oops!

Now it was Sunday evening and Edgar had somehow been hoodwinked into attending another Gail Ann Griffin social event. Tricia checked her watch. She still had two hours before she was due to rendezvous with Stefan at the Coach and Horses, a divey pool bar on Sunset where, as prearranged, they would pretend to be strangers meeting for the first time, he would ascertain that she was naked under her short rayon floral-print dress from Pier 1 Imports, follow her into the ladies' room and insist she fellate his titanic penis. Tricia ran her fingers along the inside of her thigh, shuddering.

Spread out on her desktop were renewal contracts for Edgar's clients. Agencies were required to sign new acting clients for one year, then normally renewed the contract for three more years, according to the rules of the Screen Actors Guild and AFTRA (the union with jurisdiction over videotaped television shows). Signing contracts gave most actors a sense of security and professionalism, but the chief purpose of the documents was to protect the agent from working clients inclined to jump ship for a better agency and stiff their old reps on the obligatory 10 percent commission. In order to hold a client to their agency papers, signed copies *must* be kept on file at SAG, AFTRA and Actors Equity, the live theater union. Tricia kept scrupulous track of client contracts, typing up renewals for Edgar's signature twelve weeks in advance, plenty of time for unreliable, scatterbrained actors to sign and return them in SASEs so Tricia could file them with each guild upon the commencement date.

Starting tonight, however, she would be implementing a revised system. The client would still receive his or her copies of each contract, and a set would be retained for the office. But the all-important guild copies would be filed not with the contract departments at AFTRA, SAG and Equity, but in Tricia's briefcase for subsequent distribution to the paper recycling bin at the house on Orange Grove Avenue. Tricia's laughter rang through the empty suite.

Jason knew he had seen Doll Babcock somewhere before, but it took several minutes of the loud, ill-coiffed comedienne running her mouth for him to remember the HBO special he'd watched with Andre shortly after moving to L.A. They'd only turned it on because of Sandra Bernhard, but as it turned out, Sandra was basically only there to introduce four female stand-ups, the least funny and most annoying of them Doll Babcock and her tired schtick about how she was too funny to be a country singer and not pretty enough to be a Nashville hooker, with extended riffs about her abusive ex-boyfriend and feminine moisture problem.

The real purpose of the dinner party became crystal clear as last-to-arrive Doll and her massive publicist Tammy were instantly set upon by both Edgar and Gail, who had somehow reacquired her Tennessee accent. Doll got a screwdriver from Ryan, asked Turk how it was hanging, rattled off a few jokes Jason recognized from her act, and compared the mansion to Lyle Lovett's place "back home," prompting Tammy to ask if this was Gail's house.

As Gail conducted her guests to the dining table for the first course, the personal manager explained that it was a friend's home, but up for sale. "And with all the entertaining I do, I've been in the market for a bigger place," Gail brazenly claimed, "so I thought why not try it out with a little soiree. I guess y'all are my guinea pigs!" she chirped, looking directly at Tammy. Jason saw a scowl ripple fleetingly across the morbidly obese publicist's face at the word *pigs*, but Tammy was soon happily grazing on stuffed artichoke salad and asking Wendi how many movies she'd produced.

Jason missed the necessarily brief answer to this query because it was time for him to take his seat. Since there was no room at the grown-ups' table, Gail had set up a lovely service for three on the patio, where Jason and the help would dine on slightly smaller portions of the same menu. Jason thought the condescension of this gesture outrageously demeaning and would have gladly eaten the admittedly scrumptious meal in his room, but Ryan and Wren didn't seem to have a problem with it, so he joined them by the pool at the very table where Hank had kissed him two nights ago and wondered for the hundredth time that day why Hank hadn't called and why telling Hank face-to-face that they could never see each other again was beginning to seem so much less heartrending than not hearing from him because Hank hated and regretted and wanted to erase what they'd done.

Ryan and Wren were guzzling champagne and talking about Turk Marlowe. Everyone in Minnesota thought he was awesome! "He's, like, way too gorgeous," Wren opined. "I sensed a lot of really dark sexual energy when I read him. It was so weird—he said in another life he and I would have been married, and that is so not what I was getting, spiritually speaking. Anyway, I told him I'd just done a whole past lives workshop and it turns out I was a nun in sixteenth-century Spain, so the chances that I was married to him are, like, zero." She plowed a forkful of poached salmon through her garlic mashed potatoes, her infatuation with uncooked food apparently having been a passing fad. "But he said there might be a part for me on his show," she revealed to no one's surprise.

The telephone's ring trilled through the open sliding-glass door. Jason excused himself, hurrying behind the wet bar before the machine picked up. "Hello?" he blurted. No response. He lowered the stereo volume a few decibels. "Hello? Is anyone there?"

"J-Jason?"

"Yeah . . . who's this?"

"It's Marina," came the halting, teary reply.

"My God, Marina? What's wrong? Where are you?"

"I'm here . . . at home," she said, breaking into an alarming sob.

"Are you hurt? What's happened? Do you want me to—?"

"No, I'm okay. I mean, I'm not, but . . . please come up and—"

More sobs.

"I'll be right there."

" 'Kay." She sniffled and hung up. He stood with the phone in his hand, staring stupidly into space. He noticed Gail watching him from the table. Suddenly she was at the bar, looking tense.

"Is something wrong? That wasn't Fawn or that mother-in-law, was it?" she demanded in a low voice.

"No," he said, replacing the receiver. "It was a friend. I have to go up the street and see her."

"Okay," Gail replied brightly. "We'll miss you."

Sure. Mmm-hmm. "The dinner is really delicious," Jason said, heading for the front door. "Can you please have someone save my plate for me and I'll finish it when I come back?"

"Of course, darlin'," Gail purred. "B'bye."

Jason quickly crossed the driveway and started up the embankment, his brain worriedly buzzing with possible reasons for Marina's extremely agitated state. Had Mermaid decided to shelve the album? Impossible, especially after the show at Caesar's. What if something had happened to Nabisco?

Oh, God, why hadn't he thought of this—Hank must have told her! Panic shot through Jason and he steadied himself on a handy shrub. As much as he hated to conceive of it, that had to be it. But Hank wouldn't have—*couldn't* have brought Jason into it. If he had, there was no way Marina would have just called him over like this. Was there? Yes, if Hank had told her they'd had sex and she didn't believe him and wanted to ask Jason herself if it was true. *I am so fucked*, he thought, emerging into the Stetson-Rietta backyard. Their villa, once a shimmering symbol of a warm and welcoming new world, now loomed forbiddingly against the starless sky. He walked across the lawn, drawing a little strength from his belief that Hank would have absolutely, definitely, unquestionably called him if this bombshell had in fact been detonated.

He found Marina in the music room, an oversize rag doll tossed in the corner of the purple sofa. Nabisco sat on the piano bench, watching her with a worried expression on his truncated pug face. "Marina? Oh, God, you didn't—" Jason picked up the opened bottle of Bacardi Premium Dark Rum, down almost an inch from the top. There was an empty glass and a diet Coke can on the floor. Jesus, this was bad . . . Jason had driven her back to drink!

" 'S'okay," Marina sighed. "I puked it all up." She extended her index finger and flexed it. "Another little trick from the fabulous eighties."

He warily sat beside her. He smelled mouthwash. She took his hand. That was a good sign, right? "What happened?" he asked.

"I don't know," she whispered, her wet eyes fixing on a point somewhere on the opposite wall before flicking back and meeting his, horribly beaten and confused. "How could I have not known?"

"Known what?" he pressed, but he knew, oh, yes.

"That I have a gay husband!" she bawled, not so much embracing Jason as shriveling into his arms, weeping. He held her tightly, relief at his own obvious omission from whatever had transpired making him so giddy he almost forgot to react.

"I don't understand. Why would you think that?"

"It's true. Trust me," she groaned. "God, what a nightmare . . ."

"Marina, why don't you tell me exactly what happened?" Jason said, thinking he could really use a rum and Coke himself but realizing that would be insensitive.

She sat back and pulled a tissue out of her jeans to blow her nose. "Terry and Chip said they didn't need me tomorrow so I flew back this afternoon. I knew Hank was working all weekend, so I had the driver take me downtown to his office. And he was there . . ." She trailed off to Jason's immediate consternation.

"With . . . a guy?" he stammered.

"No. I mean, not exactly," she continued. "Of course, it's Sunday so there's no one else on the whole floor. He was at his assistant's desk on the phone to someone in Tokyo or Australia or something, so I went into his office and sat at his desk and the computer was on and it was showing these little cartoons of *The Simpsons*. What do you call that?"

"A screen saver?"

"Yeah. So I was waiting for Hank to finish his call and my fingers were just sort of resting on his keyboard and I must have hit one of them, 'cause *The Simpsons* disappears and this other thing comes on, and first I thought it was some bank deal or whatever, then the word *asshole* caught my attention," she said. "So I start reading what's there and it's this whole X-rated conversation. 'Suck my cock,' 'I want to fuck you,' that kind of shit. And I, like, have no idea what's going on *still* until this message flashes onto the screen. It said something like 'Are you still there, BadBoyHenry?', which is Hank's real name. Well, the Henry part. And I realize he's been . . . *typing* dirty to this person and I figure what the hell, so when this other person says 'You've got me so hot and horny I'm gonna make you finish me off,' I still haven't quite caught on and think he's doing this with a girl, so I type in 'Tell me how you want it, bitch,' like I'm Hank. And I get this back"—she paused, trying to remember the exact wording—" 'Your fist around my cock while you spread my cheeks and rape my thirsty man-cunt, that's how I want it.' "

Jason gasped, horrified that Marina had been exposed to, much less forced to repeat, such filth. "What did you do?"

"I was so *shocked* I just typed in the first thing that came into my head," the frazzled pop star admitted. " '*I'm gay?*' " she said incredulously, miming typing. "And I get something back like 'Call it whatever you want, dude, but my balls are boiling over. Let's do it!' So I'm just sitting there, completely numb, like someone threw ice water in my face and I hear Hank still on his call. And I just keep staring at the screen until *The Simpsons* starts again and then I get up and leave."

"What about Hank?" Jason asked.

"I don't know if *his* balls boiled over after I left or not," she cracked humorlessly. "I said something about a dinner with the record publicist and walked out. And I still was thinking, like in the elevator, that it had to be some kind of mistake or game or something because my husband couldn't be queer, so I went down to the garage where his car was, 'cause I have keys to it, too, and I searched it. For evidence."

Jason felt a drop of sweat bead on his temple and start to trickle down. He wiped it away with his knuckle. "Did you find anything?" he asked in a scratchy voice.

She dug something out of her pocket and handed it to Jason. It was a laminated membership card for the Dungeon, "a private club

for in-shape men." Jason turned it over. A squiggle that could easily
be Hank's signature was scrawled under a pledge to release the Dungeon from all liability on behalf of its members and staff and to
practice safer sex under penalty of expulsion. Jason had first learned
of these raunchy, quasi-underground clubs in an article in a 'zine of
Andre's called *Spunk*, but did not recall Hank mentioning that he
frequented them during their postcoital chat Friday night. "It was
under the driver's seat," Marina said. "And this was in the trunk."

She passed him a folder he instantly recognized as the Tom of
Finland documentary press kit Bryce had given him at the job interview. It must have slipped out of his bag when Hank drove him
to Chianti. He decided explaining the true origin of the folder, which
contained six rather explicit eight-by-ten reproductions of the artist's
phallocentric oeuvre, would do nothing to help the situation. He
made a point of opening the folder and peeking inside, then put it
aside along with Hank's Dungeon card.

"I know snooping through his stuff is, like, despicable and pathetic," Marina said, her voice starting to quaver again. "I'm not
gonna do it here. If there's more to know, I just don't want to know
it. Not that I really needed *anything* besides what I read on that
computer. I always wondered who the hell would be hard up enough
to try to get off like that and now I know . . . a big butch closet
case stuck married to *me!*" With that she burst into fresh sobs.

Nabisco lay down on the piano bench and watched Jason awkwardly try to comfort Marina. "Was I retarded to not have seen it?
What about that gaydar shit?" she implored, her fingers tight around
his arm. "*You* didn't have any idea, did you?"

"It was a complete surprise to me," he answered truthfully.

"How could he marry me? Why didn't he tell me?" she asked
through heavy tears.

"I don't know," Jason said. "Maybe he wanted to, but he was
too scared. Maybe he thought that the love he felt for you would
make those feelings go away."

"Oh, Jason. You are so sweet," she cried, hugging him. "I
shouldn't have dragged you into this. I'm such a shitty friend I didn't
even ask about your new job on that TV show with the goat."

"I didn't get to start, 'cause the show was canceled."

"That sucks. Do you need some money?" she asked, fumbling

for her purse and knocking over the bottle of rum which Jason had thankfully capped. "Let me just write you a check—"

"No, really, Marina," he interrupted, his guilty conscience now actually causing him physical pain. "It's okay. I got another job, starting Tuesday. At a video company."

"Are you sure?" she asked skeptically.

"Positive. Thank you. Look, Marina, what about this?" He uprighted the Bacardi bottle.

"I kind of lost it in the limo and pulled over and bought it on Sunset. Take it with you. I don't want it anymore. If I fall off now, I can kiss any shred of hope for a comeback bye-bye. And since that's *all* I have, I better try not to fuck it up, huh?" She swiped her cheeks dry and called Nabisco to her side.

"Have you talked to Hank since . . . ," Jason began.

"Nope. I'm not really sure what there is to say. Even if he's bi, it's not gonna work. Hey, maybe I can write a song about it. It'd make a great B-side, right?" She started to laugh but of course segued to tears almost instantly. Nabisco licked a few of them off her cheek. "I feel like such an idiot! How could I have not known . . . every time we had sex, he was *servicing* me . . . thinking about God-knows-what . . . I really, really loved him, Jason . . ."

"I know," Jason whispered, unsuccessfully attempting not to cry himself, because after all Marina was devastated and despite her assurances teetering on the brink of alcoholic collapse, and there was every reason in the world to believe that at least recently *Jason* had been what Hank was thinking about while he "serviced" his soon-to-be-ex-wife.

"How'm I going to get through this fuckin' new album and tour . . . by myself? I can't do it, Jason . . . How could he do this to me? We've only been together two years . . . He had to have known. What am I gonna do?" she sobbed.

He held her. "I'm sorry. I'm so sorry."

"Hey, it's not your fault. You didn't recruit him," she said, managing a tiny smile which he could not bring himself to return.

She wanted to take a shower and crash, so he let himself out, taking the rum and Tom of Finland material. There was no need for Marina to torture herself with the press kit, which was admittedly emblazoned with the Aquarius Images logo in numerous locations and thus easily connectible to Jason. The enormity and overpowering hideousness of the Marina situation rendered him oblivious to the mega-volume music throbbing from Fawn's house until he was halfway across the driveway. Specifically, a twelve-inch remix of Madonna's "Over and Over," despite the fact that *You Can Dance* had not been one of the tasteful, low-key dinner party selections he'd programmed into the CD changer earlier that evening. He squeezed between Gail's Bronco and a Jaguar convertible and hurried into the house.

Dinner was obviously over. Remnants of dessert littered the table and the guests had adjourned elsewhere—namely, the living room, outside on the patio and, from the light spilling into the end of the hallway that traversed the west wing of the house, the junior master bedroom, to coin a Syd Swannism. Jason smelled cigarette smoke. Over the rampaging disco beat, he somehow heard a splash. They were swimming?!? After jumping behind the wet bar (abandoned in thorough disarray) to lower the stereo volume, Jason marched outside and gasped. A pair of tits belonging to Edgar's date, Kendra, bobbed naked on the surface of the water as their owner splashed around swigging champagne from a flute suspiciously resembling the set Maggie had bought for the kitchen. Ryan Olstrum, apparently relieved of his bartending duties as well as most of his outfit, clambered out in plaid boxers clinging dripping and enticing to his pert ass, and scurried over to a chaise lounge that someone had stocked with unauthorized fluffy towels from the master bath. Edgar sat on the side of the pool, bare calves and feet submerged, enjoying a doobie with Igor the mercifully clothed director. Jason turned on his heel and headed inside, out for Gail's blood. He spun around when he heard the tinkle of broken glass. "Oops!" Kendra gurgled, standing on the pool steps in her panties, holding a broken stem in her hand.

Jason shoved past the caterers clearing the dining table and found Gail in the living room with Tammy the porcine publicist. "Oh, Jason, you're back," Gail throatily declaimed. "Why don't you have a crème brûlée, honey?"

"Gail, what is going on here?" he asked as diplomatically as possible.

"Just the party," she replied defensively, smirking at Tammy. "Have you met Tammy? She's huge in PR."

Three-hundred-pound Tammy, obviously too tipsy to catch Gail's insulting pun, laid a heavy arm on Jason's shoulders, her cigarette smoldering inches away from Andre's shirt. "Gail, you know the cutest young boys!" she marveled glazedly, liquory breath candied with Extra spearmint gum blowing into Jason's face. "Are you an actor, too? Need a publicist?" she laughed, pulling him to her fleshy side.

He smiled back politely, but now she was staring through the glass wall at Ryan and his wet underpants. Jason took advantage of this diversion to escape Tammy's clutches. He grabbed Gail's arm and guided her toward the main hall/dining area. "Jason, this evening has been a *smash.* I'm *this* close to signing Doll Babcock to a five-year contract!" she trilled, sticking two barely parted fingers in his face.

"So close the deal and pack everyone up," he stunned himself by snapping. "This is *not* what you told me it would be! I need everyone out of here before this gets even more out of hand." He looked toward the junior master bedroom. "What's going on down there?" he demanded.

She rolled her eyes and threw her hands up. "I've got to find Doll."

"If any glasses or dishes or anything gets broken, someone's going to have to pay for it," he direly informed her, but Gail was already flouncing away.

Goddamn her! He lunged forward, instinctively driven to turn the stereo off and the lights on to hasten the end of this soiree, but instead found himself drawn down the west wing to see exactly what was transpiring in the room at the end of the hall. He pushed the half-closed door open and Turk Marlowe was on the bed snorting a line of cocaine from Wren's bare breasts while next to them Wendi Barash used the more traditional rolled-up dollar bill on her own line, which she had sprinkled on the framed Jean Harlow photo that *had* been propped artfully by Maggie on the nightstand. Wren noticed Jason first and shrieked.

"Jason! Hi! Uh, Turk? . . . ," she blurted, slapping the syndicated TV hunk on the shoulder. He looked up, eyes dilated, hand still on

Wren's left tit as Wendi spasmodically attempted to replace Jean Harlow and dump the evidence into her purse.

Jason was past the point of caring enough to be shocked. "I need you guys to get out of this room," he said in a flat, tired voice.

Before Jason could cross through to see if anyone was getting blown in the bath area, from behind him came an angry voice. "Well, isn't this cozy!" Gail spat.

Simultaneously, Wendi flew off the bed to the privacy of the bathroom, Wren crawled backward away from Gail's most prominent client in search of her wayward chiffon blouse, and Turk stood, carelessly adjusting his most prominent attribute in the crotch of his jeans. Jason's eyes shifted from the outrageously identifiable boner to Gail, who strode past him and stopped three feet from the bed, her arms rising from her sides as if possessed with their own urge to destroy Wren and Turk. She regained control of her limbs and snapped them into a fold across her chest.

"I *hire* you to entertain very important clients at a business function and *this* is what I get?!?" Gail barked at Wren. "Well, Miss Psychic Powers, *I* see a new personal manager in your future! Put your clothes on and get the hell out of here." Wren scampered out the door, still half-topless.

"You really told her," Turk remarked.

"I guess I should expect you to whip it out for any star-fucking little coke whore you—"

"Oh, there you are, Gail!" Doll Babcock interrupted.

"I sure am! Where have you been hiding, honey?" Gail switched gears from Skull-fry to Suck-Up with such lightning rapidity Jason thought he could actually feel the insincerity whoosh past his face.

"Tammy and me are fixin' to head down to Bar One and rustle up some action," the comedienne announced to Jason's great relief. "Wanna come along and tell us how you're gonna manage me right onto my own TV show?"

"Well, yes, ma'am, I do believe I will," Gail drawled. "Let me go ask the others," she said, pointedly ignoring Turk. Jason waited for Doll, Wendi and Turk to exit the bedroom, then followed them. He set about killing the music, shoving every dimmer switch to full blaze and opening the front door.

Out, out, out! he wanted to scream, but people were actually leaving. Wren had of course been the first but was trapped in her car, blocked in by Edgar's Jag. Jason saw her through the windshield of the Escort, twisting her hair around one finger with jittery, stoned intensity, when he helped Ryan carry out boxes containing Gail's leftover booze and dining accessories (and nothing else, Jason had ascertained after a quick inspection).

Ryan and the obese publicist were the only two guests to bid Jason good night. Gail waved and blew kisses from the driveway, pointing her thumb at her mouth and index finger at her ear to indicate she'd call Jason. He shut the door with his back and heaved an exhausted sigh. He flicked all the lights off from the control panel by the door.

The party was over. Tomorrow was plenty soon enough to deal with straightening the place up. According to the taped phone conversation on the answering machine, Maggie's husband would not even be able to meet her in San Antonio until then, so the danger of discovery was at a minimum. And if the pissy old battle-ax did happen to show up, tough shit. Jason was dependent on Fawn and Company for absolutely nothing, thanks to Aquarius Images. He grabbed the Tom of Finland press kit from the wet bar cabinet, where he'd stashed it with Marina's Bacardi, and carried both items into the acceptably tidy kitchen, cleared of any traces of tonight's menu including any leftovers that might have made up for his dinner being aborted. He poured himself some diet Coke on the rocks, adding a healthy shot of rum, went into his room and prepared for bed.

Naked, he took a sip and turned down the sheet, but just as he was about to collapse onto his pillow, headlights swept by outside his window. He'd neglected to close the gate, and now Gail or one of her playmates was back to retrieve something left behind. Jason went to the door in a pair of cutoff sweats and peered through the peephole. At Hank.

What the fuck . . . Now was as rotten a time as any. He opened it and the feelings he had been able to damn in the abstract for the past forty-eight hours—the feelings he was determined to sacrifice because there was no alternative—crushed him with their immediate, merciless return.

"Hey," said Hank.

"Hi."

Hank was in jeans, construction boots and a Ralph Lauren dress shirt with rolled-up sleeves. "Sorry, it's so late. I just, um . . . Marina knows about me."

"Yeah. I talked to her tonight," Jason replied, sliding one bare foot around on the smooth, cold floor.

"Did you tell her about us?" Hank asked, sounding alarmed but almost hopeful.

"No! Did you see her or not, Hank? She's a complete wreck."

"I didn't see her. She called me. Jason, can I come in?"

"I don't think—" Jason began, but Hank was already walking past him to the dining table, where he slumped into a chair. "Hank, after she left your office, she went out and bought a bottle of Bacardi and poured herself a cocktail."

"Oh, Jesus Christ. Shit!" His head dropped to the table, his face buried in his muscular forearms. "I gotta go see—" The chair screeched against the floor as he shoved back, leaping to his feet.

"She spit it out," Jason quickly added, feeling guilty and manipulative for scaring Hank, though he probably deserved it.

Hank took a step toward Jason. "What?" he asked, confused.

"When I got there she told me she made herself puke it up as soon as she swallowed it. And I'm sure it's true. I took the rum back with me."

"Thank God," Hank breathed, sinking heavily into the same chair.

"Whether or not she can keep from drinking again, this is . . . catastrophic for her right now," Jason said, not believing that he needed to inform Hank of this fact. "She's questioning her whole life now, including her career and the album. Everything. And I had to sit there and listen and watch her be destroyed by this because she thinks I'm *such* a good friend and thinking about what we'd done to her made me sick!" Suddenly Jason was crying.

"Please don't say that," Hank begged with a terrible, wounded look in his eyes. "We didn't do it to hurt her. I —"

"Well, she's hurting! So why don't you just go home and be with her, Hank, because—"

"She doesn't want me there. She told me not to come home until she left," Hank said.

"Left for where?"

"Didn't tell me. She's taking Nabisco and leaving town. She asked me to deny that I was gay and I said I couldn't and she said there was nothing to talk about. Jason, I swear I didn't do it on purpose. I just left on the computer—"

"Hank. I know what happened. She told me everything. All about 'BadBoyHenry' and his little chatroom buddy. And about the membership card she found in your car. Which I thought was kind of interesting. So do you hang out at sex clubs very often?" Jason asked, trying to be flip and above it but sounding way too bitter to carry it off.

"No," Hank answered very quietly. "You've gotta believe me. All that shit is over with. The stupid chatroom . . . I was just fooling around. I swear. A guy gets horny. That's all it was. The only thing that means anything to me is you. Jason, I love you."

Okay—he wasn't supposed to say that. This was definitely not the time or place or female friend's husband Jason had had in mind when he'd imagined those words being said to him. The only thing this situation had in common with any recurring romantic daydreams was Jason's immediate heartfelt impulse to say, "I love you, too."

"You can't," was what Jason said. "We just can't do this. I can't do it to her, and I'm so sorry but I need you to go. Please." He closed his eyes, because if he kept looking at Hank sitting there on the chair with his rolled-up sleeves and his hair stuck up on one side like a miniature state of Utah, Jason would start crying again and that was to be avoided at any cost.

"All right," said Hank. "But can I kiss you goodbye?"

There was no acceptable response to this question. Jason froze, eyes still shut, transmitting mental signals for Hank to go, walk out the door, turn around now—Jason heard nothing except his own ragged breathing. He opened his eyes and Hank was right there.

Jason's arms remained stiff at his sides as Hank's hands moved tenderly from Jason's shoulders down his back, pulling the two of them together, and when Hank's lips met his and Jason opened his mouth and kissed back helplessly, hungrily, he grabbed Hank above each wrist and pushed his arms away. "Let me hold you," Hank whispered, pushing back.

"No . . . please," Jason coughed out, breaking loose for his room. He sat on the bed in the dark for what seemed like an hour until he heard the front door bang shut. Hank's car sped down the driveway. Jason heard the tires squeal as he turned onto Vista Laguna but was unsure whether Hank turned right, toward his house, or left down the hill.

The glass of rum and diet Coke sat on the nightstand, nearly full. Jason chugged it down without a breath then went into the kitchen for another. He would have gladly chased it with a couple dolls, but an inspection of Andre's medicine cabinet revealed nothing but fossilized Carmex and a box of suppositories.

He woke up at eleven the next morning, oddly calm. A quick swim washed away a mild hangover and he reclined in a deck chair, drying in the breeze, thinking that the place looked pretty decent postparty and that tomorrow at this time he would be at Aquarius Images making a damn good wage futzing around with sexy videos and probably getting taken out to lunch by Bryce since it would be his first day.

There wasn't much cleanup to do, so even though he'd arbitrarily left the living room for last, it took Jason no time at all to discover the sofa. He backed away from it, horrified, snatching up the cordless phone on the run back to his room, where he dug up Gail Ann Griffin's number, dialed and stomped back to the living room as her phone rang.

"Gail Ann Griffin."

"It's Jason." He stared at the couch.

"Hello! Jesus, I have to tell you, last night could not have gone better! Doll Babcock's signing with me. Muchas gracias, darling. I was just about to write you a note."

"Well, I saved you a stamp. Gail, the sofa is ruined!"

The teeniest incriminating pause. "What sofa is that?"

"The white sofa. The only sofa here. The back of it is . . . *splattered* with red wine! Did a whole entire bottle tip over? Why didn't you tell me about this?"

"Jason, I had no idea!" she insisted. "I'll call my upholstery cleaners and have them up there first thing in the morning."

"And what about the cigarette burn? I told you no smoking and you ignored me and I turn the cushion right side up and there's a hole burned right through it!"

"Please try not to get upset—"

"Gail! That sofa is brand-new and unbelievably expensive and *totally fucked up!* What the hell am I supposed to tell Maggie Burke?" He was circling the gargantuan couch like a marine biologist trying to make sense of a beached whale. Oh, good Christ. There was a pink ring soaked into the arm of the sofa, perhaps from the bottom of a champagne flute full of, say, pink champagne?!?! Just goddamn wonderful.

Gail was recommending Jason channel his anger into a more focused place. "When is Maggie coming back?" she asked, like he was five years old and retarded.

"I don't know. Probably this week," Jason snapped.

"Then you need to find out exactly where she got the sofa and I'll replace it. Problem solved. Let me know and I'll cut you a check," Gail said in the warm, nurturing tones she'd used with the actors during the showcase Jason had house managed. "I'm so sorry about this, honey. But I'll take full responsibility, 'kay? B'bye." She hung up. He wondered how much the couch cost. Five thousand? Ten thousand? It didn't make two shits' worth of difference. Gail Ann Griffin wasn't giving him a dime and he knew it. Jason hurled the phone into the scorched sofa cushion. It rang in midbounce.

"Hello?"

"Hi, is this Jason? Bryce Barger here."

"Hi, Bryce, it's me." Jason tumbled onto the sofa. Maybe he could artfully arrange one of Maggie's dreaded throws over the stain before he left for work in the morning.

"Jason, something pretty major has come up for me. Just this afternoon, in fact," Bryce began.

"What is it?" Jason asked, hoping it wouldn't delay his start date more than a few days.

"I've just been offered president of worldwide marketing at Soloflex. It's an incredible opportunity for me and I don't think I can pass it up. I had this meeting today scheduled with them for a while, but I never thought it would amount to anything, especially an offer like this. I asked them about bringing an assistant on with me, but apparently there's already a full support staff, not that you'd have wanted to move to Oregon, anyway—"

"Oregon?" Jason interrupted, his chest tightening as realization dawned sickeningly. "What about Aquarius?"

Bryce sighed. "The guys over there are pretty pissed at me. I have to start at Soloflex next week and . . . I'm sorry, Jason. The position you would have filled there is kind of in semipermanent limbo for now."

Ah, yes. *Semipermanent limbo.* That fun-filled district where Jason was apparently spending the rest of his life.

"Tricia, you look fantastic," Violet said, meaning it, as the agent's assistant released her from a friendly, honest-to-God hug. "Is that a new hairstyle or have you been on vacation or what?"

"None of the above," Tricia said, laughing. "I guess I just find summer in L.A. very alluring." So that was it. She was getting laid regularly. "Can I get you a cup of tea or a soda while you wait for Edgar?"

"No, thanks. I'm fine," said Violet. She picked up *Variety* from the reception room coffee table to read as Tricia pranced off, promising her it would only be a few minutes.

Tricia tapped lightly on Edgar's door, then cracked it. "Violet Cyr is here," she said softly to her boss, who was presently engaged in an obviously high-stress telephone conversation with one of the two actors besides Ione Skye who'd left him in the past two days. Edgar, looking as haggard and pale as she'd ever seen him, held up three fingers, indicating he'd be off in as many minutes. Tricia nodded and went back to her desk. Edgar wanted her to send gift baskets to the defecting clients, a gesture she considered gauche and futile. Tricia knew one of these clients happened to be diabetic. She ordered an all-chocolate extravaganza for him and promptly forgot about the other two. A busy subagent like herself hardly had time to worry about ex-clients, anyway, she reasoned, picking up the phone to call Stefan.

Violet checked her watch. This meeting Edgar had called had been labeled "urgent." But so far he'd kept her waiting fifteen minutes. She knew it had something to do with the script he'd messengered to her yesterday, a lurid, graceless "erotic thriller" called *Prying Eyes* about a voyeuristic married couple spending their vacation at a wine country inn owned by Voyeuristic Wife's ex-lover, who's looking to get *his* rich, masochistic wife bumped off. Very 3 A.M. Cinemax, decided Violet, who'd been asked to look at Brittany the Voyeuristic Wife, which, despite the nudity and bad dialogue and the name Brittany, was at least a lead and demonstrated that Edgar was paying her a modicum of attention in the wake of *Chillin' with Billy*. Now if he could perhaps open up the field to screenplays that didn't suck.

"Violet, you can go in now," Misty announced.

Edgar greeted her at his office door with a passionate embrace in which she could feel the dampness under his arms. His eyes were slightly bloodshot and his normally glossy dark brown hair drooped lifelessly around his ears like he'd sworn off blow-drying. "Come in, gorgeous," he said. She paused to wave to Tricia, engrossed in a phone call with what looked like her hand up her skirt . . . No. It couldn't be. Violet went in and sat down.

"So how've you been? I know how tough it is when your show goes down," he told her. That'd explain all those supportive phone calls and auditions, I guess, Violet thought sourly, continuing to smile.

"It's been okay, really. But I didn't work long enough to feel like I need a vacation or rest or anything, so I guess I'm eager to see what's next." She pulled the script out of her bag. "Thanks for sending this over."

"What'd you think?" he asked, his tone indicating the answer should be pretty fuckin' favorable.

"It was all right," Violet shrugged. "A little cheesy . . . didn't you think?"

"Cheesy . . . ," Edgar repeated. His vaguely annoyed expression transformed itself into a standard shark-toothed grin in under three seconds. "Yes, it is kind of cheesy. But so was *Fatal Attraction* and look how much that made." Violet nodded agreeably, unsure if and why he might be taking this personally. "I sent your tape over to the director yesterday. He called this morning and they're very interested. Very, very, very interested. To be honest, I expect to get an offer for you for Brittany by the end of the day."

"An offer?" Violet was shocked. "Without auditioning? Without *meeting*?"

"Hey—I was surprised myself. But it's not the kind of thing an agent wants to argue with," said Edgar.

"Why are they in such a rush?"

"They're about to start shooting. Within the next week from what I understand. The lead actress dropped out a few days ago and I thought, what perfect timing. 'Cause here you are, available. The money's not terrific, but it's nothing to piss on. And they'll probably agree to points, too."

"Points? What kind of distribution is this going to have?" Violet asked. An inordinate amount of discussion seemed to have taken place while she had been supposedly casually perusing this script.

Edgar sighed, rolling back in his chair till he hit the wall. "Violet, it's the lead in a goddamn movie. You should be jumping for joy."

"I'm sorry, Edgar, but—"

"I don't want to be out of line here, Violet. And you know everyone here thinks you're extremely talented. But that series, that *Chillin' with Billy*, is the joke of the town. Nobody blames you, of course, but it's one of those 'credits' you're going to have to rise above. And you do that by working again. As soon as possible."

"It's not that I don't want to work. This movie, there's nudity and I wouldn't have any time to rehearse and . . ."

"Do you have a problem with nudity?" Edgar asked.

"Well, no, not exactly. I mean, depending on the project, but—"

Edgar cut her off. "That can all be worked out in the contract."

"I need to think about this. Is it shooting in town? Could I go in and talk to them about the part?"

"Uh-uh. Everyone's up at the location in the Napa Valley. It's the most beautiful fuckin' place in California. Look, Violet, my friend Wendi is producing the picture. She's a woman." Oh, Jesus. "It'll be a great experience for you." Violet said nothing. Ten minutes ago she was laughing at this tacky script and now she felt like if she didn't star in the movie, she'd never work again. "As your agent, Violet, I've really got to advise you to take this."

"Maybe it is the best thing . . ."

"It is. Trust me." He picked up the phone.

"Edgar?"

"Yeah, doll?"

"Were you ever able to find anything out about the Aldo Spackle movie? *You Lucky Bastard*?" She felt like a complete loser for bringing this up but maybe, just maybe . . .

"Yeah, I did. There's no further interest, Violet. I'm sorry."

She nodded and put *Prying Eyes* back into her bag. It looked like she had a shitload of memorizing to do.

Silverlake was a trendy, lower-rent neighborhood east of Hollywood and south of Glendale, fraught with rather extreme local color, where the generally simple laws of L.A. geography broke down into a dizzying web of intersecting parallel thoroughfares and hilly streets slicing the eclectic urban landscape into irregularly shaped blocks. Jason drove up and down one such block a total of three times without spotting the Dungeon, although he'd checked the map in the Thomas guide with the address in the phone book and he had to be in the right place.

He slowed down, unable to pull over because the otherwise deserted street was completely lined with parked cars despite the fact that it was almost midnight on a Tuesday. A door swung open in a windowless gray storefront and a buff bearded guy in a torn Bundeswehr tank and Levi's emerged and headed down the sidewalk in the opposite direction. That had to be it. Trepidation thrummed through Jason's stomach, along with a pang of excitement reminiscent of but much stronger than the ones that had accompanied his Video Xplosion smuggling maneuvers.

Another pass around the block yielded no spaces, so he turned up a nearby residential street and parked in front of a crumbling Spanish house, its porch and small, weedy lawn like an overexposed photo in the glow of the overhead streetlight. Jason checked himself in the visor-mirror and wrenched The Club into place on the steering wheel. He was ready.

It had been a hideous day and a half. After Bryce's apocalyptic phone call, he'd stayed on the besmirched white sofa for over an hour, staring at the water in the pool glitter obliviously in the sun. Then he had a rum and diet Coke and fell asleep watching *Geraldo*. He woke up in the dark, starving. There was no food in the house, so he drove to Pavilions and spent $25 of the $186 he had in his checkbook. Combined with the fourteen bucks in his wallet, that left

him with $175 and a little over half a tank of gas. Another rum and
diet Coke sent him to sleep that night until he awoke two hours later
and ralphed his guts out in the vicinity of the toilet.

While scrubbing the servants' bathroom Tuesday morning, Jason
hit upon the idea of temp work. His office skills were average at
best, but he had a car, could type around forty words per minute,
use a few computer programs and effectively answer phones. *Wren*
had been getting work through temp agencies when he'd first moved
into the Orange Grove house, for God's sake. How difficult could it
be? Hopefully not as difficult as actually getting an appointment at
the agencies themselves—out of the seven he called, only one agreed
to see him on Wednesday. He'd have to wait ten days to two weeks
to test at the others.

Chip Reeves was still in New York. Violet wasn't home. Jason
left messages for both. He called Marina's private line on the off
chance she'd changed her mind and stayed in town. Her machine
picked up, outgoing message unchanged. He spent the evening in
front of the TV thinking about Hank and how he had fucked everyone over. Replaying every minute of their night together with a
queasy mixture of regret and relish. Wondering how many guys
Hank had been with and if he was with one now right up the hill.
(*All that shit is over with.*) Fuck him! (*The only thing that means
anything to me is you.*) Jason slid off his bed and found the Tom of
Finland press kit. (*Jason, I love you.*) He opened the folder and
pulled out the laminated Dungeon card.

Jason thought there might be a secret password or something to
get into the club, but upon entering the dimly lit vestibule plastered
with safe-sex pinups featuring the lovably butch kids from Colt Studios, and handing Hank's membership card to the nipple-ringed
Brian Grillo-lookalike behind the glassed-off window, the only thing
Jason had to come up with was six bucks. "Enjoy yourself," Nipple-
Ring said, buzzing him through a second door upon which was
posted NO COLOGNE, NO DRAG, NO DRESS SHIRTS.

Braced for a writhing sex tableau of every possible gay perver-
sion, Jason instead found himself in an empty cubicle lined with
coin-op bus station lockers. On a black-draped card table was a
fishbowl full of condoms and mouthwash in a large plastic jug with
a self-serve spout, next to a stack of Dixie cups. Flickering candles

and thunderous industrial "music" enhanced the sinister atmosphere.

A curtain of black mock-leather strips hung across the doorway leading to the recesses of the club. Jason took a stick of peppermint Extra from the pocket of his 501's, folded it over three times and put it in his mouth. As he stepped through the curtain into a pitch black corridor, a person of indeterminate age, size and looks brushed past Jason with a muttered "Excuse me," his hand clumsily squeezing Jason's crotch in what was certainly no accident. Jason recoiled, nearly tripping over his own feet as he retreated down the corridor, which turned sharply before splitting into two forks. Jason took the left-hand choice and found himself in an open area with television sets showing porn bolted to the ceiling and two guys sucking each other's dicks on a carpeted wooden platform for an audience of three other guys standing by whacking off. Shocked, Jason came closer, hanging back a safe distance from the other three, unable to take his eyes off the live sex show.

The men on the platform were naked—a horse-hung, dark-haired swimmer's build and a horse-faced blonde with mucho muscles and a thick spark plug hungrily devouring each other in an ever-changing series of positions. Were they lovers who got off exhibiting themselves in a semipublic place? Or did they even know each other? Despite the fact that neither one was exactly a dreamboat, Jason felt himself stiffen. He watched the blonde slurp the other guy's nuts into his mouth and slowly work a finger into Swimmer's Build's asshole.

Jason realized he was now standing roughly abreast of the three other spectators. To his left, a lean, long-haired skateboard type with his shorts around his ankles leisurely fisted his rigid cock, while a discreet glance to the right revealed some cute brand of Latino whose sculpted, hard-nippled pecs fought for attention with the stunning uncircumcised penis jutting from his unbuttoned Levi's. Jason's eyes locked with the Latino's for a second, then Jason looked back where, in the reddish light bathing the platform, the blonde was now squatting over his pal's face.

Jason felt someone touching him and jumped. The hand the Latino wasn't using to pump himself was tugging at Jason's gray T-shirt, pulling it out of his jeans. Then his small, hot hand was sliding up Jason's belly. Skateboard had moved up against the platform and was now helping feed Swimmer's Build's titanic bone to Horseface. The third guy who had been watching was now on his knees trying to suck Skateboard. The Latino moved closer, guiding Jason's hand to his lubed-with-something dick. Jason shook his head and backed away, terrified at how easy this all was and how hard he was getting. He darted out a different door than the one he'd come in.

Now he was in a long corridor filled with what looked like side-by-side bathroom stalls. A man who might have been gorgeous ten years of partying ago, nude except for sneakers and bike shorts, eyed Jason appreciatively and puffed on a cigarette. The man nodded toward the nearest door, pushing it open with a creak. Jason kept walking. The doors all had wide holes or slots cut into them to encourage voyeurism and God knew what else. Jason peered through one.

Two white guys were kneeling on the floor, orally servicing a beefy black stud whose encouraging cries of "Eat it, motherfuckers!" were audible over the hellish, screeching music. A stiff cock everyone was ignoring protruded through a glory hole from the stall on the left. Jason stepped over and looked through the slot in that door. The guy shoving himself through the hole was having his sagging bare ass whipped by a tattooed leather clone wielding a belt from Miller's Outpost.

I've gotta get out of here, Jason thought, turning a corner into another dark hallway. Low moans and the sound of flesh slapping against flesh seemed to come from behind the plywood walls but could just as easily have been special effects on the industrial sludge hit parade, which continued to offend from a hidden conspiracy of speakers. The corridor had become a maze, and Jason was reminded of the Kiwanis Club Halloween House of Horrors he used to attend as a kid every year in Dayton. The tacky-but-hallucinatory quality was virtually the same, as was, for some reason, the musty, musky smell. Jason felt suddenly very sad that Hank had ever been in this place.

The passageway dead-ended into three curtained doorways. A scary bald man, bare chested under a motorcycle jacket, came up behind Jason and went through one of the doorways. Jason went into another one. It was a shabby evocation of a den, lit only by the Jon Vincent movie silently flashing across a TV set. On the broken-down garage sale sofa, someone totally naked except for hiking boots rode up and down on the condomed cock of the hairy guy below him. A mustachioed third-wheel stood to the side, then moved in to fondle the fuckee's smooth chest and pointy erection. He was batted aside by Hairy Fucker, who apparently didn't like to share. Jason was ready to call it a night and retrace his steps to the front door. But when he emerged from the room, he nearly collided with a hugely hunky, shirtless muscle-stud who gave him what looked like a sneer and went into the room Scary Bald Guy had entered earlier.

Jason waited three seconds, then followed him in. His breath caught in his throat as a warm front of ripe, steamy body heat from what must have been at least ten mostly nude men crammed into a twelve-by-twelve-foot cubbyhole blew across Jason's face. At the vortex of this fleshstorm knelt a beautiful young boy using his mouth and both hands to try to simultaneously stimulate the six large dicks wagging in his face. Jason watched in disbelief as two of the organs disappeared between the boy's lips at once. Scary Bald Guy was also on his knees, whacking his own grotesquely large penis as he buried his face between the sturdy buttocks of one of the six fellatees. Jason felt hands on his ass and spun around, straight into sneering Shirtless Muscle-Stud.

Except now the sneer had been replaced with a lascivious grin and Shirtless Muscle-Stud had a thick, sexy arm around Jason and was backing him against the wall and pressing his massive pecs against Jason's chest and covering Jason's neck with violent kisses and Jason was running his hands over giant shirtless muscles and he felt his pants being undone and pulled down, underwear, too, and Jason looked down at his own cock naked and erect and now the beautiful young boy was swallowing it and sucking it with exquisite velvety precision and there was the acrid stink of poppers and he had Shirtless Muscle-Stud's dick in his hand and was rubbing it faster and faster and faster and it was fat and felt great and was spurting across Jason's fist and forearm and he kept pumping and jacking until Shirtless Muscle-Stud was gone and still the blow job continued, relentlessly, almost painfully, and there were more big hard dicks and pecs and nipples and rippled hairy stomachs and now he was surrounded on all sides by a solid wall of men and a finger slid into Jason's butthole and he was going to cum he had to cum and he looked down and Beautiful Young Boy was gone and Scary

Bald Guy was sucking Jason's dick and fingering Jason's ass and Jason pushed against his bald head trying to dislodge him but he put his hand around Jason's cock and roughly jacked it and would not let go and Jason was still going to cum but it was as if his penis had gone numb and he shot and shot all over Scary Bald Guy's face and slack, pasty white torso and felt nothing and finally the despicable bald troll released his penis and Jason yanked his pants up and misbuttoned the fly and pushed his way out as Scary Bald Guy tried to kiss him and Jason's hands were wet with someone's cum and he wiped them on the plywood wall of the corridor as he staggered toward the exit.

"Have a great night," the guy at the window said. Jason barely heard him. Outside. Fresh air. Away. He hit the sidewalk and had to zigzag around two incoming marine types who responded with a friendly, "Careful, buddy," which just made him think of Hank and feel worse—difficult, since at the moment he quite possibly felt as degraded, shameful and miserable as he ever had in his entire life. Where the hell had he left the car? He froze, panic-stricken, and checked for his wallet and keys. Shit!!! All right, front pocket. Thank God they were still there. Never again. Never. Never. He would spend tonight under the shower spray, although he doubted he'd ever feel completely clean again. There was his car. He heard another one turn onto the street behind him and quickened his pace. This neighborhood wasn't exactly the greatest.

The vehicle that had turned, a battered El Camino, braked to an abrupt halt parallel to Jason, who watched with exponentially mounting unease as the lights were turned off while the engine still ran and the passenger-side door opened and a black guy climbed out and walked toward him aiming a double-barreled sawed-off shotgun.

"Empty your pockets," he ordered, staring at Jason with stupid, contemptuous eyes that blazed white against his dark, dark face.

Oh God oh Jesus oh holy fuck just do what he says stay calm I'm gonna die right here on this street oh Christ! Jason slowly passed him the wallet, fighting to suppress the trembling in his hand. The scumbag tore it away and dropped it into the front pocket of his dirty white painter's pants. "Now gimme your watch." Jason did. "I tole you t'empty y'fuckin' pockets." With that, he pushed the barrels of the gun into Jason's crotch.

"Okay, okay," Jason babbled, fumbling out his car keys and some change that jingled to the ground.

"Which one is it?" the man demanded. Jason pointed at the elderly Subaru, finger shaking. "Shit," grumbled the gunman.

"Kill him. Shoot him. Kill him," came the El Camino driver's voice.

Jason involuntarily took two steps backward, away from the gun still aimed at his balls. The human turd stared at him with raw, murderous disgust, then ambled off toward the Subaru. Jason turned and started walking at a carefully controlled pace back the way he'd come. "Git back here. Git the fuck back here right now, you faggot." Jason increased his speed, his heart battering against his chest, and dared to glance over his shoulder. The lowlife was standing by the Subaru, aiming the shotgun at him. Jason whipped his head forward and sprinted away. A shot exploded into the quiet-as-death night and Jason did not hear himself cry out. He wasn't even sure he hadn't been hit until he stopped running.

Part III

"I wish you could come with me," Violet said, giving her just-delivered Numero Uno pizza one stab with her fork before deciding it wasn't worth it and eating with her hands.

They were in the mansion's breakfast nook. Jason nibbled his slice of pizza. He hadn't had an appetite for anything all day but Darvoset, which, it occurred to him, probably shouldn't be mixed with the wine they were presently having with dinner. Oh, fuck it. *I narrowly escaped death,* he reminded himself, taking a long sip of Freixenet. "I'll be okay, Violet. You've already done so much for me and I'll miss you, but work is work. Anyway, now that I'm getting paid, I should probably stay here."

When Violet had handed him the mail a few hours earlier there had been a letter for him with an Ohio postmark. For a fleeting moment he actually thought it might be from his family, despite the fact that his last name had been left off the address. As stunning as that would have been, the reality was only slightly less astonishing —a check made out to "Jason" for five hundred dollars along with a note from Giles Burke.

Dear Jason,
Your idea worked, man. Fawn and I flew up to Dayton yesterday to
chill out for a while. Thanks for house-sitting and everything.

Giles.

This brought several questions to mind, such as whether or not the
impetuous separated lovebirds had evaded Maggie in San Antonio
and where was Andre and exactly what role had he seized for himself
in the drama, but Jason was in no condition to speculate. All he
knew was that without that five hundred bucks it would have made
a lot less difference if those assholes had blown him away last night.
Violet was going to take him to the bank to deposit the check after
they ate.

She'd been with Jason the entire day, since approximately
2 A.M., half an hour after she'd been awakened by the call he'd
placed on a policeman's mobile phone at the corner of Hoover and
Santa Monica asking if she could come to Silverlake and pick him
up because he'd just been mugged. Tomorrow she was driving up
to Calistoga in the Napa Valley to start *Prying Eyes*.

"For once my mother's unhealthy interest in my career is actually paying off," she'd explained that morning after giving an outraged lecture about how *incredibly fucking stupid* it had been for
him to be "tomcatting around the scuzziest neighborhood in town at
one-thirty A.M." (Jason, who'd already been convinced of his own
stupidity by the gun-toting security patrol he'd run into—hired by
the local nightspots to cut down on damaging publicity engendered
by murdered patrons—while fleeing his assailants, listened and
agreed repentantly.)

"She got a look at my contract yesterday," Violet continued,
"and called Edgar and demanded they put in costume approval, a
private dressing room with my own phone, and some other things
that I guess never crossed Edgar's mind. And she never once mentioned Dave or the breakup, even though I know she's talked to him
because I saw his grooming van's phone number written on Saturday's paper when I was over at Mom's. So maybe this is sort of a
new beginning for us, you know? Where she treats me with the
respect she'd give, say, a nineteen-year-old flunking out of beauty
school."

They'd spent the afternoon out by the pool, Jason moderately zonked on Darvoset (another plus for Violet's mother, who'd sent them over via messenger earlier), doing nothing, Violet in the next lounger, sometimes holding his hand, reading her *Prying Eyes* script and occasionally quoting particularly overripe dialogue to him.

"Do you like your pizza?" she asked.

"It's great," he smiled, reaching for a third slice he didn't really want, trying to reassure her that he was okay so she could go do her movie without worrying about him. The cops who'd taken the report had told him there was usually at least one mugging per night in that area, many ending in deaths that never made the papers. They also told him that the gunman had called him back to shoot him—what other reason could there be? He'd taken everything else. When Jason had tried to go to sleep last night, the walk back to his car replayed itself in stark, high-contrast monochrome again and again, always with the same new ending—instead of leaving Jason and walking to the Subaru alone, the mugger orders him over to the car, opens the trunk, and aims the shotgun at Jason's head—

Stop it! That didn't happen. You're okay. It could have happened but it didn't, so stop torturing yourself—Violet was saying something about the couch. "Sorry, I didn't hear you," Jason said.

"I said your best strategy is to deny knowing anything about it to Maggie. I mean, she's going to think you did it, but there's no proof. If she throws you out, you can stay at my place. Just call my mom and she'll let you in."

"Thanks. You're the best."

"Hold that thought until you've seen *Prying Eyes*."

Violet drove off at nine the next morning, leaving Jason with half a large Slaughterhouse Five foil-wrapped in the fridge, six Darvosets and a fifteen-foot, ten-thousand-dollar sofa ready for the Goodwill truck. He thought about what in his life he had control over (not a hell of a lot at this point) and what was most important to him right now (a job at Mermaid Records) and decided the two areas intersected. Barely, but they did. He popped in his advance cassette of *Ghost in the Fog* (minus "You Don't Know") into the stereo and fast-forwarded to "Broken Mirror," the favorite song of Marina's she'd first played for him in her car the night they met. He listened to it once, rewound and picked up a notebook. The phone rang. He answered, hoping for Marina.

"Hello, there. Lewis Burke speaking. Is Maggie about?"

Oh, shit. "No, she isn't," Jason replied cheerfully.

"She's flying in sometime today and I thought it was this A.M. The Bel-Air tells me she hasn't checked back in yet, but I thought she might have stopped up to the house first."

"I haven't see her, sir," said Jason, suddenly compelled to blurt out the couch confession, certain that absolution in warm, midwestern tones would be forthcoming. He restrained himself, took a message for Maggie to call Lewis in Dayton, hung up, restarted "Broken Mirror" and began to write.

"Well, of course I've noticed it," Tricia admitted to Conan Carroll, twisting a lock of hair around her index finger and darting her eyes nervously around the agency owner's office in a splendid performance as The Employee Uncomfortable Discussing Her Boss With His Superior. "But I really have no idea what the problem could be. I mean, I like to think Edgar and I are friends, but he doesn't confide much of anything personal to me."

Conan sighed and swiveled in his chair, staring absently at a framed photograph of himself and Jennifer Holliday. "It's just bizarre, honey. His bookings are way down *and* he lost six clients in a week. I've worked with him for five years now and there's never been anything like this, and The Business has had some miserable slumps. I know he's still in there trying, God bless him. He did just sign Turk Marlowe and he says he has an in to Julianne Moore, who's fabulous. But this past month or so, I dunno . . . That Cicely Tyson disaster made me want to set my hair on fire! Do you have any clue about what might have happened in there?"

When Conan had called her at home last night (Stefan made her override the answering machine despite or possibly because of the fact that they were in bed with one end of a double-headed dildo deep in her vagina and the other up his ass) and asked if he could discuss something privately with her first thing the next morning, she'd been terrified that somehow he was on to her. Stefan, however, correctly guessed the boyish talent czar was merely trying to figure out Edgar's recent, swift skid down Mount Agent. Tricia had an answer ready for the Cicely Tyson question, and now hesitated for maximum effect before offering it.

"I was at my desk, so I didn't hear their whole conversation, and this might be way off base, but . . ." Conan tilted forward in his chair, wide-eyed. "I had to go in to tell Edgar about an important casting phone call and I overheard him telling a joke to Ms. Tyson."

"What joke?" Conan wanted to know, his expression deadly.

"Let's see if I can remember it. Oh, yes. 'What do Michael Jackson and Kmart have in common? Little boys' pants, half-off.' "

"Oh, fuck me! She's probably on the board of his Foundation for Dying Tots or something. How could Edgar have been so stupid?" Conan hissed.

"Please don't tell him you know about the joke. He'll know it came from me," Tricia pleaded.

"Don't worry, honey. This whole little chat will stay strictly between us." He patted her hand.

"Conan, I'm sure this is just some odd pocket of bad luck Edgar is going through. He'll rise above it soon. The feature he packaged, *Prying Eyes*, starts lensing this week," she added brightly.

"That's great, Tricia. Hon, I know it hasn't been easy working with Edgar lately and you've really done a beautiful job keeping things together. Keep it up. It hasn't gone unnoticed, you know. The next opening we have, it's going to be agent time," he said, pointing at her.

She smiled with soft, self-effacing charm. "You have no idea how much I appreciate that, Conan."

That night, Jason woke up from a dream that Maggie was in the house. His eyes immediately focused on his digital alarm clock: 1:13 A.M. There had been no sign of the old bitch all day, and Jason had spent his time productively, popping a Darvoset midafternoon and screening a couple of Aquarius Images sample tapes which led to swift, orgasm-induced sleep. He was now thirsty, so he left his room in white Jockeys and headed toward the foyer/dining area, where there was Perrier in the wet bar fridge. Before he could step down behind the bar, he heard footsteps echoing from somewhere inside, very quietly. But they seemed like thunderclaps in the cavernous, utterly silent house. Pure terror, completely undulled by the numbing shock he'd felt when the mugger climbed out of the El Camino with the shotgun two nights ago, stabbed at Jason, lung-freezing and voracious.

Someone had broken in and they were in the master bedroom wing off the kitchen and if they found Jason they would kill him. He felt tears boiling up and instinctively moved forward to crouch down behind the bar and tripped and landed soundlessly on his knees. His hand, already shaking, reached for the phone next to the sink and found only an empty base. Oh, Jesus, no! Where was the fucking receiver? The living room. Violet had been over by the stained couch talking to her mother before she left that morning.

He had to find it and call the police. Or maybe he should run out the front door. What if there was someone else outside, in a getaway truck? He heard the footsteps again. They didn't seem to be getting closer, but what the hell did he know? There was no way he was going to go near those footsteps by heading back to his room to use the phone there. He looked behind him, through the sliding glass doors to the pool. No, the backyard was totally enclosed. He'd be trapped. He had to get to the living room. It was less than twenty feet away. He grabbed a full bottle of liquor from the half-open cabinet as possible protection and went for it, his barefoot slaps against the floor ringing horrifically loudly in his ears.

Jason rounded the corner into the living room, where the sofa sat like a huge snow sculpture by moonlight. He saw the cordless receiver on the glass-cube coffee table at the exact second he clearly heard footsteps coming toward him. He wanted to dive for the phone but was almost involuntarily pulled back against the column next to the glass wall facing the patio. He did not recall raising the liquor bottle over his shoulder like a club but that was its position when the dark figure of the intruder passed in front of him, his back to Jason, walking with slow, ambling steps, which made it very easy for Jason, once he overcame paralysis, to step forward and bash him in the head. Weren't expecting that, were you, you cocksucker? Jason silently screamed as the bottle shattered across the back of the prowler's skull, overpowering the room with the medicine odor of vodka.

The intruder fell to his knees. Still gripping the jaggedly severed bottleneck, Jason skirted past him to the phone. 911. 911. 911. He misdialed twice, then finally got it right just as the man on the floor rose and lurched toward him. The phone slipped through Jason's sweaty hand and when he squeezed it to keep from dropping it, he hit the disconnect button.

The mugger with the sawed-off shotgun. It was him. The flat, animal eyes that had peered through Jason's every conscious thought of the past forty-eight hours, terrorizing him with barely averted death, viciously locked with Jason's. Of course it was him, Jason's mind blithered. He had the gate control and Jason's key ring and there must have been mail or something in the Subaru with this address and one hand was still clutching the back of his head but the other was reaching into those same grubby white pants and pulling a pistol out—

"You dead meat, faggot—" the human scum was able to growl before Jason screamed "Fucker!" and stabbed the jagged bottleneck into the pig's throat as far as it would go. The gun hit the floor and went off, scaring the shit out of Jason. Driven into a new zone of emotional meltdown, he shoved the mugger away from him with both hands, sending him cartwheeling backward against the white couch. He took a shambling marionette step toward Jason, clawing at the fountain of blood pumping from his neck while making ghastly, wet wheezing noises before plummeting face first onto an outcropping of sofa.

Jason bent down for the phone and hit redial. Three quick beeps, two rings, and he was giving the address to the emergency operator. "Someone broke in and attacked me. I hit him with a bottle—"

"Sir, try to stay calm. Police are on the way. Is there anyone else in the house?"

"No, just him and me . . ." Oh, Christ. Oh, fuck. What if there was someone else? What if the asshole driving the El Camino Tuesday night was in there, too? Jason's head jerked around in panicked, paranoid glances.

"Sir? Sir!" the operator demanded.

"I'm still here," Jason said. He noticed that his hands were sticky with blood, which had also lightly splattered his bare torso.

"I suggest you go outside to wait for the police if there's any chance another perpetrator—"

"Okay, I'm going," Jason interrupted. He scampered to the front door, unbolted it with wildly unsteady fingers and dashed into the cool night air in his briefs, still holding the receiver as he went down the driveway. Before the connection was completely eroded by distance, he gave the operator his number and clicked off.

He nearly screamed when he saw the El Camino parked in the driveway. Empty. He danced past it, not wanting to touch it, not wanting to think what its driver had in mind for Jason when the sonofabitch walked out of whatever shithole he called home earlier that night and got into it and drove from his blighted neighborhood for a little Beverly Hills fun with Whitey.

Jason made it to the bottom of the driveway and stood shivering behind the open gate waiting for the police.

"Next time you better Scotchgard," the goateed fat guy from the coroner's office quipped to Jason as he and a uniformed colleague wheeled the dead mugger out in a body bag to a waiting meat wagon. Jason, feeling not the slightest bit tranquilized by the two Darvosets he'd popped after the cops had questioned him and okayed a shower, crossed from the dining table to the living room, where full-powered recessed lighting showcased the spectacularly besmirched couch, which looked like it had materialized whole from the photo insert of some lurid true-crime paperback. Jason had a momentary image of Maggie examining the sofa then angrily turning on him: "The police explained about all the blood and that's well and good, but how did this *wine* get on my sofa, young man?"

"He's a friend of mine. I want to see him," a familiar voice said somewhere by the front door. "I live next door," Hank told one of the cops before rushing to Jason's side. He stared at the couch, open-mouthed. "Jesus Christ, what happened here?"

"Somebody broke in and I—I killed him," Jason said, hearing the words spoken and having Hank there enough to make him start shaking again. He thought he might actually topple to his ass on the glass-strewn, vodka-puddled floor, but then Hank's arms were around his shoulders and Jason anchored himself against Hank's business-suited torso, not caring what the cops might think.

"What'd you use? A chain saw?" Hank asked in a low voice. Jason looked at him. His thick Italian lips were firmly, seriously set but there was a glimmer in his eyes. He gave Jason a long hug. "I was driving home when I saw flashing lights and cop cars. You sure you're okay?"

"Yeah. I think." They went out and sat by the pool while Jason told him the whole story, leaving out the part about Hank's membership card to the Dungeon inciting it all.

The Beverly Hills cop in charge of the investigation emerged from the house with a carbon of the police report. "We're about wrapped up here. Like I said, it was clearly self-defense. A detective may want to ask you some questions in the next few days, but I honestly doubt it." Jason nodded. "We'll send a tow truck tomorrow for the El Camino. No ID on the deceased, but we radioed in the name on the registration and it's some puke who'd been doing time for armed robbery, just got paroled. Goddamn courts. You gentlemen have a peaceful evening."

Jason thanked the cops and they left. For the third time in less than a week, he was alone after midnight with Hank, who insisted on walking through the whole house to check that every window and door was locked. "Jason, let's go to my place. You can have one of the guest rooms. Or how about a hotel?" he suggested, noting Jason's pained expression.

Jason knew it was ridiculous, but he couldn't bring himself to go back to their house with Marina out of town. And a hotel would be even worse. But he couldn't send Hank away, either. Or explain any of this to him. So he shook his head, then leaned back against the wall and covered his face so Hank wouldn't see his tears.

"Jason, I'm not leaving you." He gathered Jason in his arms and walked him to his room. The pills were starting to work, or maybe it was just the inevitable crash of nervous exhaustion, but Jason felt himself spiraling down, barely aware of Hank pulling off the sweatshirt and jeans Jason had thrown on after scrubbing the blood from himself in the shower earlier. In fact, the only sensations that registered were Hank's wonderful, sweet smell and the warmth of the strong arms in which Jason slept cradled until morning.

He knew she'd be showing up, so it was almost a relief when Maggie drove up the next day around noon, her Lexus closely followed by Syd Swann's Rolls-Royce. The driveway was clear, the only trace of the El Camino (impounded earlier that morning) a spidery oil stain on the gray asphalt.

Jason saved the document he had up on Andre's computer and opened the front door to Maggie, a key pointing from her right hand, her witchy chestnut shag improbably twisted into a chignon. One step behind her, Syd sported diamond earrings and a Maude Find-layesque jacket that fell to the back of his knobby knees.

"Jason," Maggie said, the hint of surprise in her usual flatly imperious voice indicating she hadn't expected to find him here.

"How are you?" Syd inquired, pasting on a minimal smile.

"All right." Jason stood aside so they could enter. "Have the police called you, Mrs. Burke?" he asked, figuring with some surety by her calm demeanor that they had not.

"Police? What on earth about?" Maggie demanded sharply.

"There was a break-in last night," said Jason. "Around one a.m. I woke up and found someone in the house," he added, watching Maggie's jaw drop. "He had a gun." She stood there, mouth gaping, gold reflecting from one of her molars. Her eyes, normally narrowed to disapproving slits, were wide and shocked beneath dyed brows. Jason decided he liked her much better this way.

She found words after a few seconds. "Well, was anything taken? Was there damage?"

Syd Swann regarded her with what looked like religious awe before pivoting his focus to Jason. "Are you okay? Did they hurt you?"

"Yes, Jason, how are you?" Maggie was finally moved to ask, actually hooking a liver-spotted talon around his forearm.

"Nothing was stolen. But there was some damage," Jason replied.

"Oh, good Lord, what?" Maggie cawed.

Enjoying this far more than any conversation he'd previously had with Maggie, Jason said, "He dropped the gun on the floor and it fired." This elicited a little squeak from Syd, who, in the face of the terrifying account, had taken Maggie's free hand. "So there's a bullet hole in the living room wall. That was after I smashed him on the head with a bottle of vodka." He paused, giving Maggie the opportunity to interject "Not the Stoli!" But she didn't take the bait.

"Anyway, he came at me, so I stabbed him with what was left

of the bottle. And he died. On the white couch. Here's a copy of the
police report." He handed Maggie the carbon, which she fished out
her glasses to read while walking toward the living room with Syd
at her heels.

Jason had no real desire to see the bloody sofa again, and the
house's formidable acoustics amplified Maggie's shriek of horror to
such a degree there was no need to be standing next to her to savor
the full effect. She came clattering back, one hand pressed to her
middle. "Oh, Jesus Christ . . . that's disgusting! I need to sit down,"
she announced, white faced, as Syd helped her into a dining chair.
"The blood . . . everywhere . . . ohhhh," Maggie moaned. "We'll
never sell the house now," she said miserably.

"Of course you will, Maggie," Syd assured her, patting her
shoulder and avoiding eye contact with Jason. "Did you know I
leased the Sharon Tate house a while back? Just think of how many
people died *there!*"

"I want that sofa out of here today!" she spat, wringing her
claws and encouraging Jason that she probably would not be examining the cushions for cigarette burns or anything else. "Horrible,
just horrible!"

Jason wondered in what way, if any, her reaction would have
differed if he'd been the one killed. "I'll be in my room," he told
them. As he headed down the hall, he heard muffled conversation
between Syd and Maggie, and a minute later there was a tap on his
closed-but-unlatched door.

"Come in."

Maggie did. "Jason. Dear, I just wanted to make absolutely sure
you weren't injured in any way by that . . . man last night." Syd
must have really put the fear of litigation in her to warrant the use
of "dear."

"I'm really fine, Mrs. Burke."

"Because we'd be happy to pay for a checkup with a doctor, or
even a psychiatrist, if need be. My family knows several excellent
ones here in town." Yeah, I bet they do, Jason thought but said
nothing.

"I know you've been through a dreadful ordeal," Maggie continued, "but I really need to ask if you happen to have heard from
Giles or Fawn. Or even Andre. You see, they seem to have vanished

into thin air," she said, lightening the confession with an incredibly phony titter.

"Nope. Sorry." He shrugged and began typing.

Violet returned to her motel room (and yes, that's what the place was, a motel, despite the branding-on-redwood sign reading WHIS-PERING PINES RESORT AND LODGE) around 2:30 A.M. She'd been up since six for a 9 A.M. makeup call the previous morning, and she was exhausted but didn't feel much like sleeping with a stomach full of the greasy combination pizza someone had finally ordered to feed the starving cast and crew sometime after midnight. Marc Singer, who played Violet's diabolical lover in the film, had been justifiably complaining about the lack of food since nine that night, but by the time it arrived, he'd quit the movie, providing a rather spectacular capper to her first day on the *Prying Eyes* set.

Igor the director had engaged Mr. Singer in a colorful screaming match, replete with threats of severe physical violence from both parties, but had been unable to prevent the early eighties heartthrob from storming out of the Victorian house serving as the movie's principal location and screeching off into the night in his red Isuzu Trooper. Violet stood by, stunned but inordinately relieved that she might be able to at last get out of the slutty black nightgown she'd been costumed in for hours and get some sleep. Igor had other ideas.

The imperiously crude auteur of countless episodes of Stephen J. Cannell telecrap not to mention *Ernest Goes Bossa Nova* called for another setup and, while gobbling down the truly awful pizza, proceeded to revise the shooting schedule to accommodate the de-parted star, resulting in a new call time of 7 A.M. for Violet tomor-row. Or four hours from now, to be precise, she mentally noted as she robotically undressed.

Violet had enjoyed a breathtaking drive north into the Napa Valley Thursday morning, and nothing else since. While she was checking in at Whispering Pines, the querulous old poop behind the desk informed her that the production company had classily insisted on a personal credit card deposit from everyone staying there in case of "room damages." The old poop also passed along the latest draft of *Prying Eyes*.

To Violet's dismay, it was even less comprehensible than the one Edgar had given her earlier, with the added bonus of a new kinky sex murder prominently featuring her character, Brittany. Violet dozed off and woke up with a backache from the lousy bed. She went out to find some dinner and drove around for an hour in a futile search for a restaurant open past 9 P.M. She ended up eating half a sack of "fun-size" peanut butter cups and a pint of coffee Häagen-Dazs from a convenience store.

Then today. As difficult as it was to devote serious artistic thought to a character named Brittany, Violet had hoped to imbue the unfulfilled voyeuristic housewife with some darker layers and textures as well as emphasizing what little sense of humor Brittany had been given in the script. Unfortunately, Igor's performance-lite directorial "technique" made the *Chillin' with Billy* production week seem like a summer at the Old Vic. He was inarticulate, sloppy and apparently horny as hell, if the mind-boggling array of big-titted bimbette extras and bit players slinking around the Victorian was any indication.

The private dressing room Violet had been promised turned out to be a walk-in closet in one of the house's bedrooms. And what good was costume approval? She *hated* what they'd put her in today, but since there were no other choices, she'd had to wear the tacky getups and would now have to continue with them to match the footage they shot, providing of course Marc decided to come back and they weren't required to scrap the entire day.

Back in makeup at seven? That had to violate some SAG turnaround rule. She'd call Edgar in the morning. Now she just had to get to sleep as quickly as possible. First, the hot shower she'd been craving for hours. She adjusted the taps in the cheap plastic tub to the correct temperature, then stepped in, aiming her face at the shower spout. She pulled up the thing, closed her eyes and felt a dribble splat against her forehead and run down the middle of her face. Bob Hope's noontime piss had more pressure behind it. *First-class accommodations, love,* she could almost hear Dave cracking, which made her even madder. She cranked off the water and crawled into her crummy bed.

Hank had offered Jason the use of the Stetson-Rietta house during the day, and after factoring in carelessness, Maggiedom, and Hank's incredibly sweet, no-pressure behavior since the break-in (nothing more physically inflammatory than a kiss on the cheek), Jason decided to take him up on it. Hank was at work the whole time anyway. Not that there was any danger of a relapse into transgression—it was obviously possible to remain just friends with Hank. However it was still probably a good idea not to use the home gym together, Jason reasoned as he exercised alone Saturday night, waxing nostalgic for the innocent lust his workouts with Hank used to evoke. He showered, resisting the urge to sniff Hank's sleeveless white T-shirt (or "wife-beater" as Andre called that particular style of undergarment) hanging on the towel bar, then gathered up his stuff and crossed back to the Burkes'.

The driveway was vacant. Jason let himself in and turned on the nighttime lights. There was no more white couch. He went into the living room and saw that a small Oriental rug now covered the bloodstained floor, the glass-cube coffee table squatting in the center like bad modern sculpture. Jason wondered exactly what happened to ten-thousand-dollar sofas gone bad. Surely the couch was too profoundly tainted in Maggie's eyes for reupholstery. What had she done? Called the Salvation Army? Sold it to a gallery as dadaist urban art? Oh, who cares, he thought, glad to be rid of it.

From its hiding place in the cupboard below the TV, Jason's answering machine blinked three messages. Jason hit Play. The first one was Hank, "just checking in." Next, Violet: "Hi. This is a fucking nightmare. Call me."

And definitely saving the best for last, another intimate peek into the wacky world of the Midwest's richest harpy, Mrs. Margaret Burke. "Is the machine off?" Lewis Burke asked, impatient.

"I don't *know,* Lewis. I can't *find* the damn machine. Remember?" Maggie testily replied. "You're the one who told me they shut off after you pick up a call."

"I said I knew of *one* that did. Why the hell don't you ask the kid where he keeps the friggin' thing?" Jason had never heard Lewis sound so pissed.

"Where are you, Lewis? I'll phone you back."

"I'm, uh—oh, Jesus, there's no number on this and I don't have my portable—"

"Then just get on with it!" Maggie snapped. "What is so

damned urgent that you have to spend ten minutes haranguing me before—"

"Fawn is pregnant."

A silent beat, then: "Oh, my God! How do you know? Are they there? Did he take her to Dayton?" Maggie squawked.

"Doctor Toussaint just called. Apparently, Giles and Fawn have been here a few days. I don't know where they were staying, but Fawn collapsed ill yesterday and Giles took her to see Peter, who ran tests and diagnosed severe morning sickness. He estimates she's in her second month. He felt that you and I should be told."

"Well, I should hope so! Peter Toussaint has been our family doctor since I had Giles," Maggie snorted. "Certainly the least we can expect is loyalty. Actually, Lewis, this is the best news we could have gotten. Aside from that little tramp falling off a cliff." Jason snickered.

"What are you talking about, Maggie?" Lewis asked wearily.

"Fawn is pregnant! We'll insist on a paternity test and Giles will see her for the slut that she really is. I can practically taste that divorce!" Maggie's malevolent glee erupted in a cackle.

"Has it occurred to you that this baby might be Giles's?" Lewis demanded.

"No," Maggie coldly retorted. "Two months ago Fawn Farrar was here cavorting with those theater people. She and Giles were barely speaking. It's not his. And a test will prove it. Do Fawn and Giles know?"

"No," Lewis sighed. "Peter called me first."

"Tell him not to say a word to them! Not one word, Lewis," Maggie hissed. "My guess is that Fawn will figure it out and get an abortion without saying anything to Giles. Then we'll *really* have her."

"Maggie, I'm not too keen on the sound of any of this."

"I will handle this. I'll call Doctor Toussaint now. Lewis, listen to me. *Don't fuck this up.*" Click. Dial tone. Rewind. Eject. Hide in desk drawer.

The girl with fried platinum-blonde hair tweaked the wide, stubby nipples atop her ludicrously inflated breasts, which, thanks to one of the Valley's busiest tit surgeons, did not so much as jiggle despite the vigorous ramming her decoratively shaved vagina received from a tanlined, fatly endowed muscle boy. Tricia watched them.

Including her and Stefan, there were less than a dozen patrons at the Pussycat that night. Tricia found the mechanical, overlit video sex on the screen tedious and antierotic, but the mere fact that she was sitting in this filthy porno theater on Western Avenue in seamiest Hollywood with a box of Junior Mints in one hand and Stefan's huge cock in the other was almost unbearably arousing.

When Stefan had suggested they see a movie together, she could have guessed what he had in mind wasn't *Free Willy*. He was in the seat to her right, munching popcorn from the concession stand, dispensing J/O Formula Wet brand lube and issuing low-pitched commands. "Faster." "Squeeze me." "Rub the head." He fed her popcorn and she licked the warm butter from his fingers.

Tricia's right hand stiffened, and she ran his majestic penis through it, feeling the organ heat up with friction despite the oily slickness of the lubricant. "Do my balls," Stefan said. She toyed with his smooth, bulging scrotum and popped another Junior Mint.

She'd been to her doctor that morning complaining of fictitious constipation and now tucked away in her purse was a prescription bottle full of powerful laxative capsules. They would have to be administered to Edgar with utmost discretion, but the results promised to be quite rewarding. Edgar had reclaimed a little ground this past week, with the acquisition of that detestable Turk Marlowe and an upcoming meeting with Julianne Moore, a truly delightful actress who gave consistently fine performances in everything from the risible blockbuster *The Hand That Rocks the Cradle* to Altman's sublime new ensemble piece *Short Cuts*. But since Tricia was in charge of setting up a luncheon with Ms. Moore, chances were the deal would somehow fall through, she smiled to herself, giving Stefan's dick an impulsive squeeze.

She wanted to touch herself very badly, and it would have been so easy—all she had on under her skirt was a garter belt—but she knew from the steamy moistness of her muffin that climax was imminent, and she intended on delaying the pleasure as many dirty, humiliating minutes as possible.

They were a fair distance from the nearest audience member, but now someone was entering their row. "Somebody's coming," she whispered to Stefan.

"Don't stop," he said.

Tricia's grip faltered, but she bravely continued, sneaking a glance to her left. The man was sitting five seats away and looked Japanese. Tricia quickly turned to face the screen. The blonde was now on all fours, boobs defying gravity as she got it "doggie-style." From the corner of her eye, Tricia saw the Japanese man (or was he Korean?) move toward her and sit down. There was now only one seat between them.

She stroked Stefan faster, wanting him to cum, wanting the game to be over—somewhere inside her remained at least one fragment of Tricia the chubby, churchgoing overachiever from Topeka, and she was begging not to be discovered committing a sex act in a public place, even one as indigenously sordid as the Pussycat Theater. As if sensing her agitation, Stefan placed his left hand firmly over her right, trapping it at the base of his penis. As he stuffed more popcorn into her mouth she could only watch, speechless and immobile, while the Asian man moved into the seat next to hers.

Oh, God, he was watching them. He knew what she was doing. She shuddered with illicit glee.

"Grab his cock. Beat him off," Stefan ordered.

"What?!? Stefan, I can't—" she whined in protest.

"Yes, you can, Baby Nastypants. You're very good at making men cum," growled Stefan. "Do it."

He slowly decreased the pressure on her right hand so that she was once more free to massage his steely phallus. Staring straight ahead at the screen, upon which Platinum Blonde's lover thrust in and out of her dilated anus again and again and again, Tricia raised her left hand and swung it over and down into the Asian's lap.

How could Stefan want her to do this? How could it turn him on? But Stefan's dick was now harder than ever, his breath quickening. Tricia's hand crept across a flabby, trousered thigh, encountering a lump in the crotch region. A sudden bloom of power seemed to fill her chest and she knew she *could* make this horny pig tourist cum. Stefan had unleashed something in her, and now he wanted to see it at work. She wanted to do it for him—she would have done anything for him—but she also wanted to do it for herself.

She pinched the man's zipper between thumb and forefinger and yanked it down. She felt his hand hovering, trying to help free his erection, but Tricia needed no help, her fingers plunging into his fly, through the nearest opening in his underwear, her hand closing around his penis, amazingly small and unthreatening next to Stefan's. She hauled it up through the fly and masturbated him. Two hands, two cocks, two men in utter submission to her. Edgar Black didn't have a chance!

Jason didn't recognize the old bubble-topped Mercedes that came up the driveway but heard familiar barking halfway to the front door, where the peephole revealed Nabisco Stetson prancing around the bridge as he waited for Marina to catch up. Still stunned from the answering machine bombshell an hour before, Jason scrambled to admit the sundressed pop star and her ultra-cute pet.

"Oh, my God!" Marina exclaimed without preamble, rushing to Jason and enveloping him in a fierce hug. "I'm so glad you're okay!" Nabisco nonverbally echoed this relief by hopping up on his hind legs and pawing Jason's knees.

"Hi," was, stupidly, the only thing he could get out.

She released him but tightly held both of his hands. "Hank left me a message and told me what happened. I drove down right away."

"Where were you?"

"Betty Fonseca's house in Pacific Grove. You must have been so scared," she said.

"Well, it was over pretty quickly both times, but yeah—"

"*Both* times? What do you mean?"

"The guy was the same one who mugged me Tuesday night," he told her, not sure what she'd heard.

"Fuck, you're kidding! Oh, honey, I didn't know you were mugged, too! How horrific!" This called for another hug. "All Hank said was that your car got stolen, then someone broke in and you had to—" Tears shone in her eyes. "You've got to tell me everything. I mean, if it isn't too painful."

"I'm really okay," he had to insist for several minutes before convincing her. She was starving and wanted to go eat, so he grabbed his house keys and they went outside.

"Is this new?" he asked about the Mercedes.

"Oh, no. I've had it for years. I just never drive it. Do you like it?" For some reason she was standing on the passenger side.

"Yeah, it's gorgeous," he said as Nabisco took a quick piss on a rear tire.

"Good. It's yours." She pitched the keys over the roof of the car and he stumbled forward to snatch them out of the air. "You know, to drive until you get something else."

He was flabbergasted. "Marina, I can't—"

"Oh, bullshit. You need a car. This has been just sitting in our garage. You can drive a stick, can't you?"

He hadn't used a manual transmission since the summer after his freshman year at Ohio State, but it came back to him like it was the most natural thing in the world to be driving a Mercedes-Benz through Beverly Hills with Marina Stetson and her dog next to him in the front seat. He only popped the clutch twice maneuvering down the mountainside to Sunset, and except for some minor gear grinding, the ride to Kate Mantilini was otherwise free of mortifying operational mishaps. By the time he drove up to the valet in the parking garage, he was in love with both the idea of driving the Mercedes and the car itself.

They went into the restaurant, an angular ponytailed host immediately slicing through the half-dozen clotheshorses in varying shades of chic milling around the entrance. "I'm sorry, but we can't allow that dog—oh, hello, Miss Stetson! How are you tonight? Table for two?" They were shown to a booth, where Nabisco curled up unobtrusively next to Marina and nibbled at a piece of bread.

"So how's the new job? Are they being nice about the whole justifiable homicide thing? And how're you getting to work?" She asked in rapid succession, forcing him to admit that yet another entry-level show-biz position had slipped through his fingers. "Wow. Tough week, honey," she remarked with an adorable absence of irony.

"What about your week?"

"It was good for me," she said after a beat. "I used to go up to the Monterey Peninsula a lot with my dad when I was little. And I always thought someday when I was rich and famous, I'd buy the biggest house right on the ocean and never, ever leave. But if I'd

done that, I wouldn't have anyplace to run when things turn to shit."
He looked at her sadly and she shook her head, smiling some. "By
the time I drove up there, I'd almost convinced myself I could live
with it."

"You mean Hank being gay?" Jason asked, knuckles of guilt
giving his esophagus a preemptive clench.

She nodded. "I came up with this whole rationale that he'd been
that way when I met him and we still spent two really great years
together and we could sort of do this open marriage kind of thing
—like don't ask, don't tell—and how important was sex to me anyway and he was leaving messages on my machine and at Betty's
in San Francisco and, uh—well, thank God I wised the fuck up
before I hit him with that idea."

"Have you talked to him at all?"

"No, and I really should, I guess. I left him a note when I was
up at the house. You see him, right?"

"Yeah. I mean, a little."

"I just can't right now. You can tell him I'm going to New York
in a couple of days to work with a vocal coach Terry my producer
recommended. But don't tell him I'm staying with Terry and his
wife until I leave."

"Okay."

"Hey, look at this." She took a sheet of paper from her purse
and passed it to him. It was a concert schedule on Mermaid letterhead. She began the *Ghost in the Fog* tour in Las Vegas the first
week of October. Seventeen dates were booked, including New
York's Beacon Theater and the Wiltern in Los Angeles.

"Marina, this is fantastic! They must love the album."

"Well, Chip seems to be really excited about it. Betty's going
to play guitar on the tour, which makes me feel a lot better. And if
you're free, maybe you can come with us."

"On tour?" he sputtered through a gulletful of iced tea.

"You'll probably have a job by then, but if you don't or Chip
flakes out and there's nothing at Mermaid, I really want you to come.
I mean, I know we talked about the whole assistant thing and it's
weird, but believe me, baby-sitting me on that tour will be a real
full-time job."

"You are too good to be true."

"I'd probably be dead right now if it wasn't for you," she replied simply. Her hand found his next to the bread basket and he looked into her eyes and was dizzy with what he saw there. This near-mythic moment was undercut in the nick of time by Nabisco propping his forepaws onto the table and sneezing. Jason and Marina both laughed. "Don't worry, baby-pie. I love you, too," Marina crooned, planting a kiss on the pug's neck.

Their waitress arrived with aromatic pasta entrées. "I wanted to tell you," the girl said to Marina, "I heard your new song on the radio while I was in Seattle last week. I loved it!"

"Really? On the radio? What song?" Marina asked, giving Jason a befuddled look.

"I'm not sure of the name," the waitress frowned, grinding pepper onto Jason's linguine. "But it sort of went like this . . ." She segued into a rendition of the chorus of "Broken Mirror" while Jason and Marina sat in amazement.

"That's 'Broken Mirror.' It's my favorite song on my new album," Marina told her. "But they told me the first single was definitely going to be 'Ghost in the Fog,' and that's not even supposed to be released for a month."

"Well, I heard it and it was great. I'm sure the album will be a big hit," the waitress gushed. "Would either of you care for fresh Parmesan?"

As they chowed down, Jason made use of the lull in the conversation to obsess about what the premature debut of "Broken Mirror" would do to his recently hatched plan. He hadn't told Marina or anyone else, but from the minute Violet took off for her movie, Jason had been listening to his rough mix of "Broken Mirror" over and over, jotting down notes, brainstorming images and constructing a scenario that owed equal inspiration to his descent into the Dungeon, the subsequent bloodbath at the mansion, and several hours' viewing of stylized Aquarius hunk tapes. With format aid from one of Andre's never-cracked books on screenwriting, Jason had cobbled together a music video script for "Broken Mirror" that he intended to send to Chip Reeves this week. He wanted it to be entirely his own idea, something that, when and if Chip showed it to Marina, would be a genuine surprise. It was the only way Jason could come up with to express the initiative and enthusiasm with which the prospect of a record company job filled him, and now, if "Broken Mirror" was being bumped up as the first single, a video could already be completely conceived, rendering his ideas useless. "When do you think you'll start shooting videos?" Jason asked, fighting the urge to tell her about his script.

"Around Labor Day. I think I have a meeting with them about it in New York on Wednesday or Thursday. Videos are such an incredible pain in the ass. I've *gotta* make sure I've got good hair," she sighed. "Seattle. Whatever," she shrugged.

The conversation inevitably worked its way back to the dead mugger and how Jason could possibly continue to stay in a house where something so gruesome had occurred. "Well, Giles is paying me to be there now, and I actually feel, you know, less scared and violated and everything since I killed the guy and it's not like I'm always right where it happened, because I'm not really supposed to go in the living room anyway."

"Oh, my God! I didn't even ask you what Maggie said about the whole thing. Did she freak out?" Marina became livid as Jason recounted yesterday's scene with Maggie and Syd Swann. "That coldhearted douchebag! After all you've been through, she worries *to your face* about whether she's gonna be able to unload that mausoleum? Jesus Christ." She distractedly dabbed a piece of bread from their new basket into a leftover pool of arrabbiata sauce, then looked up at Jason with a very Pop-Tartts smirk. "I just thought of the most brilliant prank."

She wouldn't tell him what she was going to do, just that he should "stick around the house tomorrow and pretend we've never met." He began to figure it out the next morning, shortly after Maggie arrived at the mansion. He'd just had the pleasure of telling the plutocratic prune the Mercedes in the driveway was his loaner when the phone rang.

Jason answered. "Hello?"

"Syd Swann for Mrs. Burke, please."

"One moment." He primly put a hand over the mouthpiece. "Syd Swann for you."

She all but snatched the cordless from him. "Yes, Syd?" Jason went toward the kitchen and paused just out of Maggie's view—the house's acoustics made eavesdropping effortless.

"Wonderful. When are you going to show it? . . . What kind of a situation? . . . Next door? . . . I see. Syd dear, let me explain something to you. Your personality conflicts with potential buyers are really not my concern . . . I don't care, Syd! If she's interested in the place, she's going to see it! . . . *So don't come, Syd.* I'm fully capable of showing her around myself . . . No, Syd. Selling this house is my top priority . . . I'll be here all day. Send her over." Jason heard her hang up, then stomp off to the bathroom.

Twenty minutes later, a black Corvette came slithering up the drive. Jason, en route from the servant's quarters, encountered Maggie, who'd been fussing over something in the junior master bedroom, as they both headed to answer the front door. "I'll get it," she said, cutting him off and opening the door to reveal Marina Stetson, superstar.

She sported a metallic green leather jacket over a sleeveless black V-neck top and black Norma Kamali knee-length skirt, bare legs and black pumps. Hair up, makeup flawless. "Hi, I'm Marina," she said, removing her sunglasses and holding them in the air next to her head.

"Hello. I'm Maggie Burke. Welcome," she added with a smile that looked bizarrely incongruous if not just plain goofy on Maggie's hatchetpuss.

Marina walked straight past her to where Jason was standing a few feet away. "And this must be Mr. Burke," Marina said sweetly. Jason bit his inside lower lip not to laugh.

"Euh . . . no," Maggie replied, immediately covering her annoyed tone with a weak titter. "This is our caretaker, Jason."

"Wonderful," Marina grinned. "Then he can come with us while you show me the house to make sure I don't miss anything."

"Certainly," Maggie agreed. "Let's begin, shall we? The realtor's office tells me you live next door."

"Yes, that's right. My career keeps me out of town a lot, but after my world concert tour this fall, I plan to settle down for a while. That's why my husband and I are looking into expanding into a second house."

Presumably wishing to dispense with the utilitarian and unglamorous immediately, Maggie led them to quick peeks at the laundry room, servants' bath and Jason's bedroom. "So you're involved in the music business," Maggie said, actually sounding interested.

"Mm-hm. What a stunning kitchen," Marina commented. "I was in a band a few years ago called The Pop-Tartts."

"It seems like I must have heard of that group," Maggie lamely replied, opening the massive built-in refrigerator-freezer for Marina like some Terry Sweeney sketch with Nancy Reagan prize-modeling on *The Price Is Right*.

"Well," said Marina in a vaguely disappointed way, "we did release three albums, one went gold, one went platinum. We were nominated for two Grammys and won an MTV Video Award. Then again, you're probably not young enough to have been into that type of thing." She shrugged and gazed out the window over the sink.

"I love those albums," Jason quickly interjected in a burst of inspiration. "And I've really enjoyed your solo career, too."

"Aren't you sweet," Marina said, patting him on the shoulder with a wink Maggie was unable to see. "I'd love to see the rest of the house, Mrs. Burke. It's just breathtaking." Maggie visibly unclenched and shot Jason a look that was almost grateful. "How long have you lived here?"

"Oh, I don't live here. No one does." So much for gratitude. "Well, except Jason here. You see, my son and daughter-in-law bought the house some time ago, but they never moved in and now they're divorcing, so we're selling it. Completely furnished. It's all included in the asking price."

They were now in the master bedroom. "Oooh. I hope that won't be a deal breaker," Marina remarked, peering into the adjacent closets and dressing rooms.

"Pardon me?" said Maggie.

"I have to be honest with you. I love the house but I absolutely despise everything in it. Whoever decorated this place should be horsewhipped."

The sickly feeling that came over Jason when Marina had entered the very boudoir in which he'd acquired carnal knowledge of Hank was miraculously soothed by the vision of Maggie Burke helplessly impaled and squirming on Marina's wickedly subversive skewer. Maggie's speechlessness gave way to stammering, apologetic reassurance. "Well, certainly, uh, Miss Stetson, the furniture is hardly *compulsory* . . . if it's not to your taste."

"I can't imagine it's to anyone's taste. It reminds me of the sets from *Barbarella*. And what's with these French subway posters? They don't match anything. I'm sorry, Mrs. Burke, but that decorator ripped you off." Marina exited through the sliding glass doors to the patio.

"Jason," Maggie barked, seizing his arm with one hand, the other twisting and clawing her red cardigan sweater from inside the pocket. "Is this *woman* really some sort of star?"

"Oh, yes," he nodded solemnly. "She's very famous. I read that her new album is supposed to be one of the big hits of this fall."

Maggie sighed, exasperated, and went out to the pool area. Jason followed, wishing this once-in-a-lifetime diva duel was being videotaped. "This view is just spectacular and so is the pool," Marina was telling Maggie. "And I love these," the singer declared, picking up one of Maggie's infamous throws from a deck chair. "I bet you picked these out yourself, Mrs. Burke. They're gorgeous." Shaking the throw out in front of her, Marina took a few steps toward the pool.

"Yes, I did actually choose the throws," Maggie replied, pleased. "There's the most exquisite little shop near the Design Center—"

Marina dropped the throw into the pool. "Oh, I'm such a klutz. I'm so sorry, Mrs. Burke."

"That's all right. No, let me get it." Maggie squatted down at the edge of the pool and tried to reach the throw. Failing, she got on her knees, leaning precariously over the placid, deep blue water. Marina exchanged a naughty glance with Jason, then stepped back and fired a kick at the air just above Maggie's bony ass. She and Jason both squelched laughs as Maggie made it to her feet, holding the drenched throw at arm's length and still managing to splatter herself.

"I'll take care of that," Jason offered. Maggie gladly handed over the throw, which Jason wrung out over the pool and arranged across the back of a lounger as Marina and Maggie went inside to continue the tour.

The west wing proved to be well stocked with sitting ducks for Marina ("Movie star photos? Oh, I get it. We're in *Tinseltown*. That is so beyond lame.") and by the time she'd seen all three bedrooms on that end of the house, Maggie's nerves were clearly numbered. She tried to speed Marina through the sunken den and living room area, but as a prudent mansion-shopper, Marina had a few last questions.

"That's a really odd place for a coffee table," the petite eighties icon observed. "And that rug—is something wrong with the floor underneath?"

Everyone stared at the glass-cube coffee table and the Oriental rug in question, Maggie of course deliciously oblivious to the fact that Marina knew damn well the spot had been occupied by the bloodstained sofa up until yesterday. "No, no, no. In fact, we're expecting a new sofa to be delivered this week," Maggie fabricated.

Marina's face remained expressionless except for one raised eyebrow. She gracefully dropped to her knees, flipped up the edge of the rug, and began inspecting the floor. Maggie shot Jason a panicked glance. "Really, Miss Stetson, there's no—"

"Wait a minute. What is this . . . *blood?*" Marina exclaimed.

"Oh, nonsense," Maggie laughed, imploding.

"Look at these stains. This is dried blood. What the hell happened here?" Marina demanded.

Jason moved forward for a closer look. "You know what that is? That's paint," he said to Marina.

Taking her cue, Maggie shifted from flustered to imperious. "Jason, why is there paint on this floor?"

"Probably . . . from . . . Fawn. She used to paint . . . those pictures of hers sitting right here so she could see the pool," he explained.

"Oh, yes, that's right," agreed Maggie. "Another good reason my son Giles left her. Well, Miss Stetson, you've seen the entire house. I can briefly walk you through the garage on the way back to your car."

"I don't need to see anymore, Mrs. Burke. I'm prepared to make an offer," Marina said. Jason's eyes controlled a strong desire to bug out of his head.

"Y-you are? Well, that's marvelous," Maggie trilled.

Marina held up her hand, silencing her. "But first I need to see it completely empty. No artwork, no furniture, nothing. I can't even *think* past all this obnoxious crap." The hand moved to her temple and began massaging it.

"I'm not sure I understand what you're asking . . . ," Maggie began, trailing off. Jason, however, understood exactly what Marina was asking and came perilously close to blowing it all by erupting into a fit of mirth.

"Clear it out," Marina said. "I need every last ugly stick gone. I mean, the maid's room and laundry area are fine, but the rest of it . . ." She shook her head. "I'm sorry if that's inconvenient, Mrs. Burke, but it's really the only way my husband and I will be able to make that kind of commitment." Maggie just stared at her. "It's up to you," Marina smiled. "I'll be in touch with Syd's office. It was nice meeting both of you. *Ciao.*" She sashayed out the door without another glance.

"God, I hate show business," Maggie said.

He'd only intended to cruise over the hill to Mermaid Records' Burbank offices and drop off his "Broken Mirror" video script to Chip, but driving the Mercedes proved to be so therapeutic for his self-esteem, Jason repealed his own ban on using Marina's car unless it was *absolutely necessary* and took a tremendously enjoyable ninety-minute detour along Melrose and Santa Monica Boulevards then back up to Sunset Strip, accompanied on the elderly but perfectly serviceable tape deck by an advance cassette of *Very,* the new Pet Shop Boys album due for release in two months that Terry Davidson had given him at last night's dinner with Terry, his family and Marina at the producer's way-cool Hancock Park home.

They'd spent a magical evening eating meatless lasagna, drinking wine (Pellegrino for Marina) and telling Terry and his wife about Marina's tour of the mansion earlier that day. Terry responded with primo music industry gossip items concerning Whitney Houston and the Stone Temple Pilots. After dinner they reviewed the proofs for the final layout of the *Ghost in the Fog* CD cover and booklet, for which Marina gave Jason full credit—the John Dugdale photos were nothing short of gorgeous.

Now, as he turned onto Doheny Road from Sunset, heading back home, Jason found himself arriving at the unlikely conclusion that his life had radically improved almost from the very moment the twin barrels of the sawed-off shotgun had been thrust into his crotch early Wednesday morning. The Grand Guignol defilement of the already ruined sofa, his sudden burst of creativity in the music video medium, the trade-in of decrepit shitbox for valet-able glamour-coach—all were undeniable results of the mugging, an event that in the rosy glow of hindsight was quite possibly the best thing that had ever happened to Jason. Certainly his friendships with Hank and Marina had never been stronger. And if it had taken a near-death experience and justifiable homicide to get there, tough titty.

He effortlessly commandeered the Mercedes up the hill, going left off Schuyler Drive and climbing Vista Laguna before sharply banking right into the mansion's driveway. The gate was open. Maggie. Jason had planned a tranquil afternoon making tapes and reading *The Case of the Not-So-Nice Nurse*, a hilarious lesbian Nancy Drew spoof he'd just picked up in West Hollywood, while pretending not to wait for a life-changing phone call from Chip Reeves. He could do all that sequestered in his room while Maggie ran amok elsewhere, he supposed, curving up and around to the carport where he was startled to see not only Maggie's Lexus but also a huge van into which uniformed laborers were loading ugly, high-priced furniture and accessories!

Oh my God. Marina's prank worked. This initial thought he put aside for a more logical explanation-to-come, although it certainly hadn't by the time Jason had crossed the driveway and entered the house. Blue-suited movers buzzed about, packing boxes and removing art from the walls under the exacting supervision of Maggie Burke and her J. Crewed acolyte and partner in interior misdecoration, Rochelle, who waved without looking at him when Jason traversed the rapidly emptying foyer/dining area and said hello.

"Uh, what's going on?" he inquired with utterly false nonchalance.

Maggie sighed. "Surely you remember. You were standing right beside me when that singer insisted they had to see the place *stripped* before she'd make an offer." Oh, boy. "Everything but your room should be cleared by tonight. The Stetsons can come by tomorrow, and if things go well, we won't be needing your services for very much longer," she smiled nastily.

Don't count on it, Cruella, Jason fired back mentally, a warm glow suddenly burgeoning through his body like organic Darvoset. Maggie and Rochelle diverted their attention to the bedrooms and disappeared into the west wing. Jason went into the kitchen for a diet Coke, which he promptly forgot about upon the discovery of a file folder on the black marble countertop. Labeled STETSON, MARINA/RIETTA, "HANK", it appeared to be the official Syd Swann Realty dossier on the couple, including copies of contracts, correspondence and a Buyer Information form on pretentious, gold-trimmed letterhead.

Clipped to this sheet was a half-page *People* magazine wedding photo of Marina and Hank, the bride resplendent in an antique lace gown, the tuxedoed groom sporting 1991's popular muffintop hairstyle, luxuriant curls fading into shaven back and sides. Obviously completed after the stormy villa transaction Marina had told him about had been finalized, the form listed their occupations, estimated yearly income, Social Security numbers and DMV registrations. Under "Comments" had been typed the ominous "See S. Swann."

So Maggie had done a little research before authorizing the furniture purge. The notion of her prying into Marina and Hank's lives sent a thin icicle of dread through his guts, but he knew they were beyond her reach. Marina had made no promises the day Maggie had shown her the house and was obligated to do not a damn thing. He couldn't wait to call her in New York with this delicious success story.

The day passed in endless hour-long blocks, each one marked by a different talk show host on the giant-screen TV set, which, thank God, Maggie was obviously going to let stay. Muting the commercials, Jason overheard snippets of Maggie's conversation with Rochelle through his bedroom door, the most interesting of which concerned a cruise Maggie felt Giles would be very eager to take with his parents *and* Rochelle (who in addition to being a snotty prep bitch-kitty was apparently the eligible bachelorette of Maggie's dreams) "after all that divorce nonsense is cleared up." He managed to catch the phone the few times it rang, but it was always for Maggie, who remained at the house until everything but the servants' room, kitchen and laundry area were bare.

As soon as he heard the gate shut behind the moving truck and Lexus, he began to dial Marina's hotel in New York. Call-waiting stopped him. Andre's voice on the line floored him. "Howdy, stranger! Did you and Hollywood miss me?" Five stinging retorts immediately popped into Jason's head but were withheld, allowing Andre to prattle away that they had *just* landed and Jason would absolutely not *believe* the *soap opera* Fawn had been at the center of and how she was *dying* to see Jason and could he meet them at Marix in an hour?

Sure. Why not? Andre Nickerson—truly a sick ticket. One phone message had been the sum total of his communication with Jason the past two months, but did Andre even attempt an apology or explanation? Heavens, no. He was much, much, much too busy co-starring in *The Fawn and the Fairer*, the sizzling real-life drama Jason was lucky enough to be rejoining tonight!

The absurdity of it all was actually irresistible. Andre doubtlessly expected to dazzle Jason with Giles and Fawn's romantic shenanigans, naturally unaware that not only had Jason instigated their jet-set neo-courtship, but because of the latest Maggie 'n' Lewis Burke answering machine bombshell, Jason had a more complete understanding of this particular soap than any of its dysfunctional participants. Not to mention the fact that he personally felt the events of his own life this summer easily out-dished the Burkes' cutthroat family circus.

He had no idea how to handle the admittedly incendiary answering machine tape. The last thing he wanted was to be more deeply entangled with these people. But for the moment, his living arrangements were basically at their mercy. He changed, taking care to avoid mixing any of Andre's clothes in with his outfit and deciding the best strategy was to reveal as little as possible about himself and what he knew about Maggie, Fawn and Giles.

His arrival at the restaurant could not have been more perfectly timed. He pulled the Mercedes up to the valet on Flores Street just as Fawn and Andre were alighting from *their* Mercedes and so was able to enjoy the full, Ray-Bans-tilted-down-the-nose astonishment of Andre's reaction to Jason's car. "I guess we don't need to ask how *you're* doing!" Andre snorted with indignation a lot less mock than he would have liked Jason to believe. He was blonde and tan and worked out in a UT Longhorns tank top, ludicrously tight jeans and ropers. He squeezed Jason into an Egoiste-scented hug.

"Hi, sugar!" Fawn chirped. After she released him, he flicked his eyes down to her hand. Sure enough, Giles's twenty-carat cock-substitute glittered like a small Christmas ornament. "Thanks for house-sitting. Let's go get a table before it gets too crowded. I am starving!"

"*Where* did you get that car, young man?" demanded Andre, jabbing Jason in the shoulder repeatedly as they climbed the steps to the patio café.

"I'm borrowing it from a friend," Jason said, hesitating before adding, "my car was stolen."

"That old clunker?" Andre gasped. "You're kidding. Oh, honey, that must have been terrible for you."

They were advised of a ten-minute wait and proceeded to the bar. Fawn told the waiter no drinks for her, then started scarfing chips and chunky salsa. Did she know? Jason wondered.

"God, it's good to be back!" Andre sighed, plucking a Kick-Ass Margarita frozen no salt from their waiter's tray. "There were some mighty fine mens in Texas, let me make *that* clear, but I missed all my WeHo eye-candy. Check that out—I've been seeing her and her shaved balls at the Sports Erection for years . . ." Andre smacked his lips as the gym rat in question brushed past. Fawn chomped on, oblivious.

Andre refocused on Jason. "So has Mag the Hag been driving you up a wall?" Jason nodded, sipping his own drink. There was no reason to downplay the shitty situation Andre had knowingly stranded him in. "Well, still, it's better than that dingy room on Orange Grove Avenue with Laverne and Shirley and Retardo-Pup, right?" Jason shook his head. "Oh, for fuck's sake, Jason! I know I deserve a good heinie-paddling for subletting your room to Stefan, but I honestly didn't think it would cause any trouble. Pinky-swear," he added, dabbing his extended little finger with his tongue. Jason couldn't help chuckling.

"Okay, look," Andre said, pocketing the sunglasses to show that he meant business. "Stefan paid three months' rent up front."

"Andre, that is so—" Jason began.

"Just listen. I'm staying at Fawn's apartment on Burton Way with her, but you'll probably be able to join me there very soon because . . ." He pulled Jason aside and whispered, "I think Fawn is going to move in with Giles. They're getting back together. *Look at that ring.*"

"Y'all quit whispering!" Fawn ordered. "Andre, what are you tellin' him?" She put a protective arm around Jason's shoulders.

"Why, nothing, Fawn. I think that the *r-o-c-k* speaks for itself," remarked Andre pertly.

"All right, all right," Fawn sighed, as if she were Sharon Stone finally giving in to a gaggle of pesky reporters outside the Golden Globes. "Giles and I are *considering* a reunion—I haven't made up my mind yet. This is a li'l present he gave me . . ." Wrist limp, fingers wiggling, she displayed the ring.

"Don't tell me that's real," their server said as he swapped Fawn's empty salsa cup for a full one. Fawn giggled, Andre nodded, and Jason gulped down the rest of his strawberry margarita.

"Andre, enough about us," Fawn pleaded. "Jason, how are you doin', darlin'? How's the video store?"

"I don't work there anymore. I've been interviewing and meeting people and I think I'm going to have a job at Mermaid Records really soon," he admitted, knocking the wooden drink rail and telling himself he really was not embellishing.

"Fabulous! You can give them Fawn's CD!" Andre thoughtfully exclaimed.

Their table was called. As soon as they were seated, Andre whipped out a compact disc. Titled simply *Fawn Farrar*, it featured a cover photo of Fawn in pearls and a red, cleavage-friendly evening gown reclining in what appeared to be a haystack. On the back was a black-and-white shot of a moody, airbrushed Fawn (who, to Jason's knowledge, couldn't play so much as a tambourine) leaning reflectively on a piano. "This looks great," Jason said brightly, opening the jewel box and sliding out the booklet. Instead of lyrics, it contained five pages of Fawn pix and liner notes by Andre (who else?) which Jason elected not to put himself in the high-pressure position of actually reading.

Instead, he turned his attention to the CD itself. Along with

Fawn's preciously art-directed name and the "Aida Productions" logo, a single song was listed: 1. "I'm All Cried Out."

"Just one song?" Jason couldn't help asking, although he did resist the urge to add "All this fucking hoopla for one lousy song?!?"

"It's all we had time to record," Andre replied defensively. "And Fawn wasn't feeling well, and then Giles showed up . . ."

A waitress asked what they wanted to start with. Fawn requested nachos with everything and, to Jason's alarm, a pitcher of kick-ass on the rocks. Okay, maybe they were for him and Andre. "It was the most romantic thing I've ever seen," Andre was gushing. "Giles drove up in a Porsche Carrera and practically swept Fawn up in the middle of rehearsal. And then they vanished for two whole days! I was worried sick."

"You were shacked up with that stripper from the Bonham," Fawn reminded him.

Before Andre could snip forth a response, three margarita glasses were slapped down in front of them. The waitress filled Andre's, then Jason's, then Fawn's. Fawn did not protest. She raised her glass. "Bottoms up, sweeties!" Andre clinked his glass against hers, then turned to Jason, who looked suddenly distressed.

Fawn began to drink. "Oh, Jesus . . . Fawn I don't think you should be doing that!" Jason blurted out helplessly.

"Oh. And why the hell not?" Fawn asked, clanking the glass down on the table, obviously pissed.

"Because you're pregnant."

"WHAT?!?" Fawn and Andre screamed.

The tape did not go over well. Jason had played it for Andre and Fawn three times since they'd bolted from the restaurant sans dinner or appetizers and tore back to Vista Laguna. The first time, they'd all been clustered around the television stand in which Jason kept the machine hidden. Upon hearing Lewis Burke tell Maggie their family doctor's diagnosis, Fawn nearly went into a fainting spell and had to be helped to one of the servants' quarters' twin beds, where she listened to the rest of the recording, her face contorted into a horrified mask of disbelief. When Maggie offered her prediction about her daughter-in-law discovering and aborting the pregnancy, Fawn shrieked.

Andre, so used to magnifying the mediocrity of Fawn's life into melodrama, was rendered speechless by the raw, deep-rooted import of this development. He was the one who rewound the tape and played it a second time, after which he all but attacked Jason. "How long have you known about this!?"

"Just a few days," Jason stammered, knowing he was now in it big-time but refusing to take any shit. "I had no way to get in touch with you guys."

"And why did you wait till we were sitting down to *dinner* to tell us about this?" Andre said accusingly, looking to Fawn for backup.

"Hey," said Jason, "this is pretty personal, don't you think? Not to mention none of my business. I just didn't exactly know how to bring it up."

"Don't blame Jason, Andre," Fawn groaned. "Baby-sweets, I know this puts you in an impossible position," she told Jason. "But this is not gonna come back to you. I promise. Now play it again. I have to hear it one more time."

So she did, finally breaking into tears at Maggie's "little tramp falling off a cliff" line. "That evil goddamn fuckin' dried-up nasty cunt! The bitch! The lousy, vicious coozebag! What did I ever do to make her hate me so much?"

Andre comforted the sobbing heiress. "It's all right, honey. To-morrow you'll go see Doctor David DeLeon and he'll start taking good care of you and your little angel. Giles'll be home at four o'clock and we'll go meet him at the airport. And just remember, we've got the old witch on tape. Jason, give me that cassette." Jason ejected it, put it into its case and handed it over. It vanished into Andre's pocket.

Fawn dried her eyes on one of Jason's pillowcases and suddenly they were flashing fire. "Maggie Burke, your ass is grass! You go ahead and try to make Giles choose between you and me, lady, and we'll see who comes out a loser. Come on, Andre. I want to go back and try to catch Giles in Dayton before he goes to sleep."

"He's at his brother's. I've got the number," Andre said, helping her to her feet.

The doorbell buzzed. "Oh, God, is that her? 'Cause I will take her *down,* baby or no baby!" Fawn snarled, placing one hand over her stomach and clenching the other into a fist.

"It can't be. Nobody came up the driveway. We would have heard," Jason said. Fawn and Andre followed him through the dining area to the front door. There was only one person who could have just walked up, and, as the peephole revealed, it was Hank.

Trapped between Fawn and Andre and the door, Jason felt an indefinable panic about Hank crossing paths with the two of them, but since he could think of no earthly reason not to answer it, he had to.

Hank was in cutoff sweats and a red T-shirt and carried two bags from which wafted the delectably pungent aroma of curry. "Hi," Jason said, amping surprise. "These are my friends, Fawn Farrar and Andre Nickerson. Fawn owns the house. This is my friend Hank, who lives up the street."

"How wonderful to meet you," said Andre. Hank shook his hand, then did the same with Fawn while Andre turned to Jason with one of his "You bad, bad girl" looks.

"I just thought I'd drop by and see if you'd had dinner yet," Hank said to Jason. "But if you're all hungry, we may have to order more."

"Oh, no. We were just leaving," Fawn assured him. "Jason, sugar, thank you." A tense, lengthy hug. "We'll be in touch. Don't say anything to you-know-who," she whispered.

They said goodbye to Hank and walked out, Andre continuing to make incredulous, worshipful faces at Jason while mouthing something queeny until Jason gave a final curt wave and shut the door.

"Okay—did I miss the yard sale?" Hank asked, looking around.

The only place to eat was the poolside patio table, where they split chicken tikka and seafood vindaloo over saffron rice and Jason told Hank about Marina's encounter with Maggie and its decidedly dramatic consequences. "That's so fuckin' perfect," Hank laughed. "Does Marina know yet?"

"No," Jason said. "I tried the hotel in New York before I went to Marix and she was out. I left word for her to call me before her voice lesson tomorrow." Hank nodded and forked some leftover chunks of chicken breast onto a piece of naan, which he rolled into a sandwich and ate in large, pensive bites.

"So, what's up?" Jason finally asked.

"I was just thinking you're the only reason I have any idea where she is or what she's doing. She left me this note that said something like 'Came back to see Jason—he's got Mercedes' and that's the only communication we've had since that night. She ain't ever gonna forgive me and I don't blame her. Is she okay?"

"She seems to be really good," Jason said. "They've planned the tour and Betty's going to go with her and Marina's excited about it."

"That's cool to hear."

"Hank, she said she wants to talk to you, but she can't. Right now. I really think when she gets back, she'll want to see you and—"

"Jason. Listen to me. I don't expect Marina to be able to deal with this, or me, or for us to be friends or any of that bullshit. She's within all her rights to never want to see me again. I'd just move out tomorrow, but I get the feeling she's probably going to be doing that, so if I did it, too, we'd be just like your fucked-up friends Fawn and What's-His-Face."

"You guys could never be like them," Jason said quietly. "So, where would you move?"

"I don't know. Los Feliz, Larchmont. Somewhere closer to my job. I guess I should call anybody but Syd Swann and list the place." He stood up and unself-consciously stretched. Something cracked and his T-shirt rode up several inches, exposing lean, ripped flesh. Jason sighed and started clearing the table.

Hank clapped a hand on Jason's shoulder and squeezed. "Look, buddy. The last thing I want is anyone thinking I'm looking for sympathy. Marina's the one who got shafted here. And I'm really sorry I got you involved. It was shitty of me."

Jason did not trust himself to reply, because at that moment more than anything he wanted to say that his involvement had been entirely voluntary and since the touch of Hank's hand had just now prompted an instant semiboner, Jason decided on a simple nod to get the forbidden Italian love-Jesus out of the house as quickly as possible.

Hank's already-somber face fell a few more notches. He closed his eyes and seemed to pitch forward slightly, his hand still on Jason's shoulder. A giddy bolt of terror spiked Jason, who knew if Hank collapsed into his arms it could be all over. Instead, Hank stepped back and stuck his hands in the pockets of his sweats and said he had to go.

They went into the house, which now resembled a cavernous art gallery after severe NEA cutbacks. "Thanks for dinner," Jason said. "And for calling Marina and having her come down and see me. You've both been so great." *I just wish you were the same person.* Wait a minute, he thought, that would make them George Michael.

"Jason, I'm glad you're okay after getting mugged by those assholes and the break-in and what happened over there"—he cocked his head in the direction of the living room "—but it's probably, you know, better . . . if we don't see each other anymore."

"Not even as friends." Jason didn't bother to phrase it as a question because he knew.

"Can't do it, buddy. I gotta go." He started walking to the door.

"Where?" Jason was acutely aware that no matter what he did or said, it would be a mistake.

"For Christ's sake, Jason, what do you want from me? What do you want me to say? Out. Away. Someplace. I don't fuckin' know."

"To the Dungeon?" Jason asked softly.

Hank's hand dropped from the doorknob. "How do you know about that?"

The flash-forward to Hank in a gabled Los Feliz duplex starting his life over with a string of beautiful bar trash was heartbreaking, appalling, unbearable. "It doesn't matter. I want you to stay," said Jason. Once he'd actually gotten those words out, it took no effort at all to cross the foyer to where Hank stood motionless at the door and envelop him in a thermonuclear, full-body-contact kiss.

They broke apart, hearts hammering at each other, shirts shoved aside, their hands already reclaiming pecs, stomachs, asses. "What about Marina?" Hank murmured, his lush, sexy lips grazing against Jason's quiveringly responsive neck.

"I don't know," Jason admitted, Hank's biceps hot and huge in his hand. "I can't think that far ahead."

"Then don't try." Hank crushed Jason against him. Jason felt

Hank's thick penis straining against the sweatpants, wedged into Jason's own aching crotch. He had to have it. *Violet, forgive me,* he silently implored before dropping to his knees. Jason tugged at the laces cinching Hank's waist as he mouthed bulging heat through the gray poly-cotton. Hank stopped tousling Jason's hair to help—the knots in the drawstrings were obviously too gnarled for Jason's shaky fingers.

Jason hooked his thumbs into the now-relaxed waistband and dragged the sweats down to Hank's knees. The cutoffs fell to the floor and Hank kicked them aside. His snowy white briefs were so radically tented they'd begun to pull away from Hank's waist, revealing tufts of dark hair sprouting below his muscle-framed navel. Jason inserted his index finger into the gap and yanked downward, eventually freeing Hank's dick, which bounced against his abs and continued to bob up and down until Jason trapped it between his lips and hungrily swallowed the gorgeous thing.

"Hey, Jason," Hank interrupted. "Is there any furniture left in your bedroom?"

Tricia slammed Edgar's TV booking binder onto her desk and flipped to the *G*s. It had been a most frustrating week. Somehow Edgar had gotten that useless Arye Gross a series regular role on the new Ellen DeGeneres show, *These Friends of Mine.* And while Tricia was in the rest room, a call from Julianne Moore had gone directly to Edgar, resulting in today's lunch appointment that could very well result in the signing of that up-and-coming film star, and a corresponding feather in Edgar's recently besmirched agent's cap.

Then Edgar, who'd been strutting around all morning in his new tan Pierre Cardin suit, stopped by her desk with an extremely minor request. "I'm meeting Julianne at this restaurant in Beverly Hills, Martini's, and I don't know where the hell it is. Somewhere on Wilshire. Find out and double-confirm the reservation."

"Right away, Edgar." According to reviews she'd read in the *Los Angeles Times* and *Buzz,* Martini's was a beguiling mélange of hearty nuovo Italian cuisine and Sinatra-era hipster chic located just off Rodeo Drive. She dialed 411 for the number, then called the place, gleaning both the address and Edgar's confirmed reservation for two at one o'clock. She was already half out of her chair to deliver the information to Edgar when the solution came to her.

As a new restaurant, Martini's could very easily be staffed with rather inexperienced people who could very easily be confused about certain things, such as the address and how to use the reservation book. Perhaps they were so incompetent, they could very easily instruct prospective patrons to look for a fictitious silver awning decorated with a martini glass to identify the place. Very easily indeed, Tricia clucked to herself, shredding the memo slip she'd just written and jotting down a Wilshire Boulevard address that couldn't possibly exist because it was only two digits away from a casting office the agency dealt with. Below, she added "1:15." Someone at that place had made quite a blunder!

She peeked into Edgar's office. He was ordering from a Crate and Barrel catalog. "Hold on a second, will ya, hon?" he told the operator, hitting a button. "Yeah?"

"Here, Edgar. They told me Julianne had to change the reservation to 1:15. Look for a big silver awning with a martini glass on it."

"Great. Hey, Tricia. I was up till four a.m. I'm gonna need more coffee. Here," he said, handing over his forty-four-ounce plastic java tankard, which presumably meant he intended to drink as opposed to douche with it.

Between the built-in fifteen-minute tardy and the guaranteed wild-goose chase to find Martini's, Tricia calculated there was a 75 to 80 percent chance that the meeting would be aborted. If only she could up that to one hundred . . .

On her way out of the break room, she ran into Ari Rosenblatt. "Hey, Tricia. Misty and Eric said you've seemed kind of down these past couple days. Is everything okay?"

"I guess I've been a little preoccupied," she confessed. "Edgar's having a bit of a rough time."

Ari nodded. "But this Julianne Moore thing is great. Everything's gonna be swell. Edgar needs to take a chill pill. By the way, we're all going to Q's to shoot some pool after work, if you're interested."

"That's sweet of you to ask, Ari, but I can't. Maybe some other time." She offered him a lovely smile and hurried back to her desk. Oh, yes, Edgar needed to take a pill all right. What a smart idea. She retrieved her purse and wriggled out the small orange prescription bottle of laxatives.

Her plan had been to dose Edgar before some overblown night on the town with his girlfriend, but since that featherbrained blow-up doll Kendra was in Napa shooting the reprehensibly cheesy *Prying Eyes*, the opportunity to do so had not arisen. (Which reminded her—Violet Cyr had left several increasingly perturbed messages about her dissatisfaction with the shoot; Tricia would have to meet Violet for dinner and see that she leave Edgar immediately after *Prying Eyes* wrapped.) Besides, why embarrass Edgar in front of some disposable peroxided tramp when his humiliation could be tied to an exciting, successful potential client like Julianne Moore?

According to the label, only one capsule was to be taken at a time. She wondered what five would do. Something very unpleasant indeed, she imagined, nearly chortling aloud as she tapped the sea green capsules into her palm.

She transferred an up-the-ass smoke-blowing call from network casting in to Edgar, then returned to the break room/kitchenette. It was empty and the coffee was done. Tricia poured it from the glass pot into Edgar's convenience store bladder-buster. Make that bowel-buster, she smirked, carefully unscrewing each of the five largish capsules and sprinkling their contents into the steaming coffee. She added two extra drops of vanilla to offset any unusual taste the laxative might impart, but Edgar's blend was so strong to begin with, she doubted he'd notice a thing. The capsule shells went down the drain, the plastic splash-guard top went onto the cup and the coffee went straight to Edgar's desk.

By the time he strolled past her desk without so much as a "See ya at four" he'd consumed all forty-four ounces.

Maggie Burke's nails were not quite dry when the phone rang in her Hotel Bel-Air suite. "Damn!" she muttered, picking up. She knew she should have worked a visit to the Korean girl into her schedule today.

"It's Giles, Mother."

Maggie suppressed a sigh of disappointment. Lewis had already informed her that Giles had returned to Los Angeles, not to mention the fact that she was expecting an important call from Syd Swann's office about when that insane Marina Stetson might be available to view the house Maggie had emptied at a cost in the high four figures. Nevertheless, there was no reason Giles should be let off the hook. "We were worried sick about you! Where have you been?"

"Just away," he replied like a defensive, inwardly terrified teen. Maggie smiled and stretched her skeletal frame across the bed. Where the hell was room service with her lunch, anyway? "Mother, I need to see you. Tonight."

"What's the problem, Giles?"

"I'll explain everything when you get here. Can you come to my house at seven?"

"No. I'm going to a baby shower in Hancock Park at five. With Rochelle. You remember her? The very attractive girl you met at the Hermening wedding in Grosse Point? Well, she lives out here now. Getting her master's at USC. She's just a delight, Giles—"

"What time can you be here?"

"By nine, I suppose. Giles, can't we discuss this over the phone? Why are you being so melodramatic?"

"My place. By nine. I'll see you then." It took Maggie a moment to realize the click in her ear was Giles hanging up on her. That disrespectful little layabout! How dare he? Maggie put down the phone, trying to figure out what on earth Giles was up to. She wished she could believe it was some idiotic passing fancy, that he wanted her to invest in a film he hoped to direct or something equally sophomoric. But she knew that petulant tone of his. This *stank* of Fawn Farrar, and Maggie did not like it one little bit.

Edgar had to cut off some mummified Beverly Hills broad in a Cadillac in order to jump into the far right lane on his second pass around the block where that fucking restaurant was supposed to be. The old bag responded with a honk, which erupted into a total bitch-fit on the horn when Edgar slowed to five miles per to scan the building for the awning or any other sign of Martini's. Edgar waved his middle finger out the sunroof and came to a complete stop.

This had to be it. 8672 Wilshire Boulevard. There was 8670 next door. Hold the goddamn phone—there was no 8672. Jesus Christ, how the fuck did this happen? He snatched up the slip of paper on which Tricia had written the address. Maybe she got the numbers reversed . . . unlikely, since she'd sooner whack her left nipple off with the office paper-cutter than make a friggin' mistake. One-twenty? Fuck!

He made a fast right, then an immediate U-turn and waited for the light to go green so he could back west on Wilshire and look for fuckin' 8762. He felt around under the Jaguar's ivory leather seat for his cellular phone, yanked up the antenna and punched in the office number. It started ringing. Oh, great. Now he had to take a shit. Another dickwad behind him started honking. The light was green. Edgar turned left onto Wilshire. Why the fuck wasn't Big Tits at the front desk answering? Finally . . . "Your Pacifica Tech cellular phone service has been discontinued due to nonpayment of a delinquent account. To reinstitute service, please dial our billing office at 310—"

"Goddamnit!" Edgar barked, hurling the phone into the backseat as he noticed strange and urgent sensations in his lower digestive tract. He had to take a dump—*right away.* There was a Starbuck's on the next block. He'd pull over and—fuck! A Volvo station wagon with a "Practice Random Kindness and Senseless Acts of Beauty" bumper sticker cut him off, then *stopped* on a yellow light. "Stupid cocksucker! Fuckin' moron! Ohh, Jesus Christ . . . ," he moaned as not one but two gigantic loads of liquid shit torpedoed out of his ass. It soaked his silk bikini briefs, straight through his light tan slacks. It squished up the butt crack of his ass and ran past the backs of his thighs and dribbled down to his socks. And it smelled. Although not a religious man, Edgar could not stop screaming "Why are you fucking with me?!!!?" over and over again while glaring heavenward through the sunroof.

The whole thing took less than two hours, from initial phone call that morning to Jason's return through the mansion gate as manager, visual media promotions, Mermaid Records. Chip Reeves had given the "Broken Mirror" script to his pal Jillian, who ran Mermaid's video department, the same day Mermaid learned that through spontaneous play by two Seattle deejays, the song was now number six in that market. Clearly it should be released as the debut single from

Ghost in the Fog. Jillian faxed the script to a director she had in mind, and he agreed that Jason's concept, a nightmarish odyssey through sexual temptation ending in violent death for the scumbags stalking the heroine, was exactly right for the new, darker image the album dictated for Marina.

Jillian, a ditz-of-steel Glenne Headley-type, explained to a blissed-out Jason that Chip had intended to save him for an A&R position, but he realized upon reading the "Broken Mirror" scenario that Jason's talents might be employed in a more timely manner in VMP. Jillian told Jason she'd enjoyed some of The Pop-Tartts' singles in college, but found Marina's first two albums atrocious and had been baffled when Mermaid signed her last fall. *Ghost in the Fog*, though, had been a huge surprise. "I know you two are very tight," she said with a sardonic eyebrow-raise, "but so are Chip and I, and he's too smart to recommend anyone shitty."

That was it. The job was his. It would entail coordinating the making of all Mermaid videos by serving as liaison between artists and their A&R and the freelance production companies and directors Mermaid contracted out to. It involved extensive communication with music channels and club video suppliers and occasional travel to New York and London. "It also isn't a bad way to break into directing, but you didn't hear that from me," Jillian added. The position paid a flat salary of $775 per week, no overtime, but full benefits and an expense account if necessary. He was to start next Monday.

Chip was in New York with Marina, so Jason left a note with his assistant—"I start with Jillian on Monday. Thank you thank you thank you!"—and went back to Vista Laguna, where he found Andre in his bathroom, packing. Jason said hi then darted into the servants' quarters, where he was relieved to discover Andre hadn't begun excavating the closet. Jason slipped off the shoes he'd borrowed for the interview and laid them next to Andre's other pairs on the floor.

"Love-muffin, we have to talk," Andre decreed, marching into the bedroom with a box of toiletries. It had been two days since Marix and the answering machine tape, during which Jason had heard nothing from Aida Productions. "Where did you get the Benz and *who* was that deliciously fuckable stud we left you alone with the other night?"

So Jason told him. Not everything, of course—Andre certainly could not be trusted with the truth about Jason and Hank, or Marina's real estate prank. But Jason did tell him about meeting Marina and her husband, the trip to Vegas, the mugging, the bloodbath in the living room, and the job he'd just gotten. He felt the balance of his resentment toward Andre evaporate as Jason recounted this tumultuous if edited version of the summer to Andre's reliably campy overreactions to it all, particularly the mugger's death ("Oh, good Christ! It was kill or be killed, honey! I'll never feel safe in Beverly Hills again!"). After all, it could have been argued that, neglectful dillettance notwithstanding, Andre had made possible everything that had happened to Jason the past two months, resulting in Jason's dream job.

And because of the job, Jason was now truly free. The Aquarius Images fiasco would not repeat itself. And although Jason made Andre promise not to mention Jason's friendship and/or association with Marina and Hank until he'd officially started at Mermaid, who really gave a shit at this point what anyone knew? Jason would begin looking for his own apartment immediately. He'd ask Violet for a move-in loan as soon as his job started.

After a respectful thirty seconds to let Jason's revelations sink in, Andre dished the latest in the Fawn saga. He hadn't seen her since yesterday, when she left for the airport to meet Giles's flight. The star-crossed marrieds had spent the night chez Giles in Bel-Air, and this morning Fawn had called Andre to request his presence at Giles's house at seven o'clock sharp. "She wouldn't say anything else. It's all so *Wild Palms*!"

Jason helped Andre load the rest of his things into his car, submitted to a reprise of congratulations then overwrought sympathy for "the hell you've been through," showed Andre the bloodstained living room floor, and said goodbye. Jason picked up the phone and dialed the Whispering Pines Lodge and Resort. He asked for Room 217.

On the third ring, "Yeah . . . who is this? Hello?"

"Violet? It's Jason. Were you asleep?"

"Mmm. It's okay. What time is it? Oh, shit. Sorry. I was up all night again."

"Do you want to keep sleeping?" he asked timidly. "Cause I can call back later or—"

"No, I really had to get up anyway. And I didn't even set the alarm. So what's up?"

"Well, I just got a job at Mermaid Records."

"That's so great! Congratulations. So they liked your video script?"

"Actually, yeah. I start on Monday. In visual media promotions. Can you believe it?"

"Of course I can. See, everything worked out great. Aren't you glad you didn't screw it all up by having a fling with Hank?"

"Oh, yeah." There would be time to analyze and debate the dizzying messiness of the Hank situation when Violet got back to town. Jason changed the subject. "So how's the shoot?"

"This is how it is. Before I fell asleep around noon today, I'd been up forty hours straight, the last, oh, six of which I spent in panties, push-up bra, garters and fishnets tied to a bed in a room so infested with fleas a special intern was assigned to spray Off on my body as soon as Igor said 'cut.' And then when that bastard called a break, they all just walked off and left me there. I swear to God, I almost pulled a Marc Singer, who by the way, they haven't replaced yet."

"Why didn't you? It sounds hideous."

"I can't quit, Jason. Not after *Chillin' with Billy*, the fastest-canceled sitcom in history. And especially not when the thing I'm most known for is kicking Turk Marlowe in the balls. I have to stick with this. In two weeks it'll all be over. Supposedly, the new male lead is starting tomorrow."

"Who is it?"

"I have no idea. Christopher Atkins? Andrew Stevens? Jeff Griggs? You tell me. You're the one who worked at the video store, which is the only place this piece of crap is gonna end up. If I'm lucky," she sighed. "Look, I don't want to bring you down. I'm thrilled for you. You're gonna blow that record company away. I'll finish this fucking movie and come home and we'll go out and have a huge emancipation celebration somewhere disgustingly decadent."

"You got it. So what are you shooting tonight?"

"Nothing. Your pals Wendi and Igor are hosting a mandatory party, supposedly for the investors or exec producers or some bullshit, and I have to put in an appearance. Which reminds me. I need to borrow a dress from one of my costars. I'll try to call you in a few days. Congratulations again. And tell Marina I think I heard her new song on the radio and I really liked it."

"I will. Try to have fun tonight. Bye."

Violet hung up, tied her sleep-snarled mane of dark curls back with a velveteen fashion accessory, and walked down the creaky staircase at the end of the motel's second-floor landing to Room 120, where she found Kendra propped on pillows painting her toenails and watching a soap.

"Hi, Violet. I pulled out a few things I thought might be good for you," Kendra said. She wedged cotton between the last of her toes and did a chicken-walk to the bathroom. "I think we're about the same size." Except my boobs don't have their own gravitational pull, Violet mentally added. Kendra returned with three choices for Violet as well as her own selection for the evening, a strapless white sheath that when donned would presumably cover Kendra's woo-woo although God only knew. Wondering why in hell anyone would travel to a film location to shoot a four-day role like Kendra's with an entire wardrobe of evening wear in tow, Violet thanked her and took the black Alaia into the bathroom to try on.

Violet regarded herself dubiously in the chipped mirror. On the slightly taller, fuller-figured Kendra, this thing must be a traffic-stopping obscenity. On Violet it was merely dazzlingly trampy. What the hell. It would have to do. She slipped out of it, redressed and told Kendra it was perfect.

"Goody! So do you know where the party is, Violet?"

"I have the address. I'm not sure how to get there, exactly."

"Why don't you drive with me? I've been up to Wendi's place before. It's kind of in the mountains and it's *really* easy to get lost," Kendra advised.

"Okay, sure. That'd be swell," Violet smiled. Kendra had certainly been very sweet to her since they'd met on the set yesterday. The girl was no Linda Ellerbee in the brains department, but Violet appreciated having some sort of a friend, even though Kendra's role as an aerobicising murder victim would be completed by the end of the week.

At least this party should have some decent chow, Violet reminded herself hopefully as she began the laborious beautification process that preceded any show-biz function, no matter how fringe, because a girl never knew who she might run into or what casting needs they might have in the near future.

The twilight drive up into the hills was actually relaxing, despite the En Vogue cassette Kendra shoved into the LeBaron convertible's tape player and cranked to near-max volume as soon as she started the car. Since conversation was impossible, Violet sat back and marveled at the sylvan perfection of the wine country, vowing to return one day under better circumstances. Kendra had turned off the main road some time back, and as they climbed higher and houses and passing vehicles became more scarce, Violet became concerned that the bobbed blonde was so busy lip-synching to "Free Your Mind" she'd gotten them lost.

She needn't have worried. "Oops! It's right here!" Kendra giggled, wrenching the LeBaron into a very hard right, nearly missing the driveway. Expensive cars were parked in a haphazard line all the way up to the house, a towering A-frame built into the side the hill, its facade a geometric pattern of softly glowing windows. Kendra squeaked into a spot between a Town Car and a Cherokee and had to shimmy over to Violet's side to exit the convertible.

They clomped up redwood stairs to the front porch and Kendra gave the brass knocker a couple of raps. When no one answered, she shrugged and tried the door. It was unlocked. Pot smoke, Eagles music and the aroma of dim sum greeted the two women as they entered the house. The two largest knots of people seemed to be clustered around the first-floor fireplace (straight ahead in the sunken living room), and on the second-floor mezzanine, near sliding glass doors that probably led to some kind of outdoor patio area.

"Hi, Heather!" Kendra waved to a beautiful young girl in a pert French maid's getup behind a buffet stocked with haute-Chinese noshables.

"Did you girls carpool? That is so cute," Wendi Barash said, appearing from somewhere wearing a leather jumpsuit, an aging Tarzan in Armani Exchange on one arm. "Walt, I'd like you to meet my gorgeous star, Violet Cyr, and this is another fabulous actress, Kendra Michaels. Ladies, Walt Taylor, my dear friend, dentist"— Wendi flashed her caps—"and motion picture investor."

"How ya doin'?" Walt said, passing his joint to Wendi so he could shake hands.

Wendi hooked Violet around the waist and guided her toward the food as Walt and Kendra got better acquainted. "Wanna puff?" the hostess asked Violet before taking one herself. "You might end up with a rich husband tonight. Most of the guys here are loaded."

"Is this your house? It's very nice," Violet felt obliged to say.

"Thanks. I'm renting. Oh, damn, there's somebody I *have* to talk to. Help yourself to food, drinks, anything else that catches your eye. I'll be back to introduce you to more people," Wendi promised, moving off toward the fireplace.

Violet hated Chinese but was so famished she took a chance on the chicken salad and what Heather the French maid assured her was a vegetarian eggroll—no mystery meat. A separate table of wines was available in the living room. Violet poured herself a glass of white and sat down near some people she recognized from *Prying Eyes*, who made small talk about scenes that had been recently shot until Violet turned back to them after locating a spot to lose the remnants of her fairly inedible dinner plate and discovered the two actors and the assistant director had vanished.

Replacing them was a hot-looking man Violet had noticed earlier. He introduced himself as Jack and asked about her role in the film. "I play a voyeur-homemaker tricked into murdering my ex-lover's sadomasochistic wife. So I've really been able to draw a lot from my own life, which is so great for any actress," she joked charmingly. Jack laughed and momentarily touched her knee. Violet smiled back, admiring what she assessed as warmly handsome Semitic features as she realized with a strange little flutter that he was the first guy she'd even noticed since the breakup with Dave.

"So, is this the first time you've worked for Wendi?" Jack asked, peering at her cutely over his wineglass.

"Yeah, it is. I just did this ridiculous TV series that was canceled, and before that I was in New York doing some Broadway and a couple of films and a soap and things." She felt like she was babbling.

Jack patted her knee again, told her how nice it was to meet her, and excused himself to join a pair of bimbos across the room. So much for that. Jesus Christ, what am I doing here? Violet asked herself. And who were all these goddamn honeys strutting around like the place was a Victoria's Secret catalog shoot? The house was starting to fill up, although Violet counted only a few *Prying Eyer*s among the new wave. The cantilevered design of the house enabled Violet to scan both the second and third floors from the living room, and she did so, hoping to locate Kendra and perhaps get the hell out of this Night in Alpine Brentwood.

The music had changed to Prince and seemingly doubled in volume as Violet wended her way through clouds of various smokes and colognes to the stairs near the front door. She climbed up to the second floor, resolving to give mingling one more attempt and check out the rest of the house, which had been furnished with equal parts Eddie Bauer Showroom and Benson and Hedges Home Collection catalog.

She leaned against the mezzanine railing, idly imagining how things might be on *You Lucky Bastard*. Who had gotten her part? Two guys were watching her from across the living room, at the opposite railing. They were young but cheesy and thickly coiffed. One waved. She waved back, mentally choreographing an escape route should they begin to cruise her way. She felt cool hands on her shoulders and jumped.

"Hi, doll! Havin' fun?" Wendi inquired breathlessly. Violet turned around and tried to look festive.

"Oh, yeah. Great party!"

"Have you seen Igor yet?" Wendi asked, reflexively rubbing a finger under her phony nose.

"Uh, no. I don't think I—"

"Then come on! He's outside," Wendi urged, dragging Violet back through the sliding glass doors, where Igor held court in a hot tub. "Look, honey! It's Violet!" Wendi announced. She deposited the actress at the edge of the bubbling tub then disappeared instantly, leaving Violet to savor the chunky director wading toward her, brandishing a magnum of champagne, gold medallions glistening between hairy breasts.

"Violet, my darling! Come in, come in! The water is beautiful! So relaxing, eh, girls?" His topless spa-mates emitted cries of agreement.

"As tempting as that sounds, Igor, I'll have to pass," Violet demurred pleasantly, shouting to be heard over "U Got the Look," blaring from a nearby speaker.

"Have some champagne with us!" Igor bellowed. He jerkily sloshed some into a plastic flute and handed it to her. "A toast! To a truly great actress! Violet Cyr! You will be a big, big star!" Igor and several of the chicks raised their flutes to Violet, who did the same back to them and faked a swallow, having noticed a large lipstick stain on the rim of her flute.

A giggly scream from one of the tub girls heralded Violet being splattered with water. She danced back, thoroughly annoyed, and watched as a heretofore unseen guy surfaced between the screaming girl's legs and stood up, revealing a tanlined set of naked buttocks. The ensuing commotion in the tub gave Violet a window to make her exit. She pitched the champagne into a trash can and edged her way back into the house. Thank God, there was Kendra.

The bosomy blonde was arm-in-arm with Walt the studiedly rugged dentist. "Hey, Violet!" Kendra called as she approached them.

"Does your friend want to join us?" Walt asked Kendra, with a nod toward Violet.

Violet was immediately hopeful. "Oh, are you guys going someplace else?"

"No, we were actually just going outside to look at the moon . . . and everything," was Kendra's oddly fragmented reply.

"I'm really exhausted," Violet said. "I think I'm going to find somewhere to lie down. Don't leave without me, though, okay?"

"Oh, sure, Violet. I'll find you," Kendra promised. "See ya."

There had to be a bedroom somewhere, or even a den with a couch where she could crash. That glass of wine downstairs had really knocked her out. She opened a nearby cracked door and tentatively stepped into the dark room, simultaneously tripping over something on the floor. She crouched down and discovered a high-heeled shoe. Straightening back up with her hand on the wall, trying to find the light switch, she heard the unmistakable sounds of sex rising through the music.

"Oh yeah oh baby oh *yes! My* pussy's on *fire!*" was clearly audible, with accompanying masculine grunts and groans and some frenzied bedspring action. Violet got out fast, giving the door an irritated half-slam. It was like spring break around here, for Christ's sake.

She was near the stairs to the third floor so she went up and found a simply appointed guest room containing a sleigh bed with a quilt folded invitingly at the foot. She hoped Kendra would be able to find her, but if not, Violet would just stay the night and let Igor worry about getting her to the set in the morning. She clicked the bedside lamp to its lowest setting—darkness would have been preferable, but she didn't want to wake up with strangers copulating on top of her. Violet kicked off her shoes and was about to lie down when the door opened and a man stepped into the room.

"What the fuck are you doing here?!" Violet demanded in a tightly controlled voice.

Turk Marlowe smiled at her with such warmth and genuine good humor that she realized he was much more of a psycho than even she had believed. "Hi, Violet. Is that any way to talk to your new costar?"

"What?" But she knew. And it couldn't be. It was just not possible . . .

"Edgar didn't tell you I was coming? Since he represents me now, I'd've thought . . . oh, well, who gives a shit? When I found out you were the other lead in this thing I had to sign right up." *Edgar?* Edgar put Turk Fucking Marlowe into a film with her? Her fury so neatly transferred itself from the asshole standing in front of her to that slimy, dead-rat-blowing turdlick of an agent she was struck mute.

"Don't worry," Turk continued, elbowing the door closed behind him. "I'm not still pissed about you racking me in the nuts over at *Leather & Lace.* I haven't had a woman turn me down since I was thirteen years old, Violet. You know how sexy that makes you?" The distance between them suddenly decreased by three feet. He was very tall and slabbed with muscle and there was no way she was going to be able to fight him off this time.

"Don't come near me!" she spat, hating the unintentional quaver of fear that undermined the command.

Turk stopped, his left hand absently fondling the footboard. "That's going to be a little difficult, don't you think, considering the scenes they've got us doing. Like the one where you and I make love on the floor while your husband's asleep in the bed next to us? If the schmucks watching this get half as aroused as I did reading it, this'll be the biggest hit since *I Spit on Your Grave*. Can I start calling you Brittany now?"

He'd backed her into the corner of the bedroom and there was nothing in reach to use as a deadly weapon, much less any knick-knacks to toss at his grinning, sociopathic face. So she started to scream. "Help me! Anybody, please, help—" His hand clamped across her mouth, the ball of his thumb wedged painfully between her jaws. Her impulse to bite the shit out of him was mitigated by the fear of ingesting possibly HIV-tainted blood. Turk pinned her arms to her side and heaved her onto the bed.

"We're gonna be great together, Violet. I've been dreaming of this from the first second I saw you. I'm gonna make you—"

Because her face was mostly pressed against the quilt, Violet could not see what happened next. She only heard Turk stop talking, then he leapt off her as another voice said, "You're under arrest. You have the right to remain silent. Anything you say can and will . . ." There was a cop in the room, handcuffing the son of a bitch!

"Thank God! He attacked me!" Violet exclaimed. "But why are you here? How did you know that he would—"

The Brian Doyle-Murrayesque cop stared dispassionately at Violet. "Ma'am, you're under arrest. You have the right to remain silent . . ." He whipped out another pair of cuffs.

"Do you know who I am?" Turk yelled.

"No, sir, I do not. Ma'am, anything you say can and will be used against you—"

"Wait a minute!" Violet stammered. "What is going on here? Why are you arresting *me?!?*"

"Prostitution. You have the right to an attorney . . ." She was handcuffed.

"Fine, Giles. You have a tape of a private conversation between Lewis and me. And you got to put on a little show with it in front of these two," Maggie said coldly, flicking her wrist in Fawn and Andre's general direction. They were gathered in the living room of Giles's house (which Andre had successfully begged the very resistant maid into cleaning at the last minute that day); the answering machine tape (which Andre had dubbed from micro to standard-size cassette) had just finished playing through Giles's speakers. "What do you expect me to do?" Maggie went on, one imperious note short of full-blown sarcasm. "Deny that it's our voices?"

"Maybe I expect some kind of explanation about why you're trying to destroy my marriage," Giles angrily replied, sipping his Rusty Nail.

Genuinely taken aback by this unprecedented show of defiance, Maggie chose her words with care, feeling the smug stares of Fawn and that meddling pansy Andre. "Giles, you've been . . . hurt, and your father and I only want to spare you from any more pain in this . . . relationship."

Fawn had remained silent next to Giles on the black leather sofa, but now she tightened her grip on his arm and spoke up. "For your information, Maggie, I love Giles, and if you gave a good goddamn about him, you would not be on that tape talking about aborting his child!"

"But we *really* don't know that it's his baby, now do we, dear? Although I'll be more than happy to drop the subject until we see the results of the paternity test," Maggie said, throwing her hands up faux-amicably.

"No baby of mine is going to take any paternity test. You can just forget it, Mother! I will *never* allow it," Giles told Maggie, pointing his finger at her for emphasis while Fawn quietly began to weep. "Fawn and I are moving back in together, with or without your approval. If you and Dad don't like it, that's tough. Because I don't need you or your money. I've got my trust fund. All I need is Fawn. And our child. So you can stop worrying about selling the Vista Laguna house."

"Well, isn't that wonderful," Maggie hissed. "I spend months trying to unload that albatross and you finally decide to move in after all. That's just lovely."

"We are not moving into that house," Fawn informed her, blotting the last of her tears with a fingertip. "You expect me to raise a *baby* in a house where someone was murdered? Giles, sugar, I just don't understand how she can be so . . ." Fresh tears.

Giles put an arm around Fawn's shoulders and patted her. "The Vista Laguna place is still for sale. But I don't want Syd Swann showing it anymore. We're listing it with Fred Sands Estates. And they won't be needing your help."

"I see." Maggie got up and snatched her purse from the coffee table. "And did you give that sneaky little deadbeat Jason a big fat reward for taping my phone calls for you?"

"No, as a matter of fact, and he didn't ask for one, either," Giles told her. "Look, Mother. Jason is our friend and I want you to lay off him."

"And he's hardly a deadbeat," Andre added from his perch on an ottoman. "He was just hired by Mermaid Records to produce videos for Marina Stetson."

"Oh, is that so? Marina Stetson?" Maggie asked.

"Yes. They happen to be very close friends."

"Of course they are," said Maggie. Without another word she walked briskly out of the house, a particularly poisonous expression spreading across her hawklike features.

Violet had been in a jail cell once before, but the *One Life to Live* prison set at ABC studios in New York hadn't had A.T. IS A DEAD MUTHAFUCKER scrawled on the wall in foot-high letters or an unpartitioned toilet bowl in the middle of it.

Since the municipal pokey boasted only four cells, normally plenty to handle the occasional post-wine-tasting DUI, the bust at Wendi's severely taxed the constabulary's resources. Despite vociferous protests, Violet was locked in a cell with ten other women, Wendi not among them. Violet had an embryonic idea of what was going on but had been unable to corroborate it with anyone during the half-hour ride to the police station in a paddy wagon. Apparently

taking their Miranda rights seriously, the vanload of party guests
(chaperoned by two armed cops) turned a collective deaf ear to Violet's initial outraged insistence upon an explanation. From her dis-
advantaged position seated and handcuffed near the back door of the
vehicle, she unsuccessfully scanned the crowd for Kendra or Turk
or Wendi and stopped talking when an inbred-looking policewoman
told her to shut up.

They weren't going to let her make a phone call, but she made
herself cry and the young cop who'd taken her prints and mug shot
relented. Without a second's deliberation, she dialed her mother and
got the answering machine. Dropping the teary waif routine, she
clearly and calmly outlined the situation and asked her mother to
please fly up immediately. She'd been hoping to pump the sympathetic policeboy for information about what in hell was going on,
but he became annoyed when, after Violet, every other collar started
yammering to use the phone and he brusquely tossed her behind bars.

She found Kendra in a corner of the cell, hugging Walt the
dentist's jacket closed over her bra and panties. "Oh, God, Violet,"
the disheveled vixen sobbed. "They got you, too! I don't know what
I'm gonna do . . . this movie was supposed to be a new start for me.
Wendi promised! This is my third bust and I'm gonna end up in the
slammer. I just know it!"

While comforting the aspiring starlet, who was using the dress
she'd loaned Violet as an oversize black hankie, Violet learned much
about Wendi. Ms. Barash, up until this evening, had also been using
Prying Eyes to make a new start, or more precisely an expansion to
motion picture producer from her ongoing stint as Hollywood's pre-
eminent madam. Kendra herself had been earning as much as two
thousand dollars a night "entertaining" various actors, producers,
studio execs, attorneys and network bigwigs from Wendi's ultraex-
clusive client list. "But a girl can't go on doing that forever. I mean,
you only have your looks for so long and I want to raise a family
someday and just get a nice job starring on some soap. A couple of
series regulars on *The Bold and the Beautiful* used to do it, one even
worked for Wendi. So I thought, Why not me, too? And now I am
so in deep shit," Kendra wailed.

"So Wendi Barash is like the Industry hot ticket when you want the best hookers in town?" Violet asked, realizing she was most likely the only person in the cell who did not fall under that classification.

"Well, yeah," Kendra nodded, futilely dabbing at her fatally smudged mascara. "If they find her address book and client file and everything, it'll be the biggest scandal you ever saw."

"But my agent said he was one of Wendi's best friends. How could he not . . . know." Oh, Jesus Christ.

"Who's your agent?"

"Edgar Black at Conan Carroll," Violet told Kendra, guessing what was coming next before Kendra could confirm it.

"Wendi introduced me and Edgar. He did my deal for the movie. He said he was packaging the whole thing, whatever that means. Wendi'd set up a lot of girls with Edgar, but she told me I ought to date him for free, 'cause he'd really help my acting career. So I did," Kendra confessed, shaking her head sadly.

Violet had never been involved in a package before, but she was familiar with the concept: an agency receiving fees from a studio or production company for putting together (or *packaging*) key elements of a film or TV series—stars, writer, producers, director. Normally an agent would promote a packaged project as such to a client, because such projects were exempt from commission for the packaging agency's clients. But Edgar had never mentioned this to Violet, not because he wanted to chisel her out of 10 percent (although she certainly wouldn't put it past the scumbag) but because *she* was the final piece he needed to complete the package.

Now the last-minuteness of the *Prying Eyes* job made infinitely more sense—whoever Edgar had booked as the female lead must have bailed at the eleventh hour, forcing Edgar to plug in some other sucker from his roster, namely Violet, in order to collect his fee. Much the way Marc Singer (surely another Edgar client) had just been replaced by Turk Marlowe. So not only had Edgar knowingly sent her off to star in a piece of kinky slasher shit produced by the kingpins of a notorious prostitution ring, he'd paired her romantically with her attempted rapist.

She sank down to the floor next to Kendra, folding her legs beneath her to keep the chill of the cement off her ass. Closing this fruitless, bitterly humiliating chapter in her career would not be that difficult, she told herself, shutting her eyes and taking a few stabilizing deep breaths. All she had to do was clear up the misunderstanding with the authorities, and then murder Edgar Black.

Violet had dozed off and was dreaming that her mother was nagging at her about having walked off *Prying Eyes*. "Don't tell me to be calm," Mom yelled. "I'll be calm when I see my daughter!" Which made no sense because in the dream Violet was sitting right there next to her by the picture window in her mother's house in Calabasas.

"Violet! Violet!" She woke up with a stiff neck, confused by the oddly angled conjunction of bars and cement floor in front of her face. She tilted her head back and saw her mother and one of the deputies on the other side of the bars.

"Oh, my God. Mom!" She exclaimed, snapping to alertness and standing.

"Honey, I'm right here," Evelyn Cyr said, clasping Violet's hand with one of hers since her other arm was busy holding a stack of file folders and videotapes. "Let her out of there this minute!" her mother insisted to the cop who, remarkably, complied.

Evelyn yanked Violet from the cell and into a pulverizing embrace. "Are you okay, baby? Did they hurt you?" she whispered.

"Mom, thanks. I'm fine. What time is it?" asked Violet, her watch having been confiscated before her incarceration.

"It's just after four a.m. I was out seeing *Sleepless in Seattle* with Merna and Bev. *They* liked it but I kept watching that Meg Ryan and wondering why on earth is this bland woman a movie star and thinking how much better you'd be in these romantic comedies she's always—"

"Mother, please—"

"Then I came home and got your message and went straight to the airport. It took longer to drive here from San Francisco than the flight did. I can't believe they had you in a prison cell!" Evelyn wailed. "Come on, we're going home now."

"You're releasing me?" an incredulous Violet asked the deputy.

"Yes, the charges against you are being dropped for now, pending the investigation. Follow me, please," he replied in an embarrassed monotone.

Violet glanced back into the cell, her eyes meeting Kendra's.

"I'll get this dress back to you," Violet said, feeling absurdly guilty for being sprung ahead of her new pal, recovering hooker or not. Kendra nodded and waved. Violet could think of nothing to say but "Good luck."

On the short walk to the office, she asked her mother how she had pulled this off. "I just showed them all this evidence I brought with me that you are a working professional actress, not some call girl. I have your *Chillin' with Billy* episodes and your demo reel and photo and résumé and of course my scrapbook . . ." She stopped moving and opened up a leather-bound photo album stuffed with precisely laminated clippings, theater programs and pictures tracing Violet's career back to mortifying teen gigs on *Knightrider* and *Alice*. "And this script you left at my house," Evelyn added, indicating an earlier draft of *Prying Eyes*. Violet couldn't help feeling sorry for the cops who'd had to endure this impromptu show-biz biography.

"Thanks a lot, Mom. You did great," Violet told her, signing a form the desk sergeant gave her to reclaim her valuables.

"Do you know what finally pushed them over the edge?" Evelyn whispered.

"My Ultra-Maxi with Wings ad from 1987?"

"I told them since they'd let that Marlowe animal go, they'd damn well better show the same respect to my daughter."

Violet had briefly mentioned encountering Turk just before the arrest but was unaware of his fate after seeing him hauled into a different paddy wagon. "Did you *see* him leaving?" Violet asked, figuring if her mother had, Evelyn would have ended up next to her in the cell, booked on assault charges.

Evelyn shook her head. "No, but I had a hunch." Off Violet's expression, she continued defensively, "Well, Violet, I didn't become strip poker champion of my dorm at Bucknell without learning how to bluff."

The cop in charge approached Violet. "You may be called in to testify when this case reaches court, so don't leave the state without notifying us."

Yeah, right, Violet thought, soberly nodding in agreement. They went outside and Dave was sitting on the hood of the white rental Taurus. Violet stared at her mother. "Now Vi, please don't get mad. We needed someone to drive your car back down, didn't we?"

"I'm not mad. But I can drive my own car back," Violet said, suddenly on the verge of real tears for the first time that whole night.

Dave ended up driving most of the way back to L.A. Violet checked out of the motel, offering no explanation but "I'm quitting the movie" to the querulous old poop at the front desk. Evelyn took off for the San Francisco airport after Violet extracted a vow of silence from her. "No press conferences, no *Hard Copy*, and especially no contact with Edgar Black, Conan Carroll or anyone at the agency. Got it?" Violet demanded. "I'm going to handle this myself."

"Yes, dear. But I already put in a call to my lawyer . . . ," Evelyn halfheartedly countered.

"That's all right, Mom. Just don't discuss it with anybody else." Evelyn swore she wouldn't.

It was sunrise when she and Dave left Napa. There was a horrific amount to talk about, but she figured that Dave still owed her an apology and besides, she was completely obliterated so she folded her sweatshirt into a pillow and went to sleep. When she awakened, they were on a freeway and Dave was holding her hand.

She was starving. They stopped at McDonald's but couldn't get fries or Quarter Pounders because it was before eleven, so Violet settled for hash browns and a scrumptiously unhealthy Sausage McBiscuit with Egg. Dave sat across from her in a plastic-backed swivel chair, his Doc Martened foot nestled comfortably between her Reeboks. He drank black coffee.

"Violet, I'm sorry."

"For what?" she asked innocently.

"Come on now. We both said some pretty stupid things that night," he said, folding his arms across his broad chest.

"Especially you," she remarked through half a mouthful of hash brown.

The jaw clenched familiarly, and he let out one of his slow-burning sighs. But when he looked at her, she saw unmistakable warmth beneath the impatience. "Look, you've been through a lot of shit and I don't want to get into another row with you in front of a portrait of bloody Mayor McCheese, all right? We scrap and we fight and sometimes we act like cunts to each other and well, I've been thinking that maybe it'll always be like that. But I also think

I'm always gonna love you and I don't imagine you'd fancy a guy who was well behaved and didn't break your balls from time to time. Am I right, then?"

"No, Dave. I actually think I'd fancy that quite a bit," she replied. "But right now this is what I've got." She edged forward in her swivel chair and gave his thigh a squeeze. "And I'd be lying if I said it didn't look pretty damn good right now."

His hand went beneath the table and absorbed hers. "So tonight you won't be charging me?"

"I ought to kick your ass for that. Fortunately for you, kicking Edgar Black's is my top priority. And the little plan I've concocted for that involves you."

"What plan would that be?"

So she told him.

As much as Jason wanted to believe his employment nightmares were over, he had profound difficulty accepting that he was actually Mermaid Records' new manager of visual media promotions. So he fabricated an excuse to call his alleged boss Jillian the next day but could read nothing ominous into her "See ya on Monday."

Marina seemed plagued by no doubts whatsoever regarding the situation, as the FedEx delivery that afternoon indicated. Inside was a Pierre et Gilles card with a purple-inked "Congratulations" scribbled inside in Marina's spiky handwriting.

> *They faxed me the video script and it's awesome. We're shooting it in L.A. first week of Sept. Chip & Jillian love you and I do, too.*

The card was taped to a barely scuffed and completely undented Pop-Tartts lunch box identical to the one last seen at his mother's infamous Labor Day garage sale.

Issued in 1984, several months after *Pandora's Box* was released, the exquisite Thermos-brand collectors' item was crafted in sturdy metal and featured a delightfully rendered painting of the band in concert on the hinged side, while opposite was a majestic group portrait at the Acropolis, setting for the classic "Pandora's Box" video. The edges of the lunch pail were decorated with frolicky individual panels of the girls, including Marina with severely moussed New Wave hair saucily sipping a Slurpee through glistening, luscious lips. Jason clicked the lunch box open and was amazed to discover the original Thermos emblazoned with each band member's head floating beneath the Pop-Tartts logo. He picked up a Paramount Hotel note sheet Marina had put inside.

Don't let your mother near this. These things ain't easy to come by!

Jason set the lunch box up on the big-screen TV in his bedroom and for the millionth time imagined the destruction that would be wrought if Marina found out about him and Hank. After he was offered the job at Mermaid, he went through the day beginning to believe that he could now build his life from scratch minus Hank and deal with this sacrifice by flinging himself into his work and constantly remembering the importance of protecting and supporting Marina and finding a new video store and renting lots and lots of porn.

But then Hank asked him to come up to the Stetson-Rietta house that evening, and the dining room was filled with candles and there were red roses for him and a delectable dinner of stuffed poblano chiles, shrimp in cream of cilantro, and chicken asada quesadillas, prepared by the since-departed housekeeper. "Cause last time you got hired we went *out* to eat and look what happened. To the job, I mean," he added, scratching his sculpted shoulder self-consciously.

"Thanks," Jason said, unable to resist kissing him.

Hank put on a wonderful CD Jason had never heard by someone named Sheryl Crow and they ate and talked about neutral things like Fawn and Giles and Maggie. Jason hadn't spoken to Andro directly but had received a message the night before claiming Giles and Fawn had read Maggie the riot act and that the "desiccated cuntosaurus" would never bother Jason again. "Even though that's great, I'm still going to get my own place as soon as I can," Jason said, dipping a quesadilla strip into the heavenly chipotle salsa.

"Someplace closer to Burbank?" asked Hank.

"Yeah. Not the Valley, though. I was thinking West Hollywood, maybe somewhere in the hills. All I really need is a single."

"Sounds good, bud. So are you gonna do that over the weekend?" In the candlelight, Hank looked like some ridiculously beautiful liquor ad in *Out* or *Vanity Fair*.

"I probably should. Why?"

"Because the bank is sending me to Toronto on Thursday and I thought maybe you'd want to come." He looked smolderingly into Jason's eyes. Jason quickly took a large bite of food and proceeded to chew it very slowly.

Then he dabbed his mouth with a napkin and said nothing. He and Hank away together in a different city. You could pretend for a few days at least that it was real life. But he couldn't. "I'd love that, Hank. But I don't know. I don't think I should. Can you understand?"

Hank nodded and stood up, walking around the table to where Jason sat. He put his hands on Jason's chair and pulled it back, then straddled it and sat on Jason's lap, facing him. He laid his head on Jason's chest and stroked his hair. "I know it's fucked up, Jason. But we'll work it out somehow. Whatever way you want it, buddy. No pressure. I swear to God." They held each other.

"Hi, Tricia. It's Violet returning Edgar's call." Actually, two calls. Near-frantic messages she'd found on her machine when she got back to her apartment the day before—Edgar had heard there had been "trouble" at the *Prying Eyes* shoot and was concerned about Violet. Concerned about how she might connect him to Wendi Barash and her carnival of whores, to be exact, Violet had mentioned to Dave, rewinding the tape and flicking on the midday news, which coincidentally featured a segment (no names mentioned) on the bust and its "possible links to a widespread Los Angeles prostitution syndicate."

Violet let Edgar sweat for a day before calling back, using the time to catch up on her sleep and to compose a first draft of an important letter. "Jesus Christ, Violet! Are you okay?" Edgar squawked.

"Oh, I'm fine, Edgar," she replied, sounding worn out but truly touched by his concern. "A little shaken up, but completely okay." YOU ROTTEN PIGFUCKER, she jotted in the margin of her notebook.

"Violet darling, you've gotta understand I knew nothing about any of this prostitution crap! It shocks the hell out of me that movie professionals like Wendi and Igor would be mixed up with this sleazy shit." *You're good, Edgar. You ought to represent yourself.* And you just might have to, because after I finish with you, you deceitful turd, you won't have a single client left. "Don't worry about a thing, Violet. It's clearly force majeure. You're off the movie. And believe me, we're already looking into a lawsuit."

"I really appreciate your looking out for me, Edgar. And of course you didn't know what was going on with Wendi. I *never* thought you did." EDGAR BLACK R.I.P. DIRTBAG TAPEWORM FUCKING ASSHOLE.

The relief in his voice was pathetic. "Violet, you're a trouper and a hell of an actress." *You have no idea, fuckface.* "Now I want you to come in, we'll have lunch, we'll get you back out there and you'll book. Hold on for Tricia." Jesus Christ.

"Violet, I'm so sorry. They actually put you in jail? Unbelievable."

"I'm really fine, Tricia. And I just got back from a long drive and I need to rest. So please tell Edgar I'll come talk to him next week, okay?" Violet sweetly requested.

A strange beat of silence. "Violet . . . ," Tricia said in a hushed tone. "Can you meet *me*? Tonight?" What the hell was she up to?

"No, Tricia, I honestly need to take a break. Next week, okay?"

"Call Aldo Spackle."

"What?!"

"Call him. Aldo Spackle. At Sunset/Gower." She hung up.

Violet dug through a mound of papers on her dinette and found Aldo's office number. Her hand quaked as she dialed. "Grantville Spackling," a female voice answered.

"Hi. Is Aldo there? It's Violet Cyr."

"One moment." A dead hold. Thirty seconds later. "Sorry, violins . . . what?"

"It's okay, Frankie," Aldo's voice jumped in. "I'll take it." Frankie hung up. Violet realized she'd stopped breathing. "Violet, it's really the nuts, you calling like this."

"What do you mean?" she interrupted stupidly, overcome with a rush of hope.

"Your agent said you were doing another flick. So the studio was pressing me to go with Kim Basinger. But the deal just fell through. When are you finished your shoot?"

"I'm—um, oh jeez—I'm finished now, Aldo! Wait! When did you—talk to my agent?"

"Just a few days after we met that night. Right after your show with the goat got canceled." Oh, no. No way could she have been reamed that royally. It just wasn't possible.

"And he said I wasn't available for your movie." She stopped pacing and collapsed into a chair, wondering if she had any tequila on hand.

"Yeah, he was kind of a butthole about it. I thought maybe you were sore at me for making a pass at you. Sorrreee. Anyway, we start in two weeks. Wanna be in it?"

"Yes!" she shrieked. "Sorry, Aldo. I'm a little on edge today. Hello? Aldo?"

"Yeah, I was just getting a pen. I need to send you the script. If you could meet me and Adrian Pasdar, you know, the lead, for drinks tonight, that'd be the nuts. I guess I've got to schedule a screen test or something. Fuckin' studio. Okay, where are you?"

They made plans to rendezvous for Kahluas at Tiki-Ti in Hollywood at nine-thirty. Which gave her eight hours or so to finalize her surprise for Edgar. Of course now, in light of her deduction that Edgar had railroaded her into *Prying Eyes* at the expense of a chance to star in Aldo Spackle's *You Lucky Bastard*, the letter she'd written would have to be slightly revised. The restraint she'd attempted to employ was clearly unnecessary. By the time Dave arrived at her place, it was ready.

Dear Friends and Colleagues,

It is with great sadness that I must publicly come forth and admit to you, the film and television community, my failure as a talent agent, an entertainment professional and a human being.

I have lied. I have misrepresented myself. I have consistently put my own needs before those of my clients. I have used my position to humiliate and mistreat my underlings. As a client and close associate of Hollywood madam Wendi Barash, I have participated in the predatory exploitation of young women that is, because of men like myself, an unfortunate cornerstone of this business.

I cannot go back and erase my years of unconscionable behavior. But I can apologize to everyone who was hurt by my greed, lust and incompetence. And I can attempt to redeem myself by leaving the Industry and devoting the rest of my life to charity and social work. I am truly sorry for the pain I have caused and the careers I have damaged and destroyed. I do not ask for your forgiveness, only your prayers.

I hereby resign from the Conan Carroll Agency.

Sincerely yours,

Edgar Black

"Christ Almighty, Violet. This is fucking brutal," opined Dave. "I love it."

"Great. Did you get me what I need?" she asked tensely. Dave had been at Edgar's house performing his regular biweekly dog grooming. Only this time he'd stopped by Edgar's catastrophically messy desk and filched an agency client contact list and several stray signature samples.

Violet excitedly scanned the list, dated a month ago. Tricia's compulsive handiwork was obvious—not only was every single agency client's full address there in alphabetical order, but if the actors had personal managers or publicists, those addresses were listed, too. Without this document, she would have been forced to limit her attack on Edgar to the contents of the latest casting director address guide, purchased that morning at Samuel French, as well as the editors of *Variety* and *The Hollywood Reporter*. Now she could launch a multipronged assault that would effectively annihilate Edgar in front of his buyers *and* his product.

Of course none of it would have been possible without Dave's last bit of booty, a thick stack of agency letterhead with Edgar's name engraved on every sheet. "Dave, this is fantastic!" Violet gushed.

"It's bloody first-degree mail fraud. Are you sure you want to go through with this?"

"Oh, yes. And we need to be finished by nine because I have a meeting tonight with Aldo Spackle and the star of his new movie.

A movie Edgar refused to let me go in on because he'd already decided to plug me into his little Napa Valley prostie-package." She tossed everything into a shopping bag, along with a roll of stamps and several boxes of plain envelopes. "Next stop, Mom's laser printer."

Maggie did not have much hope invested in the mansion security cameras, but since she'd paid in excess of ten thousand dollars to install the system after that meddling twit Jason slaughtered the Negro on her sofa, she decided it was only sensible to review the tapes and see what the little freeloader had been up to when he wasn't busy stabbing Maggie in the back.

The Burkes' insurance broker had recommended the cameras for protection against lawsuits in the wake of the "justifiable" homicide, and Maggie, who had very strong suspicions that the person Jason killed was actually his drug dealer or some other type of illicit acquaintance, had felt no obligation to inform her house sitter that strategically placed, motion-sensitive ultra-hi-tech video cameras would now be monitoring activities throughout the house, including his bedroom.

She sat in her hotel suite with the video the security company had just messengered. The morning after Giles and Fawn made their ever-so-heartfelt stand against her (and Maggie learned that not only had Jason provided the idiots with a private taped phone conversation of hers, he'd conspired with that despicable Marina Stetson woman to play their little furniture prank), Maggie phoned her consultant at the hyper-discreet, mega-expensive security company and demanded that anything out-of-the-ordinary that had been seen by those cameras be edited onto a cassette for her immediate review.

The consultant had called this morning and asked if she considered sex to be out-of-the-ordinary. Maggie had told him, "Absolutely."

She tried to insert the tape into the suite's VCR several times before realizing she had to turn the power on. The channel three and TV/VCR switch factors compounded her confusion but she was ultimately able to achieve picture without requesting room service. The tape was silent but in color. It began at the front door, where a tall, muscular man stood, looking back toward the foyer. Momentarily,

Jason joined him and they instantly began a torrid kiss. So he was a fruit, just like his nancy-boy friend Andre. Unfortunately, the good old days when footage of someone performing homosexual acts was enough to ruin not just their career, but their entire life were long gone. Mermaid Records was doubtlessly crawling with pansies already.

Now Jason had dropped to his knees and was pulling the other man's pants down. The camera angle prevented Maggie from seeing exactly what was happening, but of course she could figure it out. She wondered if men did it differently than women, if there was some technique—

There was a cut to the camera in the servants' bedroom. Maggie sat up in her wing chair, feeling an odd sensation of breathlessness. This was obviously continuous action from the front door scene, because Jason's partner entered the frame in the same red T-shirt and white bikini underpants. Jason followed, apparently playing the female role in this liaison, as evidenced by his enthusiastic fellatio. The highly sophisticated camera zoomed in and auto-focused so the two filled the screen. Maggie stared, fascinated. The tall, dark, masculine one was certainly attractive, she thought as he pulled off the T-shirt, revealing an exceedingly well-built, lightly furred torso. He was probably a fashion model Jason had "cruised" somewhere in the West Hollywood gay district. In fact, she thought she recognized him, perhaps from a catalog? It *was* rather unlikely . . .

Now completely nude, Jason's chum pulled the boy into his arms and they toppled to the twin bed writhing and kissing and tearing off Jason's clothes. Then they stood and Maggie got her first look at Jason in the buff. Jason's penis was long and plump and jutted stiffly upward, and she eyed his sleek, toned form with its long, hairy legs and tight white buttocks appreciatively, but it was the other who really interested her. There was something so familiar about that handsome face.

When he knelt on the bed and Jason went down to the carpet and fell upon his considerable endowment, suckling and tonguing and nibbling it, the man's identity plinked into Maggie's head almost audibly. Without pausing the tape, she scrambled from her seat and flew to the armoire in the bedroom, returning with the Syd Swann Realty folder marked STETSON, MARINA/RIETTA, "HANK". One look at the *People* magazine wedding photo convinced her Jason's sex partner was in fact Marina Stetson's husband. Did Marina know he liked to fuck boys? More importantly did she know one of those boys was her little pal Jason, for whom she had doubtlessly exerted her influence to land him a job at her record company? While anything was possible in this moral cesspool of a city, somehow she didn't think so. Maggie smiled to herself, actually feeling happy for the first time in what seemed like years.

On-screen, Jason and Hank French-kissed while masturbating each other. Now Hank was sucking Jason's penis. Not a sight many wives would care to witness. And witness it Marina certainly would. Maggie would mail it to her as soon as she could make a copy of it. Giles, who wasted hours of his life with video discs and tapes, had the duplicating equipment at his house and she could invent a reason for him to show her how to operate it. She'd already made a preliminary step toward rapprochement with an apologetic phone message to Giles earlier that day. She supposed she should send his blonde bitch of a wife some sort of lavish, baby-themed gift today as well. After all, it would do Maggie no good to be estranged from them if she had any hope of monitoring or manipulating what went on in their ridiculous lives.

She watched Jason and Hank, their sweaty muscles tensed as they climaxed into the air and onto each other. She rewound the tape and viewed the entire encounter a second time. Then she dialed her massage service and asked if it would be possible to schedule two masseurs at the same time, and might these gentlemen want to put on a little show for her before her rubdown? Of course the answer to both questions was yes.

Tricia arrived at the office early and picked up the *L.A. Times* in the lobby newsstand on her way up. She'd been obsessively following the Wendi Barash case since the bust several days ago. Tricia was disgusted at her own cluelessness. Edgar had been hobnobbing with Wendi and her "friends" for almost a year—how had Tricia not put two and two together and come up with whore? It had been unbelievably obvious what business the Encino-based "producer" was actually involved in! Oh, well, no matter. Tricia was presently combing her old appointment calendars and phone logs to compile a detailed history of Edgar's association with Wendi and her referrals, most recently the spectacularly vapid Kendra. As soon as it was complete, Tricia would furnish this dossier to the LAPD vice squad, who were now spearheading a potentially incendiary probe into the affairs of Wendi Barash, or as the press had dubbed her, "The Tinseltown Madam."

She did not bother to start Edgar's coffee because he probably wouldn't be in until around noon, if at all. He'd been mostly out of the office since the ill-fated Julianne Moore luncheon. Tricia was unsure *exactly* what had transpired, just that the meeting never took place, Edgar never returned to the office that day, and she'd been asked to schedule a full detailing of the Jaguar the next morning.

The first call came seconds after Misty the receptionist went on duty and switched the agency phones over from answering service-forwarding. "Did Edgar quit or something?" Misty buzzed Tricia to ask.

"No," Tricia immediately replied, then added, "I mean, not that I'm aware of." Maybe he *had* quit! "Why do you ask?"

"Because I have people on two lines asking if he did!" the petulant message-taker snapped, hanging up. Tricia went back to her Wendi research, curiosity mildly piqued.

Within half an hour, a full-scale Situation had erupted. The agency's main number was ringing off the hook, Tricia had three lines on hold, and all the assistants but Janice Twickenham were rampantly speculating amongst themselves about the rumor that Edgar had sent out a mass resignation letter. Tricia had spoken to seven clients and three casting directors who said they'd received it, and had just asked Rick Millikan's associate Stacy to fax her a copy of the letter when Conan Carroll appeared at her desk in utter consternation.

"What the Christ is going on, Tricia? Everyone and their Aunt Fanny are telling me Edgar's resigned . . . that he's written some wigged-out confession about lying and cheating and leaving The Business? And I can't get him on the phone!" Conan spluttered.

"I don't understand it, Conan. But someone's faxing me the letter now." She heard the fax machine bleeping and raced down the hall to retrieve the transmission, nipples hardening. This was unbelievable—the excitement made the Cicely Tyson incident and

even Operation Colon Blow seem tame by comparison. To think that
the day was finally here, that she had driven that smug, sleazy *bastard* out of the company!

The fax dropped into the receiving tray and she snatched it out.
Good Lord. Agency letterhead. So it was true. She scurried back to
Conan, everything a-tingle.

Conan's assistant Eric reached him at her desk simultaneously,
thrusting out an envelope. "This just came in the mail!" Eric
squealed. It was the same letter. Conan tore it from his hand and
read it as Tricia's eyes gobbled up the fax.

"Oh, my God!" Conan gasped. "Is he fucking bananas?"

Tricia read the letter again. The words seemed a bit too eloquent
for Edgar, but it was definitely his signature. The man had simply
lost his mind. This was wonderful. Wonderful and sublimely appropriate and terribly, terribly sexy. Oh, good Lord—The orgasm shot
through her like an exploding bullet. She reached for the edge of the
desk to steady herself, her other hand flying up to her mouth to stifle
an involuntary whimper.

"Are you all right?" Conan asked. He and Eric were staring at
her. Ari Rosenblatt and Brenda the office manager were there, too.

Tricia, still riding the last wave of pleasure, quickly stepped behind her desk on rubbery legs and plucked a tissue from the box
next to her phone. "Yes, of course, I'm fine. I'm just stunned . . .
that Edgar . . ." She trailed off dabbing her damp forehead.

"You're dead, Tricia. *Do you hear me,* bitch? *I'm gonna rip
your head off!!!*" They all turned to behold Edgar Black. He was
unshaven, nutty-eyed, in jeans and a Planet Hollywood T-shirt. He
remained poised for one second in the doorway to the reception area
pointing at Tricia, then he came at her.

For the first and quite possibly last time in history, the muscles
Conan and Eric spent countless hours toning and enlarging at the
Sports Connection were put to practical use as they blocked Edgar's
charge and forcibly restrained him from leaping over the desk at
milk white, open-mouthed Tricia. "You back-stabbing twat! *When*
have I humiliated and mistreated you? Let me go! Let me go, goddamnit!"

"Edgar! Calm yourself or I'm going to slap your face!" Conan
barked. "Are you saying you didn't write that letter?"

"Of course I didn't fucking write it," Edgar replied through clenched teeth. "*She* did."

"No! I didn't do it . . . ," Tricia stuttered.

"Don't you dare deny it, Tricia! Who else?" Edgar screamed. "Huh? You fucking tell me who else has access to my stationery and can fake my signature! You've been pissed off ever since I didn't make you an agent and you just sat back and waited for the perfect time to *fuck me!*" He lunged toward her again. Conan and Eric dragged him back.

Tricia's intercom beeped. "Is Brenda there? AFTRA's on line three for her," Misty said.

"Take a message," Brenda ordered.

"Misty, please hold all of Edgar's calls," Conan said. "Let's go to your office, Edgar." Conan guided him by the arm away from Tricia's desk.

"You're fired! Get out," Edgar hissed at Tricia. "I oughta sue your ass off . . ."

"Edgar." Conan yanked him into the office and slammed the door.

Ari and Eric were whispering to each other. Brenda looked up from the letter Conan had received and regarded Tricia coldly. "I didn't write that letter," Tricia insisted, wringing her skirt. The three of them said nothing and slowly dispersed.

They all thought she did it. Oh, God, what could she do? Naturally there was no proof but if *everyone* . . . Stefan. She had to call him right away. He'd know how to handle this. She dialed Kinko's and he answered. Thank heavens. She related the story to him in hushed tones, trying to remain calm and coherent.

"Fax me that letter and then call me back. Listen, Baby Girl, everything's going to be all right." His deep, soothing voice was first aid for her nerves. She carried the fax to the machine and punched in the Kinko's number. It began to transmit.

"Tricia, please come here," Conan said from down the hall. She left the machine to its business and followed Conan into Edgar's office. Edgar, seated in the guest chair recently occupied by Cicely Tyson and Tricia's spermy panties, gave her a murderous look.

Conan kicked the door closed. "Did you send this letter out?" he asked dispassionately.

"No," she whined miserably.

"You're lying!" Edgar snapped.

"Edgar, please. Now, Tricia, Edgar obviously didn't write this letter himself. So how do you explain it?" Conan crossed his arms and leaned back against Edgar's desk, a dark "don't-fuck-with-me-Missy" expression on his youthful face.

"Conan, I can't explain it," Tricia replied through an indignant, helpless sigh.

"Neither can I, Tricia. That's why we're going to have to let you go," said Conan. "Please pack up your things." He opened the door. She looked from one to the other, saw there was no argument to be had and exited.

"We should call the lawyers, Conan. This is forgery! It's libel," Edgar yammered.

"I think I'd rather discuss your relationship with Wendi Barash," said Conan.

Tricia ducked into the break room and called Kinko's. "Stefan, please," she begged when someone named Tyreesha answered.

"Sure. Hold on."

She waited for what seemed like five full minutes, twisting the coiled cord around her finger, expecting Eric or Ari or, God forbid, Edgar to walk in at any moment. Oh, no, sir. They were all huddled up together talking about her sabotage. Edgar had truly cracked and sent the letter himself. That had to be it. But she'd driven him to it, and if Conan started sniffing around, he would indubitably discover some of the things she had been up to and then—

"Hello? Tricia?"

"Yes, darling, it's me. I've been fired. And there's no way I can make them believe—"

"Listen to me. It doesn't matter. We'll take off for Mexico tomorrow."

"Oh, God, Stefan, yes. I want that so much!"

"So do I. Look, I read the letter. Edgar is finished. Destroyed. That rat's asshole is history in this business. So take your stuff and go. Wait at the mall. Buy things for the trip. Have a drink. Just try to relax, Baby Girl. And then go back there tonight and do the jalapeño thing. A little farewell present for that prick."

"Yes, Stefan."

"I'll meet you at the house after I get off. Around ten. And if my cock's any indication right now, we're going to have a very nasty celebration."

"I love you," she said, although she knew he'd already hung up.

Brenda was waiting for her when she got back to her cubicle. "You can use this box to clean out your desk. And give me your keys." She smacked the box down and held out a charm-braceleted hand.

"Sorry. They're on my other key ring at home," Tricia said, defiantly staring Brenda and her bargain-basement dye job in the face.

"I'll need to have them back before you collect your last paycheck," Brenda informed her before stomping off.

It took only a few minutes to gather the small number of personal items. She went into the kitchen and added the dishes that were hers to the box. After stowing her sunglasses in a desk drawer (the ostensible reason she'd come back to the office), she left without speaking to anyone. Four years of service down the toilet, she thought, riding the elevator to the parking garage, yet all she felt was a curiously liberating excitement seasoned with a satisfying dash of contempt. If it took getting fired to send her and her soulmate on a rapturous getaway together, then fire away!

She deposited the box in her trunk and stood by the VW for a moment, debating whether to go home and drive back to the agency that night, or to kill time at the Century City Shopping Center. The notion of spending the rest of the day waiting for Stefan at the house with Heathcliffe and possibly Wren was unbelievably bleak, so she took Stefan's suggestion and had a strawberry daiquiri at Houston's, then purchased a Mexican travel guide at Brentano's, a daring black bikini at The Broadway, and two kinds of massage oil at The Body Shop. Passing by the multiplex box office, she realized there was time to see a film and ended up watching *Romper Stomper*, an NC-17 drama from New Zealand about a love triangle involving violent racist skinheads. Tricia found it instantly compelling, and Russell Crowe radiated raw star quality as the tattooed gang leader. She did not even flinch at the graphic scenes of brutality, so caught up was she in the admittedly trite romance of the picture, casting herself and Stefan as the abused, runaway rich girl and the vicious, hateful, yet secretly vulnerable and unbelievably sexy skinhead she was powerless to resist.

The movie ended, leaving Tricia feeling nihilistic and tough. She was ready for her final visit to the agency. Fired. How dare they? And she was glad to take credit for that letter. Stefan was right. Edgar was ruined. It wouldn't be difficult for her to find another job. Edgar had many enemies in The Business and she was certain one of them would be delighted to hire her.

Although she was absolutely prepared to run into her ex-colleagues and feed them the sunglasses excuse, Tricia prayed that the agency be deserted. The jalapeño idea, which she and Stefan had conceived of during a fiery anal interlude two weeks before, was just too fitting a send-off to go unexecuted. In any case, there was no need for stealth. Either someone would be there or they wouldn't. She unlocked the main door and entered the reception area. All was quiet. Neither sound nor person confronted her as she made her way back into the suite.

Edgar's door was closed, but she of course possessed a key. She hesitated briefly before inserting it, struck by a vision of him at his desk, snarling at her with those savagely insane eyes from earlier that day. However, something told her he'd probably made it a very short day. She opened the door. The office was empty. Exhaling hard in spite of herself, she went to her cubicle and removed the sunglasses from her drawer along with a jar of jalapeño nacho slices labeled to indicate maximum hotness.

Disappointment stung Tricia when she discovered Edgar's enema kit was not under the sink in his adjoining bathroom. It had to be there! She'd made him two pots of coffee just days ago. Where the hell had he put it? She urgently scoured the tiny lavatory to no avail. It was maddening! When would she get this chance again? There, alone, nothing standing between her and sweet success . . . she sat down and began tearing through his desk drawers, the frustration becoming unbearable. She wheeled Edgar's chair toward the credenza and roughly slid back the door, revealing Edgar's bowel-cleansing paraphernalia: K-Y jelly, a funnel, and a heavy-duty plastic bag attached to several feet of tubing culminating in a round-tipped latex nozzle. Unspeakable.

She did not want to touch it but knew she must. Using a handy tissue, Tricia pulled the nozzle from the heinie-hose and after double-wrapping it in Kleenex, slipped it into her pocket. She then opened the jalapeño jar and reached inside the mass of pickled peppers to retrieve another nozzle, identical but for the fact that this one had been marinating for ten days in spicy, sizzling jalapeño juice. It had required an exhaustive search of Westside health food stores to locate an exact duplicate of Edgar's preferred disposable butt-plug, but it had been well worth it, she smiled to herself, fingertips burning a little from the few seconds it had taken to pop the nozzle onto the tubing.

Tricia meticulously arranged the enema kit on the shelf the way she'd found it. Arousal washed over her and she found her hand involuntarily creeping beneath her skirt. If only Stefan were here . . . He could ravish her right on Edgar's desk—a literal fuck-you to that abhorrent loser. Through her dewy panties, Tricia sought out her clitoris. Oh, how she despised Edgar! A noise from somewhere in the agency startled her and she sat up, her elbow banging a white head shot box on the edge of the credenza shelf. It hit the floor upside down.

Without moving a molecule, Tricia listened, counting one chimpanzee, two chimpanzee, all the way up to one minute. She heard nothing and was now unsure that even the first sound had been real. She turned the spilled box over and replaced the few dozen photos that had fallen out. The broodingly handsome face in the shots impelled a second look. Tricia lifted one from the box and stared at it. "Sheldon Kristoff" was the name printed on the lower right of the picture.

It was Stefan. Or his twin brother. She flipped the photo over and studied the Conan Carroll Agency résumé. M.F.A., Yale Drama School. Various theater credits—*House of Blue Leaves, Lysistrata, Equs* (sic)—in Boston, New York and Los Angeles. Under Television, one credit: *Another World*, the role of "Trey" (three episodes). This simply could not be Stefan. *Whose past she knew absolutely nothing about.* How could he be a Yale Drama graduate? And a client of this agency? Why would he have changed his name? Why was she even entertaining these questions? Sheldon Kristoff was not

Stefan. She re-examined the photo, telling herself the two men really looked nothing alike.

But how would Sheldon look with a beard? a creepy voice inside her head murmured. That was easily remedied. She snatched up a Sharpie from Edgar's sty of a desktop and sketched in trim facial hair like Stefan's (it's not him) on Sheldon's face. First Tricia's lips began to quiver, then separated mutely. The marker dropped from her hand.

"Oh, God! Oh, my God!" she moaned.

"I didn't think anybody was left up here." Tricia screamed and pivoted in the chair, colliding into the side of the desk. Janice Twickenham put a hand to her shriveled breast and stepped backward startled. Her wig was askew, and she'd lost her regulation spike heels.

"Janice! You scared the hell out of me!"

"You gave me quite a fright yourself, Trish. And it wouldn't take much to finish me off completely, you know. I wasn't feeling well this afternoon so I took a little nap in Sam's office." The octogenarian diagnostically patted her maroon wig. "Ah, fuck it. Wait a minute. Before I went to sleep, they told me you were fired."

"I just came back for my sunglasses," Tricia blurted, ridiculously adhering to her original plan.

"Oh, I see," Janice said, as if forgotten sunglasses made it perfectly sensible for Tricia to be snooping through Edgar's office. "So long, kid. I'm hitting the road."

"Janice, wait!" Tricia hurriedly came around the desk, clutching the photo. "Do you recognize this actor?"

Janice slipped on the bifocals hanging from her neck and peered at the picture. "Sheldon Kristoff? . . . Oh. Oh, my. Yes. Yes, yes, yes. I'll be damned . . ."

"Who is he?" Tricia all but shrieked.

"That was years ago. Quite a while back, anyway," said Janice, slowly entering Edgar's office and sitting down. "My memory's not what it used to be, but this is one kid I'm not gonna forget."

Tricia took a deep breath and resisted a voracious urge to shake Janice's wig right off her. "Was he a client of Edgar's?" she forced herself to ask calmly.

"Oh, yes. Very talented, but one of those unstable artistic types.

Anyhow, he got a big contract role on one of those New York soaps . . ."

"*Another World*?" Tricia prompted.

"No. It was something else . . ." Janice said, her creased brow becoming even more furrowed.

"But the résumé says *Another World*," Tricia insisted, hysteria seeping into her voice.

"Well, that's not it! And it wouldn't be *on* the résumé because Sheldon never played the part. Now are you going to let me finish, because I've got places to go—*All My Children*, that was the show. He got cast on *All My Children*, big contract role. Edgar did the deal and he would've made a lotta dough, but it all fell through and they decided to cut out the character or kill him off or some crazy horseshit. *After* the deal closed, mind you."

"So they had to pay him—Sheldon," Tricia inferred, having not a gleam of an idea where this was heading.

Janice waved a gnarled finger at Tricia. "No, they did not, because Edgar hadn't gotten the contracts signed in time. They were just laying on his desk for weeks. And then the whole thing went straight to hell. If Edgar hadn't fucked up, they would have had to pay Sheldon around a hundred grand."

"What happened to him?" Tricia whispered.

"He got zilch," Janice informed her. "All those years of studying and working and paying his dues and his big break went right down the shitter. And then Sheldon found out Edgar was responsible," the crusty secretary confided. "My theory is Edgar's assistant at the time told Sheldon. She was kind of sweet on the kid. Sheldon just couldn't take it. Had to leave The Business. And you know where he ended up?"

Kinko's. My house. My bed. "Where?"

"The nuthouse, that's where. Nervous breakdown," Janice said, shaking her head at the picture. "Why'd you draw a beard on him?"

Tricia didn't hear the question. She had taken another Sheldon Kristoff shot out of the box and was staring at it. "How could I have never heard about this?" she asked, looking at Janice with wide, dazed eyes.

"No one ever talks about it around here," Janice replied. "Edgar made Conan and Sam promise never to mention it. And since Edgar made a bunch of fat deals for other clients around the same time, Conan just forgave him for lousing things up. But wherever he is, I bet that Sheldon Kristoff never did. I gotta get out of here, kid. See you tomorrow." She dropped the head shot on her chair and shuffled out the door.

Tricia steeled herself against the full-scale revolt of her nerves. Even if Stefan had been Edgar's client, even if he'd suffered a mental breakdown, even if he had *initially* sublet Andre's room to carry out some sort of revenge plot against Edgar, it didn't invalidate what she and Stefan had shared. The things he had done to her, the things they had done to each other.

And the things you did to Edgar while Stefan goaded you on? asked the creepy voice. It had all been because Stefan/Sheldon wanted Edgar destroyed. And now he had been.

"That rat's asshole is history in this business." That's what Stefan had said when she faxed him the resignation letter that day. In the two months they'd been together, she'd never heard him sound happier.

It couldn't be. For the love of God—She dialed Kinko's. "Kinko's on Wilshire. This is Mohammed."

"Stefan, please."

"Stefan is no longer with us, madam. Can someone else help you?"

She slammed the phone down and sprinted out of the office. Not too late. Not too late. *It doesn't have to be too late!* It took forever for the elevator to reach the parking garage. She made up for lost time by recklessly tearing over the speed bumps, en route to the exit. She jerked the VW Golf to a halt at the barrier arm and shoved in her parking card. The arm raised and Tricia yanked the card upward and out with such ferocity it snapped in half. She floored it onto Avenue of the Stars, tossing what was left of the card out the window.

Stefan would be at the house. He probably only quit because of their trip to Mexico, Tricia babbled to herself, spasmodically reaching behind her for reassurance that her shopping bags were still in the backseat while doing sixty down Olympic. She ran two red lights before barreling onto Melrose from Crescent Heights. Stefan would

be at the house and she would explain to him that she knew everything, she understood how Edgar had hurt him and it was okay because she hated Edgar, too. And Stefan would weep tears of relief
before making searing mad love to her and they would go away
together because it was meant to be and the alternative was un-
thinkable—

The driveway was empty. No Saab. No Stefan. Still, that didn't
mean . . . Tricia pulled in just enough to be off the sidewalk, and
went flying out of the car to the front door, pounding on it as she
turned three separate keys.

"Stefan! Stefan!" she cried, slapping on lights and careening
through the small house, past the kitchen where it had all begun and
down the hall to his room. She flung open the door and a strangled
moan escaped her throat. Everything was gone.

Not exactly everything. Ben-wa balls, blindfolds, a textured vibrator, handcuffs, condoms, Astroglide and a double-headed dildo
sat near the air mattress Jason had left. Tricia crumpled to her knees,
sobbing, beside them. She picked up Stefan's house keys and
squeezed them in her fist until her palm started to bleed.

"Let me get my mail," Marina said, braking the Vette and reaching
through the window into her ornate wrought iron mailbox for a thick
handful.

She'd just flown in from New York and had called Jason from
the plane to ask if he'd mind spending his last day before Mermaid
with her. Upon arriving at Vista Laguna Drive, she'd gazed around
the starkly barren Burke house and lapsed into a giddy giggling fit
at the result of her sole interaction with Maggie, while Nabisco
bounded across the expanses of black slate floor, growling to himself
with the pleasure of freedom after spending hours on the plane in
his travel kennel.

Marina had regained control and told Jason exactly why she
needed him. "It's Hank."

"What about him?" Jason asked, suppressing pangs of guilt.

"I haven't seen him since . . . that day and I want to. I think I
want us to be friends. Maybe not this minute, but, you know, soon.
I mean, I'm still really pissed and hurt about it, but I don't think
I'm that confused anymore," she said, hopping onto the wet bar.

"I've been sort of asking myself, if Hank's knowing he was gay two years ago had meant we never would have met and had what we had, would I go back and change things now? And I wouldn't. The timing of life really, really sucks sometimes." Jason nodded. "But if you don't have any control over something, you should just let it go. I don't want to lose Hank completely and I don't see why I have to. Am I crazy?"

"No." Somehow, this news made Jason feel unreasonably happy.

"Anyway, Hank's coming back from Toronto today, but I don't know when, so I was gonna ask if you could come up to the house with me in case he's there now. It'd just feel a little less weird."

Jason happened to know Hank wasn't coming until 5:40 P.M. but decided against sharing this data. He told her all he had planned was a meandering apartment search, which he'd gladly postpone.

"False alarm," she sighed as they pulled into the empty carport. "Let's just drop off these bags and then hit Cobalt Cantina for brunch, all right?"

Jason carried her luggage inside and upstairs. He put it in the bedroom, then joined Marina in her music room where she was sifting through the mail from the box. "Let's see what this is," she said, referring to a padded envelope. "Bad handwriting, my home address, *and* it's marked PERSONAL. If I'm already attracting stalkers, maybe this comeback deal isn't so far-fetched after all."

She slit the parcel open and pulled out a VHS videocassette and a sheet of notepaper. "What the hell? . . . Jason, look at this."

The note was on Hotel Bel-Air stationery, which would have indicted Maggie Burke even if she hadn't signed it, which she had. "My dear Miss Stetson, My security cameras picked up something you'll find very interesting." *Security cameras?* What security cameras?!? Holy shit! Oh, Jesus, he and Hank . . . The note fluttered from his fingers when he looked up to witness Marina inserting the cassette into her VCR.

"Do you think she's mad about the whole furniture thing, maybe?" Marina laughed. "What the hell could she want me to see?" She zapped on the TV and hit channel three.

No! Jason almost screamed. He had to think fast! His hands

immediately went to Marina's MTV Music Video Award, presented
to The Pop-Tartts in 1986 for the sumptuous and frisky "Stop! You
Tease Me" video from *Kung Fu Grip*. He picked up the heavy,
pewterish globe—the trajectory to the television screen was totally
unobstructed. He had already killed once this summer—surely he
could take down a twenty-seven-inch Sony. Jason froze with the
award over his shoulder, ready to hurl . . .

CBS/Fox Video? What the fuck was going on? He and Marina
watched as *The Rose* began. "She sent me *The Rose*?" Marina asked
rhetorically. She hit Stop and ejected. "Look, it's the movie." She
held up the tape for Jason to see, tapping her fingernail against the
label. He'd lowered the MTV statuette enough to evade suspicion,
and now clunked it back onto the table, bewilderment easily overpowered by nearly opiate relief.

"She's pretty wacko," Jason offered, shrugging.

"I'll say. So this is like her ugly, retarded way of warning
me that I'm gonna end up back on drugs, dying onstage during a
concert?"

"That must be it," Jason agreed.

"Wow," Marina said. She handed the cassette to Jason. And
picked up the rest of the mail. "What a twisted old bitch."

Conan Carroll accepted the caffe mocha with cream (for which Eric
had just minced down to the bakery) and a piece of chocolate cake
from his assistant, then closed the door and glided across his lavishly
carpeted office to where Violet was seated on an overstuffed purple
Italian sofa. "There we are," he cooed. "Coffee and cake. Our lovely
receptionist Misty had a birthday yesterday."

"Thanks," said Violet.

"No. Thank *you*, honey, for bearing with us this week. And I
think you'll find it was worthwhile," Conan winked, dashing to his
desk for a deal memo. "We closed first thing this morning. Three
hundred forty-five thousand dollars. Single card, main titles, second
position, all paid ads, private trailer, transportation to and from the
set, wardrobe approval, first-class hotel, rental car and per diem
while on location, blah blah blah. Violet Cyr, finally you are the
movie star you deserve to be!"

Two days after meeting with Aldo Spackle and Adrian Pasdar, Violet had auditioned for the studio and was immediately approved and cast as Lucy in *You Lucky Bastard*. Rehearsals began in ten days. It was definitely the nuts.

"Let's hope it works out better than my last epic."

Conan shook his head and briefly massaged his temples. "When I think of what you went through up there . . . oh, Violet. I am morally and legally obliged to inform you that since Edgar Black is leaving the agency, you're free to walk, too. And I wouldn't ask for a dime of commission off this movie deal. But I really hope you'll stay. We all adore you here."

"Well, I do feel better now that Edgar's not going to be with you," Violet admitted sweetly. "I know the resignation letter was a hoax, but I never really got the feeling he cared about my career. So I'll stay. If you do me one favor."

"Name it," Conan smiled, taking her hand.

"Drop Turk Marlowe from your list. I couldn't sleep at night knowing I shared an agent with that psychopathic motherfucker."

In a twinkle of his blue eyes, Conan had computed that the chances of Turk earning $34,500 or more for him this year (*Leather & Lace* was still commissionable by his previous agent) were about the same as Anne Archer telling the truth about her age. "Consider it done, doll." They shook hands.

"You know, at one time, Edgar was a very good agent," Conan added thoughtfully. "But this summer he really started to slip. To be honest, Violet, I was seriously considering letting him go *weeks* before this letter thing. But that's what really pushed him over the edge. I'm afraid there was a certain amount of truth to the letter. The whole Wendi Barash angle—I don't have to tell *you* about that. I just pray that he gets the treatment he needs," Conan clucked, not wishing to go into detail about the full-throttle emotional collapse that had taken place the day after Tricia had been terminated for sending out those goddamn letters. The vision of Edgar on the floor of the break room, pants around his ankles, howling obscenities while trying to insert ice cubes into his anus before they'd had him dragged off the premises by building security would haunt Conan forever. Jesus, maybe he *had* written the letter himself . . .

"And I noticed Tricia's cubicle is cleared out, too. What happened to her?" Violet asked, genuinely curious.

Conan shrugged winsomely, propping his Kenneth Coles up on his desk. "She left us. On to grander things, I imagine. That Tricia was a very bright girl, but she really didn't have a head for show biz, y'know. So . . . let's definitely ink in lunch at The Ivy before you start your big movie, missy!"

Tricia finished filing the paperwork then went to the minifridge for a well-deserved Diet Dr Pepper. Working at her new job unsupervised was a luxury for her that was paying off handsomely for the company—Tricia had already booked eight people on jobs just that day. Drat, make that seven. Natasha hadn't called back to accept in the allotted twenty-minute confirmation window. There was already a note on Natasha's Rolodex card indicating she had a history of availability problems. Tricia would be forced to type a memo to the manager of the modeling agency. But first, she beeped Amber as a possible fill-in.

She sipped her soda, reflecting once more how satisfied she was to be back in a pivotal role in a productive workplace. Tricia certainly was not the type of person who'd feel comfortable chiseling the state out of unemployment benefits when she was perfectly capable of working (although collecting those benefits would have been complicated by the fact that she'd been fired, not laid off, by Conan Carroll). Nor was she one to be crippled by a minor bout of depression (manifested in this case by not leaving her room for four days after Stefan's departure except for an abortive suicide attempt with a bottle of Wren's dolls that had resulted in a grisly vomiting incident). No, no, no, no. Tricia Cook pulled herself up by her bootstraps, washed that man (and the vomit) right out of her hair, and re entered show business posthaste.

Of course the modeling agency wasn't *precisely* show business, but it would suffice until this ridiculous blacklisting problem, obviously inflamed by the unexpected local media frenzy about Edgar's allegedly forged resignation letter, cleared up and everyone in the gossipy Industry stopped condemning her as the culprit in what *Variety* called an "unprecedentedly massive and vicious hoax." And although she'd lost her insurance and other benefits, this current job paid in cash, thereby nearly equaling what she'd taken home as Edgar's assistant.

The phone rang. "Good evening, Sweet Sophisticates," Tricia answered in the sultry voice suggested by her boss, Tito. The man on the other end, a regular client according to the discreet, account numbers-only customer log, requested a model for a night of "misbehavior and light discipline."

"Naughty girls need love, too," Tricia quipped, flipping to Wren's card in the Rolodex. It was only fair that she give her first crack at this. After all, Wren had been considerate enough to help Tricia land this job.

Tricia had been utterly oblivious to the fact that her housemate had been getting spanked by wealthy men at private parties since Wren had been dumped by her personal manager, Gail Ann Griffin (who, Tricia had been appalled to read in the trades, had just brokered a million-dollar series deal for the horrid Doll Babcock at Carsey-Werner). "It's not prostitution. It's more like performance art," Wren had explained, applying makeup while Tricia forlornly scrubbed down their bathroom. "And the modeling agency I go through needs someone to work the phones."

Since the Wendi Barash story had become a national news phenomenon, Sweet Sophisticates Models and Escorts seemed to have picked up the slack left by Wendi's now dormant operation, enjoying a substantial boom in business. Tricia had just been assigned the peak 7 P.M. to 3 A.M. shift. This was going to take some adjustment biologically, but it didn't really matter when she got her nine hours of sleep, did it? And Wren was of course correct. It was *not* prostitution. Modeling and escorting and getting one's fanny paddled were certainly not illegal. Whatever else the ladies and she-males of Sweet Sophisticates wanted to do with clients was their creative prerogative.

Oh for crying out loud. These were awful! Tito had asked Charmaine, the girl who worked day shift, to compose some classified ads to run in the *L.A. Weekly* and *Los Angeles* magazine, and the bubblehead had failed spectacularly. Tricia sighed and began correcting her mistakes. Then there was the matter of the Rolodex cards. At least 70 percent were typed on the wrong side. She'd have to write another memo to Tito. I mean, this is insane, she told herself. The one thing she would not put up with was unprofessionalism.

"Hi, this is Jason."

"Your own phone number?" Andre gasped. "Ooooh, honey! You *have* arrived!"

Jason silently agreed, eyes scanning his office, just big enough to hold a desk, a guest chair, TV/VCR and the enormous Marina Stetson promo poster Chip Reeves had sent down for him. He loved it, naturally, but felt that hanging it immediately would brand him an unmitigated Mariniac to the point of dorkhood. He decided to prop it under the window behind his desk, facing the wall, at least until after today's lunch with Marina.

"What's up, Andre?"

"I am on the go fourteen hours a day. Thank Christ Fawn and Giles found a house. It's a five-bedroom Tudor estate in Brentwood. With this very private and adorable guest cottage for me. It's two blocks from Joan Crawford's place! How scary is that, especially since I'm going to be their nanny."

"What do you know about raising kids?" Jason asked mildly.

Andre snorted, hurt. "We just got back from Rizzoli's and bought around thirty books on the subject. Naturally I'll be breast-feeding." He cackled delightedly.

"So Fawn and Giles are a happily married couple again, just like that?" asked Jason, wondering if he should be taking personal calls during his first week of work.

"Mmm-hmm. Everything's going to be fab, Jason. There's at least a ninety percent chance the baby will be white. Oops! Thinking out loud. And you would not believe Maggie Burke. Nicer than *shit*. She sent Fawn this whopping basket from the most expensive tot boutique in BH. I still don't trust the old buzzard farther than I can kick her, but as long as she's out of my hairdo, I'm a happy gal. Before I forget, honey, we want you to join us for dinner very, very soon."

Jason surveyed his calendar. Saturday he was spending on Catalina with Violet and Dave to celebrate her starring role in Aldo Spackle's *You Lucky Bastard*. Sunday, a party at Terry Davidson's. Monday and Tuesday nights he was going to video shoots with his new boss, Jillian. "What about next Wednesday?"

"Sounds delish. I'll have to check with The Pregnant One. She wants you to cruise through the new place. Then we can have a movie screening. Ooh, I know. I just taped *The Rose!*" Andre exclaimed.

"*The Rose*? Really?" Jason asked with laughably phony casualness.

"Mmm-hmm! I must confess I rented it from your ex-boss, mammoth Marilyn. Only because the store is right near Fawn's GP, the *muy* dreamy Doctor DeLeon—"

"Andre, I just remembered something I forgot to do, so can we talk later?"

"TTFN!" Andre blew a noisy kiss into the mouthpiece and hung up.

So that was it. That had to explain Maggie's bizarro snafu with the videotape. Somehow—it must have been at Giles's house—she'd mixed up Andre's rental tape with whatever she'd been planning to obliterate Jason with, doubtlessly him in a hidden-camera video entitled *The Joy of Gay Sex with Hank Rietta*. Which meant that *that* tape had been sent back to the video store—

He dialed Video Xplosion, feeling his forehead and underarms break into a terrified sweat. Lori answered. Sweet, apple-cheeked Lori. She would help him. "Hi, this is Andre Nickerson," Jason said, femming it up. "And I think I did something monumentally stupid, which was, um . . . returning one of my own tapes in one of your cases."

"Which case would that be, sir?" she chirped.

"*The Rose*?"

"Okay, let me check on that." The brain-softening sounds of K-LITE, Marilyn's mandated hold station. It had to be there. The chance of a 1979 Bette Midler movie being rented twice in the same week was zero. "Andre? Hi, it's Lori again. I've got that tape right here, and it's *The Rose*, all right. So I guess everything's okay."

"Is that the only copy?"

"Yes, we only have the one."

"Could you check to see if I rented anything else with it?" Jason asked, mutilating a handy paperclip.

"Sure." Fingers on a keyboard. "Nope. That was it. And your last transaction before this was in June."

"Great. Thanks." He hung up and closed his eyes. Now this really made no sense. But the fact remained—a tape of his and Hank's most intimate moments was out there. And Jason was just going to have to live with it. Somehow, destiny had diverted it from Marina's mailbox and he just had to be grateful for that. He had to let it go. Ever since that blood-freezing moment in Marina's music room, Jason had been dressing and undressing in the servants' bathroom, keeping all the lights off, knowing he was under surveillance. He had to get out of that fucking mansion this weekend, even if it meant paying more rent than he wanted to for a decent apartment. Someone rapped on his half-open door, and he jumped. "Did I scare you?" Marina giggled. "I thought record execs usually took naps *after* lunch." He got up and they exchanged hugs. "Wow, Jason. This is, like, tiny."

"I love it," he said. "Thanks again."

"Ah, come on." She dropped into the guest chair. "Hey, guess what? They booked me on *Saturday Night Live* in October. I know the show sucks—"

"I actually think Melanie Hutsell's really funny," Jason interjected supportively.

"Anyway, they still get a lot of the top acts as musical guests, so it's kind of cool."

"And 'Broken Mirror' gets released next week," Jason said, waving the one on his desktop at her. She crossed her fingers. "It's already number forty-seven nationally, before the official debut. That's amazing. And the album is going to do even better."

"Believe me, I could sit here all day and let you boost my ego, babe. But we need to eat. And I've been meaning to ask, how's the apartment search going?"

"Not great. But I've committed to picking out a place this weekend. How 'bout you?"

She nodded. "There's a little house in Santa Monica I think I'm going to take. A rental. It's near the beach and there's a yard for Nabisco and a skylight and nice floors and . . . it's good."

"Do you need help moving?"

"No, sweetie. But Hank and I were talking, actually about the divorce, which my publicist is going to announce the week *Ghost in the Fog* comes out—the drama, but we decided we'd really like you to move into our place on Vista Laguna for a while anyway, or as long as you want. You know, until you find a place you really, really like."

"I thought Hank was staying there until you guys could sell . . ."

"Oh, he is. But there's four extra bedrooms, and he's not there very much, but I know he'd like the company. Please say yes."

"Okay." He smiled.

"And Hank really is a terrific guy, Jason. Who knows?" she added with a raise of her eyebrows, smiling back. "Maybe you two will hit it off."

"Well, I guess anything's possible," Jason agreed, reddening and closing his office door behind them.

Ronald woke up with a stiffy and had just what the doctor ordered for it hidden in his dresser under ten pairs of creased and folded designer jeans. He hopped out of his waterbed and retrieved the tape, prancing nude into the living room of his third-floor condo on Moorpark Avenue and carefully inserting it into his VCR. Since discovering the video a week ago, he must have watched it a dozen times and somehow it defied all known laws of porn by becoming *more* exciting with each viewing.

It had started out as a normal evening at home with a Bette Midler double feature rented from his gal-pal Marilyn down at the Video Xplosion. But after laughing, crying and singing along with *For the Boys*, he'd found an unexpected miracle where *The Rose* should have been—a home video of that hunky little closet queen Jason having hot, steamy man-sex with a gorgeous muscle stud! It was the most nut-bustingly erotic twenty-six minutes Ronald had ever seen, so much so that he'd actually lost control and soiled his autographed Barbra Streisand coffee table book. And it had been worth it.

Ronald wanted to tell Marilyn about Jason's outrageous indiscretion, but realized that no one else must ever know this tape existed. It was just too precious. So he'd hurried to Tower, bought a copy of *The Rose*, and returned it to Video Xplosion in the appropriate case.

He spread an old towel onto his couch and sat his naked heinie down, baby oil and remote at the ready. The tape started. One question remained in Ronald's mind (besides who was that other hung, hairy butt-stud and how could Ronald get a piece of *that* action?!?). Had Jason switched the tape with *The Rose* by accident, or was it a deliberate act of exhibitionism? Either way, thought Ronald, pinching his nipple with oily fingertips, that Jason was one sick ticket.

· A NOTE ON TYPE ·

The typeface used in this book is a version of Janson, a seventeenth-century Dutch style revived by Merganthaler Linotype in 1937. Long attributed to one Anton Janson through a mistake by the owners of the originals, the typeface was actually designed by a Hungarian, Nicholas Kis (1650–1702), in his time considered the finest punchcutter in Europe. Kis took religious orders as a young man, gaining a reputation as a classical scholar. As was the custom, he then traveled; because knowledge of typography was sorely lacking in Hungary, Kis decided to go to Holland, where he quickly mastered the trade. He soon had offers from all over Europe—including one from Cosimo de Medici—but kept to his original plan, returning to Hungary to help promote learning. Unfortunately, his last years were embittered by the frustration of his ambitions caused by the political upheavals of the 1690s.